Not Just Pretty

By

Burt Hurlock

For my brother Jimmy

PREFACE

All vessels, aircraft, and military and financial surveillance capabilities in *Not Just Pretty* are in use today, except ekranoplans, which have been retired by both the U.S. and Russian military. All named U.S. government agencies exist and operate as described, and all cited anti-narcotics operations, major financial institution money laundering settlements, and every account of collaboration between U.S. government agencies and drug trafficking organizations is documented.

Glossary of Terms and Acronyms

AG	Attorney General of the United States
CPOT	Consolidated Priority Organization Target – A major, DEA targeted criminal enterprise
DEA	Drug Enforcement Administration
DICE	DEA Internet Connectivity Endeavor - DEA data base with more than one billion records
DOJ	Department of Justice
EC	Electronic Countermeasures
FAST	Foreign Deployed Advisory and Support Team - DEA tactical units
FBI	Federal Bureau of Investigation
FinCEN	Financial Crimes Enforcement Network
GANTSEC	Greater Antilles Section of the U.S. Coast Guard
Go-Fast	A high speed boat used to ferry contraband
HITRON	U.S. Coast Guard Helicopter Interdiction Tactical Squadron
LEDET	Law Enforcement Detachment - specialized deployable maritime law enforcement team
NSA	National Security Agency
OCF	FusionCenter or Fusion, research/deconfliction unit of the DEA's Special Operations Division
OIG	Office of the Inspector General of the United States
OSHA	Occupational Safety and Health Administration
PATT	Proactive Asset Targeting Team, a special Fusion research team
RHIB	Rigid Hull Inflatable Boat
SAR	Suspicious Activity Report identifying suspicious financial activity
Semper Paratus	Always Ready - the U.S. Coast Guard moto
SIGINT	Signal Intelligence – clandestine signal and communications monitoring
SOAR	160th Special Operations Aviation Regiment
SOD	Special Operations Division of the DEA
SPSS	Self-Propelled Semi-Submersible, or Narco Sub, used to transport contraband

PART 1

CHAPTER 1

Coleman U.S. Federal Penitentiary, Sumter County, Florida

"Phoenix Perdue, is it?" she said, closing the door. He knew her face, from a past too distant to recall.

"Phil, ma'am."

"Pardon?"

"I go by Phil, ma'am," he said, rising the way he was taught, the past she evoked dissolving out of reach in the clank of his shackles.

"Please sit down," she said, her eyes judging him. "You don't look like a boy from North Georgia." He could tell she was drawn to him, the way folks were.

"That was years ago, ma'am," he answered, taking his seat, the slurry of chains settling on his extremities.

"Barely five. Not *that* long ago," she continued, "that you murdered your uncle." She was so familiar, so very familiar, though he was sure they had never met.

"If you don't mind me askin', ma'am, what do *you* know about North Georgia, or my uncle?"

"More than you might imagine, Phil, but that hardly matters now, does it?"

"Ma'am?"

"Tomorrow. Surely you don't expect another stay." She had that hard-baked Yankee thing going on. All business in her tailored grey suit and severe brown lipstick, but he could tell it was an act, like the drag queens he saw from the window of Pedro Morales' pickup truck on the drive through the Port of New Orleans all those years ago.

He knew a bluff when he saw it, just one instinct of many honed by the odyssey on which he embarked on that early June day, the day of his uncle's murder; a long day, he recalled, a real long day, that ended when he touched down in the darkness on a rough jungle landing strip beside a mangrove swamp on the northern tip of Colombia's Guajira Peninsula.

"I ain't givin' you what you come fer, ma'am," he said, smiling at the reflective glass in the cold cinderblock wall of the detention room. He liked her, liked that he could see right through her, and that she gave him that feeling from a different time.

"And what *have* I come for?"

"You know, ma'am."

"Besides your story, I'm sure I don't. I'm just a reporter, Phil, from the *Atlanta Constitution*. Criminal justice is my beat."

"Sure it is, ma'am," he said, taking her in. "And I'm Geppetto. Come on now, this ain't my first rodeo."

"Elaine. Please call me Elaine."

"Is that your name?" he asked, knowing by how she said it that it wasn't.

"Is it true you're *The American*?" she asked in a weary, inured-to-celebrity sort of way. He grunted and smiled.

"The Gentleman Gangster, the Caballero, don't they call me that too, ma'am?"

"Yes."

"Well, if you must call me names, ma'am, I'd be much obliged for you to use that one." He didn't care much for the names, but he knew they were important, to his followers and to his enemies. The names had lives of their own, like Robin Hood, or the "hooker-with-a-heart-of-gold," wishful symbols of misplaced faith, preserving the myth of noble savagery - the idea that lost wretches like himself could be lovable, misunderstood cads.

"Or just Phil, ma'am."

"So you are *The American*. You *did* unite the cartels."

"No ma'am. I didn't, but they stopped killin' each other for a while, if that's what you mean."

"While eluding interdiction, and altogether multiplying the volume of contraband reaching U.S. shores."

"You sure know a lot for a little ol' reporter from Atlanta, Elaine." She stole a glance at her handlers behind the mirror, to make sure, he reckoned, they registered his confession.

"You want to tell me about it?" she said, extracting a shorthand note pad and pen from a black leather satchel. It was new, purchased yesterday he figured, and the stiff leather cover snapped shut like a mouse trap, the buckle tethers wriggling like post-mortem reflexes.

"There's nothin' to tell, ma'am, beyond what I already said."

"That you deny killing your uncle as well as the federal agent, for whose murder you're sentenced to death."

"Yes, ma'am."

"You're sort of out of time, aren't you? I mean 6:23 tomorrow morning isn't so far away." She was a lousy interrogator, even in her good cop role. He liked that about her, too. Despite her facade she was still transparent, because she was new, and naïve. It kept taking him back, the siren song of innocence from a past he could barely remember, beneath her contrived exterior.

"I don't know about that, ma'am. I don't count on tomorrows no more." She approached him from the far side of the table and leaned forward on her hands, her familiar clear eyes angry, and knowing.

"They won't stay your execution again, you know that, right?" But he knew *they* would, and not for fancy lawyering, a successful appeal, or the fifth chances afforded death row inmates.

"Come on, ma'am, *you* know why I'm still alive, and why I might could stay alive a while longer."

"No, Mr. Perdue, I'm quite sure I don't," she snapped. "Perhaps you could enlighten me."

"Because you and yorn behind the glass 'll keep me alive, and it's Phil, ma'am. Just Phil."

"Is that so."

"Yes, ma'am. Because you need me alive."

"I need you alive only long enough to write your story. Don't you want to set anything straight? Tell your side, for posterity?"

Posterity? He wasn't even sure what she meant. He never planned on returning, and never reckoned on setting things straight, or needing to. How he ended up in Colombia, why he hadn't been executed yet, and whether he would leave in a pine box or on his own two feet – all of it mystified him.

"Whether you die on schedule at 6:23 a.m. tomorrow, or your own people get you first, you're a dead man, aren't you?" She was right about that, but why, he still didn't know. "The story is you sold out your own, to spread your power, and they put a price on your head for it."

"A price on my head, hunh? for uniting the cartels and increasing shipments...and making them richer? Isn't that what you said?"

"Then why is there a price on your head?"

Why indeed, the unsolved mystery to which he reckoned he owed his life.

"Who wanted you dead badly enough for you to turn yourself in?" Now they were making progress.

"Promise to print it if I tell you, Elaine?" he posed, pulling at the threads of her fraying alias.

"Of course, I will, that's why I'm here," she said excitedly, stealing a glance at the mirror.

"Well, it ain't that easy, see?"

"Why not?"

"Cause once I tell, y'all will put me down like a lame horse."

"You think it's that important?"

"I reckon so, or why y'all keep askin' me?"

"Who's *y'all*? This is for the paper."

"For goodness' sake, Elaine. Just 'cause I talk slow don't mean I think slow. *Y'all, you, the Feds*. If y'all *knew*, you wouldn't be so worried. What's got you so worried? What is it y'all need to know so bad?"

"I'm not worried," she protested. "The authorities aren't either," she said, clawing her way back into character. But she *was* worried, despite all her bluster. The last thing she or anyone at DEA or Justice could afford was to have him dead, not before he talked, because they suspected, Phil had come to believe, it was someone among their ranks. They suspected an insider of conspiring with his *Americanos* to defeat interdiction to the considerable advantage of the cartels and themselves. They figured he knew who it was.

It was a native Southern lilt she was struggling to suppress that accounted for her familiarity, though why she was suppressing it he couldn't say. Perhaps she was afraid to sound feminine, or sympathetic, or maybe even weak, but he'd never talk, and not for invincible resolve, but because the secret he pretended to keep he didn't know himself. Strange, he thought, how caught he was between battle lines he never saw, concealing people he never knew, vying to kill him for crimes he never committed, and betrayals of which he was innocent. All along he had done right by everyone, deserving or not. That's what he told himself, and that's what he believed.

But after three years among the cartels and two more in prison, he was growing impatient. He began the return journey that landed him in prison in full-fledged flight, fearing for his life. Now he saw it would never end without a confrontation. Maybe he'd survive it, maybe he wouldn't. At least he'd know who he was fighting. Settling scores was never his thing, "but comes a time," his daddy used to say, wearing out his favorite Ralph Waldo Emerson, "*to do what we must, and call it by the best names we can.*" It was remembering those words, as he sat there before the familiar and mesmerizing Elaine, that he saw how his daddy, with all his short-comings, had warned him of things to come.

CHAPTER 2

Lost Lake, Georgia - Five Years Before

"There's an ill wind blowin' through Georgia, son, and it ain't from the North this time," his father had said. His daddy had been a hard man, set in his ways, and Phil felt wrong agreeing with him sometimes, but there was no denying it. Things *were* changing. He'd heard talk of it long before that fateful day in June, but paid it no mind. Seemed like ministers and school teachers were about the only folks around preaching tolerance for the growing Hispanic community. Migrants didn't venture to the lake much, or ever, as far as Phil could recall, until the day Pedro appeared in the distance before Boat Church.

Staring down from the road on the slope that plunged to the water's edge a half mile across the lake, Pedro Morales had stirred something cold in the dead air around Phil's boat. He couldn't actually see Morales watching him from the shadowy cab of his red pickup truck so much as feel him, as sure as he felt the sun's warm rays descending from the ridgeline on the lake's eastern boundary. The day would be a scorcher, Phil could already tell, especially for the first Sunday in June.

Phil had been lying in wait, beneath the long shadows of the tall pines on the shoreline, not just for his first glimpse of Katie McLean, who had been on his mind, but for the flotilla of sparkling, rumbling mahogany that would make its way down the lake. It was a ritual passed on from his daddy – the close inspection of his winter's work, to make sure it measured up in the broad light of day.

Before too long the six and eight-cylinder engine blocks, some fast-approaching centenaries, would thunder to life inside neat little boat houses nestled by the water's edge, coughing blue smoke, and belching clear lake water from the glistening chrome exhausts he had spent the winter polishing. One by one, like waking beasts, the boats would roar to life, the winter-parched planks of their copper-painted hulls swelling and healing in the tamed Tallulah's pristine headwaters.

It was not technically a lake at all, but one of four man-made bodies of water engineered by Georgia Power between 1911 and 1925, when the Tallulah River was harnessed for hydroelectric power by a series of dams that brought to heel one of the East's few whitewater wonders. The project and others like it inspired *Deliverance*, a disturbing 1970s movie with Burt Reynolds that glorified a banjo duet and made inbred hill people infamous. The mighty Tallulah once churned and gushed with animal spirits through two thousand unobstructed vertical feet, from its source in the blue-ridge to the sea; and where once the feral full moon dance of the Cherokee Tribe filled the forests with primal jubilation, vulgar mansions had sprung like a dandelion blight, sprouting on the land in patches of ostentatious lean-tos, where the idle rich passed listless hot summers in addled peace.

Sleek with coiled power, the languid lake boats to which Phil owed his living slipped their stocks, and fell into a disorderly formation pointed at the bay where he was drifting. The burnt umber timbers of their plumb bows and raked sterns glowed orange in the sun, their glistening decks spraying sunlight like fireballs across the glassy calm. Slowly, deliberately, the magnificent armada of wood and light throbbed its way in uneven synchrony from all points on the shoreline to rendezvous with a rickety pontoon boat, packed with a preacher, acolytes and a teenage choir. It was the season's first gathering of Boat Church, a ritual unique to Lost Lake, because there were few better ways to gather a community of faithful cast across the shores of a picturesque lake deep in the Bible Belt. Moved to keep up appearances and possessed of the wherewithal to commune in antique boats, it was an earnest, drifting celebration of the Lord. There, by persuasion of a floating pulpit, from the center of Redemption Bay, the local Baptist preacher held forth, exorcising demons on hot summer Sundays.

Phil liked watching them come, not just for the satisfaction of seeing his work, but for the many ways they arrived. Some alighted on the congregation and circled in ritual acknowledgment of the lake's true-believers, while others idled lazily to prayer. Still others rushed forward on breathless planes, anxious to exalt in His majesty at the pontoon pulpit.

He hardly ever missed Boat Church, and not for want of the Lord. It was a spectacle, a natural wonder. Once Preacher Small got going, the lake's simple serenity surrendered to *emm, hmming* and *praise God-ing,* that carried on the water in waves. The preacher filled the pauses with narrow if well-intended hellfire and brimstone hyperbole, his words burbling in mangled phrases through the pontoon boat's faulty public-address system.

Phil's new ride was ready just in time for Small's season opener, and he felt more than a little proud as the mountain shadows receded, revealing him to Small's flock. Against all odds the experimental craft had worked on its maiden voyage, even if riding it had scared him half to death. He rode it like a motorcycle, his legs astride the engine housing, which resembled nothing so much as a fuselage by how two stunted yellow wings sprouted from both sides of its base. Repurposed water ski bindings held his bare feet to the wings, and when the wakes of Boat Church congregants came through, she rocked from wing tip to wing tip, the sparkling wet exhausts gurgling ghoulishly from where they sprung like gamecock feathers from her transom.

It was the summer after his daddy passed, which made him by succession the keeper of the Lost Lake fleet, conserver of its beauty and preserver of ancient engines. Maybe Katie would catch sight of him in the shoreline shadows, and sneak him one of her smiles, a smile made sweeter for landing undetected by her perpetually scowling father.

There were few events besides the Fourth of July boat parade that glorified Phil's work more than the season's first gathering for Boat Church. The bright work was at its best, orb-shaped chrome vents gleaming like giant globules of iridescent mercury, waterlines crisp and clean on hulls as dry as coconut husks, and the throaty growl of massive, perfectly tuned engines, detonating in resonances as familiar to him as family voices. But the moment never lasted. As the season wore on, from clear across the lake, he would catch himself wincing at the sound of misfiring spark plugs, drifting timing, and flagging fuel pumps, that he calibrated especially tightly to keep the engines clean and powerful. The perpetual deterioration of the boats kept him in business. They were as temperamental as they were stately, in endless need of nursing until sometime after Labor Day, when anxious, Atlanta-bound owners returned them to his care.

It was between house calls to shabby-chic boathouses up and down the lake in the service of his mechanical charges that he indulged his lust for speed, relentlessly inventing new ways to cover more distance in less time. His specialty was hydroplanes. Each new design piled on power and sacrificed stability in the endless tradeoff between friction and weight. The design of the craft on which he presently perched was a radical departure he felt ashamed for not inventing himself - a Cold War relic devised and discarded by a long-forgotten foe. It bore no resemblance to the planing mono-hulls of his adolescence, nor to the generations of catamaran hydroplanes with which he had won county sprints and set amateur speed records. This *thing* was altogether new, more conspicuous, and that was bound to distract from the sermon as Preacher Small whipped up rapture in his Redemption Bay opener. Phil knew the congregation, maybe better than Small himself, and knew that lusting hearts and wandering eyes would be coveting the savage splendor of this new machine, even before he cranked the ignition. It sounded more like a ram jet than the throaty grumbling inline sixes to which the crowd was accustomed, which he knew would win converts even before he put it in gear.

"I don't figure anyone will believe it when they see it," he told himself with growing anticipation, "and every kid on the lake will want one by next summer." He knew Katie wouldn't care.

"Male diversions," like football and fast cars, and cold beer and trashy women were "obvious and plain," she once said as they pulled away from the gas dock. "With all this..." she went on, ice cream pooling on her chin, "God-given and free," she said, gazing on the mountains, "what's so dern great about stinky, noisy boats?"

"You mean stinky, *fast* boats," he wanted to say, but she would never understand. Maybe no one would.

The problem with speed, Phil liked to say, was its inverse proportion to stability, and the challenge acceleration presented to balancing competing natural forces.

"Goin' fast, really fast, is an act of violence," he liked to tell onlookers before he raced, a statement on which he made good by shredding glassy-smooth bodies of water. Phil and the boats and drivers he raced against shattered the silent splendor of every nearby mountain reservoir at least once a year; except his engines were louder, and faster, screaming ear-splitting anarchy on cruel concoctions of oxygen, avgas and accelerants that left spent fumes drifting like stage effects on the water. He guessed he knew by the end of last summer how the obsession his daddy raised him on diminished him in Katie's eyes.

"It *ain't* the worst of male vices," she had assured him, even if she said it mimicking his drawly mountain-speak.

"When you say *ain't*, Katie," he scolded her, "makes you sound dumb as me." He liked her Southern Belle strength, her lilting elegant innocence, despite how coarse it made him feel. He was not the sort her momma or daddy had in mind, now or ever, and he knew he and Katie were different, even then.

CHAPTER 3

Coleman U.S. Federal Penitentiary, Sumter County, Florida

No telling how different they would be now, the years and continents and customs separating them. She wouldn't know the inside of a jail, he reckoned, nor seen the flash of a muzzle pointed in her direction. He was glad she was spared all that, he thought, as Elaine paced in silence about him, steeling herself for more questions.

He had cared for others since Katie, in one way or another, and regretted leaving them behind. Some got hurt, or worse, and some were better off, he assured himself without really knowing. No telling how many more he didn't know who paid some kind of price for how he had helped the cartels. It was careless and indifferent, and indefensible to have paid no mind to the consequences, which he could scarcely have imagined. He had sold no drugs, never murdered, and trafficked in contraband just a handful of times, and outside U.S. territorial waters, which eased his conscience and absolved him most days of guilt. *Shameful* is what Katie would say, and maybe she'd be right, but there was no undoing the past. The best he could do right now, he came around recently to thinking, was to keep from repeating the mistakes, if he ever got the chance. And for that, as usual, he had no plan.

As Elaine continued to circle, he swore himself to renouncing the sins of which he knew he *was* guilty - the careless going along to get along without regard for the consequences. He had indulged his skills at first for the thrill of it, realizing only later how the attention it brought him conferred with it powers he never imagined - power to threaten, power to make peace, and power that made friend and foe alike want him dead. That was gratitude for you. All he did was make the cartels faster and more elusive – all of them – and so long as they all prospered by it, and prosper they did, they fueled his ambitions and acceded to his popularity. Turning himself in achieved no better outcome – the reward for two years of cooperation and incarceration was death by lethal injection, if his captors and Elaine were to be believed. *The nail that sticks up gets hammered down*, he had been warned along the way, and he would pay with his life for doing what he thought was expected of him. God but not time was on his side to make amends, though he was beginning to get the feeling he might have that chance.

It was low to think he was doomed by the father he idolized, and by the beleaguered estate to which he owed his former living and unusual skills, but the truth spoke for itself. Five years ago, on the Friday morning before the Boat Church season opener, Uncle Mortimer had come to call. It was Uncle Mort, his mother's brother, and the local town banker, who brought him the news. It was bad, but not insurmountable, Phil reckoned, if the bank gave him time to round up some money from friends. It was with this in mind that he planned to call after Boat Church on Katie's father, who despite his misgivings about Phil as a match for his daughter, had always been encouraging, and sometimes even kind. It was with Katie in his heart and her father in his head that he straddled his speed machine, waiting on the *General Lee*.

He recalled how he had daydreamed about her all winter to rueful country ballads on the local mountain radio - where she might sit and how she would look there on the sparkling teak deck stringers he had burnished back to life. Her face had vanished, lost with recalling, like the scars he had sanded smooth from the planks of the *General Lee*. But he saw her still, in faceless form and coloring – her onyx hair, mahogany eyes, and tawny skin - sometimes on the gas dock by her father on Friday nights, sometimes drifting at Boat Church, which the McLeans attended unfailingly, and sometimes sunbathing on her dock, where he staged the improbable breakdown of his jet ski. The memories survived despite how it ended, late in the evening on the last night of summer, at the end of her dock in the full moon twilight. On the verge of the kiss for which they both yearned, Katie's father, Malcolm, flicked on the boathouse floodlights, to remind them, Phil reckoned, of what they both knew already - they were as mismatched as baked beans and caviar.

Malcolm's was the biggest of the lake's houses, a pseudo-neoclassical pile on Orchard Point with enough dry-stack stonework to rival the pyramids. The massive home, like the *General Lee,* conveyed the scale of his self-centeredness, which striving Atlanteans stomached willingly only because it mirrored their own ambitions. Phil never laid eyes on the first Mrs. McLean, a slight, pretty lass of the Atlanta Campbell clan, according to Phil's father, who grew up summering on a lake two dams up the Tallulah. The lake's first families embraced her deep North Georgia roots, and forgot her just as easily when lustful Malcolm's hard heart strayed. He jilted her for Katie's mother, a decades younger Colombian of doubtful breeding, who arrived home with Malcolm from a business trip to South America. She intimidated Phil, as did Duncan, Katie's step-brother – the other male McLean standing between himself and Katie.

So it was surprising, even to Phil, who had never felt sorry for anyone, that it was for Duncan he first felt sympathy. Duncan plainly disappointed his father, a state of affairs Phil couldn't imagine. "All hat, no cattle," his Uncle Mort once said, and Mort probably knew. He worked in the local branch of a regional savings and loan that McLean was rumored to own. The six-week no-show summer jobs the bank afforded Duncan came on murky authority from higher-ups, Mort said, and no one cared if Duncan came or went.

The McLeans appeared in June with a handful of the lake's first families, mingling politely with summer and year-round residents alike. With their duties done, they paraded like peacocks up and down the lake in the ravishing wooden chariots that owed their beauty and power to decades of devoted care in the Perdue family boat business. Perdue lake boat restorations were renowned for their faithfulness to the essence of the original craft. Collectors came from miles around with full wallets and empty trailers, and earnest heart-felt well-rehearsed appeals for prying loose Lost Lake Perdue-kept masterpieces. But they were journeys made in vain, for Lost Lake boats seldom strayed from home. A waiting list of patient buyers attended each one, the owner, the owners to precede him, and the ones to follow self-styled patrons, conservators of rare art misplaced anywhere but Lost Lake. No price was too high for the privilege of stewardship.

Faithfulness to the old ways meant no boat in the Perdue's care emerged in spring with less than twelve fresh coats of spar varnish, sanded between applications by ever finer grit until the abrasive used to prepare the final coat was soft as talc.

"There's no difference to the naked eye 'tween twelve coats of spar and three coats of 'urethane," Phil used to goad his daddy out of pure wickedness, "and the poly is way more durable in the sun," he added, despite a few lingering doubts. He had used it on his own boats to reduce his launch prep, but the urethane had never proved itself over more than one Georgia summer. He wasn't the first son to think his father hopelessly dated, nor the last to presume himself an innovator; and by the time Phil found himself alone in the world, weighing the bad news from his uncle as he drifted on a winged speed machine in the hush before the call to prayer, he was an old hand at building his own boats.

They all bore the signature artistry for which his father was rightly credited by inculcating scrupulous disciplines; but Phil's keen eye, his steady hand, and his natural grasp of physics were his own. Canoes and lapstrakes, sailing dinghies and fishing skiffs, monohulls and hydroplanes, Phil had built them all, designed in winter, assembled in spring and launched in summer. Had it not been for his interest in boats, the Lost Lake Middle School Library would never have added *Naval Architect* to its periodicals subscriptions. It was through an advertisement torn from the back pages that Phil had ordered *Fifty Wooden Boats: A Catalog of Building Plans*, a book that stirred his spirits like the Bible calls Baptists. The subscription was a last-ditch effort by Marion Buttersworth, the school librarian, to keep him enrolled, though "it's a wonder that boy can think at all," she would say when the heavy metal strains from his earbuds disturbed her other charges from three stacks over. But Phil knew he was the apple of her eye. How else to explain how sweetly she asked him to "keep a lid on" his favorite, *Back in Black*, which would set the library to howling the *I'm back!* chorus the moment its easily distracted occupants caught wind of it drifting from Phil's retreat in the stacks.

When Phil did finally drop out, *Naval Architect* sat at the periodicals desk collecting dust until Ms. Buttersworth called the publisher and had the issues forwarded to Phil's house on Perdue Landing, the road posthumously named for Phil's grandfather in the tradition by which many of the lake roads were named for the region's settlers. Ms. Buttersworth knew the issues would find more use with Phil than in the school library, and this furtive act stoked her dwindling hope that anything good would come of him.

She knew by virtue of intimate relations she maintained with a local law enforcer that bootlegging was back in fashion, and meth labs were multiplying like mole hills, drawing the region's malingering youth like moths to light. Her unconventional life with J.D. Dunbar, the local police chief – a life in sin, by the reckoning of Lost Lake Middle School parents - explained her familiarity with how local boys broke bad, drawn as much for the excitement of being outlaws as for the intoxication that few things offer like a tight wad of cash. J.D. worried the fledgling local moonshine and meth enterprises would soon be met by violence for encroaching on the trade routes of South American drug gangs. His officers were stumbling on traffickers with growing frequency, and "they all looked like Pedro Morales, more or less," J.D. had been heard to say. Once, when he referred disparagingly to the *cockroach effect*, Marion admonished him for using racial slurs. She couldn't have known the *cockroach effect* was a term of art in the drug interdiction world, second only to the *balloon effect* on the list of growing concerns to U.S. law enforcement and border patrol.

If J.D.'s duty was to the community, Marion's was to its youth, and she stood watch in the school library like a guardian angel with talons, setting on imperiled youngsters with travel logs and classic literature to distract them as long as she could from hasty nuptials and lifetimes of toil at minimum wage. She prayed for her wayward pupils and despaired when they slipped her clutches, though Phil felt relieved when he did. It amused him to think how wrong she had him, just because he was reared without a momma. "I would have found you another, if another measured up," his daddy told Phil more than once, honoring the woman who traded her life for Phil's in childbirth. Marion had badly underestimated his daddy - but so, too, it turned out, had Phil.

"You can read whatever you wont," his father stipulated the day Phil dropped out, "'long as it ain't trash and it don't have pi'tures. Magazines don't count. You can read those on your own time. So long as you eatin' and sleepin' under ma ruff, it's two hours before work and two hours before you turn in. You can quit when you start payin' rent." His daddy worked him harder than school, but Phil took to it. Physics, naval architecture, colonial history, even the Transcendentalists – he followed his heart. He was plunging through solipsistic strains of *Fate* and *Self Reliance,* encouraged by how they echoed his reasons for quitting school, when he caught his daddy smiling. "Make you a better boat builder, that Emerson feller will. Teach you to think for yourself, be your own man," he said before turning out the light. He had tried to do both, but evidently not hard enough. Good thing his daddy couldn't see him now, and where boat-building eventually landed him.

For reasons he couldn't place, it was looking at Elaine, who appeared stumped by what to ask him next, that brought him back to the throaty, halting gurgle of Malcolm McLean's *General Lee* and the memories of that last day in Georgia.

CHAPTER 4

Lost Lake, Georgia - Five Years Before

The inexorable throb of the *General Lee's* advance was at first barely audible over the sputtering outboard of the overpopulated pontoon boat as it coughed and hissed beneath the moral burden of its cargo. Through the gathering din of assembling lake boats the anticipation thickened for the preacher's opening sermon.

The *General Lee* was a thirty-three-foot, triple cockpit, custom racing runabout designed by John Hacker and built in 1922 by the Stanley's Cape Vincent boat yard in the Thousand Islands district of upstate New York. She was powered by a Liberty V-12 engine, a repurposed World War I airplane engine that propelled her two tons of mesmerizingly vulgar jazz-age displacement at more than fifty miles per hour. She was the queen of the lake, and a badge of honor in the extended Perdue fleet. She had been raised from the frigid, oxygen-free depths of Lake Michigan, her hand-hewn timbers perfectly preserved, and trucked to Phil's backyard where she arrived when he was a boy. His daddy revived her, hand-fashioning parts discontinued before World War II, and matching mahogany timbers, old with new, so every one matched by grain and hue. And then to auction she went, where Malcolm McLean took her, doubling the last bid as the gavel fell.

He knew, on that first Sunday in June, and his last on Lost Lake, that Katie would be there aboard the *General Lee*, her long dark legs and white-soled feet carelessly cast over his painstaking stitching of the soft green leather that cushioned the cockpits. In a big straw hat with a cool blue ribbon, and a light cotton frock that hung girlishly from her figure, she'd be perched above the second cockpit leaning back on her hands, her long black hair falling freely to the deck. She always sat that way - on the edge of her dock, on the wall at the Pavilion, and on the gleaming henna hatch of the *General Lee*. Duncan would be aboard, too, slouching close by his father in the passenger seat of the front cockpit, mimicking the reproving glare by which the patriarch consumed his surroundings, his chin aristocratically elevated to align his cold Scottish eyes with the crisp clean line of his nose.

When the anticlimactic close to the season-opening sermon sent the pontoon pulpit skulking quietly ashore, and the summer's first Boat Church congregants retreated to reunions around the lake, Phil reached for the ignition. The *General Lee,* like Marse Robert himself, had slipped stealthily away long before the preacher had prostrated himself in gratitude for the glorious gift of a new pontoon boat, arriving soon, courtesy of the generous McLeans. His words were lost entirely on the whole McLean family, whose distant fading outlines had melted with Small's parting blessings in the infernal grumbling exhaust pipes of the scattering fleet. The *General Lee* had pulled up short of her boathouse half a mile off when Phil judged worship over and cranked the engine to join the exodus.

"Gawlee," he whispered as the ignition exploded to life in the meditative hush that rode on the calm of the bay after Boat Church. It sounded louder today, but not altogether deafening, he assured himself, until he surveyed the shoreline. All eyes were upon him. In every boat, on every dock, mouths gaped and eyes squinted, even heads on the distant *General Lee* turned. It was easy to imagine what Katie was saying, for she had in Phil's company mocked her father as few others dared, and with impunity.

"I think it sounds marvelous, Daddy, doesn't it?" she would be taunting him delightfully, "and I bet it goes fast, too."

Phil had yet to perfect the transmission. The clutch needed yanking and the throttle forceful priming, and still it produced a howl like a banshee.

"The cry of the Devil," Katie's mother, Ana-Maria, would be fuming in the husky Hispanic accent that defied disguise when her emotions ran hot, which Phil reckoned was just about always. She mentioned the Devil often, at least every time he surprised her in the boathouse, tending to the *General Lee*. That's where he had seen the picture of Duncan and his sister, Katie's stepsister, Moira, captured together as children in a forgotten old sun-bleached photograph hanging deep in the shadows of the *General Lee's* slip. Duncan thought his stepmother *was* the Devil - a black-eyed, dark-skinned, raven-haired, fiery South American, twenty years younger than his mother, and Phil reckoned Ana-Maria was why he'd never laid eyes on Moira.

Phil closed the distance between the Redemption Bay shoreline and Orchard Point at astonishing speed. He could see Katie watching him over the gently rolling transom of the *General Lee*. First Duncan, then Ana-Maria, and finally Malcolm, turned to face the horrendous noise heralding his approach. The *General Lee* was dripping from her hoists in the boathouse by the time he throttled back and the cushion of compressed, ground-effect air dissipated beneath his stubby wings. The belly touched down smooth as a duck, and he glided to a stop beside the boathouse where he abruptly killed the throttle, setting himself adrift just yards from where Katie stood on the dock by her father.

"Clever lad," he heard McLean mutter. "An ekranoplan, is it boy?"

"Why, yes sir, almost. All but the shaft. Next one will be proper, with a crop duster engine. Workin' on her now. Without no surface friction, she'll go twice as fast."

"Yes, of course," said Malcolm, sounding pleased but distracted.

"Hey Phil," Katie crooned, to send her father around the bend.

"Hey Katie," he replied, swallowing his delight. "Welcome back to the lake, and you too, sir. I hope the *General Lee* ran smooth for you this morning. She ain't never looked better, if I do say so myself. I think even my daddy would agree, rest his soul."

"Yes, son, you have no argument with me. She's in fine shape. You've acquitted yourself masterfully, young man. Your father would be proud."

Malcolm McLean was first generation American and proud of it, a child refugee of the Second World War, sent to live with his kinfolk in America to wait out the coming invasion of England. The remnants of his brogue resurfaced in rare moments of solicitousness, mingling with an acquired drawl to give his imperiousness a soft edge, like a kindly old robber baron mellowed by retirement.

"But I don't suppose it's the *General Lee* that's brought you calling today, is it Master Perdue?" he said, making Katie smile and her cheeks flush.

"No, sir. Not exactly, sir," Phil replied, pausing uncomfortably. "May I speak with you, alone, sir?" he asked, glancing at Katie.

"Man-talk, is it, son?" McLean replied, faintly amused. "Why, of course," he rattled in his kindly brogue. "Why don't you run along, Katie," he instructed. Katie huffed and ran off the dock. "Won't you come ashore, young man?"

"No thank you, sir. These wings..." he said, looking down at his feet, "make her hard to tie-up. I won't take much of your time, sir."

He had told McLean everything – how Uncle Mort brought news

from the bank, soon on the heels of the funeral. The news was of his daddy's indebtedness, accumulated over years by the poorly managed boat business. Rising real estate values kept the bank lending as the Perdue's lakefront property came to be worth a fortune. But now the property would bear no more and the real estate market looked ready to falter. It gave Mort no pleasure to report to Phil that the bank wanted the land sold right away. The bank was fixing to seize the family homestead and run him out, and Phil hoped Mr. McLean, by all accounts a rich man, and connected to the bank, would help him. Phil was willing to work hard, to bring discipline his daddy never had to running the business, and to repay all its debts, if someone would just stake him. Mort had given him time, but not much, to figure a way to keep the property. Would McLean, served faithfully for decades by Phil's father, please help? Mort was returning tomorrow morning to hear Phil's plan, and failing something satisfactory, begin the process of foreclosing. There was no denying his desperate circumstances. McLean was his only hope.

Phil never forgot McLean's clear-eyed indifference, nor the tone in which he conveyed it.

"No," he said abruptly. "Pity is a poor path to advancement, young man. You will have no self-respect," he assured Phil condescendingly. Malcolm himself had found his own way in Georgia, he told Phil, arriving with much less than a few million dollars of indebted water front property. In time, he assured Phil, the method of the Lord's madness would be revealed and make sense of this misfortune. Phil should latch on to his circumstances and find his own way, "by far the best thing for young men." McLean's words had been nothing if not prescient, Phil realized, as he eyed Elaine fixating on the reflective glass pane in the cinderblock wall.

Uncle Mort appeared, true to his word, at 8 a.m. the following Monday morning. He seated himself in the rocking chair beside the massive river stone fireplace that supported the rest of the ramshackle Perdue cabin. And there Mort sat, shaking his head discouragingly, until suddenly, unexpectedly, in the driveway beyond the old rickety porch a red pickup truck appeared.

"Phoenix?" said Uncle Mort, taking a scolding tone. "Phoenix?" he said again, his voice cracking with alarm. "What's *he* doing here? Don't tell me you're resorting to *this*."

Pedro Morales mounted the porch and came through the door without knocking. His soiled red t-shirt clung snugly to his belly, and his dilapidated flip-flops barely clung to his feet. He had shiny, shoulder length hair that matched an unkempt paintbrush moustache that billowed black as night from his upper lip. He closed too fast on Phil to notice Mort.

"Mr. Phil Perdue, yes?" Pedro inquired optimistically, his heavy Spanish accent massacring the Ys by turning them into Js. "It is Pedro, Pedro Morales, you know me, yes?" said Pedro, genial as the Welcome Wagon. YES sounded like JESS, and YOU sounded like JU, like juju beans, Phil's favorite. "I see you on the lake before, and yesterday, in your new boat. She fast," Pedro continued, turning the Fs to Bs so FAST came out BAST. "Your new boat, very, very fast," came out BERY BERY BAST. "I come to see if we do business, JESS?"

The glare Mort cut Pedro caught Phil's eye, which caused Morales to turn.

"Awwe, I sorry," said Pedro, "I no mean to interrupt. I come back later, yes?" he said turning for the door, a revolver handle protruding like a duck tail from his waist band at the small of his back.

"No!" said Phil in desperation. "No, please stay. How much business you talkin' about? And what you got in mind?" Morales turned and smiled.

That's when it began, he remembered, as he studied Elaine, who was growing more familiar by the minute.

"Don't be ridiculous," Uncle Mort interceded. Morales turned.

"Is there a pro'lem?" asked Morales.

"No problem," said Phil. "How much business you got in mind?"

"Quite a lot, my frien'," said Morales, winking at Uncle Mort. "Maybe more than you can handle, yes?"

"Absolutely not, Phil," Mort interjected. "The bank will not launder drug money." Phil never forgot how the expression drained from Morales' eyes, how much they looked like buttons on a coat, smooth and hard and lifeless, like plastic from a mold.

"What bank?" Morales asked.

"I owe money, Mr. Morales, a lot of money," said Phil, matter-of-fact. "I could sure use me some new business to start payin' it back. What you got in mind?" Morales grinned, a soulless sort of grin.

"Maybe I help, yes? I buy your boat," he said glancing through the window overlooking the porch, to the ekranoplan bobbing at her mooring beyond. He found Uncle Mort and winked at him again.

"No," said Mort, rising from his chair. "He's paying with drug money, Phil. You can't take that money. The bank can't take that money. It's money laundering. It's against the law and we'll all go to prison for it."

"How much?" began Morales, producing a wad of hundred-dollar bills as big as a roll of toilet paper.

"More than a million," Mort intervened, "and your money's no good at the Farmers Building and Loan of Lost Lake."

"No?" said Morales, looking defiant. The next fifteen seconds Phil would take to the grave. In three short steps Morales held Mort by the neck, stretching it like an accordion across his left shoulder. He had Mort's chin clenched tight in his left fist, and in his right against the taught skin over Mort's Adam's apple, he held something black with a distinctive crosshatched enamel handle. Phil had seen one before, a telescoping switch blade, and he saw Pedro's thumb caressing the catch.

"What Building and Loan of Lost Lake thinkin' now?" said Morales smiling at Phil.

There was no time to speak. When Pedro released the blade deep into Mort's throat, Mort's eyes bulged and the handle kicked, and the tissue in his neck yielded like soft butter. Mort squirmed for just an instant before his body went limp, and Morales laid him gently like a child to the floor. The blood spilled like milk, spreading smoothly and symmetrically in an even crimson halo like a saint in a stained-glass window, before seeping through the cracks in the knotty pine floor. Morales' grip loosened as Mort's pulse weakened, steadily subsiding until it gave out altogether. Morales crossed himself, mumbled a prayer, and reached into Mort's mouth and cut out his tongue. That blood-filled mouth, and Mort's glassy blank stare before Morales closed his eyes would haunt him forever.

"I sorry, my frien'," said Morales, breaking the silence. "He no good."

Phil reckoned he'd gone into shock, losing all sense of time, retaining but a few of the indelible, incoherent images of his final minutes at home.

"He was my uncle! You killed my uncle!" was all he could remember saying. "You killed him. Jesus-H-Christ! Why did you kill him?" he thought he remembered pleading.

"The banker, he was your uncle?" said Pedro, looking genuinely contrite. "I sorry for you, Mr. Phil. I sorry. No so nice, your uncle..." Phil must have panicked, felt sick, and buckled, because he came to in Pedro's arms, Pedro holding his head off the blood-soaked floor. *What now?* he remembered thinking, cradled in Pedro's murderous arms. *What the hell do I do now?* And then Pedro said something Phil never forgot, on which the next five years turned. He supposed those years didn't have to unfold as they had, though he had pondered enough how they could have been different to know the exercise was pointless.

"I think maybe you will be blamed, Mr. Phil, no?"

"*Me?* Why me? *You* did it. *You!*"

"Because is you, Mr. Phil, is you who owe *this* money to *him*, no *me*. I think you safer comin' with me now, yes?"

Or end up like Uncle Mort, Morales was saying, by how he wiped the blade clean on his soiled red t-shirt and drove it hard at the floor to reset the catch.

* * * * *

Was it a fateful miscalculation or destiny that sent him down this road that day – the road that led to this room, at this table, in these shackles, with Elaine.

Why he took the ride with Pedro remained altogether murky. Fear, surrender, resignation? There was just no telling, but he'd gone along to get along, and it sure had cost him.

He was partly to blame, he reckoned, for overestimating both friendships and family, for presuming goodwill from customers like McLean, and expecting forbearance from business partners like the bank, and counting on consideration from his uncle. None had hesitated to throw him to the wolves, despite his simply stated desire to restore his family's name and the luster of the boat business. So much for good intentions. But the conspiracy of coincidences to which he first attributed his misfortune was acquiring the feel of design, the inscrutable presence of an invisible hand growing palpable. He felt carried on the wave of some immutable dark force that had delivered him here to Elaine. Could things have turned out differently, he wondered.

After Mort bled out, Pedro had taken Phil on a harrowing nine-hour ride through the cotton fields and soy bean patches of

Alabama and Mississippi to the Port of New Orleans. Five hours after that they were touching down on a smudge-pot-lighted jungle airstrip on the Guajira Peninsula in Colombia, South America. The four-seat single engine Cessna had drained its wing tanks and consumed one of the two rubber fuel bladders that occupied the back seats. Morales had guided the plane to a camouflage netted clearing before cutting the throttle and letting the plane clatter to a halt in the dark.

It was a long time ago, whatever Elaine thought, and judging from the way she kept checking the mirror, she had run out of ideas. She turned on one heel, trained her cold reproving eyes on him, and lifted her chin just so, in a way Phil suddenly recognized.

"You're not *Elaine*," he said, seeing the familiar line of her aristocratic nose. "You're Duncan's sister, Katie's step-sister. You're Moira McLean."

CHAPTER 5

U.S. Coast Guard Cutter *Osprey*, Caribbean Sea

On or about the same night Phil Perdue touched down with Pedro Morales on Colombia's Guajira Peninsula, Casey Tindall passed his first night in a bunk at sea. All night he had rocked in the great ship's bowels, cradled like a baby in his lee-cloths. It suited him less than he expected. He rose before dawn to take some air and glimpsed Lieutenant Colonel Hank Gutterson for the first time. The officer emerged from his cabin down the hall with his freshly shaved scalp shimmering like an Oscar, and his handle bar mustache waxed to rebellious glory. He was suited up and ready, moving in the direction of the galley.

Tindall's condition was still deteriorating by the time he was suited-up himself, in a bright red flight suit and torso harness with a built-in, water-activated personal flotation device, or PFD, a piece of gear that was new to him. He was making his way toward the ready room when he heard a voice behind him say, "Semper Paratus," the U.S. Coast Guard motto. Tindall turned to find a fair-haired scrawny figure in a loose-fitting flight suit like his own, with

"Burbank" stitched into the Velcro name patch hanging askew from the young pilot's chest.

"You must be Doug," said Tindall, swallowing the urge to vomit.

"It's Dougie," replied the youthful pilot. "And you must be Casey. Welcome aboard," he continued, extending his hand. His grip was impressive, considering his slight build, and he followed closely behind Tindall down the narrow passageway.

The ready room sat beneath the flight deck of the medium endurance U.S. Coast Guard Cutter *Osprey*. She was the thirteenth and last of the two-hundred-seventy-foot *Famous* class cutters, christened in 1989 and commissioned in 1991, and she was presently steaming a long way from her home port in Key West, Florida. Tindall had puked all night and there was no disguising his impairment. If the distress on his face was not evidence enough of his weakened state, his sluggish gait gave him away. The dismal swish of his nylon flight suit inseams rubbing together betrayed his plodding legs, and Dougie seized on the opening.

"How glad are *you* to be here?" he said, pulling abreast of Tindall. "Welcome to HITRON. Whoa! you look like shit," he continued, "even in this light." The *Osprey's* interior lighting was switched to night ops, the dim red pall turning her insides murky, to protect the watch's night vision. Tindall groaned with the ship's roll, disconsolate but accustomed by now to her rhythm as she accelerated through her center of gravity, decelerated just as quickly, and then halted at her moment of inertia before repeating the cycle all over again. Tindall felt the pause and used it to widen his stance and sling-shot himself on the counter roll into the ready room where he collapsed in the nearest captain's chair. The chair had high padded armrests and faced forward with a dozen others. They were pointed at a screen, and divided like a movie house by an aisle. The *Osprey* had pitched all night on a quartering sea, riding long deep rollers from a tropical depression that had kept the Caribbean churning for the first two weeks of hurricane season. Tindall had never felt anything like it.

"I been shot at, crashed, and heard grown men cry for their mommas, God rest their souls, but I ain't never felt like this," Tindall whined from between his high padded armrests.

"You'll get used to it," Dougie assured him.

"I don't know..." said Tindall, straightening as the *Osprey's* Captain, Sherman Buldoc, appeared in the ready room doorway. Buldoc's reputation preceded him. He was a God-fearing, Bible-quoting mid-westerner whose life's ambition was an appointment to the Naval Academy that he never received. He settled for the Coast Guard Academy and a smoldering inferiority complex, and consequently commanded the *Osprey* like a fast attack corvette. He didn't tolerate blaspheme of any kind, especially not the Lord's name in vain, which is why the pornography running on the ship's closed-circuit television network had to be muted.

Buldoc marched down the center aisle of the ready room and turned on his heels at the front to face Dougie and Tindall. They were sitting like schoolboys, side-by-side, across the aisle. The lighting camouflaged smoke of which Tindall had been blissfully unaware until the captain started flailing at the air. The stale smell of cigarette smoke drifted like smoldering compost in an uneven haze that obscured the glinting gold borders of the *No Smoking* decals pasted about the room.

"Gutterson," Buldoc grunted discouragingly. "Where is he, Dougie?"

"Topside, checking out the new bird, Captain."

"You know about Lieutenant Colonel Gutterson, son?" Buldoc asked Tindall pointedly.

"No, sir." Tindall replied, jumping to his unsteady feet and saluting as he addressed the ship's captain for the first time.

"You can put your hand down and take a seat, soldier. You're not in the army anymore."

"Yes, sir," said Tindall, snapping his arm to his side, shoulders back, chest out. He felt Buldoc eye him despairingly.

"*Simon says*," Buldoc continued, "take a seat. You look like hell."

"Yes, sir," said Tindall, the way he was drilled, before guiding himself gingerly back into his chair. The room rumbled with the distant growl of the *Osprey's* twin turbo-charged V-18 diesel power plants, which had been making revolutions for twenty knots for five hours. Anything not bolted down vibrated softly with the background hum of the engines. Dougie's beady eyes searched the room. An object whereabouts unknown was resonating with the big block diesels several decks below, buzzing like a cicada on a hot summer night.

"So you don't know about Gutterson," said Buldoc, taking Tindall's measure.

"Well, I mean, yes, sir. I suppose I heard some things, sir," he stammered.

"You suppose?" Buldoc said, sounding skeptical. "Because you're about to fly into the night with a crazy son-of-a-bitch and you might just want to know what to expect."

If Gutterson *was* a crazy son-of-a-bitch, he wouldn't be the first helo pilot to earn that distinction, nor would he be the first to pilot Tindall. The attitude went with the air cavalry territory, and Tindall had resigned himself early in his first tour to have faith in the man at the controls. If things went wrong, his fate was sealed, with little to do but cinch his harness and commend himself to the Lord as he hurtled inside an eggshell of an airframe toward the earth.

"Yes, sir," he barked on cue, doing his best to look chastened.

"You were in the Army?" Dougie interrupted, Buldoc's reference to *soldier* finally registering. Dougie had been distracted by his unrewarded search for the buzzing.

"Yeah," Buldoc interceded. "Chaplain turned Crew Chief in the first Air Cav. Three tours in Afghanistan," said Buldoc, reciting from memory Tindall's Curriculum Vitae.

Funny how easily impressed non-comms could be, Tindall thought, like band roadies seduced by celebrity. But there was nothing glamorous about it - the long tours, the dust, the decent but boorish men, and the horrific things that happened to them so far away from home. By his third tour in Afghanistan, he had stopped volunteering, only taking to the air under orders, the thrill of combat having lost its luster.

"Chaplain to Crew Chief?" Dougie asked, looking distracted again, an unknowable mental calculus taking shape on his face. "Private Tindall preferred pay-back to prayer for performing personal penance?" Dougie finally said, enormously pleased with his alliteration.

"Sort of," Tindall replied. "A Chaplain in the 6th bought it – blown in two - moving a booby-trapped corpse, so I put myself behind a gun figurin' it weren't any more dangerous. Don't get me wrong, Lieutenant Burbank. I ain't lost my faith," Tindall felt compelled to reassure Dougie. "Just prayed on it and decided sending pagans to hell is important, too - least as important as commending the spirits of our boys to heaven." He regretted how the pride in his Kentucky farm boy inflection rose more than he intended. He wasn't the sort to apologize for his faith, but he tried not to inflict it on others, either.

"Yes sir, Lieutenant Burbank," Buldoc resumed admiringly, "Crew Chief Tindall, here, completed his tours, came out, got bored, and volunteered to join us."

"Oh," Dougie replied.

"I still know how to pray, and I'll pray over you, too, when the time comes," Tindall offered, though it came out differently than he intended.

"How was your ride out last night, son?" asked Buldoc.

"Fine, sir. Until I came aboard. I've never been on a ship before, sir. Still getting used to it." He wasn't sure he ever would, and wondered why the motion of the sea should give him more trouble than the aircraft in which he served. Maybe the defense of men on the ground distracted him sufficiently to suppress the stomach-churning movements of a gyrating gunship. Rolling in the belly of a boat with nothing to do but think about it was a different proposition.

"You've never been to sea, boy?" asked Buldoc, looking amused.

"I've seen it from the air, sir, lots a times. Just never *on* a ship, sir."

"Terrific," Dougie mumbled.

"And you've not met Gutterson either?"

"No, sir." The look of concern on Buldoc's face belied his dwindling hope. "They say he's kinda....intense, sir," said Casey unbowed.

"You heard more than that, boy," Buldoc pressed him.

"Well, sir. Yes, sir," he heard himself stutter, wondering how forthcoming of his inquiries he should be.

"Well?"

"I heard he was the first of the Night Stalkers," Tindall began, referring to the 160th Special Operations Aviation Regiment or SOAR, a highly secretive unit of airmen dedicated to supporting special warfare teams, especially in the dead of night. "...And maybe a team of SEALs died," Tindall continued, "because they were infilled too far offshore during Urgent Fury, the Grenada operation." The fixed expression on Buldoc's face offered little to dispel the sad lore.

"Anything else?" Buldoc prodded.

"He got relieved by the 160th and turned to flying crews back and forth to oil platforms in the Gulf of Mexico. He lost that job for looping his ship in plain sight of an OSHA inspector he had just dropped at a platform."

"He didn't get *relieved*," Dougie interjected, "he quit. His orders were wrong and he deviated to infill his team closer to the beach. Command ordered him back to the designated drop and a bunch of guys died, never recovered, presumed drowned," Dougie fumed. "He wasn't *relieved*." The dissolving red haze of cigarette smoke began to irritate Tindall's clean, youthful lungs, and he coughed in the awkward silence. He had heard the authorized version of Gutterson's retirement, not Dougie's.

"Truth is, son," said Buldoc, "nobody but Hank knows what happened that night, and HITRON is an all-volunteer unit, as you know. We couldn't turn a man of Hank's talents down," Buldoc explained, as if to appease Dougie, Gutterson's loyal co-pilot.

"And we have *latitude*, Captain Buldoc," Dougie interjected, "don't we, sir, there being no rules of engagement, like in wartime." Buldoc smiled, a weary, knowing, mostly-honest-bookkeeper smile.

"Here's where we are, gentlemen," Buldoc finally said, pointing a remote control at an overhead projector that illuminated the screen at the front of the room. A chart of the southern Caribbean Sea materialized on the screen, the littoral zone between the north coast of Colombia and the deep waters of the Colombian basin brightening as the projector bulb warmed. "You came aboard," the captain said glancing at Tindall, "at about twenty-two hundred, right about here." Buldoc aimed a laser pointer to international waters northeast of Panama City. "Since then we've steamed east, almost a hundred miles, which puts us right around here," he continued. He pointed to the shallows about a hundred miles west of Aruba and north of the Guajira Peninsula, a desolate, mangrove swamp-encrusted isthmus jutting north like a sore thumb into the Caribbean Sea on the border between Colombia and Venezuela.

"Hank won't like this," said Dougie, sounding nervous. "The Kessel Run again?"

"What difference does it make? That's the mission," Buldoc barked.

"He gets twitchy near GANTSEC, that's all," Dougie observed, referring to the Greater Antilles Section of U.S. Coast Guard Seventh District, an area running the length of the West Indies chain including Grenada on its southern fringe.

"Twitchy? An ex-SOAR jockey?" said Tindall. He was curious.

"Yeah," said Dougie, "he doesn't trust GANTSEC. Thinks they're bent." Now he had Tindall's attention.

If Casey Tindall had learned anything from the hellish vagaries and morphing battle lines of combat in Afghanistan, it was that you counted on your team, and that meant the team wearing your jersey. Everyone else was suspect, like the Afghan National Army, or ANA. As green-on-blue incidents spread, the home team became sacrosanct, and trust in their fealty absolute, which is why Dougie had caught his attention. Casey couldn't easily imagine how the war on drugs could be as ambiguous as frontline combat in Afghanistan, but that's what Dougie was intimating, as Buldoc looked anxious to move on.

"You boys can expect a busy day, today," said the captain reassuringly. "This low has been stationary so long the bales of pot and pails of coke are stacking like cord wood on beaches and landing strips all over Colombia," he continued. "The traffic will pick up as this low moves out and the seas die down. You'll be refueling before sun up, count on it. It should be like shooting fish in a barrel, with all your new comms and surveillance packages," Buldoc concluded, referring to the upgraded electronics with which the crew would be flying.

Tindall's ride to the *Osprey* five hours earlier was aboard a new generation of Coast Guard helicopter gunship. She was so fresh off the production line in Grand Prairie, Texas, that her interior smelled luxurious, like a showroom sports car. She was the first of the replacements for the aging *Stingrays,* which had been flying since the Helicopter Interdiction Tactical Squadron, or HITRON, was commissioned in 1998. Gutterson's ship in particular had been showing her age because he flew her like a demolition derby jalopy. He torqued the throttle on takeoff with so much topspin that he developed tennis elbow, and he rode the collective like a hand-brake. He yanked it so hard taking off from the flight deck that the *Stingray's* husky rotor blades bit chunks from the air, and sprayed static from its blades like party streamers. His landings were legend, too, alighting to the flight deck like a wrecking ball. Fussier pilots hovered daintily over the deck, oriented themselves to the roll of the ship, and touched the wheels to the landing pad with the tenderness of a kiss. Gutterson didn't see the point.

"The landing gear is built to take it," he reassured skeptics, "and so far, everyone has walked away."

Casey Tindall had arrived overnight to replace an unnerved predecessor. Rounds from a fleeing high-speed drug-runner, or *go-fast,* in drug war parlance, had grazed an oil line and perforated the tail rotor gear box of Gutterson's last ship, prematurely ending the *Stingray's* final deployment, and requiring a new Crew Chief to make the *Osprey's* HITRON unit operational again. The old bird's replacement was squeezed in the hangar deck over their heads. With her rotor blades unhinged and folded back sleekly against her fuselage, the muscular MH-65 D *Dolphin* looked poised to erupt like a burly moth from chrysalis. She had a long black, electronics-packed snout protruding from a day-glow orange fuselage, and better night vision than a barn owl, thanks to a next-generation radar and forward-looking electro-optical infrared system that projected digitally enhanced images on the inside of her cockpit windshield in zero visibility conditions. Her primary mission was drug interdiction, but she carried her weight on reconnaissance and surveillance missions, and all but flew herself using a fully integrated GPS and flight management system that certified her for all-weather and night operations. Her pilots could even maintain real-time awareness of unfolding events across her theatre of operations with full data video and radar contact uplinks from supporting elements throughout Seventh District. She could almost land herself, too, with a four-axis auto-pilot designed for steep, zero visibility approaches, which is what Gutterson thought training in Somalian dust storms was for. Part of him mourned the cost in pilot proficiency that came with automation, but he welcomed its new freedoms. The *Dolphin* was certified for single-pilot instrument flight operations, which meant he could fly it alone anywhere, and in any kind of weather.

Tindall's willingness to trust Gutterson and Dougie was not the same as satisfying his curiosity about them. In the transition from Chaplain to Crew Chief, Tindall acquired the habit of hunting down the command histories and service records of the airmen in the units he joined, HITRON included. That's how he learned HITRON was originally a classified unit founded with ten volunteers, including Gutterson, to fly the most heavily armed aircraft in the U.S. Coast Guard. The unit was based at Cecil Field in Florida, but her crews deployed for tours of up to sixty days on high and medium endurance cutters, like the *Osprey*. Like the original *Stingray* gunships, the *Dolphins* carried a mounted M240B 7.62mm general purpose machine gun. Designed for suppressing fire, it was ideal for warning shots and self-defense, but dismal for marksmanship. The gunner's offensive weapon was a semi-automatic Barrett M107 .50 caliber precision rifle, the weapon of choice for special warfare types, fitted with laser and holographic sights. They were in use all over Afghanistan, but never from the air. Precision shooting from an airborne helicopter presented obvious challenges, and the weapon was steadied by vibration-dampening suspension straps that hung like a bungee-cord hammock between the jams of the sliding cabin door. No amount of dampening, however, substituted for poor marksmanship, so the Coast Guard maintained a special bucket of tax payer dollars dedicated solely to Crew Chiefs like Tindall, to ensure they could shoot out engines fleeing in the night.

Tindall was the only ex-military Crew Chief in HITRON, and he gave as much to the marksman training program by way of his Afghanistan experience as he got. He could scarcely wait to try his hand at neutralizing engines instead of people. A single .50 caliber bullet packed more than enough ballistic punch to silence the biggest outboard engine. A few good shots was all it took to set a go-fast adrift, but not to render it harmless. Go-fast crews were heavily armed and known to resist, even in the sights of a circling gunship.

If a go-fast crew didn't die in a futile and furious last stand, it was the job of Law Enforcement Detachments, or LEDETs, to take them into custody. LEDETs were the high-seas enforcers of the Anti-Drug Abuse Act of 1986, a legacy of Reagan era policy-making that declared narco-trafficking a national security threat. Working in eight-to-twelve-man teams, they were billeted aboard Coast Guard cutters and Navy ships, and vested with broad legal powers including portable jurisdictions that authorized them to lord over vessels of their choosing on the high seas. Warships of more than two dozen partner nations including Britain, Holland, and Canada, could be reflagged at LEDET discretion, and sail indefinitely under U.S. Coast Guard ensign at the disposal of Coast Guard command center Joint Interagency Task Force South in Key West. This is how more than a few foreign warships found themselves under tactical control by LEDETs from San Diego and Miami. It was desperately needed surge capacity to fill the gap left by Coast Guard assets spread too thin to stem the tide of U.S.-bound narcotics and terrorists.

The LEDETs lowered away in a go-fast of their own, a water-jet powered rigid-hull inflatable boat, or RHIB. The massive inflatable gunwales that ringed the self-bailing hull of the RHIB gave her buoyancy to spare, and she could ship her weight in seawater without compromising her seaworthiness. The RHIB simply powered ahead on her thick gray haunches, fording the surf like a monster truck until she reached the disabled go-fast and captured her crew. Until then, the HITRON crew hovered overhead, guns trained, lest the go-fast crew have anything but surrender in mind.

And yet, despite wide latitude to exercise force, unprecedented surge capacity, and up-tempo combat footing higher than any before sanctioned in peace time, the days at sea proved endless and mind-numbing. Many a sixty and ninety-day cruise was spent waiting for the enemy to show. The LEDETs laid siege to barren waters for weeks on end. When eventually they did muster to apprehend transiting ships, they wore bullet-proof vests and bristled with antennas and heavy weapons that were mostly for show. The tools of their trade were tape measures and graph paper, the geometry-class kits serving the vital purpose of rendering captured vessels in three dimensions to reveal where fuel tanks and water tanks, and bait wells and sea lockers disguised hidden chambers packed with contraband, which more often than not were empty.

Drug runners knew that recovered narcotics were the only evidence LEDETs required to secure lengthy convictions, and go-fast crews excelled at heaving evidence overboard. Contraband found its way into the sea faster than Boston tea the instant U.S. law enforcement made contact. When highspeed chases ensued, fleeing crews worked furiously disposing of evidence, lightening their holds and picking up speed, from fifty-five or sixty miles per hour fully laden to eighty miles per hour on empty holds and smooth seas. Even so, the go-fasts were still no match over a short course for the HITRON *Dolphin's* top speed of one hundred and seventy-five knots. On speed, the *Dolphin* was a sprinter and had the advantage; on endurance, however, she was vulnerable.

At full throttle the *Dolphin* guzzled fuel like an eighteen-wheel truck. Her range was barely three hundred and fifty miles, more than the older, nimbler *Stingrays*, but shy of the four hundred miles of open Caribbean Sea separating the Guajira Peninsula, off which the *Osprey* was presently loitering, and the southern tip of Santa Domingo. Not surprisingly, smugglers knew that HITRON crews were reluctant to be drawn too far from a landing zone - ideally their support ships, but dry land counted, too. So go-fasts ran for open water, knowing their best chance was to extend the chase. Purchased and purloined fishing boats and luxury yachts crisscrossing the Caribbean doubled as cartel sentries and floating refueling stations for fleeing go-fasts in the endless cat-and-mouse game with U.S. authorities.

In the early days, HITRON notched major successes. Interdictions rose and narcotics seizures multiplied, from less than a hundred vessels and detainees per year to ten times that number. But when the value of seized marijuana and cocaine increased from tens of millions of dollars per year to hundreds of millions, the cartels raised their game. The race was on for faster and stealthier transportation to meet demand once supplied by the broken Cali and Medellín cartels. It was into this storm the *Osprey* had steamed the evening Casey Tindall came aboard, positioning herself at the point of least distance between the north coast of Colombia and Santa Domingo, the heavily trafficked route that Gutterson and Dougie had affectionately dubbed *The Kessel Run*.

CHAPTER 6

Organized Crime Drug Enforcement Task Forces Fusion Center, Washington, D.C.

Lenny Marks was a nasty bastard, and he knew it - congenitally wicked, his mother used to say. Moral? Sure. Ethical? Mostly. Mean? Always, and for no good reason. His condition wasn't the work of an abusive parent or any other form of victimization that customarily accompanies maladjustment. Some people wake up on the wrong side of the bed. Lenny was born there. Not that he detested everything, just people and their deceits, and he knew this made him exceptional at his job.

His mood today was especially bad. The Office of the Inspector General, the investigative arm of the U.S. Justice Department – OIG to beltway insiders - had just completed an unflattering review of the organization he served, the Organized Crime Drug Enforcement Task Forces Fusion Center, or OCF. Better known as *Fusion* to drug enforcement operatives, it was an unholy union of twenty-five competing federal law enforcement agencies including the DEA, FBI, TSA, NSA, IRS, Homeland Security and the U.S. Coast Guard. The OIG's breakthrough insight about Fusion was that its mission was hobbled by a dysfunctional relationship between the DEA and the FBI.

That was news? Even the most half-assed human resource manager with the vaguest understanding of the staff and organization chart could have figured that out. It took the OIG an exhaustive, nine-month, taxpayer-funded investigation to alight with a sense of wonder on the obvious. Lenny found the report's superficialities less irksome than its repercussions. It raised fear and suspicion to new heights in an organization that breathed fear and suspicion. He was outraged, as often he was, because it made the work harder, made his people more cautious, and added a distraction they didn't need. The OIG concluded that politics came before the mission at Fusion, and Lenny knew that was wrong. Territorial scuffles always accompanied the hunt for the world's most socially destructive criminal enterprises, especially when the hunters were the best and brightest of U.S. law enforcement. Fusion staff were ambitious and competitive. So what?

Fusion's eight investigative units were tasked with disentangling the endless stream of intercepts from across the globe, and spinning the morass of phone, text, email, and social media threads into tapestries of correlated intelligence - heat maps of narcotics trafficking and money laundering, to inform the intelligence picture of agents in the field. The DEA and FBI often hurried, as A-types grubbing for credit sometimes do.

But with respect to Fusion's primary mission, namely "deconfliction," to which all member agencies were equally vulnerable, turf wars did not factor, of this Lenny was certain. Officially, "deconfliction" meant eliminating duplication of effort by multiple agencies focused on the same targets. Practically speaking, it meant keeping federal, state and local law enforcement officers from descending on the same scene like Keystone Cops and shooting each other. There was no room for communications failures when it came to taking down targets, and the DEA and FBI knew it, despite how their competitive juices flowed. Second only to deconfliction, Fusion's mission was to maintain a list of Consolidated Priority Organization Targets, or CPOTs, a handy acronym the community used to describe the extended networks of the crime world's true bad guys.

Lenny was also grumpier than usual because it was intern recruiting season, or rather, intern culling season. Fusion received countless applications for just six openings. On paper they all looked the same – over-enthused and over-educated first- and second-year law school students motivated by naïve presumptions about their potential to right the world's wrongs. They would be better qualified to serve him by spending the summer in the back of a squad car patrolling the destitute neighborhoods of Miami or Newark or Stockton. Those were the last stop, the end of the line for the narcotics distribution networks - ground zero, where you saw the face of the enterprise, and might peer, if you were very good, upstream into the channels, perhaps as far as the headwaters. These school kids could work the keyboard well enough, even master the database tools, but could they *see* anything, *find* anything? What he wouldn't do for a candidate or two who had lived the streets, survived juvenile detention, and found himself convicted by a career federal prosecutor. That applicant would be someone he could use. Instead, he found himself inventing new ways to keep acutely narcissistic and thoroughly sheltered white kids challenged for the summer.

But Fusion needed people, there was no denying it. Even OIG included among its complaints that Fusion had become "unresponsive to the field." It was failing to keep up with the growing burden on local, state and federal law enforcement, because it was understaffed. But why *these* people, Lenny wondered as he glanced uncomfortably at the anxious resumés in his inbox.

Fusion staffers numbered one hundred ninety-five full time equivalents (FTEs) - some employees, and others contractors, the majority of whom were "detailees," on loan for two-year assignments from Fusion member agencies. They were supposed to be seasoned law enforcement professionals to qualify for a Fusion posting, even though "some Fusion Intelligence Analysts have little or no law enforcement experience," said the OIG report.

Fusion operated as a drug-crime law enforcement research desk, a service bureau of sorts, offering a range of intelligence "products" to "requestors," who might or might not hail from one of Fusion's member agencies. Requests came from everywhere - domestic and international law enforcement agencies as well as federally deputized state and local law men. Fusion's products came in four flavors, two of which were responsive to external requests, and two of which were highly classified, internally originated targeting initiatives. The responsive products were *Target Profiles* and *Cases and Contacts*, the former being compilations of individual biographical and financial information, including known social and professional associations, and the latter a summary of all active investigations involving the target. The two targeting products originated by Fusion were the *CPOT Briefing Book* and the *PATT Target Profile.*

Consolidated Priority Organization Targets, CPOTs, were the Masters of the drug trafficking universe – the arch-enemy of community law enforcement everywhere. Only Fusion's CPOT Unit saw the complete CPOT intelligence picture, and that changed faster than the weather in Alaska. There were never fewer than five dozen CPOTs on the unit's tracking list, and murders, captures, and extraditions kept the list shuffling.

The *Proactive Asset Targeting Team*, or PATT, generated the fourth of Fusion's products, the PATT Profile. PATT profiles were triggered by suspicious financial activity detected automatically by financial institution compliance reporting. Beginning in 1970, when Lenny was getting his start, financial institutions were required by the Bank Secrecy Act to report certain activity to the Financial Crimes Enforcement Network, or FinCEN, a Fusion member agency. The Bank Secrecy Act defined *Financial Institutions* as every kind of business that handled large sums of cash, including banks, insurance companies, brokerages, and even car, boat, and airplane dealerships. Penalties for lapses were heavy, ranging from crippling fines for lesser oversights to revoking the institution's charter altogether. Lenny's first promotion at Fusion was to the leadership of the PATT unit. From there he ascended to the leadership of the CPOT unit. He replaced himself at PATT with a protégé, who, he was forced to concede, became a lifer after joining Fusion through the summer internship program.

Lenny believed fervently in keeping Fusion intelligence products broadly accessible to law enforcement agencies, as long as the purpose was credible. He also knew the risks of sharing that information, and that those risks had to be managed. One of the curious mechanisms by which Fusion products were authorized for release involved a separate, more potent and shadowy DEA agency known as the Special Operations Division, or SOD, from which the Fusion Center Section, or *FusionCenter* operated. SOD acted as a clearing house for authorizing, censoring, and releasing Fusion product reports.

Lenny was a proud veteran of SOD, from its formation in 1994 to combat Latin American drug cartels, until he left to join Fusion. He left because SOD expanded massively, from several dozen low-key devotees like himself to hundreds of zealots who showed up shortly after September 11, 2001 to bring SOD's surveillance expertise to bear on terrorism. The mission creep that followed introduced territoriality, political intrigue, insecurity, and envy - all the loathsome aspects of human nature Lenny abhorred. He had been looking for a way out of SOD for well more than a year when the opportunity to launch Fusion presented itself in 2004. Lenny liked desperate causes and new beginnings, the way SOD had been in the early days, not least because risk-averse career bureaucrats of the kind that invaded SOD after 9/11 shied from risky endeavors and the blots they could leave on a resumé. Fusion was Lenny's chance to get back into deep research, and he took it.

Most of the time he felt glad for his self-imposed exile to Fusion. He didn't need to know how law enforcement applied his often-surprising discoveries, and he didn't want to know how organizations like SOD daily skirted ethical boundaries to achieve its intelligence objectives. Unlike Fusion, whose methods were out in the open, SOD was the sort of place that cultivated cloak-and-dagger obscurity. SOD took its secrecy so seriously that its location was itself a secret, which Lenny found laughable. Was he really supposed to forget where SOD was after reporting to work there for a decade?

SOD even encouraged the community it served to deny its existence. The Reuters News Agency reported in 2013 that Fusion analysts were told to "remember that the utilization of SOD cannot be revealed or discussed in any investigative function." The article brooded inconclusively about intelligence gathering techniques that were so secret, or so unconstitutional, that law enforcement agents were encouraged to practice "parallel construction," fabrication by another word, of evidence supplied by SOD to protect or disguise sources. The Fusion Director had distributed reprints of the article to remind his staff that news outlets were hungry for headlines, to best the recent stunning disclosures by Edward Snowden about NSA surveillance.

Wistfulness was not in Lenny's repertoire, but part of him longed for the early days at SOD, and this explained the love-hate relationship he nursed for the place. On the one hand, SOD intelligence had delivered crushing takedowns, from Victor Bout, the Russian arms dealer, to the massive bust of a synthetic drug manufacturing and distribution operation spanning thirty-five states. On the other hand, SOD operated with impunity, and so, by extension, did FusionCenter, the gatekeeper on Fusion's and Lenny's research products. Lenny had been wondering of late if something was changing. Try as he might to discount his congenital cynicism, FusionCenter's censorship appeared to be tightening, and he was bridling under its muzzle.

In principle, he didn't mind being muzzled to protect surveillance operations. SOD harbored the same fear as the World War II Polish and British code breakers who cracked Enigma, the impenetrable Nazi enciphering machine – that its methods and capabilities would be revealed. Like the Allies who sacrificed troops and convoys to keep decoded intercepts secret, SOD encouraged federal prosecutors to drop cases that risked exposing its sources.

But the field requests rejected by FusionCenter of late had grown more suspect. The new practice of rescinding Fusion's PATT reports were especially worrying. Lenny's protégé and PATT Unit Chief, Sam Rosen, had been bending Lenny's ear about how regularly SOD was burying his PATT profiles. It was natural to second guess requests for *Target Profiles* and *Cases and Contacts.* Requests like that were rejected all the time, because there was reason to suspect the requestor's intent, or the risk of a leak was too great. Fusion and SOD were rightly wary of infiltrators or *probes*, requests from in-the-field, on-the-take law enforcement officers probing for investigations of their paymasters.

But PATT reports were different. They originated not from the field, but from alerts triggered by computer algorithms monitoring FinCEN compliance reporting. Why would SOD quash internal reports? It made no sense ...unless someone at SOD was suppressing internal alerts to conceal authorized criminal activity.

Regrettably, collusion between U.S. law enforcement and drug traffickers was practically a cliché, dating back to the Reagan-era DEA. There was the Los Angeles crack epidemic, widely attributed to cocaine trafficking by the CIA-backed *Contras,* and covered in lurid detail by the *San Jose Mercury News,* the *Los Angeles Times, The Washington Post,* and the *New York Times.* Or the CIA operation that overlooked the distribution of more than a ton of pure cocaine from Venezuela to the streets of Miami, all to frame the Venezuelan chief of anti-narcotics, a formerly trusted CIA informer. General Ramon Guillen Davila said at trial that the CIA had approved his drug smuggling activities, which had the ring of truth seeing as the cocaine had been stored in a CIA-owned warehouse in Venezuela. And then there was the recent trial of Vincente Zambada-Niebla, a leader in the Sinaloa cartel, Mexico's largest, run by the infamous Joaquin "El Chapo" Guzmán. At trial it came to light that DEA officials met with Sinaloa cartel members more than fifty times between 2000 and 2012 in operation Fast-and-Furious, a debacle approved by then Attorney General Eric Holder, which supplied the Sinaloas with military-grade weapons that were used to kill U.S. Border Agent Brian Terry. These were just the publicized cases. If the DEA were colluding with the drug cartels again, SOD would almost certainly be in on it. This time the deal appeared to involve turning a blind eye to money laundering. No need to look further than his own colleagues for the duplicity Lenny loved to hate.

CHAPTER 7

Guajira Peninsula, Colombia

He would have done anything to keep sleeping, to linger in his dreams, where yesterday never happened. He had dreamed of home, his father was still alive, Katie had kissed him, and Uncle Mort had agreed to let him work out the loan. But the screeching wouldn't stop. He opened his eyes and gazed into the murky jungle canopy. One screech followed another until a crescendo of whoops erupted across the treetops. They sounded like fisher cats, except fisher cats were ground critters, and so mean they traveled alone. This was a passel of critters. They were up in the trees and having a time of it. He had slept like a baby, slung in the open-air hammock Pedro hung for him the night before. It had kept him off the jungle floor, and for that he was grateful. No telling what jungle dwellers had passed beneath him during the night after he bedded down to the buzz of a billion insects, just like he did on his sleeping porch back home. Dawn had come steamy and warm, and strangely reassuring, until the whoops recommenced, and he sat bolt upright, as much as one can in a hammock.

"Good morning, my Gringo frien'," came a mellifluous Hispanic voice. Phil turned to find a young man no older than himself, wearing reflective silver aviator glasses and army-issue jungle camouflage. He wore a matching soft brim hat with one side turned up, Australian style.

"You no so hard to guard, my frien'," he said. "Hydrate?" he asked, turning the cap on a clear plastic water bottle sweating with condensation.

"Much obliged," said Phil, draining half the bottle's contents. The water was cold and refreshing.

"In the night, you have big dreams," the young man continued. "Who is *'Katie'*?" he asked pleasantly enough. Phil hesitated, wondering how badly he had embarrassed himself.

"I talk in my sleep?" he croaked sheepishly.

"Sí," his young guard assured him. Curious, he thought, to learn something new about yourself from a stranger.

"Hey, man, I'm Phil. What's your name?" he said extending his hand.

"Miguel," said the guard, steadying something by his waist with his left hand and shaking Phil's hand with his right.

"Thanks again for the water, Miguel," said Phil, and drank from the bottle again. He downed the last gulp just as Pedro materialized in the gloom. He was humming mariachi, and greeted Phil's guard with a beaming smile. They exchanged some words in Spanish, pleasantries by the sound of it, except an amused back-and-forth that included conspicuous mention of *Katie* a few times. Back then he didn't know Spanish, but he gleaned enough from Pedro's reaction to understand that Pedro thought he knew the *Katie* Phil had been dreaming about. Shortly, the guard was dismissed, and it wasn't until the young man turned that Phil saw the long gun slung across his back, an angular, black weapon with a metal frame stock and a vented barrel.

The whoops commenced again as the guard melted from view.

"What *is* that dadgum sound?" Phil asked Pedro.

"D'ose what you gringos call howler monkeys, yes? Sone tines we call dem dinner," said Pedro, flashing his flamboyant smile. Gross, thought Phil, peering overhead. Pedro set to humming mariachi again. He had sung all day on the drive to New Orleans, accompanying mariachi radio stations he found on the dial everywhere from Lost Lake County, Georgia to Plaquemines Parish, Louisiana. His voice wasn't terrible, and there was something irrepressible and generous to his free-spirited song. It might have been comforting but for what Phil already knew of the man's propensity for violence.

"Come on, Mr. Phil," said Pedro, backhanding Phil's chest. "No more siesta for you! Tine for a wash and brea'fast, and den we go see Vlad and José."

Reckoning he had no choice in the matter, Phil swung himself from the hammock as Pedro started into the jungle, parting vegetation with his stout, sweeping arms, and feeling his way through the gloom to the opening of what looked to Phil like a man-size burrow in the undergrowth. Sunlight had begun to filter through the jungle. As they entered the warren a tunnel took shape, a thatch of vines and scrub that blotted out the meager light by which they had found their way to its entrance. They followed a well-trodden path, the soft sound of their footfalls carrying them deeper into darkness and away from the din of caterwauling monkeys. He should have been afraid, and he did panic once, hunger and homesickness-induced vertigo gripping him in the darkness on the path. But there was no escaping, nowhere to turn and no way to save himself, nothing to do but fall in Pedro's footsteps. No time passed at all before fear gave way to curiosity, and then excitement about where Pedro was taking him. The familiarity of Pedro's face and its association with home is how the bond between them formed, Phil told himself sometime later. That Pedro knew where Phil called home, and knew Phil's customers, and even Katie, made him familiar, comfortable – with no way to foresee how entangled they were shortly to become.

Just the day before he had thought a hundred times of throwing himself from Pedro's red truck, containing himself at first for sheer terror of what Pedro might do if he survived, and then because he sensed how Pedro meant him no harm. The man had shown how easy was his way with violence, but held no obvious animus for Phil, betraying every so often a kind of fraternal, shared destiny resignation of a sort Phil had never seen. When they had spoken on and off between mariachi choruses, Phil learned how Pedro had been watching him. Pedro knew all about him and thought proving it would put Phil at ease, which naturally had the reverse effect. He knew things about Phil's customers, too, especially Malcolm McLean. He could name the families that went with each lake house, knew where they lived in winter, and even what they did for work. He knew the names of their kids, too, learned he said from nieces and nephews and cousins who worked the lake house properties as gardeners, housekeepers, and carpenters.

"You see, Mr. Phil? We all workin' for *the man*, sí?" he said, raising his bushy black eyebrows. "We are brothers, Mr. Phil, workin' for *the man*!" Pedro pronounced before launching with exuberance into another mariachi chorus. Brotherhood was not among the sentiments he ever imagined harboring for Pedro, but he'd be foolish not to embrace it for as long as it took to devise an escape plan.

Through the darkness they padded, the distant howler monkeys squalling, until the tunnel widened, the undergrowth thinned, and narrow beams of steamy light dappled the earth in mosaic blotches of sunshine. From somewhere ahead came the voices of men, bantering in muffled tones between mysterious exertions. When Pedro and Phil emerged from the undergrowth, the plane they landed in the night before came into view. By the light of dawn Phil saw what a tired excuse for an aircraft it was, with oxidized paint, a smoky, pitted windshield, and a large underslung compartment that Phil failed to notice when they took off from a small private airfield somewhere outside New Orleans. Beyond the plane was a rough white landing strip that vanished beneath the horizon of a gleaming turquoise Caribbean Sea. The sound of waves on a distant shore carried on the wind as the mystery of gasping men solved itself. They stood around the plane filling the compartment beneath the fuselage with heavy black oblong bags.

Pedro led Phil toward the plane and the men paused from their work.

"Quiero presentarte Mr. Phil," Pedro announced with fanfare.

"Bienvenido, Mr. Phil!" they replied roughly in unison, advancing and smiling to shake his hand. Phil reckoned he knew the contents of the bags, but pleasantries and small-talk followed just the same, no matter that dope worth millions was littered like toys around a Christmas tree at their feet. He'd never even seen drugs, let alone used them, and always reckoned he'd dislike the sort who did. The men around him were, by all accounts back home, villains, though they looked and sounded regular enough. It was standing there, feeling out of sorts that he noticed the pervasive smell of gasoline, how heavily it hung in the air, even as they left the airplane behind and Pedro quickened his pace down the center of the pale, sand and crushed coral landing strip.

Long swaying shadows of waving palm fronds darkened the runway in shifting geometric patterns as the Caribbean sun lifted slowly over the jungle. It was Phil's first view of a Caribbean dawn, and he gawked at the towering cumulus clouds that turned out to pack more bark than bite compared to the thunderheads back home. Garish pink and blue clouds receded in orderly ranks to the horizon, perpetually advancing and forever dispersing before making landfall.

"Big storm, Mr. Phil," said Pedro, seeing Phil's awe. "She is leaving today. We go to work." There was no escaping the gasoline fumes. The smell was everywhere, even in the clear gusty sea breeze, and he breathed it like a calming elixir, because it reminded him of his workshop back home. He found in it refuge from the vastness of the sea and the strangeness of the jungle, and the lawlessness of the place and its people.

No telling how long they would keep him or what it would take to escape, he thought, as he kept pace with Pedro striding familiarly down the landing strip.

"No town for miles, banditos everywhere, and scorpions and snakes, Mr. Phil," said Pedro, reading his mind. "At night you stay in your hammock, OK?" Phil didn't need convincing. He could scarcely imagine what lay out there in the jungle, beyond the camp. Even by day the noises were like to chill your blood.

The gusty hot air and sun-bleached earth, and the din of rustling palm fronds and desiccated tropical vegetation felt all at once thrilling and hostile. This was why explorers craved discovery, he imagined, like Christopher Columbus alighting on unfamiliar lands, teeming with mysterious peoples. He never felt anything like it, and he might have been cowed but for Pedro's spirited attentions and occasional encouragement. Despite the unnerving manner of his arrival, there was no deny it was Pedro who appeared in his time of need, when there was no help to be had. Things had gone wrong because Pedro had lost his temper, and he wished to God Mort wasn't dead, but Pedro had made things right the best way he knew how - and ushered Phil to safety - Uncle Mort had provoked him, after all.

He kept pace, falling into lock-step with Pedro, who marched with purpose into the erratic, prevailing wind blowing down the airstrip. Man-sized vortices of fine coral and sand materialized near the water's edge and swerved like drunks down the runway before veering into the jungle and disintegrating on thickets of black sage and calabash. The constant noise of wind and sea and gyrating vegetation had unsettled him at first, but soon enough he acclimated, his love for the hush of the still Georgia dawn surrendering before he knew it to the frenetic restless energy of the churning Caribbean.

He meant no disrespect to his home or upbringing by it, though he was left in a bad place back home by his daddy, owing all that money. The promise of the boat business, the goodwill of its clients, and the appreciation of the skills he brought to it, proved false. Maybe that was the lesson McLean foresaw, that running off with Pedro had taught him. Sinner that he was, Pedro had looked out more for him in just a few hours than his Uncle Mort or Malcolm McLean ever did.

The only honest path to independence was your own. That's what McLean had been saying, and Phil could see that now; how sentimental memories of home, the business, the lake and Boat Church, were false idols all along. His father's debts, Uncle Mort's stubbornness, the bank's determination to foreclose, and Malcolm's refusal to help had done him the favor of sticking his nose in it. Why Pedro had come to his aid when his own people wouldn't left him altogether stupefied; and on further reflection, he felt like a rube for approaching McLean at all, for confusing flattery with approval because McLean muttered a few kind words about the upkeep of the *General Lee*. Good enough for McLean's boats, Phil supposed, but not for his money, or his daughter. Why memories of the workshop, its tools, the curling yellowed boat show pictures, the plaques and prizes and piles of parts, weighed so heavily on him from time to time he couldn't say, but with every tropical breath he took the weight grew steadily lighter.

"Come on, Mr. Phil, you come with me," Pedro said over his shoulder, as he darted back into the undergrowth between a latticework of roots holding up two tall mangrove trees. Who the heck were José and Vlad, Phil wondered, as he followed Pedro out of the wind and into the shade.

CHAPTER 8

U.S. Coast Guard Cutter *Osprey*, on-station: Kessel Run, Caribbean Sea

"Kessel Run?" Tindall inquired. "You don't mean, like from...."

"*Star Wars,*" Buldoc interjected. "Dougie, here, thinks he's Luke friggin' Skywalker, and Gutterson's the spitting image of a three-hundred-pound Sir Alec Guinness, just ask him."

"He's losing weight, sir," Dougie objected.

"My ass, he is. He's a fucking walking heart attack. Anyway, kid, you got nothing to worry about 'til Gutterson starts purring in an English accent."

"You can be Princess Leah," Dougie offered Tindall cheerfully. Buldoc turned to the illuminated chart on the wall and traced a line back and forth with his laser pointer between the Guajira Peninsula and Beata Island on the southern tip of the Dominican Republic, "... the Kessel Run," he said darkly.

"Show him why," Dougie urged. Buldoc fiddled with a laptop computer on a side table until a chart appeared, spanning the Caribbean from the Pacific coast of Central and South America to the Atlantic coast of the Leeward Islands. Overlaid on the chart were tiny red capillaries connecting land masses in a thousand permutations, with the lines concentrated like tributaries feeding a handful of larger, more heavily traveled estuaries.

"This is a composite of suspected smuggling surface radar tracks for the last five years," Buldoc explained. The red lines were especially dense in an imprecise thicket of tangled tracks extending north northeast from the Guajira Peninsula to the southern tip of the Dominican Republic.

"As you can see, this route," said Buldoc, circling the red lines with his laser pointer, "the so-called *Kessel Run* is a crowd favorite. No telling what you're likely to see in the next twenty-four hours. Go-fasts for sure, hijacked fishing boats, more than likely bigfoots, too."

"Bigfoots?" Tindall inquired, still bemused by Dougie's Princess Leah comment.

"Subs," Buldoc replied. "Self-propelled Semi Submersibles - SPSSs, technically speaking, better known as Narco Subs," the captain continued evenly.

Dougie had been distracted since Buldoc began the briefing by the relentless buzzing of whatever it was that was resonating with the engines belowdecks, and now there was something in his right hand, which he was lifting slowly over his head. Taking aim, he rifled whatever it was without warning at a table beneath the projection screen. The buzzing ceased as the projectile found a pen lying on the table. Both projectile and pen bounced off the wall and fell to the deck.

"Thank you, Dougie," said Buldoc. "Shall we continue?"

"That's better," said Dougie. "Sure."

Tindall had read a brief on SPSSs, but it never spelled out the acronym. He thought they were a variant of a go-fast.

"We heard about them for years from ground intel," Buldoc continued, "but never have spotted one in transit. Gutterson dubbed them *Bigfoots* because we had the reports but no confirmed sightings, at least not by us."

"Do they actually exist?" Tindall asked.

"You better believe it," said Buldoc. "One washed ashore a few years back, but knowing what to look for makes them no easier to find. The sneaky bastards building them know what they're doing. They run just below the surface, except for a short, sealable conning tower that has about the same radar signature as a fish trap. Can't hear 'em with sonar on account of the surface clutter, and they vent their exhaust underwater through the hull, so there's no infrared signature. And the damn things are built to sink. If you see one take a good look, because you won't see it for long. The crew will don their life jackets, open a bank of seacocks and bail out the top like jack rabbits. The whole damn boat will be gone in less than a minute taking the evidence and any signature of her builders straight to the ocean floor."

"And that means the runners go free?" Tindall asked, as if the injustice offended him.

"It used to, until Congress passed the Drug Trafficking Interdiction Act, which made operating an unflagged SPSS a criminal offense. All you need today is clear video of the subjects abandoning ship and that's enough evidence to convict for a twenty-year visit to the big house. Just make sure Dougie, here, keeps the video rolling."

"And what happens to the drugs?" Tindall persisted.

"They're gone. The few SPSSs spotted managed to scuttle in water so deep that both ship and cargo are gone forever. We know from one seized by the Colombian Navy that they carry up to ten metric tons of cocaine worth up to four hundred million on the street. If you get one to sink herself, that's a fair day's work, Tindall," Buldoc said, "you'll have taken a hell of a lot of dope off the street."

"Usual top cover, sir?" Dougie inquired.

"Yes," Buldoc confirmed. "She could be one of the new C-130Js," he said with barely concealed pride.

Tindall knew a lot about the J variant, maybe even more than

Buldoc and Dougie combined. Returning from his last tour, he had come through London, where his group commander had an extra pass to the Defense and Security Equipment International Exhibition. All of Lockheed Martin's latest weapons systems were on show, from missile and fire control systems to an actual F-35 Lightening strike fighter.

A mockup of the J's command, control and surveillance suite was there, too. The J was a direct descendent of the Lockheed Martin Hercules C-130 that had been in continuous use by land, sea and air combat forces of many nations since 1959. With a fuselage the width of the New York midtown tunnel, and a tail gate the size of a draw bridge, the C-130 was meant for transporting heavy weapons and combatants over long distances and inserting them directly into combat. She could rain armored vehicles like Abrahams M-1 tanks directly into action from low-level passes, or orbit as a midair refueling station for both fixed-wing aircraft and helicopters. To stranded mariners, she was the angel of mercy when she materialized overhead emblazoned in Coast Guard white and orange. To enemy combatants, she was the angel of death in the forms of *Spectre, Spooky, Ghostrider,* and *Stinger*, all sub-variants of ground support gunships, armed with twenty-five-millimeter *Equalizer* Gatling guns, thirty-five-millimeter *Bushmaster* Howitzer and the *Griffin* lightweight precision-guided missile.

The C-130J was a kindred spirit to its predecessors in airframe alone. With three hundred and sixty-degree, belly-mounted inverse synthetic aperture sea search radar, forward-looking infrared/electro-optical sensors, and a gas oxygen system to keep the crew conscious while they loitered at altitudes beyond the range of conventional ground-to-air missile systems, the J was meant for high altitude surveillance and mission control. *Melissa* was the call sign of the former Air Force Combat Systems Officer, or CSO, who sat on the working end of the C-130J's state-of-the-art communications and surveillance suite. From there she commanded all air and sea elements of the Greater Antilles Section, and she could see "grass twitch on a putting green," said a Raytheon technician at the London defense exhibition. Pilots, boat captains and comms officers across GANTSEC knew *Melissa* by voice alone. She was an anonymous air traffic controller with Superman X-ray vision.

When she wasn't at 40,000 feet directing drug interdiction across the Caribbean, *Melissa* went home to a modest 1950s ranch house nestled on the outskirts of Coast Guard Air Station Elizabeth City, North Carolina. She would be in the air tonight. From the moment Gutterson and his crew lifted off from the deck of the *Osprey,* to the moment they touched back down, *Melissa* owned them.

Buldoc looked at his watch.

"Won't be long now, I imagine," he said. "You boys should get topside with Gutterson and pre-flighted. We'll be standing by the RHIBs. Good luck," the captain finished. He extinguished the projector and departed the ready room by the aisle, the way he came.

"Come on, Princess," said Dougie. "Let's find Hank."

The heavy cloud cover swirling around the stationary tropical depression hung low in the darkness over the *Osprey* as she pitched and rolled on a tumbling sea. The dawn was late and the humidity oppressive as the HITRON crew sat strapped in their seats, sweating like stranded subway riders, waiting for the call to launch. Tindall was dozing when he heard the familiar click of magneto switches from the cockpit, and the gentle whine of avionics powering up. Then he heard the voice-activated intercom on his headset crackle to life. Dougie's cool, robotic voice, was reading back wind speed and direction, radio frequencies, and finally, intercept coordinates. The blades, which had been drooping and swaying like palm fronds in the Caribbean wind, began to turn, the *Dolphin's* twin gas turbine engines engaging with a gentle moan.

In minutes the engines were screaming in pitched two-part harmony, the blades flailing impotently at the air as the *Dolphin* twitched and bounced like a bantam rooster, buffeted by the crosswind over the exposed flight deck. He saw Gutterson lower his night vision goggles and Dougie follow suit. Tindall did the same. Night vision instantly transformed the static electricity discharging from the tips of the rotor blades into sparking green streamers. Beyond the outlines of the flight deck and the superstructure of the *Osprey,* there was nothing but infinite darkness.

He felt Gutterson test the flight controls, nudging the button-encrusted cyclic between his legs, changing the rotor's angle of attack overhead until the sound of the blades slapping at the air confirmed the flight controls were free and clear. He saw Dougie dial up weather radar and forward-looking infrared.

"This is your Captain speaking," said Gutterson through the comms, "we are number one for takeoff," he announced, mercilessly masticating his chewing gum. "Everybody locked and loaded?"

"Roger that," replied Dougie. The briefest silence followed.

"Princess?" said Gutterson.

"Roger," acknowledged Tindall from where he was seated with the weaponry in the cabin behind the pilots. He was already feeling better, back in a heavily-armed, forward-deployed chopper that would in seconds be free of the rolling, pitching *Osprey*. The sophomoric hazing from Dougie and Gutterson felt strangely reassuring - a sign of the bond between pilot and co-pilot that hinted at trust and proficiency, possibly the highest proficiency in HITRON. God help him if he didn't shoot straight. Picking off outboard motors traveling at eighty miles an hour in the dark was hardly the same as laying down suppressing fire with a Gatling gun from an army Blackhawk, and he crossed himself and prayed for faithfulness to the Lord's design.

Gutterson torqued the throttle on the collective, lay the cyclic loosely in his palm, and depressed the radio broadcast mic with his forefinger.

"This is Oscar Bravo Whiskey," he crackled through the comms.

"You're kidding me," Tindall mumbled to himself, inadvertently communicating through the voice-activated intercom.

"You got somethin' to say?" Gutterson barked.

"Oscar Bravo Whiskey? like O-B-Wan?" Tindall whined.

"Quiet, Princess," Gutterson hissed. "We are hot on the pad and ready to go," said Gutterson, continuing his broadcast, his voice climbing through the cloud layer overhead and reaching into the heavens. "And who keeps us company tonight?" he inquired of the gloom.

"Oscar Bravo Whiskey, this is flight control," came a soft, sultry female voice. "Wind is north northwest at twenty-five knots, broken cover at two thousand, visibility seven miles. Cleared for take-off, squawk and ident zero, triple sixes, and proceed to target intercept. Master Luke has your numbers and radar contact downloading now. Should be on your screen by the time you're airborne."

"For goodness' sake," said Tindall through the intercom, "is *everybody* in on this Star Wars thing?" He felt the blades bite at the air, the *Dolphin* tear free of the flight deck, and Gutterson bank her hard to starboard and into the night. She creaked and popped under the multiplied gravitational forces to which she would become accustomed under Gutterson's heavy hand.

"Sweet *Melissa*," Gutterson sighed over the intercom before depressing the transmit button. "This is Oscar Bravo Whiskey, en route, squawk and ident triple sixes," Gutterson confirmed.

"Roger that, Oscar Bravo Whiskey, your target is holding course due north. Looks like a go-fast. Report back with visual contact," came *Melissa's* mellifluous voice, crackling softly through the night.

Gutterson fell silent as he climbed the *Dolphin* briskly through the darkness to two thousand feet and skimmed along beneath a churning layer of clouds heading northeast at one hundred and fifty knots. With *Melissa's* intercept coordinates downloaded into his flight control system, and the autopilot adjusting course for wind speed and direction, there was little for Gutterson to do besides ogle the GPS readout as it counted down the time to target acquisition. At seven minutes out, he disengaged the autopilot and dropped from the sky like a kestrel. With his night vision goggles on and his running lights off, the phosphorescent glow of the go-fast's sloshing track came into view, a bubbling green cobblestone trail leading directly to his target.

With Gutterson at the controls, the *Dolphin* closed fast, speeding through the darkness just fifty feet above the furrowed sea. In the noise shadow of the go-fast's burly bank of outboards, the aircraft's thundering engines were inaudible. The smugglers never knew the *Dolphin* was there until Dougie bathed them in ten thousand watts of search light, and ordered the smugglers over a super-amplified public-address system, to stop. To hunter and prey, the order to heave-to was a futile act of protocol which set the go-fast crew to frenzied work dumping contraband overboard. By the time Gutterson pulled his ship alongside the careening cigarette boat, and Tindall engaged his mounted machine gun to lay a trail of warning shots across her bow, the *Osprey* had given chase, all ahead full, lurching like a hobby horse through the sea to close on the intercepted target. If Tindall could not stop the go-fast dead in her tracks, the wind and waves and time and distance would scatter the discarded cargo across the ocean's surface like confetti before it sank, weakening the LEDET's case.

Tindall was amazed. *Melissa*, Gutterson, Buldoc and the LEDETs choreographed the take-down flawlessly. And much to his relief, he did not disappoint them, cleanly disabling a total of four powerful outboards in as many shots. The last shot inspired Dougie to dub him *Steady Hans Solo,* inducting Tindall with full honors into the pantheon of the HITRON Star Wars cast.

With the suspects in LEDET custody and the seizure of as much as a ton of marijuana and cocaine, the *Osprey* maneuvered to take the go-fast in tow. Tindall crackled with exhilaration. Perfect shooting, nobody killed or injured, and no telling how many narco dollars denied. Drug interdiction beat the hell out of combat. Gutterson disengaged from close air support as the LEDETs and suspects disappeared from view into the *Dolphin's* hangar. With the go-fast in tow, the *Osprey* eased into the wind, her flight deck steadying beneath a stiff headwind that made landing the *Dolphin* routine. Gutterson completed his crosswind leg and banked the *Dolphin* gently into an upwind approach as Tindall secured his weapons and closed the fuselage barn door. He buckled and cinched his four-point harness, strapping himself like a vital organ to the *Dolphin's* insides.

The first faint traces of light had drawn a distant horizon on the unappeased black sea. The flood lights illuminating the flight deck flashed with intermittent shadows of wind-whipped spray that lifted in ghostly billows from the passing swells, coating the gleaming ship in a frothy sheen. The *Dolphin* was over the *Osprey's* transom, seconds from touching down, when Tindall felt Gutterson holding her off.

"What's that?" said Gutterson over the intercom. He was pointing across Dougie's chest at something out in the water. "You see that, young Jedi?" came Gutterson's voice again, but changed, modulated, in a plumy British accent. The hair on Tindall's neck stood straight as the teeth on a comb. What had Buldoc said? *You've got nothing to worry about until he starts purring in an English accent?*

"Yeah, yeah, I see it," Dougie replied. "A container?"

Shipping containers fell with distressing regularity from

containerships the world over, and the heavily trafficked Caribbean basin was a minefield of semi submerged containers, floating just beneath the surface on pockets of trapped air. They flayed keels from ships like bears gut salmon, making them serious navigational hazards. HITRON crews routinely sank them, shooting holes to release the air and sending them to the bottom. But Gutterson's voice sounded anything but routine.

"Negative, Master Luke. It's under power, low and slow...and if that's what I think it is...." Tindall unclipped his harness and leaned across the cabin to peer through the night at the water. A little less than a mile off the *Osprey's* beam, a long cylindrical object was porpoising in the water, churning up phosphorous plankton as it labored through the surf. Tindall reengaged his night vision. The fluorescence of the plankton practically blinded him. The object was making headway, barely, bubbling in the swell like a boiling ear of corn.

"*Osprey*, Oscar Bravo Whiskey, breaking off approach. We have visual contact on a target off your port beam at one mile. Possible bigfoot." The *Dolphin* banked hard left in the twilight, creaking and popping as she rose, leaving the *Osprey's* bridge off her starboard wing and climbing to two hundred feet.

"Video is rolling," Dougie reported.

"Flight control, flight control," Gutterson broadcast, "this is Oscar Bravo Whiskey with a visual on a new target, approximately one mile to port of the *Osprey*, do you copy," Gutterson continued, his courtly patter reaching through the night. "Tindall," he said more gruffly through the intercom as he waited for *Melissa* to copy, "lock and load." Tindall clipped into his safety strap, released the barn door, and slammed it hard against the stop at the end of its track, unused to the *Dolphin's* frictionless, laser-aligned door. The endless open ocean unfolded beneath him, the spray and white caps glistening green through his goggles. He checked his ammunition belts, yanked on the bolt action firing chamber, then stepped into the mounted M240B machine gun and held her *closer than the girl next door*, as instructed by his Coast Guard trainers.

"Locked and loaded," Tindall confirmed.

"Flight control, do you copy," Gutterson repeated. He didn't like *Melissa's* silence, Tindall could tell, and Tindall wasn't sure he did either. The *Dolphin* closed on the object quickly and Dougie ignited the flood light, the beam skipping across the wave tops and riding the swells like a sea sprite.

"Flight control," *Melissa* finally replied, "Oscar Bravo Whiskey. Disengage. That is not a target, do you copy, disengage."

"My ass it isn't," Dougie exclaimed through the intercom as his search light landed squarely on a low, inelegant conning tower no bigger than a sideline water cooler, with bulky portholes secured by heavy fastening bolts that bulged from the tower like knots on a tree. Just beneath the surface, extending twenty feet fore and aft, a ghostly cylindrical shape lumbered through the swells.

"Flight control, we got ourselves a bigfoot, cameras are rolling, engaging uplink now. Please ident."

When Buldoc heard the *Dolphin* abort its approach, he double-timed it to the bridge. It was the one place on the ship with three-hundred-sixty-degree line of sight and the comms, radar, and data links to know what couldn't be seen. He also alerted the *Osprey's* recovery teams in case the HITRON crew needed pulling from the drink. It was just a precaution, a habit really, that he never shook after a *Stingray* in the early HITRON days banked too hard off the landing deck, caught a blade on the passing swell, and augured in like a corkscrew. Nobody got hurt. The crews followed their ditch training and escaped unharmed, but the recovery left much to be desired. Ever since, his commands excelled at man overboard recovery because he drilled them on it incessantly, tossing lifejackets over the rail on a whim, often at night, and timing the crew's recovery effort. The *Osprey's* mission was interdiction, but she excelled at recovery.

"*Osprey, Osprey, Osprey,*" Gutterson resumed on the radio, "what do you want to do now, Captain?"

"This is flight control," *Melissa* interrupted from high overhead. "Those are friendlies, do you copy? Do not engage." Dougie kept the high-powered search light on the bobbing conning tower as Gutterson turned the *Dolphin* broadside to the vessel below and brought Tindall's guns to bear. There was movement behind the ungainly portals. Without warning the hatch flipped open and filled with a head of windswept black hair, and a pair of beady eyes that stared defiantly into Dougie's light.

"This is the United States Coast Guard," Dougie's voice echoed from the *Dolphin's* public address system. "Heave-to and prepare to be boarded."

"He look like a friendly to you?" Gutterson inquired of his crew through the intercom. Tindall felt for the trigger safety lock through his gloved right hand which was already cupping the trigger guard. One false move by the man in the hatch and the safety was coming off. The vessel continued her cumbersome advance, sloshing in the swell like driftwood.

"Oscar Bravo Whiskey, flight control, do not engage, do you copy, do not engage," said *Melissa*. The man in the hatch continued to stare. His shoulders rose up through the opening and out came his arm. In his hand was a small black machine gun. The muzzle flickered. A sound like hail on a tin roof followed, then a pop as Dougie's light went out.

"Jesus Christ," Dougie shouted through the intercom.

"Shots fired, shots fired," Gutterson reported laconically over the radio.

Tindall felt the safety give way under the pressure of his thumb. He drew his sights on the man in the conning tower, placed his index finger inside the trigger guard and held it steady against the trigger.

"Disengage, disengage," said *Melissa* from on high as the machine gun in the conning tower winked again. Tindall opened fire.

CHAPTER 9

Organized Crime Drug Enforcement Task Forces Fusion Center, Washington, D.C.

Even as Lenny despaired of his former colleagues and handlers at Special Operations Division, one could not cite past embarrassments without also mentioning the victories: Operation *Mountain Express*, which broke up a major supply operation of chemicals destined for methamphetamine production; Operation *Tar Pit,* resulting in two hundred arrests in eight U.S. judicial districts and Mexico; and Operation *Impunity*, which led to a hundred arrests in nine U.S. judicial districts and the Dominican Republic. The line between darkness and light was never clear, and Lenny knew better than most that chasing bad guys often meant getting dirty.

That's when it occurred to him that the OIG's investigation of Fusion implied that someone at Justice harbored suspicions similar to his - that the DEA was at it again, using SOD to blind local enforcement to the DEA's latest Faustian bargain by suppressing Fusion reports. Lenny's present fit of outrage passed like a squall, and he turned in the calm to the intern resumés. He had to cull hundreds down to six, and the candidates were like Stepford wives, brilliant and perfect and willing. In thirty minutes, he had the six candidates he wanted, all of whom would need to clear background checks before anyone wasted time interviewing them. He would screen two himself, because he still enjoyed prying. The remainder would be screened by his staff. If the candidates he had selected passed their checks and accepted the generous offer of long-hour, no-pay summer internships, their names, addresses, and fingerprints would join permanently all the other permanent records of present and past FBI employees.

Among the powerful tools at Fusion's disposal, the most potent was DICE, a SOD-hosted data base with more than a billion records including names, addresses, business and personal associations, phone logs, internet traffic, and details of subpoenas, search warrants and arrests, not to mention case numbers, case agents, and agent contact information. The information about U.S. citizens in DICE collected by eavesdropping was supposed to be accompanied by a warrant. Foreigners, however, did not enjoy such legal protections, and DICE data included a healthy complement of overseas wiretaps and intercepts. If a few Americans were unintentionally swept up in the eavesdropping without a warrant, because they called or texted or emailed to or from places overseas, well, that was an occupational risk SOD was willing to bear, even though the information was accessible to more than ten thousand federal, state and local enforcement officers.

Lenny had been on the DICE design team and logging in was like coming home, the interface and logic tree as familiar to him as the pattern on his Kmart kitchen china. Once the interns were onboard, it was Lenny who administered the crash course they received on DICE. He also taught them Money Laundering 101, because unusual patterns in the movement of cash was the surest sign of ill-gotten gains.

They started with money laundering basics, beginning with *placement*, the process of transferring illegal spoils inconspicuously into the legitimate financial system. Then, on to *layering*, the process of moving money via bogus transactions and transfers through a series of accounts and territories. The more territories with strict privacy laws like the British Virgin Islands or Monaco, the better, to make the money hard to trace. He wrapped up with *integration*, the method by which the money resurfaced as legitimate currency. Of the three, *placement* was by far the most important for the interns to understand, especially the PATT intern, who would spend his or her summer in the DICE data base following the bread crumbs first detected by FinCEN alerts. Not that *layering* and *integration* were unimportant, but without deep knowledge of global banking systems, familiarity with tax-haven laws, and experience with the nuances of accounting conventions, summer interns were ill-suited to follow money through the high-level stations in the money laundering sphere. The work of exposing placement, however, of stitching together the countless ways criminal enterprises sprinkled money like pixie dust across the financial landscape, took hours, days, weeks. It remained the most labor-intensive part of the job, and if the interns were good for anything it was labor. Sam Rosen's PATT interns would resume law school in the fall with only a rudimentary grasp of money laundering's full complexity, but they would understand *placement* better than many experienced criminals.

Lenny had a craftier agenda as well, an agenda less about exploiting interns' energy and idealism than it was about seducing them into law enforcement. He wanted to whet their appetites - intrigue them with appetizing assignments shadowing agents tracing money through Liechtenstein, or monitoring Cayman Islands yacht dealers, or Sotheby's art auctions. Among the carrots Lenny dangled before the interns were the glamourous places they would go, and the people they would meet over a career with the Organized Crime and Drug Enforcement Task Force, or OCDETF, in the ever-changing hunt for new ways to legitimize tainted cash.

Making sure seduction prevailed over disillusionment was part of the challenge, because learning the nuances of *placement* came with a cost. Most new Fusion interns considered themselves thick-skinned and manageably jaded, but Lenny's effect was like finishing school for cynics. They would forever suspect all businesses, and every transaction, even charitable gifts. Every exchange of cash, every deposit, and every down payment and currency exchange acquired the appearance of *structuring*, the process by which professional money launderers disguise proceeds from drug dealing, prostitution, human trafficking, bribery and extortion as countless small deposits, money orders, vehicle purchases and gambling junkets.

During the Nixon administration, the Bank Secrecy Act tried to address *structuring* by forcing all financial institutions to file a Suspicious Activity Report or "SAR" with FinCEN for all transactions in excess of $5,000. That threshold was later raised to $10,000. There was a presumption that anyone with money to hide had a lot of it, and needed it moved in big chunks. It wasn't long before criminals devised elaborate schemes to launder large sums in increments below the FinCEN reporting threshold. If the interns learned nothing else it was to detect high volumes of related or geographically concentrated transactions falling just beneath the $10,000 reporting threshold. Before too long, every stranger reaching into a pocket for cash looked to Lenny's interns like a *Smurf*, DEA-speak for a self-employed nobody placing large amounts of cash in small denominations at unrelated local banks, savings and loans, and credit unions.

The interns learned a lot about *Smurfs* because they spent the summer chasing armies of them. Lenny's indoctrination included close study of the most famous *Smurf* of them all, a teenager called Luo Juncheng who moved $1.7 billion over eight months through five thousand deposits and thirty-five hundred withdrawals. Interns learned about *round-tripping*, too, the art of bogus loans and fictitious real estate trades; and *householding*, when a platoon of *Smurfs* claiming a common address, or household, disguised huge sums in the form of countless small deposits that went undetected until traced to the address. There was no denying the subtle aversions Lenny's charges acquired to the small cash-intensive businesses Americans use every day - car washes and parking garages, nail salons and convenience stores, and night clubs and bars, where legitimate cash receipts from thousands of regular patrons easily co-mingle with cash from undeterminable sources.

Lenny, the sorcerer, and his apprentices. In the best of circumstances, he created great sleuths, by appealing to their idealism, perhaps even to their patriotism. In others he aroused hedonism, opened their eyes to the lucre of criminal enterprise where they sometimes reemerged as money launderers themselves, and occasionally much worse. It had only happened a few times, but Lenny pursued these candidates-turned-criminals with special relish. The joy in retribution for misappropriating his training was its own reward. There was no predicting which ones turned. He knew only that some would, and worthy and satisfying adversaries they made.

He worked himself into a lather by contemplating the forces arrayed against him: SOD censorship, treacherous interns, even the American Civil Liberties Union had become a threat, lobbying to curtail financial surveillance on the grounds that anti-money laundering laws placed too costly a burden on the economies and institutions of more than thirty-six participating nations. The ACLU contended that FinCen enlisted banks against their own customers in a dangerous expansion of the "surveillance state." This argument was horseshit, of course. It wasn't 1776 after all, and sacrificing a little privacy to keep the gang-incited mayhem of Central

America from crossing U.S. borders seemed to Lenny, and a good many others, a fair trade.

Setting aside the undoing of criminal enterprises, financial surveillance by Sam Rosen's PATT unit at Fusion had achieved epic successes that the ACLU conveniently ignored. These included nailing the Bank of New York for laundering more than $7 billion in Russian capital flight transactions, and exposing the theft by Ferdinand Marcos of more than $10 billion in Philippine government assets. Marcos laundered through financial institutions in the U.S., Liechtenstein, Cayman Islands, Hong Kong, Monaco, Switzerland, the Bahamas and a dozen more nations and territories. There was the $1.9 billion fine levied against HSBC Bank in 2012 for laundering currency for Iranian drug dealers and terrorist groups; and the seizure of a digital currency scheme called Liberty Reserve. The list went on and on, sweeping up more than a few of the world's most revered banking names like Standard Chartered and BNP Paribas. The record spoke for itself. Fusion's little dragnet could catch anybody, everybody.

Practiced money launderers, true professionals, knew it; but they kept playing, because money laundering paid, even after the fines. Just like derivatives and mortgage trading on Wall Street, money laundering was risky but highly lucrative, besting all other forms of mainstream investments, with all the same potential for windfall and loss that had made and destroyed fortunes for centuries. A few off-the-books transactions by major banking institutions to accommodate the best and biggest clients was *de rigeur*, like tickets to a show when clients came to town. Lenny liked his work. No, he loved it - messy, intractable, and taxing as it was. A dreadnaught-steady moral compass with a healthy propensity for outrage was the only safeguard against its temptations, and as he held two resumés in his hand he knew full well the potential they held for betrayal.

On the same night Phil landed in Colombia, and Casey Tindall awoke feeling seasick deep in the bowels of the *Osprey*, Lenny Marks' computer monitor flickered to life. He clicked on the DICE desktop icon and scrolled to the *Target Name* search field, resting his index fingers on the keyboard like he was taking its pulse. He glanced at the first resumé and pecked out the candidate's name: M-o-i-r-a_M-c-L-e-a-n.

CHAPTER 10

Guajira Peninsula, Colombia

Phil couldn't believe his eyes. A fantasy world, half Robinson Crusoe, half Santa's workshop unfolded before them in the shade as he and Pedro left the gusty landing strip behind. A dozen open air structures with thatched palm frond roofs formed a loose ring of outbuildings around a big bodega-like hut. It had a raised wooden floor and a waist-high brick fire pit at the center. The fire pit vented through a hood and chimney cut and welded from old oil drums, and around the fire pit were tables and benches like the ones at the camp ground near the headwaters of Lost Lake. A handful of bleary-eyed men in filthy t-shirts huddled together at one of the tables, mumbling between yawns, when they were moved to speak at all. Two loud, gesticulating, raven-haired women raised a ruckus in Spanish as they toiled over the fire pit. They were cooking eggs and slabs of beef, the open flames licking at the oil drum hood overhead when the women turned the meat.

The smell of seared beef and frying eggs crackling on the griddle twisted his insides. Potato chips and chocolate bars from gas-and-go convenience stores was all he and Pedro had eaten on their way through Alabama, and his eyes fairly watered as he watched rice and beans spooned in great heaps on to plates from a cast-iron pot. The older of the two women looked up, her eyes fixing on Pedro. She threw her arms skyward and set without delay to caterwauling.

"Mi Pedro! Mi Pedro!" she hollered. She lifted the hem of her flowing skirts and made straight for where Phil and Pedro stood, never mind that her apron strings had her bound as tight as a roast. Phil's eyes widened with the urgency of her advance as she scurried through the tables, departed the raised wooden floor, and threw herself around Pedro. He hugged her back, and rocked with her in his arms, her eyes closed tight, and her cheek mashed even tighter against his chest.

"Mi momma, Mr. Phil," said Pedro sheepishly, smiling over his mother's head.

"Oh, mi Pedro," she said again, standing back to take him in.

So that's how mommas are, thought Phil, feeling like a third wheel. She had a million questions, and Pedro pacified her with gentle Spanish prattle, until eventually she was satisfied and gave out – or almost gave out. She found a fresh well of enthusiasm to welcome Phil.

"Mi amigo Americano, Mr. Phil," said Pedro, presenting Phil to his mother. That was as much as Phil followed, and not more than Pedro's mother needed. She put a hand on each hip and looked him up and down. He felt like a prize pig at a county fair. Then she took his hands and looked him in the eyes, and said something kind that included "Mr. Phil." It sure did sound nice, and felt nice, too.

"Come on, Mr. Phil," said Pedro, "Tine to wash up. Den my momma, she cook a big brea'fast."

Pedro's mother returned to the fire as Phil felt Pedro's hand fall lightly on his shoulders and guide him back the way they came through the mangroves to the airstrip. They were barely back in sunlight with the ocean breeze in their hair when Phil saw something he recognized lurking in the jungle. Pedro stopped beside him, inviting him to look closer.

"You build boats out here?" Phil asked doubtfully.

"Sí, Mr. Phil," answered Pedro, in full Latino lilt. "Aldough, no so much boats as fast as yours, Mr. Phil. We buy doze from the gringos in Miami and St. Juan and Grand Caymen. Come see." Pedro led him back beneath the canopy, walking toward the construction cradle Phil had seen from the airstrip. Pedro was moving differently now, a swagger in his step.

"What you think, Mr. Phil?" Pedro asked, plainly proud of the vessel taking shape in the shadows. Right away, Phil saw she was a heavy displacement hull, the sections of a stout wooden keel laid with notches cut in regular intervals to seat the bulkheads.

"A fishing boat?" Phil asked, recollecting the hull plan of the Gulf Coast shrimper he studied in *Fifty Wooden Boats: A Catalog of Building Plans*. Pedro just about split himself laughing.

"No, mi amigo. A submarine."

"Now you're funnin' me, Pedro." It was the first time he called Pedro by his name, and it came out easy, like they'd run together for years.

"No, mi amigo. No funnin' Mr. Phil."

"What all you want with a submarine, anyway?" Phil looked around the clearing, making sense of a few heavy timbers stacked and numbered on a nearby scaffold. Convex deck stringers, similar to the ones that gave the old barrel-back lake boats their torpedo shape, meant this vessel was designed to ship water over her gunwales.

"Yeah, Pedro, good luck with that." It felt comfortable now, even safe, calling him *Pedro*.

"And even if you *could* pull it off, why would you? Dern thing 'll be slower than molasses. You're wantin' to go *over* the water, not under it."

"I will esplain, after brea'fast mi amigo," Pedro said.

As they pushed on from the boat works more men in filthy clothes appeared between the mangroves and wild cinnamon and grapefruit trees. The men walked single file following a path that paralleled the airstrip through the trees. Phil paused, puzzling on who they were and where they were headed, when he saw how the path they were on bordered a canal, almost like a tow path. The men were heavily laden with backpacks and duffle bags and long guns, and the guns had husky crescent shaped magazines and ominous black vented barrels, same as Miguel's.

"Holy shit, Pedro," Phil said as he stopped and turned. "Who are those guys?" He looked down the channel in the direction the men were moving. The channel widened and the undergrowth thinned, enough for Phil to see the channel opened to the ocean. A hundred yards on from where he stood, moored in the shadows of a bend, he recognized two massive ocean-racing power boats. One had four outboard engines and the other five, each engine as big as a bank vault.

"Now *that's* some hardware," said Phil admiringly, "jiminy crickets," and he started for the boats.

"Stop," said Pedro, and by the tone of his voice Phil reckoned he meant it. "You no go near the boats when they loadin'."

"Yes sir," said Phil, the way he was taught.

Pedro's hand returned to the base of Phil's neck and guided him back toward the airstrip. Back in the sunlight, they walked another hundred yards on the packed earth and coral runway until it ended abruptly, and the beach sloped away to the sea. Pedro's hand never left Phil's neck, and steered him gently off the jungle airstrip into the soft, white sand of a pristine beach that ran as far as Phil could see - until the beach, the jungle and the ocean converged on a distant vanishing point. They hadn't gone more than a few paces paralleling the tree line when they came upon another lean-to with a thatched, palm frond roof.

"Tine for a bath," said Pedro. The lean-to had a shelf stacked high with neatly folded, conspicuously clean, dazzling white towels, and a ledge split from a bamboo stalk, with bars of used but serviceable soap. Pedro pulled his revolver from the small of his back and laid it beside some soap on the ledge. He dropped his threadbare, knee-length shorts in a pile around his ankles and discarded the t-shirt soiled with Mort's blood on the floor beside his shorts.

"Come on, Mr. Phil," he said, alighting naked from the lean-to and making straight for the surf. His gun was in one hand, a towel and a used bar of soap in the other.

Phil loved skinny-dipping, but it was the kind of thing you did at dusk, and furtively. The posse of teenagers he ran with from the Lost Lake Middle School did it all summer long, right beneath the summer crowd's noses. He had even skinny-dipped with Katie, but only once, briefly, and at night. Pedro took a different view of it. He strode across the sand like a Neanderthal, buck naked and proud, in the broad light of day. He did it so naturally that Phil wondered if everyone in these parts just dropped their drawers when the spirit moved them and headed for the ocean to bathe. It was not the habit of the men he saw wandering into the bodega where Pedro's momma was cooking, nor the ones he saw walking the path along the canal. Those guys hadn't bathed in days, or weeks more likely.

The ocean was the color of nothing he had seen, and looked like just the thing to wash off the stickiness of a night spent in the open. He dropped his varnished-stained shorts along with his boxers and Georgia Dawgs t-shirt, and headed for the water with Pedro, soap and towel in hand. He was halfway down the beach before an object in the bay caught his attention. Either his eyes were playing tricks or the swell he saw breaking a hundred yards offshore was foaming around the tail of a wrecked airplane. The vertical tail and one horizontal elevator jutted from the water, and the submerged fuselage was plainly visible beneath the crystal-clear Caribbean. The airplane looked planted like a javelin in the shallow seabed. Pity the sorry bastard who plowed that one in, Phil thought, wondering if the pilot had survived.

A few minutes later he was flopping beside Pedro, lolling in the backwash, scrubbing his hair and soaping his limbs, rinsing and rolling and bobbing like a manatee in the buoyant briny sea. It wasn't home – never would be – but the ocean felt tolerably nice. He was studying the emerald shoreline of the crescent bay when a man appeared, gesturing like a traffic cop from beside the lean-to where they disrobed. He was urging them from the water, yelling to no effect in the wind.

"Hey Pedro," said Phil. "What's that guy up there want?"

"Come on, Mr. Phil, tine for takeoff, and den mi madres' brea'fast. You will love. Come on, quick, quick," said Pedro, washing ashore, wrapping his towel like a Pharaoh about his waist, and wedging his gun behind the knot he tied beneath his belly. "Quick, quick, Phil, rápido," he said, waving Phil out of the water and making for the lean-to. Phil ran to catch him, spraying sand from his feet, and wondering at the urgency.

As they reached the tree line, the distinctive snarling sound of the throttle advancing on a propeller airplane came in uneven waves down the airstrip. By the time Phil reached the lean-to Pedro had donned a thick, white, terrycloth robe, as strikingly white as the towels. It gave him a semblance of misplaced civility amidst the pervasively grubby camp residents.

"No swimmin' in the takeoffs," said Pedro, as Phil approached with his towel around his waist. Phil followed Pedro's eyes to the far end of the airstrip where he recognized the plane they landed in the night before, the same plane the men had been loading, shimmering in the rising heat. The wings wobbled in the gusty headwind as she began her takeoff roll, and he could tell by how slowly she accelerated she was heavily laden. Halfway down the airstrip the noise wheel left the ground, but the wheels beneath the fuselage remained planted.

"She ain't gonna make it," Phil whispered to himself, making sense of the plane wreck in the bay. He glanced at the empennage protruding from the turquoise water, and that's when he saw the armed men. They had taken up positions along the tree line to the left and right of the runway and they were training their sights seaward at an invisible foe. The propeller grew louder, tearing at the air, while the wheels at the rear held firmly to the earth.

Phil stepped back from the runway, to distance himself from the inevitable crash, when a colossal roar erupted from the shoreline behind him. He spun just in time to see the two magnificent power boats he saw moored back in the jungle burst from an inlet bordered by mangroves. They headed straight for the open ocean on slowly diverging courses, throwing foam and spray in rainbow arcs, and bucking like steeds on the wave tops. He would have watched them longer - for as long as they stayed in sight - but retreating from the fast and unpromising approach of the earthbound airplane was acquiring urgency. It zoomed past the lean-to in a cloud of coral dust, its wheels growing lighter as the runway ran out. Off the threshold the wheels went, sinking in the air and grazing the beach as the power plant struggled and the wing tips wobbled and the propeller blades clawed for altitude at the air. And then, off the water, came a powerful gust and the aircraft lurched skyward on the lift of the updraft.

"I'll be," said Phil, "saved by the wind. Came right close to losing another," he thought he said quietly to himself.

"Anodder?" said Pedro, turning on Phil with expressionless eyes.

The airplane's shadow danced across the waves as it picked up speed but not altitude, and hugged the ocean, coming to a course that roughly bisected the power boat wakes. Phil's heart raced. It looked like the start of an invasion. As the engine noises dissipated and the craft receded from view, Phil saw the men along the shoreline relax and secure their weapons.

"What you mean, Mr. Phil, when you say *'anodder?'*" Phil glanced at the plane wreck in the bay.

"I meant that one, right there. You just got lucky this time, that's all."

"She no crash, Mr. Phil," said Pedro, squinting at the bay. "And we no lucky. No, dat plane, she no crash, see?" said Pedro. He looked discouraged by Phil's lack of faith. "She shot down by the Zeta, Mr. Phil, you understand? The Goddamn Zeta, you see!" There was emotion in Pedro's voice, the first Phil ever heard. That's when Pedro told him how the Zeta had taken his father, a poor, peaceful farmer, impatient with the drug trade. "So you see, Mr. Phil," Pedro eventually concluded, "we are brodders, losing our Padrés so young."

Pedro's vendetta was against the whole Zeta cartel. He'd been dispatching Zeta indiscriminately for years, hunting them like game, and it drove José nuts, because the Zeta retaliated, taking two eyes for one. The plane in the bay was just the latest casualty in the escalating feud, the gunmen in the tree line, Pedro explained, now a routine precaution in case the Zeta returned. José tolerated Pedro's compulsion though there was no telling why. He could have handed Pedro to the Zeta at will, and settled the feud forever. But for reasons unknown, Pedro was untouchable, and incorrigibly out for revenge.

CHAPTER 11

Guajira Peninsula, Colombia

Feuds between cartels were escalating throughout central America on well-founded suspicions that some were improving their position at the expense of others by collaborating with authorities. Phil had been taken by the Guajira, so named for the peninsula from which they operated, at a time when the Guajira were enjoying uncommonly good fortune. With no successful interdictions and no lost or pirated shipments in more than two years, their success was conspicuous and suspect. The Zeta, by comparison, were having a jag of bad luck. Pedro said they only had themselves to blame. They were feared for their brutality, which drew attention to the drug trade that competing gangs could live without. Even the general populous was rising against them, aiding and abetting authorities and rival cartels alike. Whatever explained their misfortune, the Zeta spread the pain. If they had to pay, so too would the Sinaloas, the Guajira, and all the other *cartelitos* that filled the void following the disintegration of the Medellín and Cali cartels. The incentive to collude with authorities diminished, went the Zeta logic, when everybody lost shipments, and they preyed on luckier rivals when their own luck turned bad. Recent good fortune, compounded by Pedro's vendetta, put the Guajira squarely in the Zeta's sights.

Phil's clothes were gone when he reentered the lean-to, a terrycloth robe like Pedro's laid out where they had been. It smelled fresh and clean, and felt soft against his skin, softer than anything he'd ever worn. The excitement of the morning's embarkations was still with him by the time he and Pedro made their way in their matching white robes back to the bodega, and he recognized the welcoming figure of Pedro's mother. She was ambling across the raised wood floor to where he and Pedro were sitting, carrying two plates piled high with steak and eggs, and a concoction of beans and rice. Phil's eyes must have widened.

"Chicharone," said Pedro with a guileless smile as his mother placed the plates with pride before them.

"What did you say?" said Phil. He felt odd sitting beside Pedro in a clean terrycloth robe accepting victuals like a king.

"Fried pork belly. You no fin' nuttin' so good in Georgia, mi amigo." His mother stayed put. She had no plans to move until she saw Phil taste her cooking.

More men filed in from the Robinson Crusoe outbuildings toward the camp tables. Pedro's mother rattled off something in exasperation, and departed for the open fire where her assistant was cracking a dozen more eggs on the griddle.

"Good, hunh?" said Pedro, shoveling food. Nothing but lip-smacking and plate scraping followed while they filled their bellies. Pedro had the vulgar habit of chewing with his mouth open, but it wasn't enough to weaken Phil's appetite. Their frenzied feeding was slowing when a loud voice with a strange accent carried across the bodega.

"Oye! Paydrow." Pedro kept eating, though he was sure to have heard his name called. "Paydrow! What-ahh-you-doin' heeyah mate! What brings you-de-town?"

It came from a wiry man with unusually long arms who was fast approaching the bodega in long, unseemly strides. He wore pressed white slacks, alligator shoes, and an iridescent blue and yellow Hawaiian short-sleeve shirt. Tucked in his armpit was a postal tube, and Pedro's eyes narrowed as the man with the twangy accent landed across from him on the bench, laying the postal tube on the table beside him.

"Who's the fresh meat, Paydrow?" the man said looking at Phil.

"D'is Mr. Phil."

"Oye, Mr. Phil, pleased to meet you," he continued, friendlier than the Good Humor man. "Blimey, Paydrow's mum can churn out the grub, can't she?" Pedro had cleaned his plate, and he left the bench for the fire pit to reload.

"So what brings *you* heeyah, mate?" said the man to Phil. He sounded like someone Phil knew, a TV personality maybe. Steve Erwin, the Crocodile Hunter, that was it. He was Australian.

"Pedro, actually," said Phil. "I reckon he didn't leave me much choice."

"Fair dinkum. These blokes never do, mate. But there's a reason. Mark my words. I shouldn't worry too much, mate. You'll fit roight in soon enough."

"Fit right in? I weren't figurin' on staying that long."

"Nobody does, mate, but you will."

"How you figure?"

"Everyone's welcome heeyah, mate, and if Paydrow brought you...at gunpoint, was it? He's got a job in mind."

"And what if I don't want to do it?"

"He'll kill you, mate, so think about it before you refuse. You moight have more fun heeyah than you think. It's like the bloody U.N., except we got no laws."

"U.N.?"

"Ooo, yeah, we got 'em all heeyah, mate – Russians, Sicilians, Filipinos, retired Foreign Legion, even Aussies like me, mate. Everyone but the Colombian army, unless they're on the dole." He had short dark hair and wire rimmed glasses, and his words came short and impatient.

"Well, I'm not fixin' to stay."

"Good on yah, mate, but where you bloody gowing? It's a hundred moiles of jungle or ocean in every direction. No mate, you're never leaving, not alive, anyway... And why? Because you're in on the secret of Colombia's busiest departure point for grass, coke and meth to your United States. By the way, my name's Ian. Pleased to meet you, Mr. Phil. Keep your head down and do as Paydrow says and you'll be fine. No harm will come to you."

Phil believed him, but he wasn't scared, not anymore. The hours between when McLean turned him down and Mort came to foreclose had been the scariest. He'd lain awake all night, staring into the abyss, wondering where he would go and what he would do. Sure, seeing his uncle murdered set him back, but it had happened so fast, so unexpectedly, that there was no time for fear, and nothing to be done but ride with Pedro to New Orleans. His debts, a body, and the rush to judgement was about all he could expect back home; and that was behind him forever, according to Ian, however long it took getting used to.

"How often do the planes and boats come and go, Ian?"

"Plenty, mate, but that's none of your affair."

"And how often do they get shot down?" Phil asked snidely. Ian smiled, an amused, crooked smile.

"Oh, roight, that one in the drink, off the beach down there. The Sinaloas brought *her* down."

"Pedro said the Zeta."

"Bugger if I know, mate. Does it mattah? Turf wars are paht of the show, mate. They're always foighting. Imagine if they sorted themselves out. What would the drug problem in American look like then?"

"I won't be here long enough to find out."

"Don't be silly, kid. You try to leave and they'll shoot you dead."

"Why? What do they care?"

"You could bring someone back, show them where this place is. Nah, mate, learn to like it. This is home now."

Phil supposed he knew all along what Pedro was all about, but the reality of a thing, especially an ugly thing, is easy to ignore until you can't, until it whups you upside the head. Until Pedro abducted him, he was just along for the ride, a bozo on the bus, sheltered by his daddy, carried by the family business to which his talents were unnaturally well-suited, and coddled in the bosom of a small Christian town patronized by wealthy Atlanteans. He never knew his momma, and his daddy died young, but he never wanted for nothing, not even his favorite school periodical, even after he dropped out. It took the colorful Australian to wake him to his circumstances, remind him of his origins, and the craziness and violence that was Pedro.

"You no listen to Mr. Ian," said Pedro reclaiming his place on the bench, his plate piled high with fresh eggs and beef.

"Why, Paydrow? Because the truth hurts?" said Ian, grinning. "Just don't ask him about his father," Ian added, watching Pedro stiffen.

"I already know," Phil replied. "He already told me."

"Strewth, you two *are* chummy," said Ian, turning to Pedro. "Good to see you, mate. I'm off to see Hoe-zay, then pissing off back to Bogotá. Perhaps a bit more qwuality time on the next run," Ian concluded, punching Pedro softly on the shoulder. "And good lahck with your new recruit," he said rising from the bench. "Keep your head down when the Zeta come 'round," he offered Phil in parting, padding softly in his alligator shoes off the wood floor of the bodega, the postal tube tucked back under his arm.

Pedro was well into his second plate when Phil found the courage to say, "I ain't runnin' drugs for you, Pedro. You might as well shoot me now if that's your plan 'cause I ain't gonna."

"Awe, Mr. Phil," said Pedro, sounding genuinely hurt. "You no listen to Mr. Ian. I already tell you that. Mr. Ian don' know shit, see? And he dangerous," he added, taking a somber tone. "You no tell him nada. You promise me, Mr. Phil, you no tell Mr. Ian nada, never. He no good, like your uncle." And just like that Pedro lost his appetite, his fork clenched tight, aimlessly stirring his rice and beans. He didn't like Ian, that was plain, and he didn't like the impression he had that Phil had taken up with him.

"You no worry, Mr. Phil. We got mucho donkeys to run the drugs. And you no good in America anyway," he added. His eyes turned lifeless, the same way they had before killing Mort.

"How you figure that?' answered Phil.

"You wanted for murder, my frien'."

"Then what you *want* me fer, dadgummit?" Pedro smiled, an uncomfortably long smile.

"You help us build boats, Mr. Phil, very fast boats, yes?" Pedro's eyes were wide and hopeful. He wanted Phil to be pleased. "The bes' tools and materials available. Even, how you say, naval architects. We have dem all," he said searching Phil expectantly.

"You brought me here to build boats, Pedro, for real?"

"Yes."

"I reckon you got pretty fast boats already, don't you?" It was one thing to care for broken down old lake boats in a shop behind his house in Lost Lake; but buildings boats for Colombian drug smugglers to evade U.S. law enforcement? That was nuts.

"Pedro, you're crazy, that's what you are. 'Sides, I build little ol' lake boats. The ocean's different - waves, wind – I don't know diddly 'bout all that. You've made a mistake, I'm not your guy."

"Sí," said Pedro confidently. "We have only the best here, Mr. Phil, and you the best. I see," Pedro said pointing to his own eyes. "We have boats, but no so fast as yours. I watch you. Your boats the fastest."

He thought of home for just a split second, and Sheriff J.D. Dunbar, and whether the sheriff would believe him if he came right out with the truth about Mort's murder. And if not J.D., then Marion, who was bound to hold sway.

Or supposing on the other hand Ian was right, and there was no going home? He looked around the bodega, taking in the outbuildings and marveling at the colorful little outpost carved into the jungle. Pedro's mother caught his eye and smiled, offering him a fresh-cooked egg, the whites hanging succulently from the sides of her raised spatula. Nobody had cooked for him in more than a year. His daddy's cooking had been tolerable enough but not legendary, bless his heart. He returned her smile before his eyes met with Pedro's.

"You can no say *no*," said Pedro. It didn't sound like a threat, "but mucho better you live here with us! And you make the biggest, fastest boats ever, right here, Mr. Phil," Pedro beamed, as if he were promising the secret to happiness.

For the briefest moment the merits captivated him. He'd be free as a bird somewhere in the tropics with unlimited time and resources to build screaming fast boats. No banks to repay, no vendors to keep current, no customers to mollify, and folks to do the cooking and laundry, as long as he stayed on the right side of Pedro. It was a Tom Sawyer dream in some ways, reckoned Phil, and how much worse than Lost Lake summer folk could the Guajira camp residents be?

"Who is José?" Phil heard himself ask.

"He the boss a dis place," said Pedro, turning his fork on a strand of pork belly caught in his teeth. "He good guy. You will like José. He take care of Mr. Phil, you'll see. He watch out for Mr. Phil after I go."

"When is that?" Phil asked, "and how long you going for?"

"I'n leavin' soon, Mr. Phil, but you be OK here with José." The news set Phil to thinking of reasons to tag along. He thought of a dozen of them between the time they thanked Pedro's momma for breakfast and when they arrived by way of a spider web of trails at a cabin set deep in the jungle.

It was the first enclosed structure Phil saw in the encampment, with a green tin roof and a raised front porch that overlooked a canal, more than likely the same one that ran inland from the ocean and meandered off into the mangrove swamp. Down on the canal was a small floating dock with a carnival ride-sized Sea-doo jet boat moored to it. The mechanical whir of an air conditioner grinding away off the back of the cabin reminded him of home. The screaming birds and the whooping howler monkeys, and the still jungle torpor wore on him as he contemplated camp life without Pedro. Pedro - the guy people spoke about in hushed tones back home, who had stared him down from the lake road, and who killed his uncle. Who, for reasons unknown, had taken Phil in, set on bending him to Guajira ways.

Pedro was mounting the cabin steps in twos as the front door swung wide and out stepped Ian.

"Gooday, lads. Fancy meeting you heeyah. It's back to civilization for me, mates," he said, and winked at Phil. "See you next time." He bounded off the porch and padded down the path for the Sea-doo at the dock, his long arms swinging as he went. Pedro's eyes narrowed as he watched Ian board the jet boat. A plume of chilled air spilled from the open cabin door, reminding him of the houses on Lost Lake, where the air conditioning ran incessantly whether it need to or not. Phil took the measure of Ian's little jet boat, figuring a boat that small wouldn't get far on the ocean. Sure enough, Ian guided the small craft inland until he vanished in the mangroves - so there *was* a way out of here, and Ian knew it.

"Pedro!" a voice barked from inside.

José looked nothing like how Phil imagined him. He was clean shaven and elegant in a pressed white short-sleeve linen shirt, with a gold pen in his breast pocket. He had close-cropped curly, jet-black hair that he slicked straight back over his head. Gold wire-rimmed readers sat low on his prominent Roman nose, and his skin was translucent and dark, like amber. His cabin was neat as a pin, with framed maps of the U.S. Gulf Coast, Central America, and South America on every wall. In a corner behind his desk was a raised drafting table with an articulated lamp that was shining on a stack of unfurled nautical charts. Adjacent to the drafting table was a book shelf filled with hard cover books, their titles in English, including a University of Houston yearbook.

Phil continued studying the cabin as José and Pedro held a spare and cordial conversation in crisp staccatos of unintelligible Spanish. José asked the questions and Pedro gave the answers. With their business concluded, José rose from his chair and extended Phil his hand. He had friendly brown eyes, and a warm, welcoming grip.

"We're pleased to have you with us, Mr. Phil," said José in perfect, unaccented English. "I regret the way you were brought here, but Pedro does things his own way, as I'm sure you have learned by now. Please accept my apologies. I hope you will enjoy your life here." It was downright eerie how happy some folks were to see him. José kept Phil in his grip, staring warmly into Phil's eyes, even as they heard a subdued knock at the door. "Entrar!" said José, keeping his eyes on Phil.

Did he say *life*, Phil was thinking when he heard the girl's soft, husky voice.

"Café?" she said from behind the door.

"Sí, sí," said José kindly, as if he were speaking to a child. The scent of strong coffee carried on the cool cabin air, the faintest trace of lavender following in the girl's footsteps. Floating like an angel, she navigated the space behind Pedro and Phil, and made her way to a small coffee table behind José's desk.

It was the lavender that reminded him of Katie, though her shiny black hair fell straight like Katie's to her waist. Hovering beside José, the girl's long slender fingers righted the porcelain coffee cup that came overturned in its saucer, and poured from a metal percolator the likes of which Phil had never seen. She finished pouring sooner than Phil hoped, and dipped in a shallow curtsy to excuse herself.

"Mucho gracias," said José. The girl turned on her heels and retreated the way she came, the ruffle on her hem whirling as she went. She was taller and more developed than Katie, and she caught him staring, returning his foolish gaze with a smirk, and pursing her soft Asiatic eyes as she closed the door and was gone.

"You will find many pleasing diversions here, Mr. Phil, though I hope Manuela will not be one of them," José said paternally. "She is my niece."

"And she do your laundry, mi amigo!" added Pedro lustily, jostling Phil's shoulder. José forced a smile.

"Don't forget these," José said, handing Pedro the same tube Ian had carried under his arm.

"Sí," said Pedro, "we off to see Vlad now. Come, Mr. Phil."

"Who is Vlad?" Phil asked after he and Pedro left the cabin. They were on the path bordering the canal by which Ian departed in his jet boat - the same path, Phil guessed, traveled by the heavily burdened men he saw on their way to load the boats that had put to sea. If he was right, they would soon encounter the cradle, where Pedro had shown him the skeleton of a heavy displacement boat, or submarine, if Pedro was to be believed.

"Vlad is chief boat builder, Mr. Phil," said Pedro picking his way down the path. The familiar sound of sawing and hammering could soon be heard through the mangroves as they approached the worksite. A dozen men were milling about, fashioning bulkheads and chiseling joints and laying up stringers as Pedro and Phil circumnavigated the cradle. The men were not to be distracted and paid them no attention. Caustic cigarette smoke hung heavy in the humid air, and the canopy overhead swayed restlessly in the breeze. They were headed for the far side of the cradle, which was oriented, Phil realized, to launch the vessel taking shape stern first into the canal. Plywood boards on a frame of hearty bamboo stalks formed a makeshift table set back in the undergrowth where a little, round man with a shiny bald head leaned on his elbows puzzling over tattered blueprints. Pegged between his fingers was a roll-your-own cigarette from which an arrow-straight column of thick, black smoke climbed the dead air, convulsing in the draft beneath the undulating canopy before carrying breezily into the jungle. Pedro hesitated before approaching the table.

"Yes, yes, what is it?" the man finally grumbled. Pedro stepped forward and the man rose from his blueprints, taking a long, slow drag on his little wrinkled cigarette. He had beady black eyes and thin tight lips. The enormous flared nostrils of his upturned nose made him look to Phil like a hog snake. His left eye twitched as Pedro advanced, and he beat at the air maniacally to disperse a cloud of flies mustering about his head. Pedro handed him the tube, extending it like a peace offering.

"Where you get *this*?" demanded the elf of a man, ripping the tube from Pedro.

"From José," Pedro replied. The man sounded Russian, or at

least the way Russians sound in the movies. He popped the cap by squeezing the tube, pried loose its tightly furled contents, and tossed it aside like a walked batter. The cool smell of fresh reproduction ink mixed in the hot jungle air along with the acrid odor of stale cigarette smoke as he spread the blueprints over the table.

"Change orders," he grumbled as he unfurled the scroll, weighting down the curling edges on one side with a straight edge and a utility knife on the other.

"They no think Vlad know how to build mini submarine?" he barked at no one in particular. "Who is *dis boy,* Pedro?" he continued, noticing Phil for the first time, and looking Phil up and down. An inscription in the shape of a crest on the blueprints caught Phil's eye.

"Dis is mi amigo, Mr. Phil, the boat builder," said Pedro by way of introduction. "He help us build very fast boats, Vlad." The inscription on the blueprints was fascinating – a decorative company logo like a passport stamp on a field of the most highly stylized geometric hand writing Phil had ever seen – the handwriting of the blueprint draftsman himself, more than likely.

"Por favor, Señor Vlad," came a soft, precocious voice, "café?"

He knew by her voice it was the girl from José's cabin, Manuela. In the open air, with her long black hair and her coffee-colored skin, her likeness to Katie was breathtaking. She carried a tray identical to the one she delivered to the cabin, with a cup inverted on a saucer and an identical serving-sized geometric peculator.

"Ah," said Vlad with uncharacteristic calm, "sí Manuela, sí" he intoned, his eyes brightening and his nostrils relaxing. Her delicate hands bewitched Phil again, righting the cup and pouring the coffee. She placed the saucer and cup near the corner of the blueprints with the imprint on it, so they obscured all the words but *Ingeniería y Construcción.*

"Dis boy, Pedro, what he know?" said Vlad, staring at Manuela.

"Dis," he said waving at the cradle, "is *grrrect Rrrussian* engineering!" he pronounced with pride. "DEA and U.S. Coast Guard never see, never catch, never!" Vlad continued, igniting a fresh roll-your-own and sucking on it hard. "And with shit materials we do this, Pedro, shit materials!" he said, shifting his gaze and looking straight into Phil's eyes.

"I believe it," Phil murmured contritely beneath his breath, but Vlad saw his lips move.

"What you say?" Vlad bellowed, his nostrils flaring and his body coiling as if he were like to strike.

"No, Vlad," Pedro interceded. "Mr. Phil say nada, nothing. Mr. Phil he build the boats, no submarines, very fast boats. Very fast, you see, Vlad." Phil stole a glance at Manuela and she smirked again, and then retreated as before, leaving lavender and blueprint ink lingering over the table.

"No, Pedro. He's right," Phil interrupted. "Vlad, here, is right," he continued, buoyed and disarmed all at once by Manuela. "There ain't nothin' like Russian engineering. It's the best." Vlad grimaced, taking Phil's measure. He pulled hard on his cigarette again, holding his breath good and long to absorbed the nicotine deep in his blood.

"But for what *you* want," Phil continued, looking at the blueprints, "there's better Russian engineering than this." He wondered when he said it if he'd pushed his luck too far. The look on Vlad's face removed all doubt.

CHAPTER 12

Lost Lake, Georgia

J.D. Dunbar crossed the threshold of his bedroom at midnight. He was six hours past due, and two hours later than when he and Marion usually shut off the lights. Marion had dozed off, leaving her bedside lamp on. She stirred as the floor creaked beneath J.D.'s heavy shoes.

"J.D....?" she murmured. "I tried to wait up for you."

She sat up, bleary eyed and mussed, her tattered edition of *Gone With The Wind* spilling from her bosom to the floor. "Why you so late?" J.D. sat down beside her on the bed, his nylon police jacket bulging where his standard-issue 45-caliber Springfield pro-rail pistol was holstered. He also carried a Glock, but it was impossible to see, Velcroed in a pouch against his belly.

"Did you have a bad day?"

"You could say that," he replied.

"What now, what is it?" she asked. He knew she could read him like a book. There was just no keeping secrets from her. He also knew all about her soft spot for Phil, and how hard she would take the news.

Marion wasn't supposed to know that Phil's uncle, Mort Ashton, was in the witness protection program, but she did because it was one more secret he couldn't keep from her. She was as good and trustworthy a woman as any, he supposed, and capitulating to her relentless curiosity was just plumb easier. She had made it her business to find out why J.D. left for work one morning a small-town sheriff and came home a federal marshal, wearing a shiny new *United States Marshal* badge, the five-point gold star beaming like a superhero insignia from his chest. He fed her a story about the understaffed local courthouse, the growing number of subpoenas, warrants and summonses, and the need for more local service processors, none of which she believed. The next day she did what needle-nosed librarians do and researched the paths by which work-a-day cops like J.D. become deputized federal marshals. What she found astounded her, and raised J.D. one notch higher in her book, if that were even possible.

J.D. had been drafted to the longest serving federal law enforcement agency in the land. Passed into law at the urging of President George Washington, in 1789, The Federal Marshal Service was created when the First Congress discovered it possessed no mechanism to enforce local and regional laws. It came as no surprise to Marion that J.D. had been called. George Washington himself wrote that federal marshals were to be "*the fittest characters to expound the law, and dispense justice,*" in order to safeguard "*the happiness of our Country, and...the stability of its political system.*" That was her J.D., all right.

Present day marshals concerned themselves with protecting court officers, transporting prisoners, coordinating manhunts for fugitives, and running the Witness Protection Program. Among a marshal's far-reaching powers was "*the power to command all necessary assistance in the execution of his duty, and to appoint... one or more deputies.*" In the Old West that meant raising a posse, or appointing town deputies to bring peace to lawless frontier towns, like Tombstone, Arizona, where Special Deputy U.S. Marshals Wyatt Earp and Doc Holliday dispatched the Billy Clanton gang at the O.K. Corral.

What surprised Marion most was that J.D. could be pressed into federal service anywhere, at any time, for any purpose. She recalled President Kennedy dispatching 127 marshals to guard James Meredith, the first African American student to register at Ole Miss. She remembered how Norman Rockwell famously depicted four Herculean U.S. Marshals escorting a spritely little colored girl named Ruby Bridges to school. To Marion it was the power to deputize that gave her pause, resembling nothing so much as the power of 19th century British naval officers to impress sailors and drag them off to battle against their will at sea.

"In the wrong hands," she had told J.D., "it raised questions. What if the wrong sort got to deputizing more of the wrong sorts? We'd end up with a town full of crooked marshals." It was just like Marion to find the dark side of a noble calling.

"I suppose," J.D. said, giving the thought its due. "T'wont happen here," he assured her. "Not in my town."

J.D. had been deputized to keep an eye on Mort, he finally admitted to Marion. A Senior Deputy U.S. Marshal from Atlanta arrived one day unannounced in search of a local handler for an individual in the Federal Witness Protection Program living nearby. Until then, even J.D. didn't know Mort's true identity. The one secret J.D. did manage to keep from Marion was his promotion to senior inspector. Only senior inspectors had the authority to handle information supplied by active informants, which Mort became when the drug trade set down roots in Atlanta. It was then J.D. learned how the Organized Crime Drug Enforcement Task Force had a gentle way of pressing protected witnesses back into service. J.D. was the right kind of low-key law man the DEA needed to handle Mort.

He became the DEA's man in Lost Lake, Georgia, albeit reluctantly, and learned more than he ever wanted about the narcotics trafficking underworld.

Mort Ashton, it turned out, wasn't Phil's uncle on his mother's side at all. He wasn't even Mort Ashton. He was Harry *the hammer* Halliday, a gangster from an outer borough of New York City. His gentlemanly manner and thinning red hair made him a natural for Phil's wayward uncle, who recovered his bearings and came home, disillusioned by life among the Yankees. Marion and Phil's father were the only civilians who knew Mort wasn't Mort, and he had been in witness protection so long there was nothing for Phil to suspect, or so J.D. had thought. Now that Mort was dead, slain on Phil's floor in the signature manner of drug retribution killings, and Phil was running, it appeared Phil knew more than he'd let on. Either he took it upon himself or had been put up to killing a cooperating witness. How he would explain to Marion that the apple of her eye was a prime suspect in the murder of his only charge in the Witness Protection Program, J.D. wasn't exactly sure.

Marion never did understand the keen interest J.D. took in the immigrants pouring into town. At first, he was just discouraged. That turned to worry, the more he learned about criminal gangs filing into the Southeast. Weed had always been around, but the cocaine and meth and heroin were new. Maybe some meth was cooked locally, but the cocaine came from points south of the border – Peru, Bolivia or Colombia - and the heroin came from Mexico, according to his briefings.

J.D. had done his homework and knew the U.S. government's interdiction record, especially in Central America. The government's modest successes, from the mid-1980s to the early 1990s, were rapidly reversed by *the balloon effect,* in agency parlance. The DEA had disrupted the so-called "air-bridge" ferrying raw cocoa paste over the Andes from Peruvian and Bolivian growers to Colombian cocaine refining laboratories, cutting off supplies of raw material. When Bolivian and Peruvian coca leaf production collapsed, the vacuum was quickly filled by Colombian growers, which *ballooned* to account for at least ninety percent of the world's raw cocoa leaf supply. It was the first hint of how adaptable the cartels would become. Push on the *balloon* here, and out popped new cultivation and processing there.

In similar fashion, the all-out U.S. war in 1990 on Mexican drug lord Pablo Escobar and his Medellín cartel created what came to be known as "*the cockroach effect.*" There was no telling Marion it wasn't a racial slur - no convincing her it accurately described a pattern of behavior. After Escobar's death in 1993, the Medellín cartel collapsed. The Cali cartel knew its days were numbered, too, and dispersed, its surviving elements not so much vanishing as splintering, skittering like kitchen cockroaches and transmogrifying into more than three hundred small, violent, disorganized trafficking gangs, or *cartelitos,* that were too dispersed for authorities to target effectively.

Would it had stopped there, but nature abhors a vacuum and so did the Colombian drug world. The *Fuerzas Armadas Revolucionarias de Colombia* or FARC, and the *Autodefensas Unidas de Colombia* or AUC filled the void left by the Cali and Medellin cartels. The brutal wars of attrition that followed so destabilized U.S. border regions that the Clinton administration came down hard again, committing more than $8 billion to a program called Plan Colombia to neutralize the proxy paramilitary hoards operating in Mexico.

A decade later, the FARC, AUC and a good many other *cartelitos* had been defanged; but cocoa production *ballooned* again, from areas like La Macarena, which Americans knew only as a trendy line dance, back into its native lands of Peru and Bolivia. Cultivation also *ballooned* south and west, and trafficking gangs followed, skittering like cockroaches north into Guatemala, Honduras and Mexico, and east into Venezuala. And so the cycle went.

"What is it?" Marion asked again, worry in her voice. J.D. had found Katie McLean walking the lake road about noon that day. He knew by her aimless gait she was stoned, and pulled to the curb to give her a ride. He would have taken her home directly, could he have been satisfied of her safety there. There was of late just no telling what went on at the McLeans, who was there or what they'd be doing. Better to keep her safe with him until she got her wits about her. She was glad J.D. stopped, and didn't draw breath from the moment she entered the car. She had seen something curious from the top of her boat house, which was straight across Redemption Bay from Phil's place. Phil and Pedro Morales had left Phil's house together in Pedro's truck midmorning Monday. Phil was still gone a whole day later. She watched all night, she said, and the house never stirred.

"Now don't you worry yourself about it, sweetheart," J.D. said, "let's just go on down there and take us a look, shall we? If I know Phil, he's found his way home by now." Right off, J.D. didn't like that Katie saw Phil with Pedro, but he reckoned there was a good explanation – just not the one he was trying to make sense of now. He was sorry as hell Katie saw what they found at Phil's. Processing the grisly murder scene became J.D.'s immediate priority, and against his better judgment, he took Katie home, calling the county medical examiner on route. As soon as the McLean's front door closed behind Katie, J.D. called the U.S. Marshals Service to alert witness protection, and issued an all-points-bulletin for Phil Perdue and Pedro Morales, driving a late model red pickup.

The Perdue homestead was swarming with law enforcement by the time he returned. More than twenty-four hours had passed since Phil and Pedro were last seen, which meant they could be anywhere by now. The only place to start was security camera footage from gas stations in widening concentric circles from Lost Lake. If they were on the move in Pedro's truck, the conspicuous red pick-up was bound to be captured on film, and offer a clue, J.D. hoped, about where the unlikely duo were going.

The *cockroach effect* did not observe borders, obeying the laws of supply and demand as vigorously in America as anywhere, including Lost Lake. J.D.'s hunch was that Pedro was in the vanguard of *cockroaches* staking claims to distribution territories in northeast Georgia. If the gangs could ingrain themselves in big city culture, terrorizing places like Los Angeles and Chicago and Las Vegas, they wouldn't stop there. And if Wal-Mart could find pay dirt in rural America, so would the gangs.

Immigrants from Central America were arriving in Lost Lake County every day now, and with them came the drug trade, including new and more dangerous narcotic cocktails, from angel dust-laced weed to heroin. Marion's middle and high school charges *were* the market. She thought she could save them by calling on their better angels, but J.D. was skeptical, especially about the presence of angels among teenagers. The only proven remedy was to strangle temptation at the source, and it was the urge to protect Marion from losing more kids to addiction that spurred J.D. to action.

J.D.'s first run in with drug smugglers was back in the eighties. Those were the days of George H. W. Bush's South Florida Task Force, which shut down the original Caribbean air and sea smuggling routes through the Caymans, the Bahamas and Leeward islands, and pushed traffickers to the overland routes through Mexico. Northeast Georgia had been accessible for a time, from the Gulf Coast ports of New Orleans and Houston, and even Miami. Coke briefly made the rounds, but it went as fast as it came when the Caribbean routes were shut down. The distances to Tijuana and El Paso and even Laredo were far too great, and the overland routes too few and too exposed for steady shipments along the main arteries east. Lost Lake's remoteness had saved it.

J.D. always said it was just a matter of time 'til drugs came back, and Marion had ignored him. There was no ignoring him now, and he didn't know how to tell her. The word from the DEA was that the Mexican overland routes were under pressure, and the bulge on the *balloon* was moving again, this time to Venezuela, with access to the old Caribbean routes and new Atlantic routes to Europe and West Africa. It meant the Gulf Coast ports were attractive again, putting Lost Lake back within reach.

Emboldened by their sophistication, traffickers were wiser and more agile than before. Decades of matching wits with the DEA and local military south of the border bred in them a chameleon capacity to mutate, shift, disperse, and reconstitute. They were trading old-fashioned territoriality for adaptability, versatility, and geographic diversity. Not that today's traffickers shied from a fight or lost their lust for blood and treasure. They were infinitely more violent, and it was how randomly and brutally they reasserted themselves that gave authorities pause, which is why Mort's inexplicable and gruesome murder was a poor omen. It had the signature capriciousness of the new millennial cartels.

If Mort's murder meant witness protection had been compromised, and Phil and Pedro were in cahoots, no telling what hell would break loose next. It would be the first sign the cartels were here to do more than sell drugs and kill each other. It meant they had been here for a while, and meant to stay - to embed themselves in legitimate local businesses, to both expand their capabilities and launder their cash, the way diversifying into South American mining made them experts at tunneling – the kind of tunnels that saved El Chapo from prison at least twice, and kept the Mexican cross-border overland routes open long after U.S. and Mexican authorities thought they were shut down.

J.D. pondered how bad it would get. One classified assessment of Mexico said, "the old institutions – police, courts, prisons, intelligence agencies, parties, and elections – no longer work. Indeed, they are manifestly corrupt and dysfunctional." It made him fear for the town. Marion worried when J.D. brooded, and that's what he was doing now.

"I'm talkin' to you, J.D." she said plaintively, sitting upright against the headboard. "What's got into you?" He told her the whole story.

"I declare, J.D.," said Marion. "I will jerk that child bald if he's taken up with the likes of Pedro Morales." The truth was far worse than she knew, maybe even worse than J.D. imagined. J.D. had returned to the stationhouse and checked the DICE data base to see what he could find by way of associations between Phil and Pedro and any other locals under investigation. There was nothing on anyone by the name of Pedro Morales. However, the Farmer's Building and Loan of Lost Lake had, in recent days, issued a Suspicious Activity Report to FinCEN for large cash deposits and withdrawals in accounts belonging to none other than Phoenix Perdue of Perdue Landing. J.D. had caught Buck Tidwell, the branch manager, just before quitting time. He was locking the doors when J.D. pulled up to inquire about the banking activity that triggered the report.

The genesis of the Suspicious Activity Report was a bit of a mystery. On closer inspection, the large deposits to Phil's account were routine, common in spring and fall when boats are bought and sold for cash. The money was disbursed as fast as it came in, to vendors Phil owed. The vendors, it appeared, had learned to live with the seasonality of the Perdue's business. "Might could be," said Buck, the bank's parent company in Atlanta "got religion about reporting compliance," seeing as the amounts exceeded the reporting threshold and had for years.

It still made no sense to J.D., there being nothing extraordinary in the pattern of the transfers, even though the amounts of cash were large.

"I can't figure it, neither," Buck said thoughtfully. "I used t'a could tell why they did what they do up there in 'lanta, but not no more. I'll be goin' on to the house now, J.D.," Buck concluded, "if you don't have no more questions."

Phil and Pedro on the lam, Mort Ashton, a.k.a. Harry *the hammer* Halliday murdered, throat cut, tongue removed in signature warning to future would-be snitches, and now the Suspicious Activity Report – circumstantially, at least, Phil was roped and tied. It was going to be hard on Marion.

"I don't believe it, J.D., I jus' don't," she said when J.D. finished, his worst fears saved for himself.

"I cain't hardly neither, but thems the facts. I's pert near sure our Phil's in trouble, but where and who with, well, there's just no tellin'."

CHAPTER 13

U.S. Coast Guard Cutter *Osprey*, Caribbean Sea

The one thing pinned-down infantry counted on in Afghanistan was Casey Tindall's rapid reaction team. Ambush was the game and teams like Tindall's were the remedy. They lived on perpetual standby to bail out unsuspecting units that wandered into trouble. Tindall's marksmanship saved more than a few units in distress, but he took no credit. It was one team, one fight. That was the job, and his combat training kicked in every time a hostile weapon turned skyward.

It was a conditioned response when he pulled the trigger and turned the man in the conning tower to a fine pink vapor that vanished in the brisk cross wind. Despite *Melissa's* protestations from the C130J high overhead, Dougie said Casey had saved them all, including the Coast Guard from the embarrassment of losing a spanking new *Dolphin* on her maiden interdiction mission. So Tindall was troubled by the uneasy mood of his HITRON crew mates and Captain Buldoc as they met in the captain's quarters.

The storm had passed and the seas were calm. The lugubrious lap of the mellowing swell licked gently at the *Osprey's* rocking waterline as she idled north northeast on a direct course for U.S. Naval Base, Guantanamo Bay, Cuba. The semi-submerged prow of the cocaine-packed bigfoot yawed and rolled like a harpooned whale, creaking forebodingly as the *Osprey's* tow line stretched and slacked on the softly surging sea. At her current speed of six knots through the water, and even less over the bottom against the set of the tide, the *Osprey* would cover the six hundred miles to Cuba in five days. That was, if the seas cooperated. A second low-pressure system creeping west along the equator from the mid-Atlantic might easily gain speed and overtake them, which would put them back in the slop. Then they'd be forced to cut the bigfoot loose before the strain of the tow separated her bulkheads and sent her with a half a billion dollars of contraband straight to the ocean floor. A slow-motion race to Cuba was on.

The size of the haul and the capture of the vessel and her surviving crew would make great headlines, maybe even a spot on the national news. Both were important to keep the Congressional spending spigots open. But the DEA valued the bigfoot even more, for what it might tell them about who was building them and supplying the engineering designs. Narco subs were the new wild card to reopening the Caribbean Sea lanes shut down in the Bush era. They were even thought to be transiting the Atlantic, delivering cocaine and heroin to Spain and Portugal. The DEA wanted their builders.

With a go-fast alongside and a bigfoot in tow, and both seizures fully intact, Tindall and the *Osprey's* crew were riding high, heading home triumphant with the spoils of war. Gutterson, Burbank, and Buldoc, however, were less sanguine.

"Truth is, boys," Buldoc started, after closing his cabin door, "we're a long way from home and we just hit the banditos hard. Could be Sinaloa or the Zeta – in any event, one a' those damn tribes is out one helluva a lot of dough. Why *Melissa* went radio silent, and why we can't raise GANTSEC I don't know, but until we figure that out, we're on our own." Gutterson grunted. "And I know what you think, Hank," Buldoc resumed. "It doesn't matter right now. If we have to fight our way outta here, the fight 'll come soon. I need you guys ready."

"The LEDETs know about the lost comms?" Dougie inquired.

"They're briefed," Buldoc replied. "If we can't raise Homeland Security we're gonna need help from somewhere. They're on the job, hailing any armored vessel in the vicinity to conscript."

"Those GANTSEC bastards," Gutterson muttered, "how long do we put up with this crap? How long before the damn DEA goes after *them*?"

"Not long, if we survive this one," Buldoc assured him. Buldoc looked scared. Gutterson's long-running suspicion of GANTSEC was looking well-founded. Tindall could tell by the body language that Buldoc and Dougie had never fought their way out of anything. They were Coasties, civil servants, trained in search and rescue, safety inspections, and the care and feeding of the HITRON and LEDET elements they hosted.

A retired SOAR jockey like Gutterson was a different story. He could have flown anywhere, been shot at by anyone, and his cool composure said so. Tindall faulted no one for fearing combat. As a chaplain he saw the worst of the aftermath, and dished it out amply as a crew chief. Knowing the fight was coming scared the shit out of everybody - SEALs, medics, marines – nobody was immune. Anyone who thought otherwise had never been to war.

But veterans handled the fear. The ones he assisted in and out of battle, and covered from the air, were trained. They knew what to do, adapted on the fly, dispersed, regrouped, kept moving, confounding the enemy's desire to pin them down. But at five knots speed made good, on a flat sea six hundred miles from a friendly port, assuming Guantanamo was friendly, the *Osprey* could scarcely be more exposed, and it was clear from Buldoc's look that he had no plan.

"Any good ideas?" the captain asked after a long pause, "besides cutting the damn thing loose and running for base?"

Gutterson leaned back in the captain's metal desk chair, folded his meaty arms and shook his head. He hated the idea.

"You mean right now, Captain? Before any sign of trouble?" Gutterson inquired.

"Would you rather wait for trouble, with no cover and no escort?" Buldoc countered, looking genuinely unnerved.

"We fight it out, Captain," said Gutterson. "With the firepower of the ship and the LEDETs, and Steady Hans Solo, here, on the fifty cal from the air?" he continued, winking at Tindall conspiratorially, "it'll be over in five minutes."

Tindall watched Buldoc circle a small unoccupied patch of his cabin staring at the floor. The captain's reticence to fight matched Gutterson's contempt for retreat - *squirting,* in battlefield parlance.

"It's the dope they'll want, isn't it?" Buldoc finally said. "They'd be fools to attack the ship after we cut the damn thing loose." Perspiration bubbled in small clear beads on Gutterson's shiny, bald head, and he exhaled, leaving little to the imagination of how he felt about cutting the bigfoot loose.

"Turn it over, just like that, Captain? to continue on its way, after the years we've been searching for one of these things?"

"What's it worth to you, Hank?" said Buldoc, staring down on Gutterson. "Is it worth dying for?"

The question never crossed Tindall's mind, not in all his tours; nor Gutterson's, judging from the pilot's frown. But it reached Dougie, who wriggled like a night crawler at Buldoc's suggestion. "I got seventy-five men to think about, Hank, none of whom volunteered, like you and Tindall, here, for combat. One stray round sets off the avgas tank and we're barbecue – all of us – except you guys, if you're safely in the air. I'm not sinking my boat to make headlines back in Florida."

For the first time Tindall pondered the dependability of his new outfit, the potency of the "force multipliers" Homeland Security promoted with such flourish.

"You're damn right we'll cut her loose," said Buldoc, "if we're still without escort or air cover and things turn hot."

"Maybe we scuttle it now," Dougie volunteered, "walk through her first and document everything on video, then sink her and scoot for home. Leave them nothing to come for." His search for a brokered peace met with Gutterson's glare, "...if things get too hot to handle, I mean," Dougie finished in retreat.

"Captain,... bridge," crackled a speaker mounted flush to the cabin wall. Buldoc turned to the intercom panel and depressed a push-to-talk button.

"Go ahead bridge."

"Sir, we have a small plane circling the ship. Single engine, high wing, fixed gear, looks like a Cessna. She's unmarked, no tail number, and we can't raise her. What do you want to do, sir?"

"Shit," said Buldoc to no one in particular, "they've already found us. It's only a matter of time now." The initiative, Tindall thought. Never lose the initiative.

"Bridge,...Captain," said Buldoc with the full force of his clenched fist mashed against the push-to-talk button. "Any luck raising GANTSEC or Navy of any kind, any nationality? I'll take a gunboat from Trinidad and Tobago at this point."

"No joy, sir. We're being jammed or something, secure comms and sat, too, sir. Big energy. Has to be nearby."

"Classic," muttered Gutterson. "It's the spotter plane. Let's go shoot us a Cessna," he said rising to his feet and steering the pull of his flight suit zipper, presently split around his generous gut, smoothly over it.

"Don't be a fool, Hank," said Buldoc. "He'll draw you from the ship and take our air cover. I want you guys on hot standby, ready to launch for close-in support if we need it, and we're cutting that damn thing loose. At least we'll be free to maneuver."

"And then what, Captain," Gutterson rumbled, his rust-colored handle bar mustache rising and falling on his pursing lips. "Why cut her loose until there's a threat?"

"And what do you suppose follows jamming, Lieutenant Colonel?" said Buldoc, returning on an impulse to the intercom. "Bridge.., Captain."

"Bridge, sir."

"Train the fifty cals on that damn plane and give her two warning bursts. If she doesn't break off, shoot her down, and monitor the comms and radar. See if the jamming lets up after we run her off. I'll be right there. No delay, understand? Unload on the bastard." He released the intercom button and turned to Gutterson.

"We can set a watch, Captain," said Gutterson, "go to hot standby, and the first sign of real trouble, we follow your plan, sir, but until then let's keep her in tow." Buldoc stood still, arms crossed, studying the floor, mulling Gutterson's proposal. Then Tindall surprised himself by interrupting.

"Sir, if I may, why don't we just hoist her aboard - ship, cargo and all," he suggested, taken with the idea's simplicity. "Then all ahead full, straight for home, and everyone wins, except the bad guys."

"Ten metric tons, son?" Buldoc replied. "No chance."

"We could offload her, Captain," Dougie joined in. "She's just plywood and fiberglass, by the looks of her. Can't weigh more than the RHIBs when she's empty."

"That 'll take hours, Dougie," Buldoc replied as the fifty caliber guns erupted from bow and stern. "We don't have hours, and it means stopping, in broad daylight. We'll be a sitting duck."

"No more than we are now, sir," said Dougie.

"We form a bucket brigade, sir," Tindall continued. "Many hands, light work, sir." He could see Buldoc didn't love it, but it meant ending the tow, one way or the other, and getting underway. Anything was better than six days at sea at five knots made good, with no one to call for help.

"Bridge...Captain speaking. Radar contacts?"

"No sir. One minute we had contacts, the next minute they were gone, sir, like radar is being jammed too. All we've got now, sir, is sea clutter."

"For Chrissake," Buldoc seethed and released the intercom. "What in God's name is going on out here. Since when did the damned drug cartels get their hands on jamming technology?"

"With enough money, sir," Tindall replied, "the bad guys get their hands on everything. The Taliban E-C'd us plenty in Afghanistan."

"Say what?" said Dougie.

"The Taliban had EC, electronic countermeasures. Not always, but enough."

"One hour, gentlemen. I'll give us one hour exactly to have that thing unloaded and on the fantail or I'm cutting her loose and sending her to the bottom, is that clear?" Buldoc barked. "And you guys," he continued, glaring at Gutterson, "on hot standby, now. Get up there." He had exited the door headed for the bridge when he paused and rounded on Gutterson from the passageway. "And if you have no comms in the air, Hank, we go to light signals, you copy?"

"Roger that, sir," said Gutterson, as all four men craned their heads skyward. They could hear the aircraft overhead. The pilot had opened her throttle, and the normally aspirated piston engine was clawing at the sky for altitude.

Gutterson and Dougie and Tindall were back in the refueled *Dolphin*, the shoulder restraints hanging loosely over their torsos, as they felt the ship's engines power back to idle. The *Osprey's* crew had mustered by the hoist, and the HITRON crew watched through the aircraft's open cabin doors as a handful of sailors disappeared over the side. Tindall barely heard the Cessna, now. It was almost out of earshot, but the air was dead and hot, and the hum of the plane's hard-working single engine still carried, if only faintly, on the wide-open sea.

Through the *Dolphin's* skylights they could see heavily armed LEDETs dressed in black where they had taken to the *Osprey's* tower. They were scanning the ocean on all four quarters through gigantic, ungainly binoculars. Large bales wrapped in white plastic began appearing on the *Osprey's* gunwales where they were hoisted in the air by sailors working in pairs, and transferred amidships. The sailors stacked them in pyramids, their exuberance rising with the pile. The hoist went into service, too, with a wide grated pallet reappearing in twenty-minute intervals stacked high with plump white bales. Each new stack met with fresh excitement, bantering sailors carrying the bales forward where the pyramids kept rising. The offloading proceeded with orderly precision until Tindall saw one of the LEDET lookouts point to the horizon, and a second train his binoculars to the spot where the first was pointing. The first LEDET whistled down to the bridge and yelled something urgent.

Tindall watched Gutterson fixate on Buldoc as the captain stepped out from the shade of the *Osprey's* wheel house and on to the sunlit flying bridge. He looked first to the flight deck where his eyes found Gutterson through the cockpit windshield, and then he raised his binoculars, leaning off the fly bridge rail to peer where the LEDETs were pointing. Gutterson buckled and cinched his four-point shoulder restraints and lay the first two fingers of his left hand gently on the magneto switches.

"Standby," he ordered, almost inaudibly. Buldoc lowered his

binoculars, leaned back from the fly bridge rail and looked straight at Gutterson. He raised his arm and whirled it like a lasso in the air.

"Here we go, boys," said Gutterson, flicking the magnetos to *on* and waiting for the avionics to spin up. He engaged the ignition, and slowly, purposefully, the blades began to turn. Buldoc departed the fly bridge and returned just seconds later with a bright orange, large-bore shot-gun device that he mounted to his shoulder and fired. A long thin trail of wispy smoke arced into the sky, rising, Tindall reckoned, to almost one thousand feet before a small parachute deployed and a brilliant red flair set to rocking and drifting, trailing a thin ribbon of smoke back toward the ocean. The seconds passed like hours as the *Dolphin* stirred to life. Gutterson rushed his checklist as the soft moan of turbines rose to a scream.

"All hands, back on board!" Buldoc's voice boomed over the ship's public-address system as the turning blades were lost to the naked eye. Gutterson had scarcely tested his flight controls before he tore the *Dolphin* free, banking hard to starboard in the direction of the threat.

At two hundred feet and a quarter mile out, the go-fasts were well in view – five of them, heavily armed, with deck-mounted machine guns forward of the helm, and mortars bristling from the stern. Each one carried a half dozen machinegun toting men, who were quick to open fire as Gutterson charged them head-on.

"Do your thing, Steady Hans Solo," Gutterson purred like Sir Alec Guinness through the intercom. Tindall was pleased to oblige. In the excitement of the moment he underestimated the breakneck closing speed, and failed to walk back his firing pattern, overshooting his targets, which passed beneath unscathed.

"I need a better angle," he reported on the intercom, bracing himself as the *Dolphin* banked hard, righted itself, and came alongside the go-fast formation closing on the *Osprey*. This time he aimed low, walking back the plumes of sea spray where his rounds met the ocean until they converged on the first of the go-fasts, and tore at her gunwales before obliterating her engines.

"One down," he reported, taking aim at the foreground of the next go-fast in line. Before he began shooting the water ahead of the remaining four go-fasts erupted in plumes of sea spray. The *Osprey* had opened fire, too. The go-fasts had closed on her much faster than Tindall expected.

"I hope those Coasties can shoot straight," he muttered over the intercom, walking back a new line of fire on the next go-fast. "We won't get to them all before they're on her." He hadn't finished the thought before the lead go-fast opened up on the *Osprey*, her forward gun raking the bridge, which lit up like a party sprinkler with the impact of the rounds. Tindall connected with the second of the go-fasts, opening a gash in her waterline, which he extended to her stern before leveling a hail of led on its engines and stopping her dead in the water.

"Two down," he confirmed through the intercom.

"Pick up the pace, Hans," Dougie replied. "The ship's taking fire." As he drew a bead on the third of the go-fasts an explosion rocked the *Osprey* forward of the bridge. A mortar round had found her foredeck. The go-fasts he disabled were still in the fight, too, training their guns on the *Osprey* and igniting her broadsides with the sparks of unremittent fire.

"No delay, Tindall," said Gutterson through the intercom, "too much more of this and we'll need someplace else to land, copy?"

And then they were in shadow as something moving fast passed overhead.

"*Osprey, Osprey, Osprey*, this is Eagle-One inbound, over," came the crisp British voice over the radio.

"Say what," said Dougie through the intercom. "Hey! The comms are up!"

"Check it out," said Gutterson, "a Lynx," he continued as a

camouflage battle-dressed Royal Navy helicopter overtook the *Dolphin*, dropped in low from overhead and opened fire on the go-fasts. The blaze of three exhaust plumes from its Sea Skua anti-ship missiles darted like bottle rockets towards the sea, where they found the last three go-fasts all at once, enveloping them in fireballs that burned to the waterline. Gutterson banked left, avoiding the thick black mushroom clouds rising off the sea.

One hour later, the *Osprey* was tracking north, northeast at eighteen knots under escort by the HMS Argyll, a British Royal Navy *Duke* class frigate. The bigfoot rode high and dry on *Osprey's* fantail as Tindall secured the *Dolphin's* cabin door inside the *Osprey's* hangar. He had just replenished the ammunition belts for the M240B machine gun when the Lynx touched down on the *Osprey's* open flight deck. Out stepped a Royal Navy officer, who crouched beneath the decelerating blades and scuttled for the flight deck apron where Captain Buldoc waited to welcome him.

"Commander Christopher Merton, HMS Argyll," Tindall heard the officer say, as the distinguished middle-aged man unfolded from his crouch.

"Captain Buldoc, Commander. We can't thank you enough for coming to our aide."

"Nonsense, old chap. Pleasure. We picked up the jamming and saw your flare," he said, following Buldoc into the shade of the hangar. Gutterson appeared in the bulkhead doorway, the collar of his flight suit dark with perspiration.

"A damn Cessna of all things, appeared out of nowhere and started circling," Buldoc was explaining. "The comms, radar, satlinks, everything went down. And then came the attack. The cartels have upped their game."

"A Cessna, you say?"

"Yes, Commander. A damn Cessna. It finally ran south when you guys appeared, and everything came back up the second it cut and ran."

The Lynx on the flight deck caught Gutterson's eye, and he stared at it covetously as he made his way across the hangar toward Tindall.

"Take a good look," he said to Tindall under his breath. "That's the only fully aerobatic rotor-wing bird in the Allied arsenal. Holds the world speed record at almost two-hundred and fifty knots, and the fire power, *man*. What I couldn't do with that."

"Yeah, they flew with us in Afghanistan," replied Tindall. "Good old-fashioned British engineering."

"Thank you, sir," Gutterson called to Commander Merton across the hangar as the engines on the Lynx' coasted down. "We're much obliged."

"Commander Merton," said Buldoc as he led the British officer over to the *Dolphin*, "Lieutenant Colonel Gutterson and Crew Chief Tindall, from HITRON. I was just telling Commander Merton, boys, how we were jammed."

"Indeed you were, Captain Buldoc, but perhaps not how you may think," said Merton, tilting ever so slightly forward at the waist.

"Not following you, Commander," said Buldoc.

"We sourced the jamming signal at twenty-eight thousand feet, coming from a U.S. command plane, according to friend-or-foe," said Merton. Gutterson grimaced.

"Sir?" Buldoc said to Merton.

"Yes. I'm sure it was inadvertent, happens all the time," said Merton cheerfully.

"*Melissa...*" Gutterson grumbled.

"I understand garage doors open for a hundred kilometers around when they forget to power off near the coast," Merton continued, thoroughly amused. "Never mind, chaps. We locked on with a guidance system and they soon saw their mistake. Nothing to worry about now. A rather good bit of target practice for the lads, I should say, though I'm sure you would have sorted it on your own," he said. Tindall knew he was being courteous. *Osprey* had been in trouble, and the way the British Navy Lynx engaged multiple targets at once was simply beyond the HITRON *Dolphin's* capabilities. The Brits had saved their bacon.

"We're pleased to escort you as far as you like," the Commander continued with a smile.

"A mistake?" said Gutterson looking directly at Buldoc, "my ass."

CHAPTER 14

Guajira Peninsula, Colombia

Floating on the mist, suspended in his hammock, Phil eased gently into consciousness after another surprisingly good night's sleep. His trusty new friend, Miguel, stood guard by his feet, his signature aviator glasses, soft-brimmed camo hat, and long gun silhouetted against the tree-filtered beams of the rising sun. The damn howlers hadn't started yet, but Phil reckoned they would, any minute, and another day would begin. Pedro would appear, dismiss Miguel, roust Phil from his hammock, and off they would march through the undergrowth, Pedro humming mariachi on the way to rendezvous with his mother and another lip-smacking breakfast of chicharone, made only as Pedro's mother could. But Miguel dropped unexpectedly to one knee, and in one easy motion swung the gun off his back and shouldered it. The sound of heavy footfalls approached through the undergrowth and Phil heard the *click* of Miguel's gun safety releasing. "Alto!" Miguel barked.

"Cállate," Pedro droned, emerging from the jungle. Miguel exhaled and secured his weapon. Pedro had scared him, though why exactly Phil didn't follow. Miguel slung his weapon back over his shoulder and departed, forgoing the usual pleasantries.

"He OK?" Phil asked after Miguel faded from earshot.

"Nobody OK!" Pedro seethed, tumping Phil from his hammock. "Let's go, *now*." He was in a rotten mood, no mistaking that, and Phil kept a step or two further back than was his custom as he followed Pedro through the undergrowth.

"I'm starving, Pedro" Phil said, trying to make conversation. "You reckon your momma's already rustled up some chicharone?" Pedro didn't answer. Nor did he break stride. "Hey, Pedro. *You* OK?"

"No, Mr. Phil. Me no OK."

"What happened?"

"You see when we find Vlad."

They crossed the jungle end of the runway and passed the bodega where Pedro's mother kept the camp fed. Shafts of light turned the ocean turquoise through fading breaks in the brooding sky, as dark and lifeless shadows spread on the heaving sea.

Beyond the bodega, opposite the open-air workers' barracks, lay a tidy, more structurally sound looking building. Not so buttoned up and secure from the elements as José's, but a darn sight better, Phil reckoned, than the workers' barracks. As he followed Pedro to the doorstep, Phil knew right where they were on account of the rough-hewn Cyrillic letters carved in a sign over the door.

"Vlad!" Pedro barked, barging into the neat little bungalow. The well-thatched roof made the interior cool and dark, and growing darker with the dimming sky outside.

"Vlad! You fuckin' useless *perro*! Get up!" Pedro shouted. His work boot found the space beneath the bed, and met the compact lump of humanity lying in it with considerable velocity. There was daylight, Phil reckoned, for just a split second before Vlad landed back in his bunk. Pedro was in Vlad's face as Vlad rolled over holding a nickel-plated revolver. It had a large caliber barrel, at least a .45, that fit neatly on the tip of Pedro's nose. *Holy crap,* thought Phil. *That bullet's comin' right fer me soon as it's done going through Pedro.*

"Back up, you fuckin' wetback," said Vlad, his smoke scorched, raspy Russian accent cool as the air in his well-appointed quarters. Pedro reached for the gun in the small of his back, but not fast enough. Vlad, pointing away with the chamber right beside Pedro's ear, fired, sending Pedro lurching backwards, taking Phil with him to the floor. Vlad leapt to his feet and landed astride Pedro, cocking the hammer again.

"Fer Pete's sake," Phil heard himself say. "Will you two quit? Put your dadgum guns down!" Vlad smiled. "Pedro first." Phil could tell Pedro was dazed, and he seized on the moment to sweep the gun in Pedro's open hand across the floor to the corner. Vlad secured his weapon and offered Pedro a hand up.

"You stinkin' communist bastard," Pedro muttered, accepting Vlad's hand. He stood there a moment moving his hand like an accordion player back and forth from his ear to establish the extent of his hearing loss. Phil rose behind him and recovered Pedro's gun from the corner.

"You give to me, *now*!" Pedro ordered.

"No," said Phil. "You two shake, and promise not to shoot each other." Vlad chuckled, then he laughed, then he hooted with delight until suddenly, gripped by coughing, he bent at the waist, his little compact body quaking from stem to stern. He appeared to be doomed until just as quickly, he recovered his composure and tucked his gun in the waistband at the small of his back. He raised both arms in submission before offering his right hand, and he and Pedro shook.

"*Now*, you give me the gun," Pedro said coolly to Phil.

“What in tarnation has got you two so worked up?” Phil asked, handing over Pedro’s gun.

“Your stupid invisible Russian sub,” Pedro began, pointing a finger at Vlad, “no so fuckin’ invisible. The las’ shipment – four hundred and eighty million dollars – caught by the U.S. Coast Guard, you stupido *puta!*”

“What?”

“Yes. Caught. At night, even.”

“Impossible,” Vlad pronounced.

“No impossible. True,” said Pedro. Phil never imagined either of these lunatics looking cowed, but cowed they looked now. They were in trouble, Phil could tell.

“Dees are *not* my designs, Pedro,” said Vlad, reaching for a sheaf of rolling papers and a bag of loose-leaf tobacco. “Dees plans are fuckin’ Colombian bullshit, from the goddamned *Empresa de Ingeniería y Construcción Maritimo de Bogotá, S.A.*,” he continued, waving his hands flamboyantly as he mimicked Pedro’s accent. He mashed a clump of stringy black tobacco into the rolling paper, turned the ingredients between his thumbs and forefingers, licked the trailing edge of the paper, and sealed it tight. “On-the-surface submarines is stupid, Pedro. I tol’ you that before. You don’t want to get caught, you build real, below-the-surface submarines, the way Vlad know how,” said Vlad leering. “And anyway, don’t you pay the stupid Coast Guard? To let the shipments pass?”

“Yes.”

“Den why they catch your fuckin’ submarine?”

“You mean *your* fuckin’ submarine,” Pedro countered. “No such *grrreat Rrrussian engineering,*” he concluded, mimicking Vlad in return. The door flew open and José crash-landed in the middle of the room.

“Who the hell is shooting?” José demanded, sounding like a harried school principal.

Phil was no stranger to gun play. The crowd he ran with back in Lost Lake liked guns, and shot at almost everything, even outside school. They had mastered for occasions of reprimand the same look of innocence and pique with which Vlad and Pedro presently faced José.

"It was an accident, sir," Phil blurted, though why, he was sure he didn't know.

"Jesus Christ," José muttered. "You *idiots.*" He looked about the room collecting himself until his eyes came back to Phil. "And *you*, making excuses for them – very decent of you, very gentlemanly, I must say. But *you* two," he said squaring on Vlad and José and looking exasperated, "*...idiots.*"

"How they catch our submarine?" Pedro asked José. It sounded to Phil like an accusation, and he reckoned by how their eyes met there was no love lost between them.

"*You* tell me," said José. "Your job is the Americans. Are you doing your job, Pedro?" By the way Pedro moved, he appeared to reach for his gun again.

"Justa cottin' pickin' minute," said Phil. He had had enough. "First Miguel almost shoots Pedro, then Vlad almost shoots Pedro, I mean, Jimminy crickets, what the heck is goin' on?"

Things had grown tense, José explained, because the Zeta were getting busted right and left, and the Guajira had been doing well, until now. The Zeta had struck the camp before under similar circumstances and the camp was on edge, expecting danger. The sub's capture, were it known to the Zeta, could briefly relieve the competitive pressure, but it was a hell of an expensive exercise in détente.

"I no give a shit about the Zeta," said Pedro.

"You don't say," said José.

"You t'ink the Zeta help the Coast Guard?" Pedro floated.

"How they do that?" Vlad demanded. Pedro's eyes narrowed.

"A spy, here in the camp, one of *your* men..." said Pedro. Vlad stiffened, his nostrils flared.

"They are not *my* men, they are *his* men," Vlad hissed, pointing at José. "If I had *prrroper Rrrrussian* engineers and shipyard workers, and we make *prrroper* submarine, nobody catch nothing." Phil marveled at Vlad's rolling r's.

"Stop it," José interjected. "Both of you. There are no spies, and they wouldn't know where to send the Coast Guard if there were. No, something else happened."

"Like maybe one of Vlad's men," said Pedro derisively, holding his thumb and forefinger an inch apart, "put a muy pequeño GPS tracker in the sub, make it easy to find." José looked at Vlad.

"Is it possible?" José inquired. Vlad lit the roll-your-own cigarette that had been since before José's arrival clinging improbably from his lower lip. Vlad sucked hard and wiped the sweat from his pate. "Is possible," Vlad conceded dejectedly.

"It's also possible the Coast Guard got lucky," José added.

"No!" said Pedro. "No, Coast Guard no get lucky. We pay dem, mucho plata, José." Suddenly, Phil caught on. Threatened by the Zeta, and betrayed by the Coast Guard, who were supposed to be in Pedro's pocket, scapegoating Vlad, transparent as it was, made sense.

"I'm sure glad y'all drug me into all this," Phil said, hoping by distraction to diffuse the tension.

"Yes," said José, taking Phil's opening. "Why exactly *is* this young man here?"

"Help us make fast boats," said Pedro sullenly, as if that hardly mattered now.

"Yeah," said Vlad. "What you doin' here?" he demanded, piling on. "What *he* doin' here?" Vlad said again, looking at Pedro.

"He build the fast boats, that's all," said Pedro, looking distracted.

Was Phil *bad luck*, they appeared to be wondering. Now was the time to show he could help.

"Remember Vlad," started Phil, "a few days back, at the worksite, when I said Russian engineering might could solve some of your problems?"

"You just kissin' my ass," Vlad replied.

"No I ain't, neither," said Phil, excited to pitch Soviet era engineering to a real Russian engineer. It wouldn't take any explaining at all. "Ekranoplans…." said Phil with a smile.

"What?" said Vlad.

"Ekranoplans," Phil repeated. "If they could carry tanks and troops and nuclear missiles, they can carry plenty of whatever it is y'all's tryin' to ship."

"Yes, but we could never build here, in the jungle," said Vlad, turning the idea in his mind.

"What's an ekranoplan?" asked José.

The cool air stirred in the darkening shadows as squalls moved over the camp. Vlad massaged his pate like he was tilling his mind as a soft rain started falling, pattering overhead on the thatch.

"Vlad, I built one in my own boat shop, didn't I, Pedro?" said Phil. "And tell you what, it goes like a bat outa hell," he added, in case anyone doubted the feasibility.

"Yes, is possible," Vlad finally conceded.

"What's possible?" asked José.

It was no surprise to Phil that Vlad knew exactly what he was talking about. Among Marion's indulgences had been an inexhaustible supply of *Popular Mechanics* back issues. One of them carried the surprising history of ekranoplans. In the late 1960s one of American's first spy satellites had spotted an enormous structure taking shape on the shores of the Caspian Sea. The *Caspian Sea Monster*, as it came to be known, bore some resemblance to an aircraft, but with conspicuously shorter wings.

"Yes," said Vlad, it was another Russian engineering marvel, developed by an early Russian pioneer of hydrofoils, whose dream was to break the surface tension limiting the speed and efficiency of even the fastest surface-going vessels, namely hydrofoils. Ground effect, a phenomenon well-known to pilots, supplied the missing ingredient. Pedro nodded his head knowingly.

"The idea," said Vlad, "is that you build wing just big enough to generate ground effect, a layer of high-pressure air between the ground and the bottom of an air foil moving fast at low altitude." José looked baffled.

"*You* the fucking pilot," said Vlad to Pedro. "You explain."

"Sí," said Pedro, forming an airplane with his hand by extending his thumb and pinky finger. "As you land," he said, flaring his hand like an airplane touching down, "the plane, she need to settle, cause the ground effect make the cushion that holds you in the air until you slow down."

"I see," said José. "So you want to build a plane that doesn't fly?"

"Is possible," said Vlad, nodding. "They go fast, fly very low, below radar, can be as big as you want... if!" Vlad stressed, "we have good materials. I mean aluminum. No more dis fuckin' plywood."

"I reckon mine got up to eighty, maybe ninety miles an hour, and it weren't even a proper ekranoplan," said Phil. "Mine still had a shaft in the water. You take the engine off that Cessna we flew in here on, mount it high and back on a modified fuselage with shorter, wider wings, and you got yourself a hundred and fifty mile an hour, radar-evading blockade runner."

"Or faster," Vlad nodded. "Is possible."

"You mean Bahamas, Puerto Rico, Cuba, even the Islands in three hours?" Pedro asked.

"Or less," said Vlad.

"How much weight will it carry?" José inquired.

"As much as you like," Vlad assured him. "The big *Rrrussian* ones have ten jet engines, carry missiles, tanks, troops, like the boy say."

"Sure thing," said Phil, "the Russians had plans for a whole fleet of 'em. A high-speed, stealth invasion force. Totally unstoppable – mines, torpedoes, submarine nets – flew right over all of 'em," said Phil.

"Dis boy," said Vlad shaking his head. "Dis boy..."

CHAPTER 15

Guajira Peninsula, Colombia

Pedro left camp the next day, entrusting Phil to his mother for care and feeding, and to apprenticeship under Vlad to complete the semi-submersible plywood successor to the one that had been captured. The promise of ekranoplans gave Pedro and Vlad common cause, and Vlad promised to think in Pedro's absence on what it would take to build ekranoplans for the drug trade, and to hear Phil out on how he had done it back in Georgia.

The longer he worked for him, the more Phil liked Vlad, entranced by Vlad's voice and the flourish with which he unfurled and studied blueprints delivered by Ian, or arriving on flights that came and went all hours of the day and night. Vlad was a purist and no fan of the company supplying the Guajira, the *Empresa de Ingeniería y Construcción Maritimo de Bogotá, S.A.* But his eye for good ideas was honest, whatever the source, even improbable strokes of genius from the *Empresa de Ingeniería y Construcción Maritimo de Bogotá, S.A.* He was a great engineer, with a big Russian heart, that apparently had room for Phil.

It embarrassed him, Vlad conceded sometime later, to be

reminded of the merits and schooled in the design of ekranoplans by an American. They were the perfect solution. Fast, low profile, and reusable, unlike submarines, that took too long to build. Just like Phil's father, Vlad's enthusiasm for talking boat design - hydrodynamics, laminar flow, power, lift and drag - was inexhaustible, especially fueled by vodka, of which Vlad and soon Phil partook in abundance. They could start planning for an ekranoplan, Vlad said, when Phil proved himself on the job site completing the next submarine. It was already behind schedule, and with the capture of the last sub, there was pressure to make a new shipment. Even after long days at work in the jungle heat, Phil found time to sketch – ekranoplans large and small, fuel tanks and cargo holds, every detail to suit the craft to its purpose. The thing better work, for his own sake, if not Vlad's.

He braved Vlad's bungalow at first just once a week, presenting plans uncertainly, testing Vlad's resolve. Before he knew it, he was there all the time, talking late into the evening, and freely into Vlad's vodka, through endless design schemes and variants. They were heavily under the influence and deep into a discussion of the Bernoulli effect when Vlad bared his broken heart – his only son, gone, unaccounted for since almost immediately after joining a Russian army unit that deployed to Afghanistan.

They agreed finally on an airfoil tapering at each end into downward facing floats on which the craft would ride as she set down and took off from the water. From his intimate knowledge of sponsons – the tiny, buoyant, ski-shaped appendages on which hydroplanes traveled like a catamaran - and the little he knew of floatplane pontoons, Phil derived a hybrid that he christened *spontoons*. They incorporated a *step* - an abrupt break below the waterline amidships, cut like a block of cheese from the cross section of the spontoon's hull, running all the way aft. As the spontoon rose to a plane at full power, the step broke the water's surface tension from the aft section of the hull. This halved the drag and shifted the angle of attack forward, standing the craft on her toes, the way Phil imagined it, where the airfoil finished the job of getting her airborne. Getting *on the step,* as all floatplane pilots knew, was the penultimate stage in transitioning to flight.

Inset fore and aft on each spontoon would be wheels, so the ship could launch with less effort from a takeoff roll down the camp airstrip. Vlad's calculations supported Phil's intuition about power, which was that a normally aspirated light aircraft propeller engine set amidships over the airfoil, ahead of a rudder and horizontal stabilizer, would be more than sufficient to get her airborne and control her in flight. The hollow airfoil would even be good for several hundred pounds of whatever, with the pilot sitting low amidships, in a cockpit below and forward of the pusher-prop. They were destined to build great things, they agreed.

After another late evening of intoxicated planning, Phil lazed in the hammock he'd come to think of as home, recently drenched by a passing shower. His head was pounding, and he buried his face and reached for his ears when the howler monkeys started in again. The sun was high, and the steam thinning when through the crack of one eyelid he saw Miguel, who tipped forward his hat, draining a copious store of rainwater, and quietly acknowledged the visitor.

"Manuela," said Miguel.

"Miguel?" Phil croaked. The putrid taste of Vlad's cigarettes lingered on his pasty tongue. He regretted acquiring a taste for them, especially mixed with vodka, but a small price it was for Vlad's friendship, he reckoned.

"Señor Phil," said Manuela, appearing through the mist, coffee and lavender following in her midst. "Vlad say you are late for work. He think perhaps you don't feel good this morning, so he send you coffee." He must have looked pitiful, and smelled even worse, if the step in retreat she took from his hammock were the measure.

Then and there, out of respect for Manuela if not himself, Phil resolved not to lower himself to the standards of care and cleanliness practiced by the men working alongside Vlad. He would build himself a shelter, at least as nice as Vlad's, and quit his existence in the elements. He might could even prevail on José to find him some new clothes, not that Manuela wasn't doing a fine job of laundering the old ones. A razor and even a haircut wouldn't hurt either. He hadn't looked in a mirror in quite some time, but he reckoned the sight wasn't pretty.

"Mighty nice of ol' Vlad," said Phil. She smiled, bent at the waist to place her tray on the ground, and poured his cup with those beguiling hands. So entranced was he by her presence that he almost fell from his hammock. He saw Miguel smirk from the corner of his eye as Manuela's face passed close by his to hand him the coffee. He barely thought of Georgia anymore, except when he saw Manuela. Her likeness to Katie was haunting.

CHAPTER 16

Guajira Peninsula, Colombia

Georgia is where Pedro said he was going before he left, "to fin' the stinkin' bastard dat give away our submarine to the fuckin' gringo Coast Guard," or words to the effect. Pedro felt certain the Guajira had been betrayed, and that the traitor lay in his midst. Why Pedro should begin his manhunt back in Lost Lake was beyond Phil, but it was hard to forget Pedro's parting words.

"You have no messages for Pedro to give Señorita McLean?" Pedro had asked, that twinkle in his eye. The taunting made Phil angry, and the anger conjured Mort, bleeding out from his throat on the floor. It also summoned Malcolm McLean's parting words: *Latch on to your circumstances...find your own way...Pity's a poor path to advancement.* He had latched on, alright, and was on his way, owing nothin' to nobody – not to his daddy or the bank, nor to his customers, or even Katie's father. It was just as Ralph Waldo Emerson said: *Nothing can bring you peace but yourself.*

Phil had found that peace indulging his gifted hands – accelerating progress on the submarine and building a bungalow to rival Vlad's, which improved his standing with Manuela, he reckoned, as much as the new clothes Ian delivered. Phil didn't much like how he came to Guajira, but he took to it fine, just like vodka and cigarettes, not to mention his surrogate parents. Pedro's *madre* grabbed his cheek incessantly around Manuela, and Vlad assigned Phil a cadre of his men, to see how he fared as a foreman - in preparation for matriculating from apprenticeship, Phil reckoned.

He wasn't too surprised when Vlad's men cottoned to him. A break from Vlad's spitting and cussing was bound to improve the general mood, though Manuela saw more in it than that.

"You show them, you teach them. They like you, I think, very much," she allowed. "The *Americano* they call you," she said with a smile. That sounded a darn sight better than *gringo*, he reckoned, to which he'd almost grown accustomed.

All cleaned up and in residence in his own bungalow, and with an attachment of his own men, his end of the worksite became a regular stop on Manuela's coffee runs. He noticed how she saved the worksite for last, appearing morning and afternoon, bringing him and Vlad individually percolated carafes of strong Colombian coffee. She served Vlad first, on his makeshift workbench, and then served Phil at the far end of the worksite, where she lingered making small talk and embarrassing him with the men.

Then came the unexpected courtesy they showed - bawdy, uncivil and unwashed as they were, the men developed something of a fondness for the novelty of his and Manuela's young courtship. The whole crew, Vlad included, began anticipating her visits, moderating their language and clearing a path when she appeared, balancing a tray in each hand. It was the darndest thing Phil ever saw, and he finally got the gumption to ask if she knew her effect on the worksite.

"Know what?" she said.

"How darn-right decent they act when you're around."

"Don't be silly Mr. Phil. They don't act decent for me. They act decent for you, because you treat them better than Vlad. José call you a true *caballero.*"

"A what?"

"A *caballero*, a gentleman."

The work on the sub progressed swiftly, and Phil enjoyed it. Vlad's workmen, after a time, brought more joy to it, too, and even Vlad managed a smile now and again, especially when Manuela lingered in the late afternoon. But Vlad's graces ended there, his brooding contempt for the pitiful skills of his men compared to the shipyard tradesmen he left back in Russia a source of endless irritation. Worse still, he doubted their loyalty, because Pedro had insinuated any one of them could be for sale. Vlad watched them closely, and urged Phil to do the same, insisting that he and Phil alone perform a final inspection of the finished submarine in search of wayward GPS beacons that might have found their way aboard on the eve of her mission.

When he wasn't hewing stringers, fitting bulkheads, and laying up fiberglass, Phil pictured the ekranoplan coming together - the stepped spontoons, the airfoil with its hollow wing compartments, and reinforced center to support the powerplant, driver, rudder and horizontal stabilizer. Vlad had tasked him with rendering a set of working drawings, and deriving from the drawings a list of materials they would need. Phil knew wood. Vlad dreamed of alloys that Ian assured him he could never procure.

"Den let him frame in wood," Vlad finally conceded, "and bring me sheet aluminum, no more dan one millimeter. And don't tell me the fuckin' *Empresa de Ingeniería y Construcción Maritimo de Bogotá, S.A.* no have!"

"What about power?" Ian asked. "Presumably this contraption wont' go on its own."

"We need airplane engine," Vlad answered, "don't know how big."

"It makes a difference," said Ian, contemplating Vlad's request. "Tell you what, mate," Ian continued, "show me this thing when its built, and we'll match her to a powerplant then."

"OK, OK," said Vlad, not to be burdened by details. "Maybe a jet, like the new Honda microjet, would be OK," Vlad proposed wishfully.

"Right-O, Vlad, maybe. Let's look at her when she's done," said Ian, taking Vlad's ask in stride, as if shopping for airplane engines and groceries was almost the same thing.

Phil took it on faith that Vlad could bend aluminum to wood, and that he had thought through sealing the spontoons to endure ocean take-offs and landings; but a jet engine – good grief – they weren't playing double-A ball now.

"Moight take me a few days to round all this up, Vlad," said Ian, looking down Phil's list. "Roight," he finally concluded before marching off the worksite. How Ian planned to deliver the extensive requisition list on his little old water jet Sea-Doo, Phil couldn't imagine, but that wasn't his problem.

With the ekranoplan drawings complete, and Vlad's submarine almost so, there wasn't much to do but wait. Word from José was the shipment to be loaded on the sub was making its way to camp. He wanted it loaded and the sub put to sea just as soon as the epoxy dried. The fuel bladder was already topped off with diesel when they sent a short run of hose down to the canal to pull water up to the cooling intake so she wouldn't overheat when they tested the engine. The spanking new Volvo diesel ran cool and quiet, according to Hoyle.

Phil chewed on his ekranoplan design as they waited for the cocaine. He had never built a boat, nor ridden in one without building a scale model first, transposing two dimensions into three in miniature before squandering building materials. In his bungalow after dinner, as darkness fell on the camp, Manuela found him piecing together a toy-sized airfoil and spontoons.

"Hello, Phil," she said, standing in the door. "You are busy?" she asked, hands pressed in her skirts. He was bent like a cobbler over a table in poor light, turning a fragile ekranoplan skeleton in his hands.

"Hey, Manuela," he said. "No, I ain't busy. What all you want?"

"Yes, you are busy. I can see. It's not so important," she said, sweeping a black tress of hair from her eyes as she hesitated in the light from the door.

"Sure, it is," said Phil, "everything's important." What a dumb thing to say - *a man 'll say anything for the right girl* his daddy had warned him, and he reckoned that was so as he gazed on her, tongue tied.

"Don't stand out there," Phil said. "Come on in." He was on his feet as soon as she crossed the threshold, pulling the thatch door closed behind her. Fugitive bolts of her shiny black hair swung wantonly along with the sway of her skirts, and his eyes went straight to her hands.

"This is a nice house you build," she said peering into the bamboo cross beams and rafters.

"It's not home, but it 'll do for now," he said, shifting uncomfortably.

"Why not home?" she asked, standing halfway across the room.

"Come here, Manuela. Let me show you something." He offered her the chair in which he had been seated, sliding it next to a crate that he could use to sit beside her.

"Come on," he said, "take a look," holding out the model. She came to the table and sat in his chair, cupping her hands to accept like the sacrament the delicate skeletal latticework of Phil's prototype.

"What is?" she asked softly. "An airplane?"

Phil smiled. He pulled the crate closer with one hand and placed the model in her hands with the other. "Almost," he said proudly. "It's a little project I'm working on with Vlad – an ekranoplan." She turned it slowly at eye level, studying its lines and angles, while Phil fixed his eyes on her hands. The spell finally broke when they caught each other's eyes. "You see, it works like this," Phil began, taking it gently from her possession. "These are the spontoons, just like the ones I use on my hydroplanes back home, and here's the airfoil joining them, 'cept it's wider and thinner, and right-side-up. You put the airfoil upside down on a hydroplane to keep her *in* the water. The idea with this ship is to get her *out* of the water, but not too far." She held her stare, not strictly taken by his artisanship, he reckoned happily.

"She is pretty," Manuela allowed.

"She's not just pretty, Manuela," said Phil proudly. "She's pretty fast."

CHAPTER 17

Guajira Peninsula, Colombia

The cocaine started arriving the next day, in short convoys of ATVs, loaded front and rear with pallets of plastic-wrapped packages of pure white, crystalline cocoa extract that glinted in the sun. The convoys converged on the camp from all directions, driven and guarded by heavily armed, unappealing men. José and Vlad met them at the worksite. The submarine waited in her cradle. They would launch her stern first into the canal when she had shipped enough cargo to hold her in the water. Empty as she was, she'd roll like a dying whale, on her side. Loading went slowly. Each bag passed, one by one, through the stubby conning tower hatch, the only through-hull access to the insides of the vessel. The hatch was barely two feet in diameter, just enough for one person, and the opening bristled with bolts that secured small portholes, the sole source of visual reference for the sub driver after the hatch closed. The bolts were padded with burlap to protect the bags from catching and tearing.

In any kind of sea, the portholes were awash. The driver relied on a compass and hand-held GPS unit to navigate most of the journey.

The portholes were to avoid passing ships, and to identify the vessels waiting to rendezvous with the sub at its destination. The sub might travel as far as Europe before positioning itself a few miles offshore to transfer the contraband to any number of smaller go-fasts for the final leg to market. As the cargo grew lighter, the driver cracked seacocks, designed for scuttling, to ship enough seawater to keep the sub upright and low in the water. Without offsetting ballast, she'd bob like a cork, visible and vulnerable to her enemies. With the last bag offloaded, the driver opened the spigots, and all of Vlad's workmanship slipped silently to the sea floor forever.

The loading went on all day and into the evening, and the sub put to sea that night. She vanished in the darkness long before clearing the end of the canal, setting a course for points unknown, except presumably, to José. Phil was glad she was gone. He disliked the look of the men accompanying the drugs, and he was glad to see them clear out of camp - guns, grim faces, ATVs and all. Manuela was nowhere to be seen, and nor were Vlad's workmen. He grew anxious in the lull that followed the departure, and steeled himself for the wait – the wait for Ian to deliver the materials - the wait before they could start work.

It wasn't as long as he thought. His second helping of chicharone, on which Pedro's mother had insisted, was settling nicely low in his belly when one of Vlad's workmen came sprinting into camp and landed at Phil's table in the bodega.

"Mr. Phil, Mr. Phil, you come, *you come*," he pleaded excitedly, pulling on Phil's arm like a school kid. He was pointing at the airstrip, and when Phil rose from the table to follow him, he took a hard right when he got to the airstrip and sprinted toward the water, waving Phil on to keep up with him. At the water's edge, beyond the runway, a cluster of men had gathered. They were looking left, to the point of land demarking the western edge of the bay. Above the trees, in the direction they were looking, rose a thick, acrid column of sooty, black smoke. A sound like fog horn carried on the wind, and the men started pointing excitedly.

"I'll be," said Phil, when he reached the water's edge. A barge bigger than any he had seen was rounding the point, only the bridge and funnel of an ocean-going tugboat visible above the gunwales to which she was lashed on the port side. A crane towered high over an eclectic assortment of cargo, from packing crates and propane tanks, to building supplies and water cisterns, and pallets piled high on a tractor trailer with roles of shiny aluminum. A man stood forward on the prow, in blinding white slacks and a colorful shirt, *and alligator shoes*, Phil thought to himself. "Ian, you *beauty*," he said out load, a favorite expression of Ian's he had acquired the habit of using.

In the weeks and months that followed, Phil lost track of time. He worked methodically and feverishly, bringing to life the vision that first gripped him back in Georgia – a vision he felt sure would favor the Guajiras. When he skipped meals, Manuela brought them to him, visiting the worksite five or six times a day with food and drink, and steaming, fresh Colombian coffee. More than ever, now, he spent his nights with Vlad, drinking, smoking, and questioning, themselves and their design. How much weight could she lose with aluminum tube framing instead of wood? How much power would she need at twice or three times the size? And with more speed and less weight, could they reduce the camber of the airfoil? Together, in their element, they ran every permutation, tobacco smoke and vodka inciting their dreams.

Vlad assigned more men to Phil, both to speed the work, and to have them learn Phil's methods and designs. Phil liked them and they liked him, and soon the new men fell in with his feverish pace, rising early, quitting late, and relying on Manuela and Pedro's mother for victuals and coffee as they worked throughout the day. The merry band of maniacal carpenters soon came to be known around the camp as the *Americanos*, as much for their devotion to Phil as to the confounded work ethic he instilled in them.

Retreating to Vlad's in the evening had been as good a way as any to heed José's warning to give Manuela a wide berth. Pedro's mother paid José's warning no heed and plainly enjoyed sending Manuela to the worksite as often as possible with staples and treats to spoil Phil and his men. Her transparent enthusiasm for the match embarrassed them both, and there was no staving off the inevitable, with or without her enthusiasm.

It was on fate and the *inevitability* of it all that Phil was pondering when he opened his eyes to find Manuela's head resting on his chest, rising and falling on his breath and with the pounding of the distant sea on the shore. She slept the sleep of the innocent, he reckoned, naïve to the trouble by which he and Pedro, and likely Vlad and José, and many of the camp's workmen had found their way into the company of the Guajira.

"She is yours now, Mr. Phil, forever," said Vlad when she moved into his bungalow. It was the kind of warning his daddy would have given, though why that came to mind puzzled him.

The Guajira camp was feeling like home, or as much like home as anywhere, and José had given the match his blessing, under pressure from Pedro's mother, no doubt. The work had gone faster than planned. The ekranoplan superstructure was all but complete, awaiting the approval of Vlad's discerning eye before he applied her skin. They would float her on the bay and tow her around a day or two to satisfy themselves she was watertight before installing a powerplant, though the engine Ian promised was nowhere in sight.

In skeleton alone, she drew the camp's attention. Everyone came to see her, from the air crews ferrying drugs out of camp, to the convoy drivers packing the drugs in. Even the most contemptible of Vlad's obstreperous workmen received Vlad's blessing to visit the *Americanos* to observe the creation taking shape nearby. She was a marvel, Phil had to admit, sparkling with Airstream camper retro coolness after acquiring a gleaming new aluminum skin.

"Just be careful, mate," said Ian on his way out of camp after seeing her, his tone atypically earnest.

"Say what?" said Phil.

"You know what the Japs say?"

"I reckon I don't, Ian. What *do* the Japs say?"

"The nail that sticks up gets hammered down." Ian usually smiled telling you something for your own good, but he wasn't smiling now, and he didn't linger either. He threw off the lines of his Sea-Doo and without so much as a backwards glance, vanished into the swamp.

Her sea trials went well, her spontoons buoyant and seaworthy, with even sizable swells passing harmlessly beneath the airfoil joining them. Vlad towed her for hours on the bay before a small audience of onlookers, and in every which way, upwind and downwind, in beam and quartering seas. Satisfied she was watertight and stable, Vlad towed her back to the canal, where Phil and his *Americanos* awaited him by their worksite. They shackled a come-along to a bridal fastened to the prow of each spontoon, and cranked her on a crude wheeled cart over a track from the water's edge back into her cradle. Phil was still admiring her dripping in her stocks when Vlad materialized from the jungle, pulling on a cigarette.

"Now for the engine and flight controls," Vlad said with a grin. It was a moment they had both awaited with some trepidation, since neither knew much beyond the obvious about flight and aerodynamics. But when they asked Ian to find them a light aircraft engine, and when Ian finally grasped what they were up to, it turned out he had more to offer than they realized. Ian had been raised on an outback sheep farm, a million miles from nowhere. Once upon a time he logged thousands of hours behind a joy stick, flying the tiny family airplane to civilization and back, and becoming a certified aircraft mechanic to maintain it.

"I have just the thing," Ian had said, when he saw her spontoons and airfoil all but complete. "I'll bring you one and show you how to use it," he promised.

Good to his word, Ian touched down three days after sea trials in a spanking new Piper Tomahawk, two seat trainer. The Lycoming O-235-L2C four cylinder, normally aspirated power plant was light and powerful, easy to remove, and ideal for mounting back to front as a pusher prop behind the ekranoplan's driver. Better yet, the Tomahawk's t-tail with high-mount horizontal stabilizer was ideal for the ekranoplan's flight controls, clear of her prop wash and ground effect, with a nice, clean angle of attack for controlling her pitch. A simple transplant from the Tomahawk's fuselage to the center, reinforced trailing edge of the ekranoplan and "Bob's-your-uncle," said Ian, they'd be in business.

"But first," said Ian to Phil and Vlad, before they disassembled the Tomahawk, "one of you needs flying lessons." Vlad wasn't about to say yes, and Phil would never say no, so the choice was easy.

"In five days I'll have you flying like a crop duster, mate. No time like the present" said Ian, clapping his hands and rubbing them together.

"If you're ready, I'm ready, so let's go," he said, turning for the airstrip. And five days later, flying from dawn to dusk, Phil had mastered the Tomahawk, especially full throttle at super low altitude, just feet above the waves, where the ground effect was palpable, and where the ekranoplan would live. Ian taught him slip turns, too, because the ekranoplan prototype would rely solely on her rudder to turn, in long, slow, skidding arcs over the waves.

"She'll turn, but not fast, mate. Just some back pressure on the yolk to induce a little drag before giving her rudder, and she'll point right where you want her to go," said Ian, pitching the plane up, pushing on the rudder, and bringing the nose around like the plane read his mind.

"The controls, here," he continued, with one hand on the yoke and the other straddling the throttle and mixture, "will go right into your little thingamy-bob. Nothing on the panel except RPMs comes over. You'll be roight at home. Got it?"

"How will I know where I'm going?" Phil asked.

"Vlad will take care of that. You'll have better gizmos than this," Ian said, pointing to the panel mounted gyro compass. As the sun touched the horizon outside his side of the cockpit, Phil taxied off the airstrip beneath the jungle canopy close by the ekranoplan worksite. He pulled back on the mixture, and starved the engine of gas until it shuttered to a stop. "Roight," said Ian, "tomorrow we take her apaht."

Ian appeared early the following day, dressed as usual for the occasion wearing brand new, dark blue coveralls, with *Ian* embroidered on one arm, and a *Quantas* patch on his chest. If Phil knew anything about building stuff, it was that nothing turns out as planned, no matter how hard you try. But the engine went on the way they imagined, followed by the empennage. They ran the controls forward to an enclosed, cramped cockpit that mimicked almost exactly the layout and dimensions of Phil's hydroplanes, outfitted by Vlad, just as Ian promised, with a GPS multifunction display showing speed, bearing, and ETA, among countless other navigational options. Vlad had taken an off-the-shelf motorcycle helmet with embedded speakers and voice activated microphone boom and wired it into the radios Ian transferred from the Tomahawk to give the pilot two-way VHF radio communications, and the ability to monitor the marine radio scanner.

On the first calm day, they launched her into the canal, and Vlad towed Phil, sitting in the pilot's seat salvaged from the Tomahawk, out to the bay. There, Phil taxied her back and forth along the beach, running up the engine and throttling it down, just a few minutes at a time, trying to get the feel of her. It was first rate craftsmanship, the controls responded well, at least as well in the ekranoplan as they had in the Tomahawk. Satisfied she was manageable and not likely to throw him, he radioed Vlad.

"I ain't going for lift off this time, just to get her on the step," said Phil.

She jumped on the step at full throttle easily, and into the air even easier, Phil discovered on the next pass. It was keeping her there that was hard. She wanted to porpoise, and nothing but full back pressure on the yoke, which Phil could barely hold for the half mile he kept her in the air, would keep her straight and level. He tried three times more and always with the same result. She was nose heavy, or felt that way, and he couldn't hold her in the air.

"I need trim," he said from the cockpit to Ian, who stood on the bank of the canal as Vlad towed the ekranoplan to where she could be hoisted and returned to her cradle.

"Buggah," said Ian. "Should have thought of that."

"She wants to nose down. Needs constant back pressure."

"No worries, mate. I'll reconnect the trim tab and install the wheel. She'll be roight by morning," and true to his word, she was. When Phil peered into the cockpit at day break the following morning, the trim wheel was mounted to the right side of the pilot's seat. By the end of her sea trials that afternoon Phil had her so neatly trimmed that she took to the air all on her own by simply advancing the throttle – on to the step, then into the air, where she'd cruise straight and level forever, he reckoned, or until she ran out of fuel.

"I can't hardly believe it," said Phil, clambering ashore beside the canal and removing his helmet. "A real ekranoplan," he said, beaming at Vlad. "*Grrreat Rrrussian* engineering!" he crowed, impersonating his mentor. Vlad smiled, his black eyes dancing, the hand he saved for rubbing his pate caressing his belly satisfactorily. "And she flies like a dream, mate," he said to Ian. "Next stop, Havana!"

"Be careful, mate," said Ian, turning to go. "And remember what I told you," he finished, sober as a judge.

He lay awake in bed that night, Manuela asleep by his side, his mind skipping excitedly through the day's events. An airplane circled low in the darkness overhead, lining up on the approach. It touched down lightly on the hard-packed coral airstrip and coasted to a stop on the inland threshold, there to be packed like a sardine can by morning for the flight back to wherever – the Bahamas, Cuba, The Dominican Republic, maybe even the Gulf Coast or Florida. Three hours as the crow flies, north, northeast or northwest, leaving the airstrip, the camp, and Colombia behind, gone by tomorrow, maybe forever.

Wherever the destination, freedom was a flight away, a flight he was now more than able to pilot himself, he realized, with room for Manuela if she wanted. The thought of leaving ignited his senses - the urge to leave filling his soul and besieging his mind, like the call of an age-old migration. Then came regret for hearing the call, for savoring the temptation to turn his back on his life in Guajira, his work with Vlad, his days and nights with Manuela, and the attentions of a mother he shared with his nemeses.

And yet, there was no denying the ill wind his daddy warned of not so very long ago began right here, in the Guajira camp, and in other camps like it dotting the central and South American coastline. This was where tons of illicit drugs began their journey to destinations like Lost Lake, sucking hard-earned dollars and fleeting youth in equal measure to gorge the appetites of men like Pedro and the men he served - men Phil served, too, abetting *their* deeds with *his* work through the gift of his own hands. *He* was the wind of which his father foretold, and his time for accounting would come, he reckoned - God forbid his lot be cast with Pedro's. That was the thought that tortured his mind and gripped his soul with the aircraft's furtive arrival. The vehicle for his escape beckoned from just yards away from where he lay with Manuela, and but for the resolve he presently lacked to rise right now and depart, the power to leave was in him. He slipped into unconsciousness with her breath on his cheek on the precarious belief that freedom would be his when he wanted it.

CHAPTER 18

Organized Crime Drug Enforcement Task Forces Fusion Center, Washington, D.C.

Whether Lenny's punishing lack of charm was the result or the reason for his lucklessness in love, he didn't long for women anymore, and there was no one special. There had been once, a very long time ago, even before college. Rachel Moscowitz had plainly liked him, maybe even loved him. She had done for him all the sweet things nice girls do, the things nice girls think boys will appreciate, and don't. Every now and then he wished he hadn't been so blind, but he was incurably insensitive, even then, and he probably found her sweetness contemptible, though he couldn't remember. It didn't last very long, maybe a few months, but Rachel had been his first, and only, until Moira.

Lenny's heightened self-consciousness peaked late in his already delayed adolescence, repelling women and fueling a nascent misanthropic nature. His mother's efforts to find him a nice Jewish girl became more desperate as his school years drew to a close. Some of her choices were very nice, always pretty, and some even showed an inclination to endure his awkwardness, to see if things could be made to work. But in the end, he found his mother's choices tiresome, and frankly, too much like *her*. Rachel wasn't that much on his mind anymore, though he knew her current street address, where her husband worked, where the children went to school, and where they attended Temple. That wasn't such a big deal, he told himself. He could find that out about anybody.

Moira, however, had been complicated. He realized now he had only himself to blame. He had managed to forget her for almost eighteen months, but now she was back, and Rachel was, too, because his intimacies evoked each other, scarce as they were. Rachel had been so gentle and kind, and Moira a bit rougher, even primal. It made him wonder how romance should feel. She was the one he had been with more than once, and the only gentile to leave him smitten. Well, that wasn't completely true. After Rachel there was a cheerleader for whom he secretly pined. A pack of mean-spirited jocks, who suspected Lenny's crush, conspired to make a fool of him, and of her, she later admitted, when she had the decency to apologize, which made him like her even more.

Lenny had punished his high school tormentors by inventing robocalling software - a program that serially dialed the home phone numbers of the offenders in the wee hours of the morning. When parents picked-up, as invariably they did, a purring sultry female voice said, "Is [insert name of offender] there? this is Delila from VIP Escorts returning his call." Getting even felt good. It was one of his few reliable amusements, even now.

The thing with Moira hadn't just been complicated, it had been professionally embarrassing, potentially compromising. Like many of his Fusion colleagues, Lenny feared she had played him, seduced him, which was a graver sin than all the other improprieties. Just the appearance of the relationship, however brief, bordered on seamy. It was true they were both adults, but his seniority, and the perception that she was selected as much *for* him as *by* him was unfair and false. He had given up on women by then, he assured himself, especially gentiles, even though times had changed and mixed relationships, even marriages, were mostly accepted. His mother would have never approved. She disapproved of everything that wasn't her idea. And yet, while the rest of the world frowned on workplace intimacies, especially between managers and subordinates, things in the intelligence community were different. If genuine intimacy - intimacy in the name of love - was absolutely necessary, the pursuit of it was strongly encouraged *inside* the community, because marriages were so much happier when the parties respected each other's secrets, and lies.

All the customary reasons to regret his relationship with Moira paled compared to the one that was on everyone's mind, which was that Fusion had been penetrated. It was the most obvious explanation for why she had been so aggressive, when no woman before her found him remotely attractive. He had given into lust, prurient desire, the oldest and most reliable of exploitable vices. His Fusion colleagues had sounded the alarms, especially Sam Rosen, his one-time protégé and current PATT unit chief, to whom Lenny had assigned Moira.

It was Moira's assertiveness, of course, that Lenny found so magnetic, and that she was bright and competent and ambitious. Her full figure and spare good looks were easy to admire, too, though he was old enough, he flattered himself, to be drawn as much to her intellect and professionalism as to her undeniable charms - charms she exercised on him spontaneously, and in the most surprising places. Everyone in the office noticed her, especially the women. He felt the sideways looks and heard the hushed hallway innuendo. It was briefly satisfying, when he thought it was covetousness, until he realized the muttering was disapproval. This triggered a relapse of the paralyzing self-consciousness he suffered in youth. Every glance and sideways whisper picked at his insecurities like a scab. The more his mind turned on office inuendo, the more love's legitimacy mattered. He believed, or had wanted to, that she genuinely fell for him, despite the prospect of the clear motive for her affections. Was she really a CPOT probe? That was the question.

CPOTs, as the Consolidated Priority Organization Target designation suggested, didn't make the list by being amateurs. They were notoriously resourceful about self-preservation, and were known to send moles to probe for Fusion investigations of their enterprises. The mole profession paid well, and good moles covered their tracks. It was possible Moira had succeeded beyond measure, and that the trail back to the CPOT whose bidding she was suspected of doing was untraceable. It would be the first time in years Lenny's cynicism failed him. And for what? For some adolescent notion of love.

Once Moira, with Lenny's help, got the hang of DICE and developed a knack for spotting *Smurfs*, she cut a swath through Fusion. Sam Rosen had assigned her to surveilling the Southeastern U.S. for structuring activities in the burgeoning commercial banking industry there. Banks were expanding all over the south, especially in Charlotte, North Carolina. Retiring baby-boomers had been beating a path to tier-two southern cities for almost a decade, and the boomers needed financial services. Regional banks were in a full-on race against branch offices and internet offerings from banks in New York and San Francisco to control their local markets, and they soon resorted to acquiring local credit unions and savings and loans.

Launching from emerging money center beachheads like Atlanta and Charlotte, the regional banks spread like kudzu across the rural south, hawking their financial service wares with folksy, hay-seed sales pitches that sounded as naïve as the banks were themselves in the sights of practiced money launderers. With IT departments scrambling to incorporate the latest security standards, perpetually a step behind changing business processes that accompanied mergers, growing middle-market financial institutions were targets of opportunity. Sophisticated laundering operations excelled at nothing so much as skipping through streams of inconsistently handled money. When it came to disguising transactions, to blending good money with bad, like colors on a palette, the banks were simply outclassed.

To Lenny it was a matter of time before some insatiable regional bank swallowed an inconspicuous savings and loan and found itself in the crosshairs of FinCEN for acting as a cartel money laundering front. The trick was being ready when it happened, to sweep up smug fat cats when they choked on careless ambition. The PATT team and Sam Rosen, assisted by Moira, worked like a wolf pack, picking up scents, following trails, and coordinating their movements to encircle their quarry.

Sam had sent Moira on a *Smurf* hunt, watching small southeastern financial institutions that never dreamed of attracting surveillance. Moira delivered, fingering scores of suspected *Smurfs*, from Memphis to Miami. Seasoned Fusion officers and local law enforcement would be called to confirm Moira's suspicions, but they couldn't all be red herrings. Somewhere in her leads big fish lurked.

Lenny's greatest lapse, for which he should have been skinned, was sharing an outdated CPOT list with her. She had asked and he accommodated, simply to illustrate where the *fusion* at Fusion happened. The information she saw was useless. Half the CPOTs on the list were already dead or in custody. It's not like it was actionable information, but it was still a careless breach of protocol.

Moira finished at Fusion shortly after Labor Day. The holiday came late while the fall weather came early, a chilling cold enveloping the Capital as an unseasonable frost settled over the District and Virginia. His skin was getting thin – thin against the air, and thin against the critical eye of his unrelenting colleagues. It felt unfair, even to Lenny, who didn't believe in fairness.

For a time he wanted her back, but there was little hope of that. Fusion was a calling, not a job, and the details of Moira's life - her wardrobe, grooming, taste for good food and fine wine, betrayed ambitions beyond the reach of public servants. It was the mysterious riddle she whispered when last they kissed, that presently had his attention.

"I left you a present," she had said.

His colleagues hadn't been wrong to suspect her. He had been unforgivably precipitous and indiscrete for his line of work, and the important thing had been to move on and hope she hadn't duped him. He would like to have proved them wrong, to have proved her trustworthy by running to ground her surveillance files himself, if only to assure himself that their suspicions had been misplaced. But he had yielded to principle, and assigned the backchecks to another team, determined for Moira to survive the skeptical glare of his colleagues. It galled him to think he was bowing to the cynicism of Fusion's B team, but it was the best way, and a decision he didn't regret.

Moira's work had born fruit. Fusion researchers collaborating with the FBI and local law enforcement had met with success, connecting four of the big five cartels to laundering schemes at money center banks in Charlotte, Charleston, and New Orleans. She had found them operating from backwaters in North and South Carolina and Louisiana. He figured on activity in Georgia, too, especially through banks in Atlanta; but those suspicions failed to materialize. Her work had silenced the skeptics, even advancing the careers of some, and this pleased Lenny greatly, not only because his confidence in Moira had proved well-placed, but because she put more bad guys in his sights.

They were all of a type - wolves in sheep's clothing - bank

executives and accountants, with happy families in affluent communities, on vestries and school boards that thrived on their munificence. That Lenny ruined families, brought shame on institutions, destroyed friendships and careers, setting whole communities on edge, mattered not a lick to him. To the innocent he felt no duty, and to the guilty he gave no quarter, lancing evil like a boil, the time and place of retribution limited only by his imagination.

It was Moira who pilloried him for the plight of the innocents, for the burden they bore long after Fusion and law enforcement moved on. It happened on Independence Day, and ignited their affair. In the closing days of training, the interns watched a live video feed from a circling drone as FBI agents raided the home of a proud, self-made building supply entrepreneur. He was turning the brisket meant for the guests at his annual Fourth-of-July picnic when agents descended on his house, guns drawn. They converged from all directions on the gas grill where the suspect was handcuffed and mirandized, family and friends bearing stupefied witness. Lenny loved the spectacle, and so did the arresting agents. The raw, testosterone-fueled exercise of authority, the drama, the action, aroused the whole cast, from the Fusion team to the local cops. They loved the clarity - good prevailing over evil, the long arm and last word of the law. Lenny preened before the shocked expressions of his charges, except for Moira, who sank conspicuously into despair. Of all the interns, she was the last he expected to be squeamish. She had celebrated the toppling of perps in the case studies Lenny presented. Reality was less palatable, apparently, and left her sober, muted, dumbstruck. Reading about a thing is different from seeing it, Lenny realized, and vowed to build more live raids into the curriculum, if for no other reason than to identify the faint-hearted.

Moira remained subdued throughout the day, gathering her things at five o'clock sharp to leave. Lenny followed her out, taking the ponderously slow elevator ride with her in silence to the ground floor.

"What's the matter?" he finally asked, having sensed her disapproval all day.

"That was wrong, sir," she hissed.

"Why?"

"Disgraceful, sir. It was disgraceful."

"Nonsense, Moira. Grow-up. The guy was laundering for the mob. A low-life scum bag who deserved what he got."

"Would they have gunned him down right there, in his own home, on the Fourth-of-July, if he hadn't gone quietly?"

"Probably," said Lenny, "I hope so."

"Isn't he still innocent until proven guilty? Or doesn't that apply to Fusion?" she said caustically.

"He'll get his day in court."

"Yeah, presumed guilty until then."

"Possibly," he said indifferently. "It's called enforcing the law. We act on the presumption of guilt. *You* know the work that goes into this. He's guilty. It's just about making the evidence stick. You know that."

"Sure, but why make all of them pay, the family, the friends? They're not willing accomplices."

"Maybe, maybe not. We'll just see," he answered, sewing doubt like the practiced investigator he was. "Come on, Mr. Marks, that's horse shit and you know it. He could have been apprehended discretely."

"Call me Lenny, Moira. I'm Lenny, and I don't give a fuck about how they come in."

"No kidding."

"Look, Moira, the only thing these guys understand is power. We lay it on heavy for a reason."

"Did you see the kids, sir?"

"Lenny," he corrected her.

"Lenny, sir,....did you see the kids, standing beside him?" Lenny didn't answer. He wouldn't have cared even if he had seen the kids.

"Rerun the tape, Lenny. Watch the kids," she said, stepping out of the building into the humid summer air. "See if you can imagine how *they'll* remember the 4th of July."

"I don't want them to forget," Lenny persisted. "That's the point."

"Right. You sure won them over, Lenny. They'll be lining up to work at Fusion." She said turning and quickening her pace in the direction of the Metro.

"Wait, Moira. Not so damn fast."

"Yeah?" she said, spinning on her heels. Her eyes looked glassy. "Can't wait to hear this."

"When they cross the line, they bring it on themselves, *and* their damn kids. *You* know that. It's not our problem. Our problem is catching them, whatever it takes."

"Whatever it takes, hunh?" The words caught in her throat.

"Look, Moira," he said, approaching her, "the good doobies work at Homeland Security, in the field units - Coast Guard, Border Patrol, TSA, where things are black and white, good guys and bad guys. Someone has to make the enforcement calls, and that's us. Don't be so soft. We light 'em up and they go get 'em. Shoot, shoot, think. Know what I mean?" The soft evening light on the glassiness in her eyes turned something tender in his chest. She saw it and looked away.

"Come on, Moira. Things with us aren't that simple. They're not that clear. You get dirty, prying into people's lives." She kept her face concealed, listening for his voice. "Look," he said quietly, "maybe you don't have the stomach for this. Not everybody does, you know." She recoiled at his condescension. It was classic Lenny, he realized and regretted at once - scorching, tone deaf and conclusive before giving her question a thought. She stared him down in silence, then with the briefest flicker of a glare, resumed course for the Metro.

"It's not an indictment," he called after her, "who knows, Moira, maybe it's a compliment..." he added half-heartedly, because he didn't mean it. "Don't you want to talk about it?" he whined.

Yes, she had wanted to talk about it, in the moldering *SinTax Bar & Grill* on the corner of the block where she lived. She ordered a bourbon, neat, and her words were slurred when she ordered a third, and Lenny knew it was time for her to go home. She needed carrying into her apartment, but then she magically revived as he lay her on the sofa. What followed opened his eyes to passion, changing his world forever by the time he woke beside her the following morning, docile and tamed against her warm soft skin.

Dawn was breaking, a pinkish hew in the east glowing against the drawn blinds as they stirred in the open window, the anxiety and restlessness with which most mornings greeted him exorcised. He was used up, exhausted, spent and revived all at once.

"Oh, God!" she said, throwing off the bed covers and bolting naked for the bathroom where she closed the door behind her. "I can't believe we did that," she said from behind the door. "Why did we do that?" she asked, reappearing in a bathrobe at the foot of the bed; but it went on all summer.

By winter she was a memory, no more or less poignant than Rachel, though he had scrolled for a time through her files because it conjured her voice. Like an overplayed favorite music cassette, her voice gradually faded with replaying, its fidelity all but sacrificed completely before succumbing to the hum of the holidays.

It was the uneasy recollection of her successes more than her charms two springs later that compelled him to revisit her files again, and to solve the riddle of the *present* she said she left him. Even Lenny had conceded that her uncanny ability to identify

Smurfs was perplexing. She had been good, conspicuously good, maybe too good, he feared, as his preternatural paranoia had run away with his imagination. Had she been *that* good, or had she been a mole as most suspected, putting herself beyond reproach by sacrificing inconsequential *Smurfs*.

Sentimentality gave way to urgency as he scanned her archived notes, *just* one last time, he told himself; and he almost missed the rose-colored editorial highlight indicating a comment buried in the body of one of her reports. The highlight was annotated with the author's initials, *MM*, for Moira McLean. Hovering his mouse on the annotation to reveal its contents, the comment *"CPOT?"* appeared.

He scrolled back to the top. The report described a pattern of deposits to a tiny bank in northeast Georgia that, she wrote, "looked like a layering operation." What the hell did she know about layering? Sam had sent her on a *Smurf* hunt and *Smurfs* didn't layer. They weren't sophisticated enough, and they didn't have access to the electronic transfer mechanisms that corrupt financial institutions use to layer. Moira should have had little more than a vague concept of it, limited to the twenty-minute parenthetical aside Lenny gave the topic during orientation. She hadn't written much, but one sentence stood out. *Besides The Farmer's Building and Loan of Lost Lake, which appears to be accepting wires to accounts in the name of legitimate businesses domiciled throughout North, Central, and South America, there are no obvious signs that the banking industry in the state of Georgia has been penetrated.*

The statement was preposterous on its face, and Moira would have known it. Banks in every state of the union had been penetrated, and she had no access to the records she would have needed to draw such a sweeping conclusion. More conspicuous still was her indictment of this one little bank. Was there some explanation for why she had it out for this piss-ant savings and loan, or was it some kind of diversion? And then he remembered, like a message in a bottle, the *present* she said she left him when they parted. It should have been a blazing signal pyre to her boss, Sam Rosen. Apparently, he missed it. Lenny's mind raced. Why the indirection, and was it true? And was it worth anything now, almost two years later.

Lenny looked at his watch. 6:30 pm. The boys at FinCEN would be long gone. He picked up the phone anyway and banged out the number for Dan Thorne's direct line. The Director of FinCEN and Lenny went back to childhood in Virginia where they had been neighbors. More often than not, Dan forwarded his direct line to his cell phone after he left the office. Sure enough, the dial tone skipped a beat as Lenny's call switched to the cellular network in search of Dan.

"Good evening, Leonard," Dan answered. Dan knew how to push Lenny's buttons, and using his given name was an old stand-by. "Working late again?"

"Hey, Danny. Got a favor to ask."

CHAPTER 19

Lost Lake, Georgia

It was June again, exactly two years since Mort's murder and Phil's disappearance, when J.D. rose before dawn, as was his custom. In the quiet of winter, he would have busied himself in the parlor making coffee, feeding the dog, reading the town newspaper, and checking both his Lost Lake and federal marshals email inboxes. But the first Sunday in June, the opening day of Boat Church, marked the unofficial start to summer. It was important to J.D. that he be visible to his citizenry on such occasions. All the lake houses would be open, their owners bedecked in new spring wardrobes to receive the ritual hellfire and brimstone from the pontoon pulpit on Redemption Bay. He left the house, as always, before Marion was out of bed. Today of all days was one to give Marion space.

On the second anniversary of Phil's disappearance the case was still stone cold. Pedro had reappeared in Lost Lake just a few months after Mort's grisly murder and disavowed any knowledge of Phil or the events surrounding Phil's disappearance. Worse yet, he had an iron-clad alibi. He had been in Athens, home of the Georgia Bulldogs – the '*Dawgs* to the intercollegiate football faithful

– visiting his Aunt and many nieces and nephews. Not a one of them spoke English, so it took a few calls to the U.S. Marshals' office in Atlanta to find a translator to confirm Pedro's alibi. Katie, who had sworn up and down she'd seen Pedro at Phil's, was discredited.

J.D. drove his police cruiser down a reasonably straight section of interstate from the town of Lost Lake to where a gravelly turnoff from a third, center lane intersected the lake road. What followed was the windiest stretch of asphalt in the northern hemisphere, with more hairpin turns and switchbacks than a coiled rattlesnake. He knew the road well enough to navigate it fast. He also knew summer folk didn't, and he was bound to encounter an oncoming car in any of the curves ahead. Every house had cars in the driveway, a notable change from just a few days past. Here and there small children were already at play in the lake. He hoped, because Marion taught him to, that a parent was nearby. Ominous clouds threatened. Rain was forecast for late afternoon, long after the season opener of Boat Church, thank goodness. Though a pity, thought J.D., that mercy should be begged and sins forgiven by a pontoon preacher when mother nature had in store a fine baptism of her own.

He reminded himself to check the police boat canopy in case the rain came early. Before long he pulled into French's Boathouse, eponymously named for Logan French, J.D.'s best friend in life, besides Marion. Logan and J.D. were reared together in Lost Lake. Logan had been something of a wunderkind when it came to stringed instruments that didn't need bowing. Guitars, mandolins, standing base – plucked, not bowed – he played with prodigious, self-taught acumen. A gifted proficient when it came to music, he was only a so-so mechanic; but French's, or *the Boathouse*, as it was known, had the only fuel dock and public access boat ramp on the lake. It was the only game in town for getting on the water without the good fortune of affording or inheriting a lake house, and it furnished the living Logan required to dedicate himself to *Logan's Last Resorts*, his blue grass band. They had played together for longer than anyone could remember, and no respectable lake wedding, Fourth-of-July barbeque or Labor Day party came off without them.

Logan wasn't likely about so early in the day, and J.D. bypassed the shop on his way to a rickety, covered catwalk connecting three dozen covered rental slips, each with a boat suspended by a boat lift over the water. The first two slips belonged to French's Boathouse service call boats. The next slip belonged to the Lost Lake Police Department, and in it sat a new Kingfisher shallow draft aluminum hull jetboat, designed for hunting and fishing in the wilds of Alaska. Her brutal, utilitarian lines were as much at home against the rugged north Georgia backdrop, especially painted green and ox blood red, the colors of the Lost Lake police force, to evoke the green Georgia pines and red Georgia clay. Nothing on the lake could match the Kingfisher's speed, not that the lake offered much in the way of places to run or hide.

J.D. eased her gently from the slip into the fingerling channel that was once a hollow, or *holler*, the way Lost Lake folks said it, flooded in the creation of the lake. He turned right, as always, idling first past each house on the eastern shore. He patrolled the lake once a week, spring, summer, fall and winter, not so much to check for break-ins or the presence of undesirables – squatters who took to empty lake houses off season - but to alert owners to property damage, loose boats, and other inconveniences as might transpire when houses sat empty nine months of the year. Fires had happened often enough for the lake home-owners association to throw in for a fireboat. The fire station being distant, and the lake roads barely passable by fire equipment, even at slow speed, there was no saving homes by the usual method. The fireboat's bow-mounted water canon projected twelve hundred and fifty gallons of water per minute, two hundred yards uphill. Powered by a supercharged V-6 engine, the canon pulled water so fast through the hull that the vessel nestled below her waterline and the shoreline was said to recede when her pumps ran. She was big enough to carry ATV mounted firefighters who deployed over a landing craft-inspired bow door. When she wasn't touring the lake to run her engines and test the water cannon, she feted newlyweds with splendorous arcs of lake water, filling the air with rainbow pallets through shimmering curtains of mist.

J.D. followed the shore south, encountering the hulk of a burned-out house with an insurance claim two years in dispute. An off-season blaze of undetermined origin claimed the whole structure long before the fireboat arrived because the house was gone by the time smoke was visible from town. A dispute with a local contractor was suspected, which J.D. knew for sure would never be proven. It paid to befriend the locals, and paid even more not to make enemies.

He was turning the Kingfisher north into Redemption Bay when he spotted the long, low shape and curling even wake of the *General Lee*. Lazy, languid swirls of exhaust trailed her on the dawn. Malcolm McLean was alone at the helm, and J.D. set the Kingfisher on an intercepting speed and course, intending to pay his respects. McLean powered back at J.D.'s approach and the boats closed beneath darkening skies, drifting closer, bow to stern, until J.D. and McLean faced each other a few feet apart, rolling on each other's wakes. The burbling rumble of the *General Lee* filled the air until McLean cut her engine, and silence filled the void.

"Good morning to you, J.D. Making the rounds, are you?" McLean inquired cheerfully.

"Good morning to you, sir, and welcome back. Yes indeedy. How fare the McLeans, everyone here?"

"Never sure, J.D. You know how it goes." McLean peered overhead, into the darkening gloom.

"Storm's coming."

"I reckon, so. Not forecast 'til later."

"She'll come when she wants," McLean assured him. He lowered his eyes and fixed his gaze on a point over J.D.'s shoulder, which gave J.D. occasion to turn. It was Pedro Morales sitting in his pick-up truck, watching them from the lake road.

"Bad news," said J.D., staring back at Morales.

"I don't know," said McLean, extending the benefit of the doubt. "He's done alright by me."

"I beg your pardon?" J.D. blurted.

"You're still hung up about the Perdue boy, aren't you J.D.?" McLean said wearily. "You never did buy Pedro's alibi, did you."

"Well now, Mr. McLean, not so much I didn't believe him as it don't square with what Katie saw."

"Ah, I shouldn't take to heart everything she says."

"Why not?"

"You brought her home that day, didn't you? You saw the state she was in. And you still believe her?"

"That don't change what she said she saw the day before, and she ain't been back to the lake since. Scared to death of Morales, I expect."

"Maybe so, J.D., but for no good reason. People in these parts have an unreasonable fear of immigrants because they can't remember being immigrants themselves. But I haven't forgotten - what it is to land on these shores with nothing but the shirt on your back. That was almost a half century ago, mind you, but I haven't forgotten. Shame on Katie. She's got no reason to fear the likes of Pedro." J.D. let it rest. McLean wasn't born to the South, but he knew what a southerner's silence meant.

"She's my favorite half-breed," McLean added to lighten the

mood, but J.D.'s silence held. "Come now, J.D., she's as much in common with Pedro as she does me, with all that Colombian blood running through her." A bug with malign intent attached itself to the back of J.D.'s neck, and he thwacked it to eternity with his palm.

"I'm sure I don't know about that," said J.D. "But don't it bother you none *how* Mort was killed, and that he was one of yourn?"

"Don't follow you, J.D."

"I mean the way his throat was cut. You reckon little ol' Phil Perdue was up to doing something like that? I mean, that's gang stuff, is what that is."

"No. I meant what did you mean by *he was one of mine*?" said Malcolm skeptically.

"Mort," said J.D. "He was employed by the bank, one of your banks."

"Yes, I suppose you're right. But *you're* a law man, J.D. You know these things happen. I have enough employees to know the sadness and misfortune that befall humanity as a matter of course, and for reasons unfathomable to most of us. It's just math, statistics, old friend."

"It don't sit so easy with me, Mr. McLean. It's my job to see *statistics* don't happen in these parts, and it so happens Mort was under federal protection, entrusted to me."

"Oh?" said McLean, but he didn't sound surprised.

"Yes. Mort's murder got the Fed's attention, at least for a while. I reckon things have quieted down," he assured himself.

"I see." He had McLean's attention.

"Not everyone reckons Phil Perdue was the murderer..." J.D. offered.

"Jesus, Joseph and Mary, J.D. Who else would it be?"

"There was talk, speculation really, that if Mort weren't safe, others in witness protection ain't safe neither."

"Is anyone safe in witness protection?" McLean inquired

ironically. "They have it coming to them if they need protection, wouldn't you say, sheriff?"

"Pardon?" said J.D.

"I don't give two figs for snitches, whatever their station, and can't say as I mind when they meet with untimely demise - in or out of federal protection. The snitch is dead, whoever killed him. The Lord may smile on you yet, J.D." The sheriff couldn't tell if McLean had just accused him of incompetence, or conspiracy. Whatever McLean meant, he was being evasive, studiously avoiding the point.

"I'm just sayin', Mr. McLean, Mort's circumstances, his situation, and how he was murdered, point more to a feller like that one on the hill, yonder," said J.D., waving his thumb over his shoulder.

"Than young master Perdue?" McLean countered. "Nonsense. What a luckless bastard, he. Come to my dock right after Boat Church, day before it happened, begging for money like white trash to save his wretched boat business." J.D. resented the reference. It cut too close, but not so close to disguise how determined McLean was to establish Phil's guilt. "I suppose he was desperate," McLean continued, "poor sod."

"I reckon he *was* desperate," J.D. concurred.

"I sent him packing," said McLean dismissively. "Best thing for him. And for Katie, mind you. He'd been stalking her like an alley cat, though they likely deserved each other. Glad he's gone, to be honest, even though Logan French can't hold a candle to him as a mechanic."

J.D. turned for a good look at Pedro, to let him know the law was watching.

"Look here, J.D., no one likes things to go wrong on their watch, but this, too, shall pass. I'm sure you'll be forgiven if you haven't been already." J.D. wasn't so sure. In some ways it would have been better if Phil *had* murdered Mort – if a random act of violence by a high school dropout explained the murder of an informant.

The targeted killing of which J.D. suspected Pedro meant witness protection had been compromised. And J.D. *knew*, because he'd talked it over with Marion, that Phil hadn't done it. He also knew there was reason to suspect the mob *was* inside witness protection. The deal Mort cut a very long time ago traded information on the rackets in the boroughs of New York, and not one lick more, for immunity and protection. He'd kept his oath. But with the drug trade resurgent, the Feds turned the screws on select protected witnesses to spill their guts if they harbored knowledge, however dated, of the cartels. The New York mob, including Harry Halliday, did. Eventually, Mort sang like a canary, but not long, because J.D. had failed to protect him. No one had been entrusted to his care since, and he half wondered if the Federal Marshals Service suspected *him* of giving Mort up. He was pondering on how events of two years past had weighed on his present circumstances when the rain started falling. Thunder one valley over echoed across the lake.

"J.D.?" It was Betty Dunphy's nasal twang, coming over the radio, tolerably audible through the crackling interference of the mountains.

"Yes, Betty, what can I do you fer?" J.D. replied, smiling at McLean, whose hand was on the *General Lee's* ignition. Her engine exploded to life, booming like a carronade, before Betty had time to answer.

"I'm taking shelter, J.D." McLean shouted over the din. "You should, too, my good man. Storm will be here soon," and he threw the *General Lee* into gear, advancing the throttle fast and drowning out Betty's precarious transmission as he steered for his boathouse.

"Come again," said J.D. into the radio as the drops grew bigger and started falling in earnest. He reached for the canopy. Dadgum if the snaps weren't rusted shut.

"It seems Mrs. Pulmutter's cat got its head stuck in a jar," Betty's voice crackled as the skies opened. "She wondered if you might come by and rescue it."

"Tell her I'll be right over, Betty."

"Will do, J.D.," said Betty, sounding accomplished. "You might should get off the water, J.D.," she added for good measure. "Looks like a storm's a comin'." J.D. keyed the mic to let her know he heard her. He gave up on the canopy, cranked the Kingfisher's jet engine and punched the throttle. He covered the mile back to French's in no time at all, drenching himself thoroughly driving into the storm.

Marion could tell when he was feeling beleaguered, and she knew it the minute he came through the door.

"Get some dry clothes," she said, welcoming him with a kiss, "and I'll get us a bourbon. You tell me all about it." He had been turning it in his mind since rescuing Lady, Mrs. Pulmutter's cat, by smashing the jar with only barely noticeable injury to Lady.

"I visited with Malcolm McLean on the lake this mornin'" J.D. said.

"And?" said Marion, her brow furrowing.

"You reckon he knew Mort was in witness protection?" Marion leaned forward and put down her drink.

"Sounds like *you* think he did. Why?"

"He wasn't so surprised when I told him. And he were none too nice about Mort, neither. Sort a made him out to be a snitch, and reckoned he had it coming to him.... His own employee, can you believe it?"

"Why do a fool thing like tell McLean Mort was in witness protection?"

"Well, it went like this. Pedro Morales was up on the lake road, sort a watching us, seemed like."

"What?" Marion replied, darkening.

"Yeah, and I allowed as how he was bad news, and McLean reckoned he wasn't. And I said he was a more likely suspect than Phil, and he called Phil white trash and reckoned Phil done it hands down."

"You fellas really got into it."

"I allowed as how there was more to Mort than met the eye, being in witness protection and all, and how that made the whole affair more complicated, more suspicious. He weren't the least bit surprised, and that's when he said Mort was a snitch and had it coming to him."

"I never liked that man, J.D. You ought not to visit with him, nor talk so much when you do."

"I know, I know. It's Pedro Morales I don't like. I never cottoned to McLean myself, neither, but I just figured him for a sharp-elbowed business man. But don't you see - how in tarnation did he know about Mort?"

"Hey, that reminds me," interrupted Marion. "You got a call today from some fella named Lenny Marks. Said he was calling from Washington, D.C."

"He say what it was about?"

"No, J.D. But he said it was important you call him back, and that he was coming all the way here to pay you a visit."

CHAPTER 20

Organized Crime Drug Enforcement Task Forces Fusion Center, Washington, D.C.

Dan Thorne at FinCEN took no time at all doing Lenny's favor. The Farmer's Building and Loan of Lost Lake identified by Moira had surfaced only briefly a couple of years back, a small blip on a very large radar screen, in the form of a single Suspicious Activity Report, or SAR, on a small local boat business that traded exclusively in cash, accepting and issuing wires often exceeding the ten-thousand-dollar threshold in which FinCEN took interest. The bank had reported no other instances of suspicious activity, certainly no mention of the cross-border transactions to which Moira had alluded. Triggering not even so much as a cursory FinCEN inquiry when it was issued, the SAR had gone stale. The business folded and the bank repossessed its assets and property within weeks of issuing the SAR.

Classic, Lenny thought. Shut down and moved on as soon as the Feds were on to them. Whoever had been operating the boat business through the Lost Lake Farmer's Building and Loan must have been working with very good information, thought Lenny, almost perfect information, to have closed up shop and moved on promptly following the first issuance of an SAR. Lenny guessed there was an insider, either at the bank or at FinCEN. Before hanging up with Dan, Lenny made one more request: personnel files registered with FinCEN for each employee at that location, and every director and officer of the bank and its affiliated entities. Bank compliance and money flows were Dan's and FinCEN's specialty. People were Lenny's. Insiders with access were always where the trouble started, and that's where Lenny looked first.

Lenny went to work in signature fashion, running a DICE search on the proprietor of the business tagged by the SAR, a one Phoenix Perdue of Perdue Landing, Lost Lake, GA. What he found was the outstanding arrest warrant for Perdue's apprehension on suspicion of murder. And it was no regular murder – a bloody, gangland style execution of an active informant in witness protection. The victim's throat was cut, his tongue cut out, an unambiguous warning to blabbermouths. The witness was supposed to have been under the watchful eye of a local federal marshal who doubled as the town sheriff, one J.D. Dunbar, who's investigation appeared to have failed in all respects. The case had gone cold. Perdue, a local lad with no record, who had never left the county, simply vanished. It lacked credibility more ways than a UFO sighting. But the speed and audaciousness with which the cartels moved was admirable, covering their tracks and stymying local authorities, by influence, deception, or old-fashioned intimidation. By which method officer Dunbar had been induced to sit on his hands, Lenny aimed to find out.

He had dialed the listed number for the Lost Lake sheriff's office, and caught Betty Dunphy leaving for the day.

"You can reach J.D. later at the house," said Betty, after trying a few failed pleasantries, and before reading out J.D.'s home phone number. What police department in its right mind gives out the sheriff's home phone number, Lenny wondered. It was his first clue about Lost Lake.

Marion Buttersworth had been nothing if not cordial. She understood the matter was urgent, and would notify J.D. promptly, though the calm in her school teacher's voice sounded nothing to Lenny like urgency. In the hours that passed waiting for J.D.'s return call, Lenny concocted a plan in case J.D. never called back. He would drive straight to Lost Lake, overnight if he had to, to confront J.D. by morning. He had mapped the route and gathered his things, and was rising from his desk to get on the road when the phone rang.

"Lenny Marks, Organized Crime Drug Enforcement Task Forces Fusion Center," Lenny answered with authority. J.D. needed to know it wasn't the Disney Channel inquiring.

"Yes, sir. I'm familiar with Fusion," said J.D., intent on sounding unimpressed. The Feds loved their titles, and J.D. could give as good as he got.

"This is Federal Marshal J.D. Dunbar, sheriff of Lost Lake, Georgia. How can I help?"

"Inquiring about an old SAR issued by The Lost Lake Farmers Building and Loan."

"Yes, sir. How can I help you, Mr. Marks," said J.D., sticking to business.

"Well, Sheriff Dunbar, I know it's old news, but that report was issued right before Harry Halliday was murdered."

"Come again?" J.D. replied.

"A Suspicious Activity Report, an SAR, from the Lost Lake bank to FinCEN, about two years ago on a local boat business. Not sure how this slipped through the cracks. It's so dated it's probably worthless, but I have to tie it out. Can I come down there to ask a few questions?"

"I know what an SAR is, Mr. Marks. What's it got to do with Harry Halliday's murder?"

"Well you might ask, sheriff. Pretty coincidental, don't you think – the murder scene and the SAR sharing the same address?"

The question filled J.D. with uncertainty, and disappointment in himself for allowing the Fusion agent on the end of the line to achieve his desired effect. Was there a dark side to Phil he had missed? Why had the boat business triggered an SAR? Marks had cards to show, and J.D. wanted to see them. He reckoned honey was better than vinegar.

"I suppose, if visitin' would help, you should come on down, if you reckon we can't cover it talking right now," J.D. offered. It was a half-hearted gambit to forgo a peril-fraught face-to-face.

Lenny hated hayseeds as much as he hated anybody, maybe a little more. After Betty, and then Marion, he'd reached his limit.

"Shall we dispense with the bull, sheriff?"

"I beg your pardon, sir?" said J.D. He didn't care for Lenny's manners.

"Sheriff Dunbar, just how big a clusterfuck do you figure you have down there? An SAR on a business whose owner turns around and kills an active informer in witness protection and then vanishes like Houdini. Any of that strike you as fairly serious?"

"Yes, sir. It was serious. Worst thing ever to happen in these parts. It's like you say, the suspect vanished without a trace." Lenny had caught J.D. off guard, and the last thing J.D. needed was Fusion crawling up his backside. Against his better judgment, and because it was fresh in his memory from his conversation on the lake with McLean, J.D. regurgitated the commonly accepted storyline. Phil Perdue had been deep in debt. He must have snapped when the informer in witness protection, carrying out the duties of his assumed identity, served foreclosure papers.

"No investigation? No witnesses?" Lenny inquired, remarking

on the conspicuous inactivity following so loaded a crime. "This fellow Perdue had no priors."

"I know it, and he weren't a bad kid, neither. There is a witness who claims she saw another man, but she's not credible, and the feller she says she saw has a passel of family members swearing to his whereabouts pert near a hundred miles away. It don't sit right with me, neither, but there's no other explanation."

"What about the SAR?" Lenny persisted.

"What about it, Mr. Marks?"

"Did Perdue get tipped off that FinCEN was wise to his laundering operation, so he killed Halliday and bolted?"

"Humpf," said J.D., stumped. "I admit, I ain't thought of that one. But how would he have known about a SAR?"

"How indeed," said Lenny, the framework of the conspiracy he suspected shaping itself around the bank, the murder, and the ingénue, Pheonix Perdue.

"Thing is," said J.D. on reflection, "Phil weren't doin' nothin' in the business he and his daddy hain't done for twenty years, least not according to the branch manager, nor his tax records," said J.D., holding to Phil's defense. Add J.D. to the list, thought Lenny. It sounded like the whole town was in on it, the same way it worked in Colombia, from the bank, to the boat builder to the sheriff.

The only way to size a covey was to flush it, and count the birds as they flew. With time against him, Lenny turned to an old favorite – a single, well-placed incendiary piece of misinformation.

"You didn't hear it from me, sheriff, and I'll deny it under oath, but you and Lost Lake are in the crosshairs."

"Crosshairs of what?" said J.D.

"The DEA," *dumb-ass*, Lenny wanted to say. "I need your help to set up a sting operation," he continued. "How about Monday, I'll come to you."

"Thadda be fine, Mr. Marks," said J.D., shrinking in the gloom at his own kitchen table.

"Whatever happened down there, sheriff, Special Operations Division is on it and the heat is coming down."

"Sure it is, Mr. Marks. I understand. Come on down. We got nothin' to…." but the line had gone dead before he could finish. J.D. held the receiver against his forehead. What a day for the first Sunday in June.

* * * * *

The hair on Lenny's neck was twitching like a divining rod. The whole town *was* in on it. Maybe that's what Moira had been trying to tell him. "Follow your nose," is what she said, just the way he taught her, and he caught himself dropping his guard, forgetting to suspect her as much as anybody. The Proactive Asset Targeting Team and his protégé and PATT team leader, Sam Rosen, was the best place to start.

"You got it, Lenny," said Sam, sounding relieved. His boss appeared to have finally come to his senses, and recognized how Moira could have compromised him. Lenny had requested PATT profiles on every individual in the FinCEN personnel files Dan Thorne had sent him, as well as Moira McLean.

"Will SOD approve and release them?" Sam asked, alluding to SOD's growing tendency to repress Fusion reports.

"That's the least of our problems, Sam," Lenny replied. "The report is for us, whether SOD approves it for release or not. What you should be asking is whether we've stumbled on another one of their half-baked, covert, sleeping-with-the-enemy operations? How will they react if they know we're on to it?"

"It depends," said Sam, grappling with their predicament, "a sanctioned covert operation, or an operation that's covert because SOD is on the take?" a scenario he and Lenny had recently suspected.

"Exactly," said Lenny, "and how will we know the difference, because they'll tell us it's sanctioned, if they deign to tell us anything at all."

"What'll we do?" asked Sam, "if the PATT reports are implicating?"

"I'll tell you what we don't do, Sam. We don't back down."

"And Moira?" asked Sam, trying to broach the topic delicately. "What if she's in it?"

"That's a risk I have to take. I can't ignore this and I won't protect her, so assume the worst, that she's in it up to her neck. If you want out, Sam, say so now. No harm, no foul in standing down."

Lenny knew the offramp he offered Sam would signal he expected trouble. They had worked too long together to misinterpret each other's subtexts, and Lenny had shared the facts as he understood them – a small, inconspicuous local bank, the revenge murder of an informer in witness protection by the proprietor of a cash business run through the bank, and not least, the tip-off from Moira. "It could be a vipers' pit," Lenny assured Sam. "We might never climb out."

As Lenny and Sam laid the ground work for upending both Lost Lake and SOD, J.D. delighted in preserving a favorite ritual - driving Marion to Sunday supper at Iguana's, her favorite Mexican restaurant.

"How was your call?" she finally asked after a considerable silence had passed since the waitress delivered the drinks and appetizers. "You haven't said a word since you hung up the phone," she noted, finishing her margarita and cutting into her enchiladas. Iguana's proprietors, the Provechosos, were among the first immigrants to settle in Lost Lake, opening Iguana's and catering first to the locals, and then to the summer folk as the restaurant built a following. The place was packed on summer weekends, except a booth near the kitchen in the back on Sunday nights that the Provechosos held for J.D. and Marion.

"Not so good, I reckon," he speculated, "though in some ways you'll be happy, and maybe not in others," said J.D., taking a bite of his quesadilla and licking clean his fingers.

"Oh no, what now, J.D.?" she asked, watching clientele come and go from the vantage of her seat against the wall in the back.

"It's complicated, but the Feds are as suspicious and disbelieving as you about how Mort Ashton got hisself killed. They're visitin' with me tomorrow." As J.D. feared, Marion's eyes brightened visibly.

"I *knew* Phil didn't do it," she said excitedly. "I know they'll get to the..." and she cut herself off.

"Now don't get all excited. They think he done it, alright, and worse," said J.D. as he looked up from reaching for his quesadilla to find Marion's brow furrowed and her index finger mashed tight against her lips, the sign by which her students, but not always J.D., knew to *hush*. Sure enough, he continued, inured by now to being *hushed* all the time.

"This feller, Lenny Marks, reckons we got us a heap a trouble down here, and DEA is fixin' to crawl up our back side. They're talkin' about settin' up some kinda sting operation," J.D. managed to finish just as he felt the toe of Marion's pump break the skin on his shin.

"Dadgummit!" he said, as Marion's distress escalated. She was running her hand like a third base coach repeatedly across her neck as she stared in fear past the high booth wall behind J.D. He leaned around in time to see Pedro Morales depart the booth behind him, making for the door on his way out of Iguana's.

"You think he heard me?" J.D. asked.

CHAPTER 21

Guajira Peninsula, Colombia

The rap on his door was so measured and soft it was hard to parse from his dream – the sort of vivid, chaotic, frantic dream to which he'd become prone. He thought he'd heard a distant gunshot, but real or dreamed, he couldn't tell as consciousness delivered him from the chaos.

"Pheel," whispered Vlad in his heavy Russian accent, standing just outside Phil's door. Manuela stirred as he moved her aside, pulled on his drawers, and came to the threshold.

"You come with me, Pheel, now. You come with me," Vlad implored gruffly, his beady eyes bulging, his nostrils flaring. It was barely light and the air was heavy, the sound of the ocean filling the gloom.

"Why are you up?" Phil asked, the aftertaste of vodka and Vlad's cigarettes pasty on his tongue.

"You come, Pheel, now." Phil threw on a shirt and sandals and followed Vlad off the threshold and down to the beach. He barely kept pace with Vlad's whirring little legs. He was moving like a sandpiper scrambling from the surf.

"Hey, Vlad, slow down, what's goin' on?" A hundred yards down the beach, Vlad turned into a grove and pushed Phil up against a tree.

"Here," said Vlad. "You take this," he continued as he produced from his pocket a hand gun. "You need this, Mr. Pheel, I teach you how to use," the glint of desperation in his dark little eyes.

"Now, come on Vlad. That's like to get me killed around here."

"No, Pheel. It save you. Let me show you. I teach you how to use," and into the barrel he screwed a mat black silencer.

"Let me see that thing," said Phil.

"You be careful, Pheel. It is loaded," said Vlad, placing it gingerly in Phil's hands.

"Awe, Vlad," said Phil, releasing the clip and cocking the slide, "you don't need to teach me. I know how to use one of these. This is a thirty-two-caliber Colt. Six in the clip plus one in the chamber. I shot these plenty," said Phil. "My daddy had the 1911 forty-five-caliber version of this. Kicked like a horse. Said it was so hard to aim you could do more damage throwing it." Phil raised the gun and sighted it. "Nice gun. What's got you all hot and bothered, anyway?"

"Pedro. He is loco. He come back last night, go straight to José this morning and kill him. Kill him in his bed, while he sleep. You keep this, Phil. You keep always, even when you sleep."

"José?... José?" said Phil, distress taking hold in the dissolving dark. "Why? Why José? Jesus H. Christ, Vlad! Why the hell did he go and do a damn fool thing like that?" said Phil, the reality of it so distant, so unthinkable.

"He say he find out José is a spy, in the camp, telling the Policía about the submarine."

"Jeezum crow, Vlad, it can't be. It just can't be."

"He is dead, Phil. Pedro is a crazy man," said Vlad, panic-stricken. "You be very careful. You be good boy and keep eyes in the back of your head. OK? And you keep this with you, always."

"Sure," said Phil, knowing full well he wouldn't do it. *Don't carry a gun 'less you ready to pull it,* his daddy taught him, *and don't pull it 'less you aim to shoot it. Pulling is same as shooting, son. Don't you ever forget it.* Maybe keeping it under his bed made sense, the way things were transpiring. He slipped the Colt in his waist band at the small of his back, same as Pedro, and ambled with Vlad back to camp through the dawn. "See ya later for chicharone at the bodega, Vlad," he said, as they parted ways at Phil's bungalow. "And thank you," he added, gripped by the fear in Vlad's beady black eyes. He had removed the gun from the small of his back to lie by Manuela comfortably, but he hadn't seen fit to let go of it. She slipped an arm over his chest and rested her hand on his neck. Only then did he lay the gun to the floor, leaving it within reach should he suddenly need it. He'd stuff it beneath one of the bed slats later to keep it concealed from Manuela.

Neither the delicate touch of her hand nor the soothing distant surf did much to settle his nerves. He lay there beneath the rafters and thatch, pondering the prevalence of betrayal. Had José really ratted on the Guajira and given up the sub's position, or was Pedro covering his ass, because he was betrayed by authorities he thought he'd paid off? Who betrayed who? And if the end came so quickly for José, couldn't the end come as quickly for all of them? Vlad thought so, and Phil reckoned he knew.

And yet, Pedro had cared for him, especially at first, *...we are brothers* were the words that had lodged in Phil's mind. Entrusted to Pedro's mother, and to Vlad and José, Phil had thrived – except he sure wished Pedro had left poor ol' Mort alive – despite Mort's intent to seize his home and business. How was *that* for betrayal, turning out your own blood, Phil was thinking as Manuela came to.

"What you thinkin'?" she whispered sleepily. She would take losing Uncle José hard.

She went ahead of him, as usual, to help Pedro's mother prepare breakfast for the workmen. Phil arrived soon after, in time to observe the ritual reunion of Pedro with his mother - the kisses and hugs and general gaiety that everyone knew followed Pedro's return from long absences. He realized watching them, with Pedro's ever-present gun protruding from his waistband, how very used to the presence of Pedro's weapon he'd become, without a thought to it turning on him. Mrs. Morales waved him over to share in celebrating Pedro's return, and as always, Phil complied.

"I come last night, Phil, late, very late," said Pedro grinning wildly, his arm resting lightly on Phil's shoulder.

"I know, I heard you land," said Phil, José's fate heavy on his mind.

"Vlad say you finish your boat, your flying boat, and she go fast, very fast," said Pedro excitedly.

"You show Pedro, after the chicharone, sí?"

"Sure, sure," said Phil. "José hasn't seen her put her through paces yet, either," he added poignantly.

"Ah, José," said Pedro, shaking his head. "He leave early this morning for go to Bogotá. He meetin' with the Gran Jefes. He see when he come back," Pedro assured Phil, waving his hand dismissively.

Vlad and Phil and his *Americanos* convened at the ekranoplan worksite shortly after dispersing from breakfast. They topped her off with fuel, and launched her into the canal. Vlad watched them in silence, brow furrowed, nostrils flared, hands squarely planted on his hips like a scold, the top of his pate gleaming with sweat. The *Americanos*, Phil realized, remained wholly unaware of José's demise, bantering enthusiastically as Phil stood forward on the port spontoon and tossed ashore the towing bridle used to haul her over the rails back to her cradle.

Without rudders in the water like a proper pontoon airplane, her steering was imprecise unless she was airborne, when her flight controls became responsive. Phil used a long pole to punt her out to the mouth of the canal. The air was still and the swell subdued, as if the ocean herself had been stunned into silence, mourning the news of José. He settled himself in the cockpit, put on the helmet, connected the comms, and switched the magnetos to *on*. He advanced the mixture to rich, and set the throttle to idle. She fired on the first crank, and nosed warily ahead on the softly scrolling sea. He gave her more throttle, guiding her around the left bank of the canal and out along the shore in the direction of the runway threshold where it turned to beach. There was Pedro accompanied by his mother, and Manuela standing close by their side. The *Americanos* and Vlad, and Vlad's submarine work crew made their way down the beach to join them. Phil powered on the GPS and radio, which he checked with Vlad, who was even more brief than usual in his brusque, clipped accent.

Proving the ekranoplan barely entered his mind as he considered Pedro's easy way with lying about José's demise. He had seen Pedro kill in the blink of an eye, and concluded reluctantly, like Vlad, there was bound to be more to come. He could run right now. It might be his last best chance. With the water so smooth and the air so calm she would fly like a bullet. On the full tank of gas she was carrying he could be over the horizon in less than five minutes, and make landfall to the east, north or west in two to three hours. But the chance would come again, he assured himself warily – the leaving part was easy. It was where he would go and what he would do after effecting his escape that crept its way worrisomely into his calculus. Gripped by indecision, idling thirty yards offshore, he took in the gathering on the beach. Manuela waved, Pedro grinned, and the imperial Vlad stood stout as a Czar, hands on his hips at the water's edge.

He zoomed out on the GPS touch screen tucked in the console before him. "Where shall it be?" he mused. Puerto Rico? Jamaica?

the Leeward Islands? Guantanamo Bay, Cuba? or dead north to the Dominican Republic? If he'd thought of it earlier, he'd have packed water and cash, and worn better clothes, hoping for a respectable reception. He signaled Vlad he was starting his run, and turned east northeast, into the only trickle of wind he could find. He advanced the throttle to full, and the ekranoplan bucked, every one of the small Lycoming's one hundred and twelve horses pounding through the fuselage and up through his seat. A small inbound swell jacked her on to the step, and the next one vaulted her into the air, where she accelerated from eighty knots to one hundred and thirty knots, according to the GPS readout. For his own amusement he poked the touchscreen GPS at a point on the southeastern shore of the Dominican Republic, automatically inserting a waypoint at three-hundred-fifty-seven miles, bearing seventeen degrees, with an ETA of a little less than three hours.

He was amusing himself with the idea that he was on his way when he rechecked the GPS and realized he was already five miles offshore without a plan. The last thing he wanted was Pedro reading his mind, and he backed off the throttle and pushed the rudder left with his foot. A long slow turn brought him back around in the direction of the Guajira camp, which reappeared strangely welcoming, on the horizon ahead.

* * * * *

"She is ready. She is ready!" said Pedro triumphantly over vodka and cigarettes with Vlad that evening.

"No she ain't," said Phil. "She's a test, a concept, Pedro. She ain't ready for nothin', right Vlad?" Vlad didn't budge, staring wide-eyed at his feet. "*Right Vlad*?" pressed Phil. "We just had to see if we could do it. Now we know we can." Vlad seemed to know something

Phil didn't, and he wasn't talking. "She'll carry me and a tank of gas, Pedro, and not much more."

"How much more?" asked Pedro, his eyes twinkling. Phil knew his own weakness for challenges, and reckoned Pedro did, too, though he was in no mood for a challenge right now.

"You no *caballero*, the way people is sayin'. You are a *perro asustado*, Mr. Phil," said Pedro, baiting him. "I want you show friend of Pedro your fast boat. He help you and Vlad build bigger, faster ones that carry more."

"Well y'all just tell your friend to come on down, and he can do as much lookin' as he likes." Vlad was somewhere distant, eyes fixed, hands clenched, feet rocking with restless misgiving. He wanted no part of Pedro or where he was going, studiously declining conversation.

"Yes," said Pedro. "My friend come tomorrow and see this thing, this very fast boat you build."

The following morning a high wing, single engine airplane that looked every bit of her fifty years touched down in the camp. Bare stretches of aluminum where the paint had been worn or cooked away by the tropical sun gave her a dilapidated, junkyard scrap metal appearance that would have given the bravest bush pilot pause. Her wheel bearings ground and her brakes shrieked as she rolled to a stop on the threshold. After fully disentangling himself from the seatbelt and cockpit, and rising to his full height beside the plane, the pilot looked to Phil to be among the tallest men ever to walk the earth. His gold pendants and neck chains shimmered on his ebony skin, and his short sleeve batik button down shirt rode tightly across his chest. His eyes lurked mysteriously behind double dark aviator glasses, while the stretch of his grin and the flash of his teeth delivered from such exceptional height made him a dead ringer for a parade master. All he needed, Phil reckoned, was a whistle.

A colossal laugh erupted from his center when he recognized Pedro, and the men exchanged hearty embraces.

"Come, Phil," said Pedro, waving Phil over. "Meet me amigo, Anton, from Kingston, Jamaica. Anton, meet Mr. Phil, builder of the fastest boats anywhere!" said Pedro, very pleased. The parade master laughed again.

"I already heard all about you, Mon," said Anton in a heavy Jamaican accent, "and Pedro, he be very proud of what he say you gots to show me." Phil squinted in the sun, looking up into Anton's aviators, then glanced over his shoulder for Vlad.

"Well, Anton, it's good knowing you, but I reckon it's really me *and* Vlad," said Phil, waving to Vlad standing in the shadows of the tree line, "that's got something Pedro wants you to see."

"Hey ya, Vlad," the parade master bellowed, flashing his teeth and extending an arm the size of a tree limb. "He still so grumpy?" Anton asked, taking Phil in over his aviators. That's when he saw Anton's eyes, as clear and blue as the sea.

Pedro led Anton with Phil and Vlad in tow to the worksite by the canal where the ekranoplan sat high in her cradle. The *Americanos* had refueled her tanks following the previous day's sea trials, and were loosening the line by which they eased her stern first into the water.

"Well, I'll be," said Anton, taking her in. "Ain't nevah seen nuttin' like it," he continued admiringly. He removed his glasses and inspected her up and down, laying his hand on the curved spontoon the way collectors admire a sports car. "How much you say she carry?" said Anton turning to Pedro. "Enough for your monthly quota, King Anton," said Pedro.

Soon the sound of ATVs growled from the jungle, moving in the direction of the worksite, Miguel aboard one and a stranger riding another, with long guns across their backs. Fore and aft, each ATV was lashed with a long overstuffed black bag, the kind that left the camp in boats and airplanes.

"Hey y'all," said Phil, as it dawned on him the bags were destined for the ekranoplan. "That dog won't hunt, Pedro. It won't. She ain't built for it."

Miguel and the other man riding the ATV pulled forward to the cradle. They cut their engines, dismounted, and unshouldered their weapons. After a brisk exchange between Pedro and Miguel that Phil failed to follow, the *Americanos* set to loading the bags into the ekranoplan wing compartments. "How much those weigh?" Phil asked Miguel, who stood there uncharacteristically stone-faced. "Vlad!" Phil yelled, seeing him in the shadows. "Tell 'em! *tell 'em* it won't work. We'll need to build a bigger one." No one was listening.

Anton looked doubtfully at Pedro, and Pedro smiled back reassuringly. "Uno momento," he said to Anton stepping in Phil's direction. Smiling and humming mariachi under his breath, he put his arm over Phil's shoulder and turned him gently away from the cradle.

"You will do this for me, me amigo," said Pedro pleasantly. "Anton me amigo, too. I promise him this shipment. Too dangerous flying to Jamaica now, so we send by your very fast boat, sí, Mr. Phil?"

"I done told you before, Pedro. I'll build you boats, but I ain't runnin' drugs, not now, not never. *You* fly the damn thing, *you're* a pilot," said Phil, as he felt Pedro's arm tighten around his neck.

"You no understand, my caballero friend," said Pedro, his eyes turning cold, same as they did with Mort. "Dis is three million dollars of pure cocoa paste, almost twenty million dollars after Anton deliver to Miami. You comprendes?" Phil squirmed, to loosen Pedro's grip, but the coil of Pedro's arm constricted like a python around his neck. "I can no help you, Phil, if you no help me," said Pedro benignly. "You will be safe, you will be fast, and if you leave now you be back from Kingston for cervezas before dinner," Pedro assured him. "And," Pedro added with a twinkle in his eye, "you be a hero, el caudillo among the Guajira!" he finished triumphantly.

Pedro wasn't wrong. Phil had studied José's charts, and cross-referenced them on his cockpit GPS. Jamaica was northwest, no more than four hundred miles, and with the twenty knot quartering trade winds from the east, he reckoned it was three hours out, maybe three and a half hours back... but who said he had to come back. While he disliked the idea of transporting the drugs, that paled compared to the points north available to him from Kingston on a full tank of gas. Guantanamo Bay, Cuba, U.S. soil, was just an hour northeast from the eastern most tip of Jamaica, just a short hop from Kingston. Or he might continue up through the Windward Passage between Cuba and Haiti, finding U.K. soil in the Turks and Caicos Islands in about two hours. He could turn himself in at either location, inform on the Guajira, and show he was innocent of Mort's murder. He knew there were risks, besides getting the ekranoplan airborne, like encountering a Coast Guard unit on Pedro's payroll, or worse yet, a competing cartel. There was just no telling what awaited out there, but the risks seemed worth the taking in light of the bad and deteriorating situation. Besides, with his head getting light on account of Pedro's headlock, what were his options.

"OK, OK, Pedro. I'll do it," he whispered. The pressure on his neck subsided, and before he caught his breath Pedro turned him to the cradle where Anton and the *Americanos*, and Vlad and Miguel and the other armed escort waited expectantly.

"Anton!" Pedro bellowed. "I give you Mr. Phil, the bestest fastest badest boat driver anywhere. He take your shipment to Kingston immediatamente, right now!" Pedro announced with master of ceremonies fanfare.

Anton grinned and the onlookers shifted with relief. A brief logistical discussion between Anton, Pedro and Phil followed. Anton would trail Phil in the air from the jalopy by which he arrived, "in case you get in trouble and need help," said Anton, as insincerely as words could be uttered. Anton would follow to keep his eyes on the shipment until Phil rendezvoused with a go-fast three miles dead south of Kingston. There the bags would be exchanged for fuel to carry him back to Guajira, *or wherever he pleased,* Phil told himself furtively.

"Hey Pedro," Phil said. "I ain't about to do a seven-hundred-mile round trip in that thing without my tools," he said pointedly, to signal his intent to return. "I'm runnin' on up to the house to get my bag. Be right back. Go on guys," he said to his workers. "Ya'll just put her in slow. And Miguel and you," said Phil to the other armed escort, "make sure them bags is tight up against each side of the cockpit, as close to center as you can," he finished, turning and loping off in double-time for the path back to camp.

He'd gone but three steps when he thought of Manuela. This might could be goodbye forever. "Dadgummit," he said out loud. He'd taken an uncommon liking to her, and she to him, saying "te amo" pretty regularly when she thought he was sleeping. He probably loved her, too, though he'd been careful not to say it. What would become of her now that José was dead – and he was leaving without even telling her. Surely, Mrs. Morales would see to her, he told himself feebly. Then there was Vlad, and even the *Americanos.* How close to betrayal was leaving all of them behind? They sure didn't begin as kinfolk, but kinfolk they'd become, and what was *he* doing the first chance he got, but saving his own skin, and turning them in if that's what it took to go free. What kind of caballero did that?

He reached his bungalow and blew through the door, went straight for the gun beneath the bed, and stuffed it in the small tool bag he carried to and from the worksite. No one would fault him for carrying a gun to a drug deal. He had hoped she would be there, but relief is what he felt when she wasn't, for what he might say to her eluded him. As low as he felt for leaving, he knew it was time to go, telling himself with dubious conviction, that she was safer not knowing – not knowing he had left, and not knowing what he knew.

"Hey, Mr. Anton," Phil called amiably from aboard the ekranoplan, pushing her off the bank in the direction of the sea. "You'll want to get airborne shortly, or you ain't never gonna keep up with me," he boasted, to quell his fear. The additional five hundred pounds of weight was palpable as he leaned into the pole, punting her down the canal; but the ekranoplan appeared to carry it well, the spontoons riding softly on the diminutive swells as they drifted in sets from the mouth of the canal.

The *Americanos* kept pace with him down the footpath, as much to burnish their association with Phil and the ekranoplan as to admire their work, Phil reckoned. No different from the way he used to wait in the shadows for the season opener of Boat Church, when his work was on show and at its very best. As he flicked on the magnetos, advanced the mixture to rich, set the throttle to idle and cranked the engine, Georgia felt close, as close as ever he remembered. Two coughs and a sputter and she exploded to life, bridling now on the swell, blades biting at the air.

He taxied clear of the canal and down the shore, following the crescent contour of the bay. More sluggish with five hundred more pounds of weight aboard, she didn't feel as low in the water as he expected. The easterly was freshening on the land effect convection. He hoped she would pop right on to her step as soon as she met the oncoming swell. To his left on the beach an audience had gathered. Vlad and his workmen had been joined by the *Americanos*, and Pedro fast approached from bidding Anton farewell. Anton's winged bag of bolts was rolling and shuddering on its way to the far end of the airstrip where it would turn to begin its takeoff roll, while Manuela, to Phil's dismay, was absent. He hoped news of the excitement might bring her to see him off, and to leave him with a memory of her standing by the sea.

He took a long last look at the beach, cinched his belts tight, and pulled his helmet down over his head. As soon as he heard Anton pour on the coals at the far end of the runway to begin his takeoff roll, he poured on the coals himself, advancing the ekranoplan's throttle to full power. With hard right rudder, he turned his back on the beach, pointing himself directly into the building easterly. In no time at all he was Kingston-bound, riding on a cushion of air, five hundred pounds of pure cocoa paste secure in the airfoil beneath him.

CHAPTER 22

En Route to Lost Lake, Georgia

"Marks," said Lenny, answering his cell phone. He was five hours into the nine-hour drive south from Washington, D.C. to Lost Lake, three hours behind him and two more to go on the endless stretch of I-81 that ran the full length of Virginia. It was beautiful country, that's what everyone said, but how many damned barns, tobacco fields, cattle herds and race horses did a man need to see? It was hot and his air-conditioning was struggling, and he wanted to be in Lost Lake early enough to go the first round with J.D. before calling it a day. It was Sam Rosen calling.

"That didn't take long," said Sam.

"What didn't?" replied Lenny, impressively curt, even for Lenny.

"That spoof you laid on your sheriff friend, about SOD coming to town? Already picked up in Colombian intercepts."

"No kidding, Sam. That's gotta be some kind of record. We scared someone," said Lenny, sounding devious and triumphant. "And I guess we know who J.D. Dunbar plays for."

"I guess we do," said Sam, "and it isn't the farm team. It's not like it came out of east central Miami. This came out of Bogotá, through a marine engineering company suspected in various narco sub building programs. And then, get this, it echoes right back to guess where?"

"I give up, Sam. Thrill me," said Lenny, encouraging the air conditioning by pounding on his dashboard.

"The Senate Subcommittee on Homeland Security and Governmental Affairs," Sam reported with considerable satisfaction. "The whole round trip in less than forty-eight hours. How's that for penetration?"

"Holy shit, Sam. Keep your head down," Lenny said, searching for every explanation but the one he knew it to be. "That's what I was calling to tell you. Your friend Sheriff Dunbar is connected."

"Who on the committee?"

"A staffer for the ranking member. An overseas call, right to his cell phone, so it's completely above board. We've got it on tape."

"It's worse than we thought, Sam," said Lenny, thinking fast. "If we've been right, and SOD is on the take, someone in Colombia thinks they're about to be double-crossed." He pounded the dashboard again, and was promptly rewarded by a cool stream of air.

"Jesus-H-Christ," said Sam. "I bet you're right. They're gonna think SOD set them up."

"Of course I'm right, Sam. Why else would I have said it? They'll trace the storyline back to me, eventually, if they don't kill each other first, and that may give us time. Still, no delay, OK? Let's move on this. How are the PATT reports coming?" They wouldn't be complete for several more days. Sam was working them as fast as he could.

What Sam *could* say was that The Farmers Building and Loan of Lost Lake wasn't much to speak of on its own, but like all mighty icebergs, only the tip was showing. It was one of three branches owned by a bank up the road in North Carolina, which was owned by a bank in Miami, which was owned by a bank in Atlanta. True to form, Lenny wanted profiles of every board member and every line executive at every subsidiary. He hated them already, without even knowing them.

The day grew hotter, the air conditioning crapping out just as he hit traffic in Johnson City, Tennessee, where he found a bounty of barbeque and boiled peanut outlets, and slim pickings among the fast-food dining options that were his staple. He refilled his tank and pushed on from the Blue Ridge into the Great Smokey Mountains, through the Cherokee to the Chattahoochee-Oconee National Forest. The deeper south he drove, the more pitiful he found the circumstances. There was no limit to the backwaters that witness protection found to hide its informants, and no surprise the drug trade was here. If past were prologue based on other god-forsaken places he'd seen, the overseas cartels were running out the local meth labs the way Japan ran Detroit out of car-making.

And that's why J.D. and Lost Lake surprised him. The sun was sinking as he crested the last hill leading down into Lost Lake proper. Long mountain shadows darkened the landscape while fugitive beams of sunlight painted wide swaths of the valley floor gold, and untended grasses billowed in waves on waning evening breezes off the hillsides. The town was tidy, with neatly mowed open spaces, freshly painted benches, and precious few barbeque and boiled peanut outlets, it pleased Lenny to see. He was unsurprised by all the pickup trucks, and driven to distraction by how slowly they moved. How did these people get anywhere, he wondered, as he punched the accelerator and passed on the left in a center lane he wasn't sure belonged to him. The driver he passed kept moseying along without the slightest inclination to road rage. He passed the Farmers Building and Loan of Lost Lake on the right, lights outs, lot empty, as inconspicuous as he expected it to be. That put him two blocks from the police station, where J.D. had agreed to meet him.

"Lenny Marks, here to see Sheriff Dunbar," said Lenny, announcing himself over the front counter to Betty Dunphy. Her head was down, immersed in a crossword.

"Well, *hey,* Mr. Marks. We've been expecting you. First time in Lost Lake? How was your drive down? Can I get you anything?"

"No thanks, just Sheriff Dunbar."

"Are you *sure* I cain't get you nothin'? Water? Coffee?"

"No, *no,* nothing, thank you," he said, cutting her off. He'd be there all night at the rate she was going. "Just Sheriff Dunbar, please," he said, forcing a smile.

"I see," she said. "He'll be right with you.... I'd be happy to heat some water if you'd prefer tea..." she persisted, because she refused to let a Yankee subvert decency - again.

"Mr. Marks?" said J.D., emerging from his office. "Welcome to town. Y'all been offered somethin' to drink, a water, some coffee?"

"*Yes,* sheriff, thank you."

"Maybe something stronger, we got us a few watering holes around town."

"No. Thank you," said Lenny. For Chrissake, what was it with these people? "Where can we talk?" he asked, dispensing with the pleasantries.

Shock and awe was the tried and true prescription for turning crooked cops. Retribution by criminal masters always scared them the most, and Lenny liked to leverage that fear. The carrot was to guarantee the informer's security and the paymaster's demise. The stick was to spread the word the informer had turned witness, and let the paymasters come for him. Lenny had never made good on the stick because he'd never had to. Retribution by criminal networks was legend, and Harry Halliday's demise would be fresh enough on J.D.'s mind. He also knew that when crooked cops turned witness it wasn't by degrees. They went arrow-straight, hoping to expose the whole criminal enterprise and cheat retribution by bringing the whole enterprise down. The failure to be thorough produced victims like Mort, and Lenny would emphasize that to Sheriff Dunbar when he eventually came around. For now, his plan for J.D. was to send him home petrified, and meet him again in the morning, after sleeplessness and terror had had their way with him.

"Just routine, hunh?" said J.D., showing Lenny into his yellowing cinderblock office, and offering him a folding steel chair that matched his desk.

"Is that what I said?" replied Lenny.

"That's what you said, before saying something about SOD comin' down here like the damn horsemen of the apocalypse."

"It's complicated, Sheriff Dunbar. I don't need to tell you that, though, do I?"

"I beg your pardon?" said J.D., leaning over from his chair on the opposite side of his desk. He was bigger up close, and smelled of chewing tobacco. "That was my witness, killed under my own nose, what exactly you insinuatin', friend?"

"Exactly that, sheriff. How does that happen? No, wait. How does it happen at the hands of a local, all-cash business proprietor with a fresh Suspicious Activity Report? Presumably, even in Georgia, sheriffs know what money laundering looks like. I need some goddamned answers...friend."

J.D. had seen this show before, and he was already tired of it. He leaned back in his chair, crossed his hands behind his head, and placed his giant, steel-toed black patrol boots on his desk.

"I don't much care for your tone, Mr. Marks. If you have an accusation to make, make it. Otherwise, I'd be much obliged if you got back into your car and headed right on back to Washington, D.C.," J.D. said, rubbing his belly where he kept his Glock concealed.

It was then Lenny realized he was on his own in a foreign land.

Betty Dunphy had locked up her desk and gone home. He was in J.D.'s hands now, and considered the ways J.D. could make him disappear in the miles of wilderness encircling Lost Lake, especially if J.D. were in cahoots with whomever actually ruled this frontier. Now seemed an inopportune time to say what was on his mind.

"On the other hand, Mr. Marks," J.D. continued, "if you'd care to show some couth while you're visitin' in my little town, wretched and uncivilized as you may find it, I'd be tickled to tell you all I know about that murder," J.D. said with a smile. "And *why* would I be willing to be so damned hospitable, Mr. Marks? 'Cause a shitload happened here that ain't come out. I can't say what 'cause I don't know, but like you say, things ain't what they appear. I'd welcome your help...if you can be civil about it."

On second thoughts, a drink at a local watering hole, and even boiled peanuts, if that's what it took, were in order. They rode in J.D.'s car, which soon gave Lenny an appreciation for riding with the sheriff through a small southern town. Dunbar knew everybody, and how he could talk. Lenny was parched and knew the life story of half the town by the time they finally ordered a drink at *Twelve Oaks Bar and Grill.* He also learned that *he's all right* meant *never mind, I don't like him either*. It's what Sheriff Dunbar said when locals didn't take to Lenny right away.

"Who killed Halliday?" Lenny asked, even before they were served.

"Not who everyone thinks," said J.D., looking up and down the bar.

"You mean the boat business owner, Phoenix Perdue?"

"Yessir. Phil."

"Why not? How well did you check him out?" demanded Lenny, presumption of the sheriff's incompetence, or complicity, coloring his tone. J.D. sighed and shook his head.

"Y'all don't know shit, do you?"

"Come again," said Lenny, unchecking his natural aggression. He felt safer in public, where the sheriff was less likely to erase him.

"Y'all up there in Washington, with your departments and committees and eavesdropping Whangdoodles, ain't got any idea how a town like this works. Look around you. Most everyone in this bar knew Phil from the day his was born. And their daddies and mommas knew his daddy and momma, and same for his grand-daddy and grand-momma. Hell, the woman I stays with taught him in school. No way he killed Harry Halliday, especially like *that*. He wouldn't know how, or even what it meant."

"Then why is the trail cold? Why no other arrests or investigations?"

"You tell me, Sherlock. Federal marshals internal investigations come down here like you, poked around some, and declared it an open and shut case. Harry Halliday, alias Mort Ashton, came to foreclose on the boat business, the way he was ordered by the bank. 'Lotta folks reckon a man 'll do just about anything in the moment his livelihood's threatened. So Phil killed *his own uncle* - that was Halliday's alias, don't you know - and then run once he saw what he done... if you believe that pile of nonsense. That's what the file says." J.D. concluded, swigging from his long neck.

"Who do *you* think it is?"

"Who's askin'?" said J.D., staring Lenny in the eyes.

"Fucking Fusion, who do you think?"

"Watch your mouth, Mr. Marks. There's ladies present. People don't cotton to language like that in these parts, or haven't you noticed." Pressuring J.D. was only getting his back up, so Lenny relented. The pause allowed J.D. to collect himself.

"What I want to know," said J.D. presently, "is why all the interest two years on? And what does SOD think they'll find here?"

"We'll get to that," Lenny said. "Tell me about Halliday. How'd the mob find him here?"

"Now you're on track. And why didn't the Marshals Service move him, or get him more protection, when he started cooperating again? Was that an oversight, or calculated? I reckon the mob had eyes on him all along, someone inside, on the home team. Someone like you, I reckon, with access to a lotta information." said J.D., swigging again. "Am I a loose end you come down to clean up?" said J.D., hand on his hip where his Springfield rode.

"You can see, sheriff, how you're the natural suspect," Lenny said. "It's your beat, your witness. He gets clipped, and life goes on like nothing happened. How would *you* explain it?"

"Yes, indeed, Mr. Marks. It's been said before, and likely explains why no more witnesses have been entrusted to me."

"Is it true?" pressed Lenny, "you on the take? Because you got a big ass - excuse me - very large, money laundering operation going on here, and you act like you don't know it, which is why I think you do. Now you can kill me and make me disappear, but we're on it, and SOD won't go away. That, or…." said Lenny, baiting the hook.

"Or what, Mr. Marks, or *exactly what*," hissed J.D., leaning in close.

"Or we let it leak that we've turned you, and the mob gets you before we do. Honestly, sheriff, I don't care either way. We'll win and they'll lose. You may want to consider whose side you're on." The hook was set.

"Tell you what," J.D. said thoughtfully, "you Feds are a piece of work. The truth don't fit whatever cockamamie crap it is you dream up in your dark corridors in Washington, D.C., so you make stuff up, invent your little stories."

"I'm tired, sheriff. It was a long drive down. I'll meet you for breakfast wherever you say," said Lenny, ending the conversation, the better to let the fish tire itself overnight on the line.

Being the unspoken accessory to Halliday's murder was getting old. By incompetence or conspiracy, all fingers pointed to him, and he knew Marion was tired of his bellyaching about it. Disparaged by the marshals, and now suspected by the Feds, his bid for a peaceful life of service had been turned on its head. The mystery of Phil's whereabouts still plagued him, and Marion even worse. A home town boy like Phil wasn't the sort to up and leave, and disappear from the face of the earth, unless he'd been killed, or unless he was guilty. Neither option sat right with J.D. He believed in a third possibility.

"You know, Mr. Marks," said J.D. at breakfast, sopping up the last of his gravy with his biscuit, "I been thinkin' on what you said last night. You reckon I'm on the take, covering for some kind of money laundering operation, and I reckon you, or someone like you, tipped the mob to Halliday cooperating again, and they killed him. That about sums it up, right?"

"The first part's right. I do think you're on the take, to look the other way on Halliday, to cover for the bank, maybe both. You're entitled to your opinion about the identity of the murderer, but Halliday's still dead, murdered gangland style on the premises of the boat business that triggered a SAR, whose proprietor fled. What am I missing?"

"What if Phil is flat-out innocent - of the murder and money-laundering?" J.D. countered. "He didn't know who Halliday was, for one, and he just ain't the sort. I think it's Pedro Morales, a local undesirable, regardless of his lock-tight alibi. He's placed at the murder scene by a single, unreliable witness - a young lady friend of Phil's, who I happened to pick up, under the influence, the day after Phil disappeared. Now, members of Morales' family put Pedro eighty miles away at the time of the murder, but only Phil and Pedro know what really happened, and the one that ain't Phil has a stack of motives, I reckon."

"Make your pitch," said Lenny. "This oughta be good."

"We got all kinda drugs up here, Mr. Marks. I know Morales is up to no good. Drugs is probably the least of it. Now, last night, you got me thinkin'. With drugs comes money laundering, which I'm sure I don't know a thing about it," J.D. extemporized, struggling with his train of thought. "What if Halliday, who worked at the bank, demanded a cut of the money you say is being laundered in exchange for keeping mum? Then he sings a little to show he's serious. So Morales, or his people, knowing it won't end there, kill him." J.D.'s theory wasn't so far-fetched.

"Morales won't talk, but Phil will, I reckon. We just need to find him."

"And he disappeared two years ago, right sheriff?" said Lenny, observing the fly in the ointment of J.D.'s proposition. "What about your witness? Who was Pheonix Perdue's lady friend?" inquired Lenny, playing out the string.

"Katie McLean," said J.D. "I reckon most folks around here believe her story, but what with Pedro's alibi, and his being not so much the forgiving type, she just clammed up. S'pose I would, too, in her shoes."

McLean – it was a common enough name – but what were the chances, wondered Lenny, ever skeptical of coincidences.

"Tell me about Katie McLean," Lenny asked. Better to be sure.

"Not much to tell, really. Not a bad kid. Not the sort to smoke grass, but she had been when I come across her. Jus' no tellin' sometimes."

"She from around here?"

"In a manner of speaking. Lives in 'lanta rest of the year, but come to the lake for the summer all her days. I known her since she was but an ankle-biter. Known her people as long as I can remember. Was just visitin' with her father on the lake yesterday morning, before Boat Church."

"Before *what*?" said Lenny.

"You know, Boat Church. It's a regular thing 'round here. I reckon you just go to regular ol' church in Washington."

"If I *went* to church, sheriff. I'm a Jew," said Lenny, going for the effect.

"I'm so sorry," said J.D., regretting instantly how it came out. "I mean I'm sorry I presumed you were Christian. You *are* in the Bible Belt, after all," said J.D. trying to recover.

"Keep going, sheriff. Tell me about the McLeans."

"I reckon they're no different than most folks around here. Mr. McLean, Katie's father been real successful doin' whatever he does in 'lanta. Married into Lost Lake through his first wife, Bonnie Campbell. The Campbells is from two lakes up. Divorced now. Katie's the only child by his second marriage. No reason for Katie to say she saw Pedro, 'cept she saw him, and got worried about Phil when he went missing."

"Any children by McLean's first marriage?" Lenny dreaded asking.

"Yes, now lets' see. There's Duncan. He still comes 'round regular. And, hold on now, it's commin' to me. She ain't been back here since the divorce. Myra?"

"Moira?"

"Why yes, that's it, Moira. How did you know?"

"Lucky guess," said Lenny darkly.

With the sheriff's knowledge of the family spanning two marriages and three generations, at least on the first Mrs. McLean's side, Lenny realized he was by no accident deep in McLean country. Moira's half-sister was connected to the murder suspect in a mob killing of a bank employee in witness protection... and of all the banks in Georgia Moira could have tagged for further investigation, she chose that one. Lenny knew he was being manipulated, though to what end he dared not speculate. Lost Lake wasn't just the locus of the Farmers Building and Loan, it had been Moira McLean's childhood summer home, "and the home of *her people*, on her momma's side," J.D. added earnestly. "She were here all summer, every summer on the lake," J.D. continued, until the McLeans separated, after which Moira and Bonnie "vamoosed," never to be seen in Lost Lake again. "Now her brother, Duncan? That's another story," said J.D., but Lenny's mind was already back in Washington, recalling events of two years past.

Moira's interest in Fusion, it now appeared, had been anything but professional curiosity, and Lenny knew the innocent annotation in her report regarding an inconspicuous little bank in Lost Lake, Georgia, had been anything but innocent. It stood to reason the affair had been a set-up, too. He tried to recall what advantage, if any, she gained by engaging with him romantically. Her indoctrination into the world of money laundering, and education about the inventory of tools and countermeasures arrayed against it was knowledge available to, and indeed, expected of all summer interns. She didn't have to sleep with him to learn the trade.

Sam wouldn't like it. Lenny didn't like it either. The feeling he had of being caught like a bug in Moira's web went from bad to worse when the sheriff got to the second Mrs. McLean, from Colombia.

"Slow down, sheriff," said Lenny, the story growing worse and more implicating by the minute. "We were discussing the prime suspect of the murder, Phil Perdue, who you doubt did it. Before we give him a free pass, why the Suspicious Activity Report, issued right before our felon in witness protection, masquerading as the bank officer, is murdered right on Mr. Perdue's premises?"

"Now *that* I don't know, Mr. Marks," said J.D. "Never did get to the bottom of it, 'specially since the branch manager couldn't see no difference in how Phil was moving money in and out of the business for years."

"Let's go ask him," said Lenny, rising from the table, his undisturbed gravy curdling at the edge of his plate.

Buck Tidwell was no more help than he had been two years before. The SAR came out of the compliance department in Atlanta. "Someone at HQ shinin' FinCEN by straightening out a branch," Buck reckoned, but Lenny doubted it. One of many thresholds for triggering a SAR was variance from established patterns. *Change* in funds flows. Buck had seen nothing out of the ordinary, and Lenny doubted Dan Thorne at FinCEN would find much either.

"Someone at the bank wanted a light shined on Perdue," Lenny concluded. "Why do you suppose that is?" he asked Buck and J.D.

"Stumps me," said Buck. "Phil and his daddy before him were real good customers, besides the debt his daddy built up on the place. But I reckon the bank's hand were in that as much as Phil's daddy's. No, Phil were a real good kid. No trouble to nobody 'round here," said Buck, swelling a little. Buck didn't think Phil murdered Mort Ashton either, but he didn't know Mort Ashton was Harry Halliday.

"Now, I know we're still getting' to know each other," J.D. said tentatively, "but sure sounds to me like that's a trick you've seen before, Mr. Marks, am I right?"

"What trick?"

"A false SAR." Lenny would no more entrust the tricks of his trade to a small-town sheriff than shoot himself in the head, especially a sheriff he already suspected of colluding with the mob, and presently intent on diverting Lenny's attention from the main murder suspect to a stereotype. It was too neat. But the sheriff was right. False SARs *were* the tool of choice for banks beholden to money launderers, routinely used to divert attention from the real thing to unsuspecting dupes. The SAR would make Perdue look guilty before the murder ever happened.

"The thing of it is," Buck interjected, "besides that it don't add up, how did he get away so easy?"

"Exactly," said Lenny. "How *did* he get away so easily? Every road and gas station from here to Timbuktu has cameras. But this guy, *Phil*, as you call him, who by your own accounts has never been out of state, just vanishes like a ghost."

"Unless he were took," said J.D. "'nless Pedro killed Mort, and took Phil with him, probably at gunpoint." Buck looked bewildered. "Now, why in tarnation would Pedro do *that*?" Buck asked.

Lenny's phone vibrated in his pocket. It was Sam.

"Excuse me, gentlemen," he said, exiting Buck's office. "What you got?"

"It's not good, Lenny."

"Give it to me straight."

Lenny never excelled at masking emotion, including now.

"How well, *exactly*, do you know the McLeans?" seethed Lenny as he reentered the room.

"Hunh?" said Buck and J.D. in unison.

"How-*well*-do-you-know-the-McLeans? Do I need to spell it out for you?"

"I reckon well enough," said J.D.

"Sure," said Buck. "I'd say I knows Mr. McLean and he knows me. Have for, ooh, I'd say twenty years, or thereabouts."

"We're acquaintances," said J.D., trying to clarify. "I told you I visited with him just yesterday, on the lake, before Boat Church. In fact, we talked about this very thing, by which I mean the murder. And I allowed as how I *still* couldn't believe it were Phil who done it, and was more like to believe his daughter's story, and he allowed as how he reckoned Pedro weren't such a bad feller after all, and his daughter weren't the most reliable in matters of the truth."

"Sheriff," Lenny interjected, because he sensed a diatribe in the offing, "what if I were to tell you he's the Chairman of Atlanta

Guaranty and Trust." Buck and J.D. stared at him blankly. "Atlanta G&T owns a bank in Miami which owns a bank up the road in North Caroline, which owns…:"

"The Farmers Building and Loan of Lost Lake," Buck said casually.

"Exactly," said Lenny through his clenched teeth. "When did you think *all y'all* were going to share *that* with me?"

"Why does it matter?" Buck asked innocently. Lenny rolled his eyes, pulled at his hair and ground his teeth. To be fair, he reminded himself, neither J.D. nor Buck could know he was wrestling with why Moira would file a tip against her father's bank, if not her own father. The conspicuous precision of her notation spoke for itself - *CPOT?* But J.D.'s failure to mention that McLean owned the bank foreclosing on the Perdue boat business shortly after issuing a bogus SAR against it was nothing if not implicating.

"Sheriff Dunbar," Lenny began with studied patience, "does it not strike you as odd that the Chairman of the bank whose murdered employee was in witness protection discredits his own daughter and vouches for the person you think committed the murder?"

"Mr. Marks," J.D. started, pacing slowly about the room, "I don't know if it's odd or not. What I do know is folks around here generally mind their own business. We don't go around spyin' on our neighbors, thinkin' up things they might be guilty of. I reckon that's your job. But I known most all the families on the lake for at least one, and in some cases, two generations, and I *still* don't know what all they do for a living. It's not my business, and the ones I do know, I don't naturally suspect them of illegalities," J.D. concluded, "y'understand what I'm saying?"

"Honestly, sheriff, I don't give a fuck how it works around here. Doesn't it strike you as odd he would vouch for the guy *you* think murdered Halliday? Or that the timing of the SAR just before the murder on Perdue's premises wreaks of a set-up?" J.D. paused. Lenny had the only working explanation for the Suspicious Activity Report, and it supported J.D.'s hunch.

"Now that you say it, I reckon it's worth a look."

"Is that what you *reckon*, sheriff?" Lenny concluded disdainfully. "I have a strong feeling you're about to know more than you ever wanted, or more than you're telling, about a whole bunch of things going on around here."

CHAPTER 23

Guajira Peninsula, Colombia

He should never have looked back. He should have stuck to his plan, and flown the ekranoplan on an empty hold and a full tank of gas to freedom after offloading the drugs to Anton's go-fast. He would regret his indecisiveness time and again in the year ahead, even though he returned to Guajira a hero, completing an eight-hundred-mile round trip in seven hours, and delivering five hundred pounds of pure cocaine in a reusable ekranoplan that took a third less time to build than a one-trick narco sub, and cost half as much. By late in the evening of his return, as the celebrations were waning, all of Vlad's men were calling themselves *Americanos*, and Vlad raised a drink to shifting all of his men and resources to constructing bigger and faster ekranoplans.

"You see, Mr. Phil," said Pedro, looking at Manuela, "aren't you glad you come back?"

Pedro had anticipated Phil's escape plan long before Phil left camp. Floating beside Anton's drug-laden go-fast three miles off Kingston, Anton's men informed Phil through crooked, gap-toothed smiles, that Manuela would be dead by nightfall if he didn't reappear in the next few hours at the Guajira camp. On reflection, it wasn't so much indecisiveness he regretted. It was the vow he made to himself to standby people who needed him, because he knew from the likes of McLean, and even the bank, how it felt to be abandoned. He could never have left Manuela in Pedro's cold-blooded hands, he assured himself. Or maybe he just couldn't leave Manuela.

In one day and one involuntary act, his life changed, and he began to feel the way he reckoned celebrities feel. All the workers knew his name and greeted him with smiles. The leaders among them sought his counsel, on subjects large and small, from dovetailing joints to layouts for bungalows of their own. And time passed. How much, Phil could not say until, before he knew it, Christmas came again, and Manuela and Pedro's mother, and the women who helped her feed the camp began preparations for the feast they served the men before sending them home to their families for the holidays. Ian kept Vlad and the Guajira workmen well supplied with materials to every specification they gave him, and Vlad and Phil reveled in their design collaboration for bigger and faster ekranoplans. By early spring the fleet had expanded to four, with payloads ranging from one to three tons, and cruising speeds up to three hundred knots, more than halving the roundtrip from Guajira to all points in the Caribbean basin and back.

Pedro reckoned the drones and surveillance aircraft operating overhead couldn't even see the ekranoplans coming and going. And even if they were spotted, there was no time to move surface interdiction vessels into position to intercept them. They were moving with impunity, the fortunes of the Guajira ascendant.

He was glad to have Manuela. She kept him honest. She still said "te amo," after she thought he was asleep, and once or twice he had mumbled, "I love you, too." He could see she was proud of him, and of the growing esteem in which he was held by the men; and she grew aware, herself, of the improving favor in which Pedro's mother and the other women held her, too. The calmness in her hands and the way she poured the coffee still soothed him, arriving as she always had at the worksite morning and afternoon, serving Vlad first, as if nothing much had changed. But Vlad knew things had changed, and in ways that generally pleased him. He still set the work schedule and drove the *Americanos* like mules, but he consulted with Phil privately and deferred to him in public, as if clearing a path to advance him among the men. Ekranoplan production soon became the pulse of the Guajira's burgeoning enterprise, and Phil, it was whispered in corners around camp, the heir apparent.

Phil couldn't figure it, but was grateful for Vlad's encouragement. It beat being on his bad side every day of the week. Manuela knew there was more to Vlad's affection for Phil than Phil's appreciation for Russian engineering. She knew the rumors of Vlad's missing son, and suspected Vlad of finding in Phil a surrogate - it explained his affection for Phil, she believed. The goodness in her soul that found sympathy for Vlad made keeping the secret of her uncle's murder harder. The next time Pedro left camp, Phil raised it with Vlad.

"You know, Vlad," said Phil, drawing on a joint and swigging on Vlad's vodka, "Manuela still thinks her uncle is in Bogotá, and I don't have the heart to tell her he's dead." Vlad stared a long time at his feet where they were propped on a crate in his bungalow.

"Mr. Phil," he began, breaking his gaze to swig on the vodka himself, "dis ganja is no good. You smokin' it more and more. No good for you, no good for Manuela, no good for the men."

"I only toke at night, Vlad, and only with you, every once in a while."

"Dat was before. Now you tokin' more and more. The men, they know. They want to be proud. They like bein' *Americanos*. Let them be proud."

"I hear you Vlad. I'll be careful. But what do I tell Manuela? Don't we gotta tell her?"

"Pedro thinks I'm the only one that knows," said Vlad despondently.

He saw how telling her could make Vlad vulnerable, if word got out around camp that Pedro had murdered José, but he reckoned he had no choice. Manuela missed José something fierce. She worried he might be in trouble, and he felt low lying to her; so that night, stoned and drunk, he swore her to secrecy and told her the truth, which went even less well than he hoped. Those soft, calm hands could throw and hit, both of which they did that night with abandon, until he put himself around her like a straightjacket, squeezing until the anger subsided, and her sobbing succumbed eventually to sleep.

By the time Manuela realized she was late, and told him so, he was piloting more deliveries than he ever intended, making roundtrips to Kingston, Havana and the Bahamas when he wasn't at the worksite with Vlad and the men, building new ekranoplans. A number of the regular airplane pilots flying routes between Central America and the southern United States had been pressed into service driving ekranoplans as well, each one trained by Phil, each one finding exhilaration flying at high speed so close to the surface, undetectable by radar and unreachable by interdiction. And the volume and speed of Guajira shipments accelerated so markedly with the thrilling elusiveness of the ekranoplans that they flew all the time, even in broad daylight. They could barely be kept full as shipping capacity outstripped cocaine production.

It occurred to Phil then that the Guajira's expertise with moving contraband, and the prevalence of excess capacity, could be valuable to other cartels; but knowing Pedro's disdain for the Zeta, among others, he paid his idea no mind. Like Phil, the ekranoplan pilots knew they had a good thing going, and like the ekranoplan builders before them, formed a special brotherhood, with feats of daring, and tales of elusion becoming the grist of revelry and storytelling lasting late into the night.

Phil loved them all – the American from Alabama, Jim Bartsch, who painted *Roll Tide* along the waterline of both his spontoons, and the former British Airways pilot, Alistair Glendenning, who went by *Glen* and flew with a white silk scarf and vintage leather flying cap and goggles. They played hard and worked hard, flew sober and celebrated drunk, and it was all more fun than a man had a right to have, Phil reckoned, except when Glendenning showed more than a passing interest in Manuela. He paid Glendenning's fancy no mind, nor did he ponder how the party might end until Ian came strolling into camp.

"You've noticed Alistair's interest in Manuela?" said Ian.

"I reckon so," said Phil. "She wants him, she can have him," he replied with bravado, surprising even himself by how coarse it made him sound – worse than Bartsch, or even Pedro.

"Look, mate, you've got biggah problems than Alistair," said Ian, who wasn't kidding. Despite how well things appeared to be going in camp, darker forces were stirring.

"You lot are getting through, and with a lot more volume. But the Zeta and a few of the others aren't having the same luck. Word's getting around."

"What word, Ian? What's gettin' around?" Phil asked skeptically.

"That the Guajira, or should I say, the *Americanos,* have cut a deal with the Yanks to look the other way."

"Oh bullshit, Ian. *You* know why we're getting through."

"Maybe, maybe not. Point is, the Zeta are wiggly. Watch your back, mate."

Ian never stayed in camp long, and he reserved his warnings

to Phil for the hours before he left. He was back on his Sea-Doo, vanishing into the swamp, just as Phil aired out Ian's warning with Vlad. Vlad nodded, folded his arms and growled, the response he usually saved for perplexing engineering predicaments. Vlad avoided politics, but Ian's warning vexed him.

They would have given it more thought were they not behind in their production schedule. The workmen were anxious to stay on plan, and the siren song of building and launching new ekranoplans proved a useful if costly distraction. More time passed and more ekranoplans joined the fleet. The finished craft resembled nothing so much as Lego mashups of production airplanes, cannibalized and reconfigured into ekranoplans of similar size and payload. Vlad had visions of a mega foil, the *schoolbus*, he dubbed it, with twin gas turbine engines, a cruise speed of four hundred knots, and the capacity to deliver two tons of cargo almost anywhere in the Caribbean basin in one hour. The *schoolbus* could never journey to Europe the way some of his submarines had, but it put the Mid-Atlantic states and New England within easy reach. Their wide-eyed ambition brought division of labor, Vlad attending to construction while Phil indoctrinated new pilots, who lined up to join the squadron.

Jim Bartsch had been, in his early days, something of an independent contractor, flying for all the cartels. He had a line on eager pilots, the inveterate risk-takers, contrarians, iconoclasts and misfits who had tried and failed at steady work. Many were Americans, regional airline commercial pilot flunkies. Others, like Pedro and Anton, were native South and Central Americans who had risen through the ranks of the cartels, learning to fly as much for convenience as for ferrying contraband. As they appeared in camp for schooling by Phil in the art of ekranoplan flying, he could scarcely ignore how the camp was changing, the new arrivals weaving themselves into the fabric of Guajira culture, their wild hare personalities inciting something feral and charged in the heretofore domesticated, and otherwise dedicated *Americanos.*

More late-night drinking, more taunting the women, even Phil developed bad habits.

"You must be careful with these new men," admonished Vlad. "They not your friends. They bring you down if you not careful." While he knew Vlad was right, he thrived on the camaraderie, despite how different the pilots were from his workmen, the self-proclaimed *Americanos*; and now everyone was calling themselves *Americanos*, especially the American pilots, who found in the name the irreverence they lived for.

Manuela grew distant. She began to show, her breasts swelling prodigiously, impossible to hide, even beneath the colorful embroidery of the loose-fitting Puebla dresses Pedro's mother lent her. The quiet, moody reserve with which she moved about the camp confounded him. She came and went with the coffee as usual, but uneasily now, the eyes of the new men upon her. He came to expect she would be fast asleep when he returned from Vlad's, or wherever he had been fraternizing. So she surprised him one evening when he came home late from carousing with his men, in the inebriated state which had become his custom, and found her awake, weeping. Vlad was beside her, holding her hands, soothing her heaving sobs.

"What the fuck, Vlad?' said Phil, shuffling toward the bed where she lay.

"Glen," said Vlad.

"Glen what?" Phil demanded.

"He try," said Vlad, sighing, "you know."

"I sure as hell don't! He try *what*?"

"You know. He come try to be with her."

"That motherfucker!" Phil shouted, lurching beneath the bed to retrieve his pistol.

"Is OK Phil," said Vlad, placing his hand on Phil's shoulder. "Is OK. I hear him. I stop him. Is OK."

"You OK, Manuela?" said Phil, seeing her through a fog. She recoiled at his sight, shooting him a withering glare, wild and dark and nameless like nothing he'd ever seen. It turned him inside out. He sank unsteadily to the floor and found the handgun stuffed beneath the bed. He shoved it in the waistband in the small of his back and staggered straight for the door.

"Phil, Phil!" Vlad shouted after him. Phil turned. "I already stop him," said Vlad, raising his fist and shaking it. "He no come back."

"You're damn right he no come back, cause I'm about to blow the bastard's brains out," Phil said, resuming his unsteady path for the door.

He doubled timed it across the camp, going directly for the outbuilding that served as a barracks for housing the itinerant pilots and convoy gunmen coming and going from camp. He blew through the door and found Glen sitting in a rickety rattan chair nursing a cut below his eye with a damp rag.

"You bastard," Phil yelled, kicking his foot like a martial arts master straight at Glen's face, sending him and the chair sprawling on their backs. Phil stood over him and drew the gun, cocking the action, chambering a round, and laying the barrel directly on Glen's forehead.

"No, no," Glen pleaded, whimpering like a baby.

"You pussy, you motherfucking pussy!" Phil raged. "Say goodbye!" Glen soiled himself. Phil secured the action, seized the gun by the barrel, and commenced pistol whipping Glen about the head. His first blow landed squarely on Glen's nose, mashing it like play dough across his face, and spattering blood. The second blow opened a deep wound across Glen's crown that seeped blood through the cane on the back of Glen's chair. The third opened a gash on Glen's temple, knocking Glen unconscious.

Phil raised the gun a fourth time and found his arms incapacitated, bound in the muscular grip of a full nelson.

"Easy," said Jim Bartsch. "Easy. The next one will kill him."

He awoke just a few hours later to an empty bed and bloodstained hands. Through the fog of events from the night before came a single, vivid memory - the knot of men surrounding him and Jim Bartsch, and Glen unconscious, blood spilling from his head on the floor - the eyes that once admired him filled with dread.

When he seated himself beside Vlad for chicharone two hours later he knew everything had changed. Pedro's mother and the ladies around the firepit eyed him warily. The *Americanos* slipped furtively to and from the bodega, a gathering of them on the fringe whispering amongst themselves, scarcely daring to glance in his direction.

"I'm sorry, Vlad. I'm real sorry. I don't know what came over me."

"You drunk, and probably high," said Vlad. His eyes bulging, his nose flared. "You not wrong," said Vlad. "You do right thing, but now they worry," he continued, waving his thumb over his shoulder in the direction of the workmen. "They wonder if you crazy man, loco," he said, spinning his index fingers around his temples, "like Pedro."

"Awe, come on, Vlad. I wasn't that bad."

"Wait 'til you see Glen," Vlad replied, cracking a smile. "He no fuck with Mr. Phil or his woman no more."

"It ain't me I'm worried about. It's Manuela." Phil looked up to find Pedro's mother holding two plates stacked high with chicharone. She looked him sternly in the eye and shook her head, placing the plates on the table.

"Manuela stay with me, Mr. Phil, at least for now, you see?" she said, lifting her skirts and departing in haste.

"Maybe you behave better, and stop this drinkin' and smokin' and be kind to Manuela, and she come back," Vlad offered hopefully.

CHAPTER 24

Guajira Peninsula, Colombia

"You kickin' the asses!" Pedro hollered enthusiastically as he loped down the crushed coral runway from where he'd parked his plane. "Now you learnin', Mr. Phil," he said with a smile, putting his arm over Phil's shoulder and walking with him toward the bodega. He was on his way to the ritual greeting he saved for his mother upon returning to camp. "You show them who is the boss, Mr. Phil!" he continued proudly.

That was never his intent, but he reckoned it was so. The men had treated him differently from then on. Not that he wanted their deference, but it grew on him. Fear had motivated them to still greater achievements, and what he lost in candor he more than recovered in pleasantries. It wasn't the worst way to go through life. Vlad was different, too. Something about the night he rescued Manuela, and Phil's unhinged rage and beating of Glen, left Vlad brooding and troubled.

"What's got you down, old man?" Phil asked that night between swigs of Vodka at Vlad's bungalow, the night of Pedro's return. "We're at the top of our game. The ekranoplans are coming out great. We're doing the work of a fleet of submarines in half the time."

"I am worried," said Vlad.

"About what?"

"Things is changin'," said Vlad staring at his feet. "José gone. Too much shipments. The pilots. The men. Even you, Phil. Things is changin'."

"Does Pedro know I know about José?"

"No. And don't tell him," snapped Vlad, his eyes bulging as they locked on Phil's.

"OK, OK. But I haven't changed, Vlad. *You* know that."

"No?"

"No."

"You carryin' the gun I give you."

"Sure I am. You told me to."

"This is different."

He was never much of a pack animal. He reckoned all only-children came possessed of the involuntary independence that burned in him. Not that he didn't have friends, but the ever-present company of his father made him accustomed to the company of grownups, and perhaps less interested or patient with his contemporaries. It's why he missed José, enjoyed Vlad, and welcomed the company of the pilots and workmen, all of whom gave the appearance of being much older. And it's why disappointing Vlad carried a particular burden, unlike any he'd born since long before his father passed. He didn't need to fit in, but he wanted for the approval of his elders.

With Manuela at Pedro's mother's, and refusing to look at or speak to him, even when she served him coffee, he had found few reasons to make it home. He had taken to sleeping on the beach, by choice or necessity, he wasn't ever sure, because he was often too drunk to know. The Zeta attack came early in the predawn hours of the very next morning following another hard night of partying.

The distinctive crackle of automatic gun fire in the woods up the beach echoed over the water. He heard a blood curdling cry, unmistakably Miguel. He was wounded, or waking the camp. It was impossible to say through his vodka-addled mind. Gun fire spread across the camp, from the inland end of the runway through the living quarters and down to the canal and worksites close by the water's edge. He reached for the small of his back, pulled the Colt, and cocked the action. It jammed, clogged by the sand where he'd lain in it and lost consciousness. By the time he was on his feet, running toward the gunfire, explosions popped off in the vicinity of the worksites, fireballs flickering and lighting up the sky.

But for the groans of wounded and dying men, the camp was silent by the time he reached it. He ran first for the women's quarters, which lay off the beaten trail between José's cabin and the central bodega. There he found Pedro's mother, on her back on the floor, small, neat bullet holes puncturing her neck and chest. Her eyes stared blankly at the heavens, an apron of blood about her torso. Manuela was on her knees, praying over the body.

"Dear God," said Phil leaning down beside Manuela. "Are you alright? Are you alright!" he said putting his arm around her. She shook it off and glared that same old glare, only darker, angrier, with accusation to spare.

"You are too late. Go find Pedro," she ordered. "Please. *Go*. Go find Pedro."

Pedro usually garrisoned himself on short stays with the pilots, and Phil sprinted from the women's quarters back to the center of camp. Miguel had been hit in the left arm and right leg, to which he had already applied tourniquets, and two *Americanos* had dragged themselves to the outside wall of their quarters, where they were propped and bleeding from chest and stomach wounds. Another lay motionless, face down in the dirt, blood clumping like slaughterhouse sawdust in the cool loose soil.

"Pedro! Pedro!" Phil yelled.

"Phil..." moaned Pedro from inside the barracks. A trail of blood led up the steps. Protruding from the threshold of the open door was Pedro's varicose veined left calf, a dilapidated flip flop hanging by a thread from his foot.

"Phil," Pedro moaned again. Phil vaulted the steps, clearing Pedro's leg, and landed inside the door. Pedro was sprawled on his back, shot through the thigh, blood squirting in jets from what Phil supposed was an artery. He dropped to his knees, pulled the drawstring from his shorts, and wrapped it tightly around Pedro's leg between the groin and the wound. It took every bit of his strength to cinch the tourniquet tight enough to staunch the bleeding.

"Hold this tight," he told Pedro. "I'm goin' to get Vlad."

The sun was high by the time Ian arrived with a doctor and medical supplies. Three, including Pedro's mother, were already dead. Two suffered critical injuries, including Pedro, and three including Miguel suffered wounds from which they would recover. A cadre of the armed guards who usually joined Miguel escorting drug shipments into camp also materialized, securing a perimeter around the camp and taking inventory of the damage. The worksites had been demolished, including two new ekranoplans, and Vlad was gone.

"Mattah of time," said Ian perfunctorily. "I did warn you."

"But why did they take him? Why Vlad?" Phil pleaded.

"I dunno, Phil. Use your imagination," Ian countered cryptically.

"You reckon they want their own ekranoplan builder?"

"Bob's your uncle, mate. And who says they took him? Who says his bags weren't packed? Who says he didn't help plan the attack?"

"You really think so? Join the Zeta?"

"Fair go, mate. But stranger things have happened. You're in the cartel world. More goes on than meets the eye." Ian paused, took in his surroundings, then leaned in close to Phil's ear. "And where were *you* when this shit happened, mate? How did *you* manage to stay clear?"

"What the fuck do you mean, Ian? You accusing me of something?"

"Calm down, mate. Don't get your knickers in a twist," said Ian, holding Phil's shoulders and looking in his eyes. "But you weren't there, mate, and people will ask. Pedro will ask. No one's above suspicion."

"Just like José," said Phil.

"Fair dinkum. Just like José."

It was dumb luck he was passed out on the beach far from camp when the attack came. It was not so lucky the attackers came from the sea, and probably trapesed right over him on their way into camp. He could have sounded the alarm if he hadn't been comatose. Pedro reacted the way Ian anticipated.

"I trust *you*, Mr. Phil. I *trust you!*" Pedro bellowed from his sickbed. "*You* and *Vlad*. You suppose to watch the camp while José gone. When *I* am no here!" Pedro fulminated.

"So, José's coming back?" said Phil coolly.

"Yes."

"When?"

"When he finish in Bogotá."

"Finish what?" Phil persisted.

Staring down at Pedro, bandaged and incapacitated, he felt the old willfulness rise in him, the cockiness his daddy abhorred, and the restless individuality Marion adored. Marinating in the old sensation of his individuality, his ability to influence people and events, he saw in Pedro's vulnerability the opportunity to exercise it. Pedro would never be so weak again, if he managed to survive at all. It was Phil's last best chance to slay the man who had killed his uncle, unsympathetic as Mort had been to Phil's circumstances, and to repay the indignity of being taken from his home; the last best chance to avenge José's murder, and deliver swift retribution for threatening Manuela. The urge to cut Pedro down, before he recovered, was overwhelming. *Nature suffers nothing to remain in her kingdom which cannot help itself*, came Emerson's words to Phil spontaneously *...we must go alone.*

"You don't reckon José's dead?" said Phil with undisguised contempt. He meant to pick a fight, and Pedro squirmed.

"What you sayin'?"

"I ain't sayin' nothin', Pedro. I'm askin'," said Phil, leaning down into Pedro's face, "is José *dead*?" As he leaned his shadow fell on Pedro, turning Pedro's skin gray and wan in the shade. Pedro winced and broke his stare to reach for a morphine syrette. The doctor who arrived with Ian had provisioned him with a healthy supply. He contracted in agony to reach for a bag from which he spilled dozens of the miniature injection ampules. Fumbling one in his hand, he broke off the tip and slid the needle beneath the skin on his belly. In seconds his eyes were rolling in his head, and the moment for confrontation was lost.

"The fuckin' pendejos Zeta. I kill every last one," Pedro muttered.

"Like José?" said Phil, unwilling to stand down.

"You doe no nuttin'" said Pedro, looking away. "You doe no nuttin' about José. Nuttin'!"

"I know you killed him," said Phil, taking a knee, and putting his face in Pedro's.

"T'ings is no always what you see," Pedro replied, forming a V with his index and forefinger and pointing the tips at his eyes.

"Like José?" said Phil, pressing his advantage.

"Yes, like José..." said Pedro, smirking, "and also, many odder t'ings."

"Oh yeah? Like what other things, Pedro?" Phil dared him. "What other things ain't what I see?" The morphine took hold in earnest and Pedro's eyes glazed.

"What else ain't I seein'?" said Phil through his clenched teeth.

"Your uncle," Pedro whispered. He was far away.

"Yeah? What about my uncle, Pedro?" but Pedro was drifting, lost in morphine dreams. Phil reached for the gun Vlad had given him and lay it on Pedro's bandaged wound. Pedro seized in agony. His eyes bulged and he howled like an animal before parting with a stream of expletives in Spanish.

"We were talking about my uncle," Phil said calmly.

"You so fookin' estúpido, Mr. Phil. *You* so *fookin'* estúpido," Pedro gasped, frothing at the mouth in pain.

"Your uncle is no your uncle," said Pedro. "You want to know his real name? You want?" He was begging Phil to ask him.

"Bull*shit*," said Phil. "Don't lay this crap on me, Pedro. You killed my uncle, just like you killed José, and probably Vlad, for all I know." Pedro shook his head.

"No bullshit, Mr. Phil," Pedro mumbled. "He no your uncle. He is Harry Halliday, big tine mafioso from New York. He in witness protection because he blah, blah, blah," said Pedro, opening and shutting his hands like Muppet mouths.

"Too bad he doe know the Guajira knows all the banks, the bank he workin' in also. Halliday, he mucho bad guy, and you never even know, Mr. Phil!" he said, amusing himself enough to produce a weak peal of laughter.

"Bull*shit!*" said Phil in disbelief.

"No, Mr. Phil," said Pedro, murmuring and drifting. "You go askin' your frien' the sheriff, J.D. He tell you," he concluded, drifting and smiling as he went. Dadgum his father, he had done it again, taking to the grave secrets that would have changed his expectations considerably, not to mention explaining his supposed uncle's betrayal.

"Who else knew?" Phil asked slow and quiet, but Pedro was gone.

When Phil emerged into daylight from the shadows of the building, he ran straight into the workmen who had gathered in a tight knot around the door. Dozens of eyes greeted him expectantly. Vlad was gone, and Pedro incapacitated. Now they were looking to him, Phil realized disconcertingly, and that was even before they learned of José's demise.

"Let's go, vamonos," he said, making his way through the men, across the camp and toward the worksite.

"Clean up the mess! Back to work," was all he could think to say.

CHAPTER 25

Guajira Peninsula, Colombia

After burying three of their own, including Pedro's mother, and speculating hopelessly on Vlad's whereabouts, or if he might ever be returned, the mood was somber. He wanted to get the men busy. *Idle hands*, his daddy always said. The women who worked the firepit with Pedro's mother were disconsolate, but closed ranks and returned to feeding the men, understanding the salve of full bellies. Absent the cheerful patter of Pedro's mother, they cooked in silence, Manuela moving in their shadows, brooding, sad, and angry.

Keep the men to their routines, preserve a sense of normalcy - that was his instinct, to buy himself time. He guessed he was at a crossroads, but it felt like an abyss, where all the choices for the first time were his, and none of them good. Thank goodness the men wanted to work, driven to bring the worksites back to their former glory, removing the shattered cradles and breaking back the unsalvageable sections of ekranoplans destroyed in the attack.

Shards of torn sheet aluminum wing sections and mangled aluminum tube fuselage ribs littered the site. Where charges were placed directly on ekranoplans in production, whole sections would need rebuilding. Where parts awaiting assembly were damaged, many, with elbow grease and a blow torch, were recoverable. Everyone worked in silence, even Phil. They knew the setback was temporary, and yearned for the routines that first brought them together, though the work in Vlad's absence felt unnatural.

Pitching in with his men, Phil was carried back to winters in his daddy's lakeside workshop, listening to country music radio, daydreaming of Katie, restoring the luster of lake boats - sanding, stitching, varnishing. It was the best of diversions then and remained so now, besides bearing no resemblance but satisfying work to the life he left on the lake. He realized now how precarious had been his existence since the day he met Pedro – from the minute Pedro marched through his lake house door. But survive he had, at least so far.

There was just no accounting for luck, he mused. Pedro got lucky, his mother had not, nor did José, nor his uncle Mort, or whoever Mort really was. And as for Vlad, there was just no telling. Only Ian, on reflection, moved with impunity, by keeping his distance, and staying nowhere long.

By the second day, the worksites were clear and the serviceable elements of the wrecked ekranoplans were back in their cradles. The *Americanos* set to, breaking their backs to make up lost time. To what end, Phil wasn't sure. He put his head down, like his men, and kept working, burdened by knowing Pedro was healing and would soon regain his strength. The same fearful future hung on all their minds – a camp ruled by Pedro, more paranoid than before, and hellbent on avenging his mother's death. Then word spread that Pedro had disposed of José, giving rise to speculation Phil overheard among the men that his own days were numbered, it was a matter of time.

He reckoned they were right. He knew by now how Pedro

worked, how thin was his skin to slights and insults, and how feverishly he exacted revenge. Suspicion stalked Pedro like a feral cat, fueling his penchant for violence. First, guessed Phil, he would strike at the Zeta for taking his mother, and having evened the score with the outside enemy, he would look to his enemies within. One way or the other - by increasingly violent strike and counter-strike with the Zeta, or by murderous internal purges - *all* of their days were numbered, and they all seemed to know it.

And so it was, in the face of futility, and with the sure knowledge of his demise, that Phil thought the heretofore unthinkable – the calculated murder of Pedro, even and especially when Pedro was still down - to protect himself and his men; and also, just maybe, to extend the Zeta an olive branch. For so long as Pedro was alive, and Phil and his men continued turning out ekranoplans, the Guajira would hold the advantage, and the Zeta would never be satisfied. Darned if his stars didn't dim, thought Phil, the faster he made boats go.

"It's a pickle, ain't it, Ian?" said Phil when Ian brought back the doctor to call on Pedro. "They'd have killed him for sure if they'd know'd he was here. And they'll come on back just as soon as he gets even. Bunch more of us is gonna die 'cause of him," said Phil confidently.

"As it was in the beginning, mate. Nothing changes. These blokes have been killing each other since someone in America smoked the first joint."

"Ain't there a way out?" asked Phil, remembering his plan to escape on the first ekranoplan test run. "I mean, why don't we both jump into one of these birds, and *hasta luego*, we're outta here."

"Where you gonna go, mate?" said Ian, looking Phil straight in the eye. "You got someplace in mind? Far away, where they won't find you, where you'll be safe?"

"I reckon so."

"Not in America, you don't, mate. I hope you're thinking of someplace else." He wasn't, of course. He didn't know anywhere else *but* Lost Lake, and J.D., and Marion, and the McLeans, and even Boat Church, and all the folks around the lake who for years relied on his daddy, and for a time himself, to keep their boats running. Surely no one had taken his place. More surely still, they'd welcome him back.

"It's a great place, Ian," said Phil expectantly. "You should come. We could ride out of here together."

"Not likely, mate."

"Why not?"

"You don't wanna know."

Pedro took a turn unexpectedly for the worse, jabbing himself with morphine when he had the presence of mind again and again. It was probably a sin to wish for Pedro to die, but wish he did, calling on Pedro frequently in the hope of finding him dead. But Pedro hung on, drifting between madness and sentience. His precarious condition kept Phil hanging in the balance, between freedom come by naturally if Pedro failed to wake, and freedom seized sinfully, by helping Pedro along. Watching Pedro's belly rise and fall with his breath, Phil imagined the ways – suffocating him with his own pillow, or overdosing him with morphine while he slept. Pedro never looked so vulnerable and peaceful as he did now, and he'd never be so easy to finish off. As the ways of killing Pedro swirled in Phil's mind, Pedro's eyelids flickered. He stirred, opened his eyes and looked directly at Phil, as though he sensed the threat.

"What if I run off?" said Phil. Pedro stuck himself again.

"We find you," said Pedro, smiling.

"Yeah? How?"

"Same way we find Halliday, your Uncle Mort. We have the eyes," Pedro said, pointing to his eyes, "and the ears, everywhere," he continued, encompassing the universe with a wave of his arms. "We find you, Mr. Phil," he said, his smile giving way to a leer.

The familiar smell of lavender accompanied Manuela through the barracks door. Her belly had swollen considerably since the last time Phil saw her. She carried a tray bearing food for Pedro, and hesitated when she saw Phil. Pedro was hungry, and in a gruff, hostile voice demanded the food, which she placed in his reach by the bed. Then, avoiding Phil's eyes, she stepped out of range when Phil reached with his hand to touch her. She stopped momentarily at the barracks door to address Pedro in Spanish.

"Sí," Pedro replied. "Sí," he said again, and she was gone.

"You like bein' at the top, Mr. Phil?" Pedro taunted.

"How long did it take you to find Mort?" Phil persisted, determined to press Pedro as he tore into some bread.

"We always know he dere. He jus' startin' to blah, blah, blah, so tine to *sssffftt*," said Pedro, drawing his thumb across his neck, "and he no talkin' no more."

"And that was your plan all along, when you come to see me? You planned to come in my house and kill him, just like that?"

"No, no, no, Mr. Phil," said Pedro, rocking his head back and forth on his pillow. "I come see *you*, Mr. Phil, to buy your boat for Vlad. See if Vlad can make such a fast boat. I plan to kill Halliday anodder time, but I find him with you, and the bank is takin' *your* work," he said with a disapproving scowl. "Den Pedro, he have a magnifico idea," he continued, tapping his temple with his index finger. "I kill Halliday to make look like *you* did, and then you have to come with Pedro! We no just get the boat, we get even better! We get Mr. Phil!" said Pedro with his old flare.

"Is that so?"

"Síí...." said Pedro in his sing-song way, "and then," he said, raising his finger like a professor, "estúpida policia no go lookin' for our eyes and ears in the witness protection program," he added, winking, "because they tinkin' Mr. Phil kill Halliday for the bank takin' his business." Pedro looked enormously pleased with himself. "You no can hide, Mr. Phil! You one of us, 'til you die."

Not a day in his life had passed, he reckoned, when he knew the full story, had the full picture of events unfolding around him. His daddy left him in debt, and had to have known about Mort; then Pedro staged Mort's death in a way that forced him to flee to Guajira. Framing him even camouflaged the cartels' informants in the witness protection program. What a fool he had been to play along, and without even knowing he was doing it. It didn't make him proud. *You one of us 'til you die...* is what Pedro said. Was he right?

And what if Vlad was right, too? What if he *had* changed? Was he more and more now a stranger to himself, or becoming the thing for which God always intended him - a fuller, stronger, more determined version of himself? It was easy to blame Pedro for putting him in distress, except Pedro never forced him. The truth was he had never resisted, not the way he should have were he truly averse to the prospects. He searched deep in his past for some furtive predilection, some formative, disfiguring event that predestined him to malign inclinations like the willingness to take up with Pedro, and now to thoughts of killing him.

What he found surprised him. Not bad advice – not even spiritual or intellectual deficit due to gaps in his self-styled education, but his nature – the irrepressible urge to chart his own course come what may against even the most intractable of obstacles, and maybe without thinking too hard. It was the call of Emerson's words, to which he had long let his heart bend, that he credited now for his troubles, for *...to be yourself in a world that is constantly trying to make you something else [is] the greatest accomplishment...* That's what he reckoned he'd done, as impulsive as that sounded to him now.

Stubborn, blind, willful – it explained pretty much all of it, he chided himself, though what he was fighting against he couldn't exactly say, nor could he say why. From school and homework, to the lake boat maintenance doctrine preached by his father, to rejection by McLean and Mort, everything he was and had been was the impulsive reaction of an adolescent to fate. *It ain't too late,* he assured himself. *It ain't too late - to think.*

Deciding what he wasn't turned out to be easier than deciding what he was. He was no Guajira, no drug runner, no *ill wind*, and no killer either. *Shameful.* He could hear his father say it, and he knew it was all his doing - falling in among the Guajira, the drinking and smoking, taking up with Manuela in sin. He had run her off with his boorish behavior when what he should have done was protect her. He had succumbed to flattery, invited attack from the Zeta by churning out ekranoplans, perhaps all as Pedro had intended. He was in it now, and deep...*you one of us 'til you die*...not the least bit the master of his destiny the way he once thought, but a pawn to forces he couldn't see, in a scheme that defied imagination.

Ashamed as his father might be, what right with all his secrets, had his father to judge; especially when, for all Phil's shortcomings, his fall held the prospect of redemption - a following - the hearts of his men, who, love him or fear him, would do what he asked when the time came.

On his next visit with Pedro, Phil arrived moved if not committed to mending his ways and resuming a righteous path, with a better idea than murder. Something needed to change, for the better this time, and the change had to come from him. The time for thoughtlessness was over.

"Pedro," he said. Pedro stirred but his eyes stayed shut. Phil proceeded on the assumption he could be heard. "This don't end, do it. They attack us, we attack them. We're all gonna get killed, sooner or later, ain't we? We just got lucky this time."

"Lucky?" said Pedro doubtfully, opening his eyes. They looked clear and vindictive. "I no see no bullet holes in *you*!"

"What are you sayin'?" said Phil, tired of Pedro's threats. Calmly, Phil drew his gun and lay it on the bed next to Pedro's bandaged thigh, a warning to mind his manners or he'd be punished again. He felt perilously close to reversing course altogether and finishing Pedro off, but commanding Pedro's attention, and lifted by hope, Phil continued. "You think I was involved? same as you thought José was involved with losing that sub?" Pedro stared at him hard. As he tried to sit up he howled in agony, and reached for another syrette, jabbing himself again in a spot on his belly with prick scars enough to look like acne.

"Listen to me, Pedro. I got an idea. We got attacked cause we ain't getting caught, right? And we ain't getting' caught cause the ekranoplans is so damn fast, right? So, I was thinkin', what if we share some with them? What if we *all* start using ekranoplans? Turn our enemies to friends." He watched the morphine take hold, and Pedro swoon. Before too long he'd drift off altogether.

"Hey, Pedro, what do you think?"

"Always the caballero, Mr. Phil," Pedro murmured.

"I don't know about that," said Phil, reminded of the temptation still fresh in his mind to snuff Pedro, "but it just makes sense, don't it?"

"*No!*" said Pedro, his eyes widening as he fought off the morphine. "You maybe caballero, but you *estúpido* caballero! You think we no get caught cause of ekranoplans. *No!* We no get caught 'cause Pedro pay to the fuckin' Coast Guard mucho plata, comprender? You understand?" He was losing the bout to stay conscious.

"Then why'd y'all go to all the trouble of bringin' me here? If the ekranoplans ain't makin' no difference, *why*?" Pedro's eyes filled with venom, even as they turned to glass. "Don't fuck with me, Pedro," said Phil, keeping Pedro focused. "I'm here and I don't want to be. You want me to keep buildin' these things, we do it my way. I'm sharing them with the Zeta. I'm not dying here."

"Yes, Mr. Phil," Pedro murmured, his eyes cold and hazy. "You dyin' here, Mr. Phil, by me or the Zeta, I no care."

More aware than ever of the thing he was becoming, new strains of Emerson rang in his ears. *Napoleon said of Messina,* Emerson had written, *that he was not himself until the battle began to go against him; then, when the dead began to fall in ranks around him, awoke his powers of combination, and he put on terror and victory as a robe.* Gently, Phil lifted his gun and bounced the barrel on Pedro's wound. Pedro awoke in startled pain, cursing a blue steak in Spanish.

"If that's so, Pedro," said Phil softly, "and I'm dying here, one way or t'other, then I ain't got nothin' to lose, do I?"

CHAPTER 26

Organized Crime Drug Enforcement Task Forces Fusion Center, Washington, D.C.

Lenny hadn't been thinking so clearly when he pulled out of Lost Lake. Moira had been up to something, and so was the damned sheriff, J.D. Dunbar. He knew it was complicated, and he knew just as well he was too emotional to make sense of it, so he reverted to the facts: the circumstances of the murder and the timing of the SAR issued by the local building and loan. The sheriff's doubts about the prime suspect sounded genuine enough, but Lenny wasn't buying the sheriff's detachment. The sheriff had motives aplenty.

The nine-hour return drive to Washington had been time enough for his nerves to settle. He believed in instincts, and Sheriff Dunbar's suspicion of Morales was striking a chord. Now that he was back at his desk, he had a narrative supporting the sheriff's doubts that made sense of the SAR. It also meant Morales was more than your garden variety mob hitman. The SAR had been issued to give Morales cover and frame Perdue – Morales and the bank had coordinated – but why? To shield Morales from suspicion, or to implicate Perdue in particular? Lenny couldn't say. Not yet. Whether Morales killed Perdue later, or took him for indoctrination into gang life didn't matter. Morales had achieved his objectives – silencing Halliday, and leaving a more credible suspect than himself, whose case wasn't strengthening in the suspect's absence.

The sheriff was right on one count, if not entirely forthcoming. Perdue's guilt was too neat. Moira's tip was troubling, too, not least for how it had drawn him in - there was no chance in hell he would have crossed paths with Lost Lake but for Moira. There was the prominence of her father, and his role at the bank that issued the conspicuous SAR. There was the meeting between Dunbar and Malcolm McLean on the lake, during which McLean purportedly favored Morales' alibi against the conflicting testimony of his own daughter – what kind of father did that? It strained credibility, if it was true at all. And last but not least, the small matter of his ruse to entrap the sheriff, which he had - the disinformation about an impending Lost Lake sting operation had made the roundtrip from the sheriff down to Bogotá and back to a Homeland Security Committee staffer in record time.

The more Lenny stewed the more the whole thing stank, and slowly, cryptically, a countervailing narrative took shape. The sheriff had a motive for defending Perdue – the sheriff *himself* was the witness protection insider who gave up Halliday, possibly even coordinating the murder. *He* was implicating Morales to divert from Perdue and the success of the undetected money laundering operation through the Farmers Building and Loan of Lost Lake. In a bigoted southern backwater, there was no easier target than Morales. Katie McLean's account of seeing Pedro with Phil was fabricated, probably by the sheriff himself, to make Morales a credible suspect. That version accounted much better for the convoluted hearsay and circumstances, but how to get to the bottom of it? *Begin at the beginning*, he had always instructed interns, like Moira. Always start at the source.

* * * * *

"I thought we agreed to a clean break," said Moira, answering Lenny's call on the first ring.

"We did. That was before your little tip on the Lost Lake Farmer's Building and Loan."

"That took you long enough. You losing your touch?"

"Why not just report it? Why not tell me, before you left?"

"I did report it. It's in the report, where you found it. God, Lenny. That was two years ago."

"When were you going to tell me you were the Chairman's daughter?" said Lenny, holding in his hands the FinCEN personnel profiles Dan Thorne couriered over. "Some big axe you have to grind, dragging SOD in to settle a score with the old man. Is that the deal?"

"I forgot how sweet you could be, Lenny. I've really missed you."

"Answer the question. Is that the deal?" Silence. "Hello? Moira? Is that the goddamned deal?"

"No."

"Or were you the family's eyes and ears, the thing everyone suspected you of?"

"What?" she asked, sounding disoriented.

"Don't play dumb, Moira. It's beneath you. Were you *probing* for what we might already know about your old man's dealings?"

"A *probe*, Lenny? Really? How absurd."

"Is it? Next thing you know you're going to tell me you know Phil Perdue."

"Yes," said Moira unapologetically.

"You *do*?" Lenny bellowed, incredulous. "Well that's just fucking great! When were you going to tell me that?"

"Well, not so much know him as know *of* him. Everyone in Lost Lake knows Phil. Why?"

"Well it just so happens he's the odds-on favorite for murdering a local in witness protection, and cutting out his tongue, you know, the way families do when someone talks too much."

"God, that's awful," said Moira sounding genuinely troubled.

"What the hell is going on here, Moira? Are you with us, or against us?"

She wasn't sure, disillusioned as she had been by Lenny's tactics during her summer internship at Fusion. Being completely honest with herself, it wasn't impossible that the footnote she buried in the report about the Lost Lake Farmers Building and Loan was a subliminal swipe at her father. Her shrink always told her to mind her subconscious. It saw, felt, and acted on things way over the horizon, way beyond conscious perception. What dark secret did she have on her father of which only her subconscious was aware?

She knew the bank was one of many in the far-flung realm of the holding company her father ruled. Duncan had worked there, after all, or been given a position there. And there was no denying she was angry - angry enough to want retribution. Years of therapy after her parents divorced bore that out. But Lenny was insinuating something darker, more complex, as often he did. She was determined to frustrate him if it was another of his absurd conspiracy theories, and she could tell he was spoiling for one of his witch hunts. If the work she did that summer caused her father some trouble, so be it, but there was no more to it than that. She refused to be drawn in or implicated.

"Follow your nose, Lenny. Isn't that what you always told us?"

"You need to come to the office. I need answers."

"Are you accusing me of something?" Lenny wasn't sure, and

law school, from which she was now a gleaming, overpaid graduate, had achieved the desired effect - she wouldn't be brought to heel. He hung up the phone. His predicament left him precious little time to gather facts before he would be forced to recuse himself from pursuing an investigation. *Their* relationship, and *her* relationships, especially in Lost Lake, were a Rubik's Cube of worrisome combinations. His judgment would be questioned, for good reason, and for the first time he questioned it himself.

* * * * *

It didn't help that the war on drugs hadn't gone well in the years since Moira filed her report and went back to school. Despite Fusion's best efforts, and the efforts of all the agencies collaborating on interdiction, more drugs than ever were reaching U.S. shores. Part of the evolving strategy was to infiltrate the cartels to gather more information about how they operated. The problem was using it. When drug interdiction task forces acted on inside tips, brutal purges followed, and the information dried up. Worse still, in a mortal game played exclusively for money, the cartels held the upper hand, offering more and paying more than U.S. agencies to informers who survived the purges. U.S. drug enforcement couldn't hold the beachheads it tried to establish. When it placed valuable human assets inside Colombia, it gave up more intelligence about itself than it gathered about the cartels.

Over time, the DEA made uneasy peace with using double agents, human intel assets who made a dangerous game of informing to both sides, preserving their value to each. These were the true mercenaries of the drug wars, supplying just enough information to ensure a contest of wits without end, and at great expense to the American taxpayer. It drove Lenny to distraction, but gave him the kernel of an idea for how to make use of Moira.

Sam finalized his PATT reports forty-eight hours after Lenny returned from Lost Lake, copying Lenny on the document he sent to SOD for review and release. Board members and officers of every member bank in the sprawling ownership of the Atlanta Guaranty and Trust Company, N.A., fit the profile of any number of usual suspects, who had turned their small and medium sized businesses over to money laundering.

"This thing stinks," said Lenny to Dan Thorne, Director of FinCEN, as he perused Sam's PATT report.

"Don't I know it," Thorne concurred casually. "We're looking at the wire traffic now. There's money in small denominations coming from everywhere running through Atlanta G&T affiliates from Birmingham to Charlotte – coming from all the usual places - Monaco, Liechtenstein, the Caymans – there's layering happening here, no question." Something in Thorne's tone wasn't impressed.

"You seeing placement, too? I'm looking at small and medium sized businesses in the U.S., the Southeast in particular," said Lenny sounding intentionally vague. "We ran a *Smurf* hunt a couple years back and didn't come up with much. We think, now, we might have missed something."

"Send me a list of company names and I'll have one of our people run them down," offered Thorne.

"It's probably nothing," said Lenny disingenuously, "a boat business in northeast Georgia using a local building and loan."

"A boat business, hunh?" said Thorne, as though it could mean something. "In Georgia? Doesn't ring a bell, at least not *that* boat business. One of the more interesting cross-borders was from a naval architecture firm in Bogotá. Let's see here," said Thorne, his fingers working the keyboard audibly through the phone.

"Here it is, the Empresa de Ingeniería y Construcción Maritimo de Bogotá, S.A. *Ever heard of* that *boat business, Lenny?"*

It sounded familiar, or maybe not. Unpronounceable Hispanic

names populated every aspect of Lenny's day-to-day routine, running together in an unintelligible vowel soup.

"Not sure, Danny. Should I know it?"

"Yes."

"Can you give me more than that?"

"No. Suffice it to say, there's a lot going on here," said Thorne, sounding curiously subdued.

"I knew it!" said Lenny. "It's a nest of bad guys. We're gonna hit them like a freight train. Some good ol' boys are going to Sing Sing before we're through here."

"I'd be careful on this one, Lenny," said Thorne, absent the encouragement Lenny expected.

"Why?" Lenny asked as Sam materialized at his door, waving a file.

"Not my place to say, really. You're on your own on this one, Lenny. Good luck," said Thorne sounding ready to end the call. "And Lenny?" Thorne added before hanging up, "be careful."*Good luck? Be careful?* It meant *your favors are all used up*.

The difference between Lenny and Dan Thorne, Lenny reminded himself, was political aspiration. Lenny had none, and Dan Thorne was a political empresario. He believed in the mission so far as it aligned with his career goals. Missions with the potential to undermine his advancement died on the vine. It's why Lenny was a career operative, and why Dan was a political appointee, chosen by the Treasury Secretary, who was in turn appointed by the President. Dan never speculated. He worked with the facts, some of which he shared, most of which he didn't. If Thorne was warning Lenny, he had a good reason.

Sam was still at Lenny's door, file in hand, staring like a school boy at his shoes outside the principal's office when Lenny looked up.

"Let me guess, Sam," Lenny said contemplatively, "Moira?"

"Yeah."

"She's become a problem," Lenny conceded.

"She always *was* a problem," Sam assured him, "from the very beginning."

"I know, I know. It should never have happened. I should never have let it happen."

"It's worse than you think," said Sam, placing the folder on Lenny's desk. "You wanna read it in private, or shall I give you the headlines?"

"Give me the whole thing, chapter and verse."

"Remember the Lost Lake sting operation story you laid on our friend, Sheriff Dunbar?"

"Sure, the one that made the round trip to and from Colombia in record time?... Wait a minute, Sam," said Lenny, snapping his fingers to trigger his memory. What had Thorne said about a boat business in Colombia? "Where in Colombia did you pick up that intercept?"

"Some marine engineering company. That's not the point," said Sam, intent on moving Lenny along.

"The hell it's not," Lenny interrupted. "What goddamn marine engineering company?"

Sam couldn't recall. It was in the transcripts and he'd get Lenny the name. The point was the second intercept, the one coming back from Colombia to the U.S. *That* intercept was a call to a staffer attached to the Senate Subcommittee on Homeland Security and Governmental Affairs. The subcommittee consisted of fourteen Senators, including Charles H. Wingate, Republican from Georgia, whose staffer took the call from Bogotá.

"Take a wild ass guess who runs campaign finance for Senator Wingate," Sam posed breathlessly. He never gave Lenny the opening to answer. "Malcolm McLean."

"No shit, Sam."

"Yeah, Lenny. Wingate's the bastard who runs on law and order and wants to cut our funding because the war on drugs is a waste of money."

"Right. Another *build the wall* guy, as if the cartels don't have twelve ways to go over, around and under it."

"Lenny," said Sam insistently, "you're missing the point. We just cycled a network and closed the loop through Wingate's staffer. What are the chances Wingate is taking drug money?"

That would make sense of Dan Thorne's reticence. Wingate was close to the President, oft cited as the President's natural successor to lead the Republican Party. Moira's father was his campaign chairman, and that put her much closer to the fire than even Lenny imagined. If she had been doing her father's bidding, probing for suspicion Fusion may have developed about Senator Wingate's fund-raising operation, Lenny's career was over, and Fusion was in for an overhaul. But the clue she left ran contrary to that theory. In fact, *"CPOT?"* which was all she had written, hardly protected her father. She had implicated him, if he was the CPOT she meant. But her notation was not specific, just a tag on the Farmers Building and Loan of Lost Lake. She could have meant any of the Lost Lake locals she knew, including the one the sheriff appeared to be protecting.

* * * * *

Moira had been sitting at home bemused by Lenny's call, wondering at his anger and impertinence after two years of radio silence. He didn't act that way unless he were hot on a trail, which meant he was bound to call back. And for that she was glad, not because she missed him, but because her father had him fulminating, and that intrigued her. How in the world had *he* gotten Lenny's attention? In matters of love he was a well-known philistine, but in business and politics he was held in the highest regard. Therapy had helped her bury the hatchet and move past a turbulent childhood, but only because she judged her father impregnable, and bearing a grudge took too much out of her. What if she had inadvertently exposed him? Whatever Lenny had found sounded worth knowing.

"Who did you mean by *CPOT*?" said Lenny when she picked up the phone.

"No small talk, Lenny?"

"Don't waste my time, Moira. We don't have much."

"We?"

"Yes, *we*."

"And why is that, Lenny?"

"I'm going down, Moira, and I'm taking you with me, so you better start singin'."

"Going down for what, Lenny? It's always the same with you – presumption of guilt. I didn't *do* anything."

What if she hadn't?

"I need to know what you meant by *CPOT* in your report." Circumstantial evidence however thin spelled conspiracy to Lenny, and the evidence against Moira wasn't thin. Her father's banks were money laundering, and the campaign finance operation of a senior Senator, close to the President, and with oversight of Homeland Security, was in close proximity to, if not comingling with drug money.

"Who knows, Lenny? It was years ago," she answered, sounding tired. "Maybe it *was* a shot at my father. I am, Lenny, according to my therapist, an angry person. You of all people should understand anger."

It was better than your average plea of innocence, and wittingly or unwittingly she had dropped a dime on her own her father when her father was nowhere in Fusion's sights. And McLean had all the makings of a big fish. Sam Rosen's signal intelligence said so, as did the information Dan Thorne scrounged up at FinCEN; and then there was Dan Thorne's conspicuous warning and hasty retreat. How innocent could Moira be?

"You regret it?" she continued.

"Regret what?" Lenny snapped. Regret wasn't in his repertoire, or so he thought.

"Us."

Yes, Lenny regretted *us* deeply. With perfect hindsight it was the biggest mistake of his life, of his career. And for the first time maybe ever, he chose his words carefully.

"Not in a personal sense, Moira, no. But professionally, yes. It was unprofessional and it will cost me my career, and you your freedom, if it turns out you're involved."

"Involved in what?"

Who *is* this woman, Lenny wondered? She wasn't just disarming, she was good. She would never concede to knowledge of her father's dealings, whether she knew of them or not, and she had tied Lenny's hands. Authorizing a CPOT investigation of his former lover's father more than strained credibility, and he was jaded and insecure enough to suspect this had been her motivation from the start – to inoculate her father by compromising Lenny, and any of his Fusion directives. Who's side she was really on would elude Lenny forever, and he knew it.

"I guess that's how it's going to be," he concluded. "But don't be too cute, Moira. I didn't show you all my tricks," and he disconnected the line. The number two pencil he gnawed at habitually while speaking on the phone disintegrated in his mouth.

"Jesus," said Sam as he reappeared before Lenny. "You ought to try gum. You're gonna die of lead poisoning."

"What you got, Sammy?"

"Mystery solved."

"What mystery?"

"How they're moving so much dope undetected."

"What are you talking about, Sam?"

"You asked me where the call originated, right?"

"Call?" It looked to Sam like Lenny was somewhere else.

"The call from Colombia to Wingate's staffer, from the marine engineering company? It came from the..." Sam hesitated and dropped his eyes, to read from the transcript he was holding. "The *Empresa de Ingeniería y Construcción Maritimo de Bogotá, S.A.*"

"Of course," Lenny noted despairingly. "The same place FinCEN identified, according to Dan Thorne."

That was news to Sam, but it didn't surprise him. If Wingate were taking drug money, an inconspicuous rural building and loan on the fringes of his campaign chair's banking conglomerate was as good a clearing house as any, maybe even better than most.

"We have a source inside that organization that says the cartels are using a new delivery vehicle," said Sam, handing Lenny a grainy black and white photograph.

"What the fuck is that?" said Lenny.

"It's called an ekranoplan, some kind of super-fast, low flying thingamajig invented by the Russians."

"No shit. First submarines, now..."

"Ekranoplans," said Sam.

"Whatever. Is Border Patrol looking for these things?"

"They will be soon, boss."

"Who's providing that intel? What's the source?" Lenny inquired skeptically.

"Can't say. A deep cover SOD asset." Lenny groaned. Their shared suspicions of SOD, which vetted Fusion's reports, tainted everything SOD generated. It was hardly coincidental, thought Lenny, that SOD should have a deep cover asset inside a Colombian marine engineering company that was looking more and more like a cartel front for financing dirty U.S. politicians. It was also the first hard evidence of collusion between SOD and yet another Colombian cartel. What the hell was SOD up to this time?

CHAPTER 27

U.S. Coast Guard Cutter *Osprey*, Atlantic Ocean – 6 Months Later

"Why are we patrolling east of the Bahamas, Captain?" asked Dougie Burbank. "...more than a thousand miles from the Kessel Run. We're totally out of the fight."

"Yeah, it's a fuckin' mystery, ain't it Dougie?" Gutterson interjected. "We catch the first narco sub, make the biggest bust in interdiction history, and the next thing you know we're divided up and put on parade like a bunch of fuckin' organ grinder monkeys touting our heroics."

"That was a long time ago, Hank. And that tour kept both your salary and your flying habit funded," Buldoc replied. "If we don't have another bust soon, HITRON gets the axe."

Gutterson, Dougie and Casey Tindall, the now famous HITRON team, had been reunited with Buldoc aboard the *Osprey* more than two years after achieving their major interdiction success. They knew exactly what Buldoc meant. During their publicity tour, cocaine had flooded into every major U.S. east coast, west coast, and Gulf coast city. Gang violence was spiking, and the U.S. faced another major drug crisis. Oversupply had driven down street prices more than seventy percent, and nobody could say why the war on drugs was faring so poorly.

"So why the hell are we out here?" Dougie asked. "And why for so goddamned long?" added Gutterson. "It's not like we've seen any action and we've been out here for months."

"Grasping at straws, I guess," said Buldoc. "They're a million theories on how so much coke is reaching our shores, but nobody knows. Some think the narcos have acquired the technology to build fully submersible submarines, which we'll never find from the air. Others think they've shifted their routes further out to sea."

"So they stick us out in the middle of fuckin' nowhere, hoping we'll catch a stray go-fast headed over to Europe? That makes a *ton* of sense," Gutterson offered. Even Buldoc knew it was a reach, but his orders were clear.

"Here's a theory for you," Gutterson ventured sarcastically. "Homeland Security is funding a bunch of other shit with cartel money, which is why GANTSEC can't find their backsides with both hands when it comes to actually catching anybody. We're out here in no-man's land where we can't get in the way. What about *that* fuckin' theory?" Dougie nodded. Casey cringed. They had all been thinking the same thing, even Buldoc, by the look on his face. And they felt more alone than ever - God forbid another drama unfold, without HMS Argyll nearby.

"Go burn some avgas and fly your mission, boys. I'll see you for debrief at 1700. Good luck."

They flew grids over the turquoise Atlantic east of the Bahamas all afternoon. No Joy. Casey fired a few compulsory rounds at stray flotsam for target practice, but the waters below were as clear and calm and empty as ever. Even drones were too precious to fly top cover in the remote waters they were patrolling.

"We've been put out to pasture," Gutterson pronounced, flopping into his debrief chair after completing the afternoon patrol.

"This is a con job. We all know it, Captain," he said speaking to Buldoc and the LEDET team leader, Mike Gregson. Gregson's appearance at post-mission debriefs was rare. When he showed, he came with fresh intel, or at least intel fresh to *Osprey's* HITRON team. Gregson was a chunk of man - tall, broad, with chiseled features that made him look to Gutterson like GI Joe. He was wearing fatigues, a side arm, and webbing that bristled with pockets chock full of who knows what.

"Something new?" Dougie asked, guessing at the only explanation for Gregson's presence.

"This oughtta be good," Gutterson mumbled. "If it's coming to *us* it's a diversion or months out of date," he muttered through the side of his mouth to Dougie.

"Now, now," said Buldoc. "This is priority one general intel from our friends at Fusion. Probably has no effect on us at all, way out here in the middle of nowhere, but it's worth its weight in entertainment value, if nothing else. Briefing packets are in your quarters. Contents go something like this..."

Buldoc went on to describe what appeared to be unprecedented collaboration among the cartels, led by a heretofore small and unimportant challenger to the Zeta. After pioneering the use of narco subs, with the help of freelance Russian naval architects and engineers, the *Guajira*, sometimes called the *Americanos*, had developed a specialty – high speed, low signature, delivery vehicles known as ekranoplans. Ekranoplans, not coincidentally, were also the handiwork of Russians that gave Soviet era war planners nuclear first strike capability.

The entertainment part was this: It was the Guajira whose cocaine packed submarine the *Osprey* HITRON and LEDET teams had captured almost three years before – the first-ever narco sub recovered with one hundred percent of its cargo. The Guajira weren't just in the drug trafficking trade anymore. They were in the shipping business, too, supplying cargo capacity to all comers, their blood sworn enemies, the Zeta, included. This was thought to explain the waves of cocaine washing ashore on U.S. soil, and the conspicuous decline in intercepted shipments, or so the brief said. Gutterson, to no one's surprise, was skeptical.

The ekranoplans, said Gregson, were being reconfigured from production piston and gas turbine aircraft. The resulting vehicles were believed to fly faster than the models from which they were derived because their stubby, cormorant-like wings, induced so little drag, and because the cushion of ground effect air on which they rode was more frictionless than a maglev train. The only resistance they encountered was fourteen-point-seven pounds per square inch of sea level atmosphere.

"You'll be lucky to keep up with one of these things," said Gregson, "let alone overtake it, or capture one." Gutterson was incensed.

"Why the hell aren't we on station back in our old patrol zone, skipper? The damn Kessell Run - that's where we nailed the sub. That's where these damn things will be. Maybe we can't catch them, but we can intercept them. All Casey needs is one clear shot, right Casey?"

"Those aren't our orders, Hank," Buldoc reminded him.

"Sir?" Casey chimed in, "what's the range on these things?"

Buldoc nodded knowingly.

"At least *someone* on your team is thinking," said Buldoc. "Nobody knows, Casey, ...they'll fly at least as far as the aircraft from which they're derived, and possibly much further, if they've been modified for long range. That's why we're out here. Some folks think they're launching from the north coast of Colombia and transiting via the Windward Passage between Haiti and Cuba, here," Buldoc continued, pointing to a wall map, "and the Mona Passage, east of Puerto Rico, here, before turning northwest, skirting east of the Bahamas, and then heading for wherever they make their rendezvous. With so much speed and range, almost every city on the east coast is an option for landing their cargos. They're likely converging with go-fasts offshore that disperse the cargos to multiple landing points."

"That makes them unstoppable," said Dougie dejectedly, "unless we catch them offloading."

"Tactically, that's right," said Gregson. "Our jobs just got so hard we might not keep them. But strategically, they could do themselves in, at least in the short term," Gregson continued.

"*What?*" said Gutterson incredulously.

"Sure," said Gregson before launching into an epistle about price wars and the dynamics of rival U.S. distributors that had nothing to do with interrupting the flow of drugs crossing their patrol zone. He would have put his audience to sleep but for his power to keep them relevant. Gregson and his LEDET team made the arrests and recovered the cargo without which HITRON was doomed.

Gutterson had his own reasons to listen. He knew that but for HITRON he was unemployable. There was no reversing his military discharge, and none of the oil and gas airlift operations would have him, even if they wanted him. His record with OSHA and three industry safety compliance bureaus made him toxic, radioactive. Any *incident* – industry parlance for *catastrophic industrial accident* – with an employee like Gutterson in the vicinity was uninsurable. The next stop for Hank was the beach.

Gregson described how the plummeting street price of cocaine was expanding the market of buyers and users, as well as the sophistication and number of distributors serving them. Fights were breaking out everywhere as distributors challenged each other for market share.

"Let 'em fight," said Gutterson. "The more spilled blood back home, the more money Congress will find for the war on drugs."

"Maybe," Gregson acknowledged, "but there's more." The intel said the instability was rattling the cartels themselves. They were struggling to move product through the changing faces of increasingly glutted and complex channels. The beneficence of the Guajira – sharing ekranoplans – to ensure everyone got product to market, had kept the peace in Colombia, but fomented conflict in the United States. Like OPEC ministers defending the price of oil, there was cartel chatter about suppressing production. "Here's what's not in the brief," Gregson continued. "SIGINT thinks the call for order is coming from inside the U.S., not from the cartels."

"No kidding," said Gutterson. "Let me guess, Homeland Security."

"Don't think so," said Gregson. "More likely a distributor losing ground at home, with something to hold over the cartels." Casey wheezed, the sound he made when he was thinking.

"What is it?" said Gutterson.

"You said the *Guajira*, sometimes known as the *Americanos*. Is that why?" Gregson looked puzzled.

"Is what why?"

"You said the call for order is coming from the U.S. Are the Guajira Americans?"

"Wait," Dougie interjected. "I thought you said they were Russian."

"These guys aren't picky," said Gregson, "but no, that's not why. We think they sometimes go by *Americanos* because there's an American who has risen through the ranks, seems to have built a following. We don't know much about him. We're not even sure he exists, but with so many disaffected U.S. expatriates freelancing in Central America, it's not hard to imagine."

"Traitor," Gutterson muttered. "What I wouldn't do to get my hands on him, but what are the chances of that, way the hell out here."

"Maybe better than you think," said Gregson. "With so many of our assets concentrated on the old routes, we expect the cartels to try new ones. Just as Captain Buldoc said, we're here to outflank them. Maybe we'll get lucky - the way our friend, the *Americano,* may not."

"Say what?" said Gutterson.

"Disrupting this market comes with a price, and the Guajira will pay it. No one wants the violence and no one likes the prices - he'll be killed by his own people. But that won't solve our ekranoplan problem."

CHAPTER 28

Guajira Peninsula, Colombia

Phil hadn't wasted a minute of Pedro's convalescence - there was just no telling how long Pedro would be incapacitated - so he had gone to work in earnest. He gambled with the loyalty of his men, ordering them to clear enough jungle to triple production, pushing them hard to produce ekranoplans faster, and encouraging the pilots to promote the superior speed and elusiveness of ekranoplans to the broader cartel flying community. He prevailed on the colorful freelance pilot of *Roll Tide*, Jim Bartsch, to extend the Zeta an olive branch by offering them a test run of his ship, and promised them a fleet of their own in exchange for peace. Naturally suspicious, the Zeta responded tepidly, wasting time Phil didn't have. Not so for other low-profile cartels and cartelitos operating more nimbly than their bigger brethren. First pilots, then buyers, appeared in ones and twos on the Guajira camp beaches, and the ranks of the *Americanos* swelled as word spread among men seeking work across the peninsula that the Guajira were hiring. If he pulled it all together, the horse would be out of the barn long before Pedro could protest.

He reckoned on leaving nobody out, on leveling the trafficking playing field among smugglers throughout Colombia, so work-a-day rank and file laborers like his men could live in relative safety without fearing the violence of rivals. The surge in Guajira shipments after the first of his ekranoplans went into service was too impressive to go unnoticed, and when he encouraged the pilot network, against every rule and custom, to offer third-party shipping, he won friends and allies among drug runners everywhere. Flanked on all sides by cartelitos buying ekranoplans from the Guajira, and using them to devastating effect, the Zeta eventually relented, sending a small attachment of pilots carrying pales of cash for training and the purchase of several ekranoplans. Thus, did Phil neutralize the Guajira's greatest threat, and create the impression of ending Pedro's feud, all while Pedro remained bed-ridden.

But it was the growing orders Phil placed with Ian for manufacturing supplies and production aircraft that alerted the Guajira leadership to something more than good fortune unfolding in the distant camp. The lessons of the Cali and Medellín experience were to keep your head down, minimize your footprint, and keep operations nimble. In very short order the Guajira were on the map, buying and processing more raw cocoa, shipping more refined cocaine, offering third party logistics and transportation, and now selling delivery vehicles. Times were good and getting better, but how long would they last before attracting unwanted attention? Only the Zeta had failed to learn the lesson of *too big to succeed*, and they had paid time and again.

Ian, flanked by Miguel, delivered the message as Pedro's convalescence dragged on, his recovery more precarious as his morphine dependence deepened.

"I've warned you before, mate," said Ian, drawing up a chair in Phil's bungalow. "The nail that sticks up..."

"I know, I know... gets hammered down. I reckon you only said it a million times."

"Then what are you *doing*, mate? Building all these bloody ekranoplans and handing them out like drinks."

"Keepin' us alive, Ian. Zeta won't bother us again, you watch."

"Fair dinkem, mate. Maybe you've made peace down here, but keep this up and a war will break out in America."

Ian must have seen it all coming, and Phil wished he had listened, but the genie was out of the bottle. A cadre of men across the peninsula had now been schooled by Phil himself in dismantling production aircraft and reassembling them as ekranoplans. As Pedro declined and lingered near death, the doctor arrived by plane and airlifted him to a hospital in Bogotá, where he could receive better attention. Muted celebration followed, and the *Americanos*, swollen in rank, and rallying around Phil, worked with such esprit de corps that the little camp on the Guajira peninsula began delivering as many as half a dozen ekranoplans per month.

Those were the hay days. Phil had quit drinking and attended to Manuela in ways he always should have. With Vlad gone, he spent his evenings with Manuela outside Pedro's dead mother's lodgings, where she continued to reside. They talked about the baby, and their hopes for the childhood it might have someday, if only they could find their way to somewhere peaceful, away from the drug trade. He had been more than content to go home alone, if that was the condition for her receiving his visits, until one night, upon saying his farewells and turning to go, she followed him. The next day, while Phil attended to his men at the worksites, she had moved her things back into Phil's bungalow. When he came home that night, dusty and tired from work, she was waiting for him on the stoop. She'd grown round and plump, and pink in the face, even as she attended to the *Americanos* with all of the care and even more enthusiasm than Pedro's mother. He basked in the contented rhythms of living with Manuela and working with his men, never imagining it would end.

* * * * *

"You gotta stop, mate," said Ian some months later. "And if you don't, we're cutting you off." Ever present Miguel, who was sitting in the shade at the bodega table beside Ian, shifted uncomfortably. Ian knew why.

"Look Miguel, I get it," said Ian. "This has been good for you, too. You make quite a team, the shipper and the shipwright, but this will all end in tears if you blokes don't slow things down." From guarding Phil as a prisoner, to filling the holds of his ekranoplans, to driving off the Zeta after sustaining severe injuries, Miguel had always had Phil's back, and not without reward. His merry band of mercenaries was the camp's sole line of defense, and they materialized and vanished without fail on Miguel's word.

"It's gotten too big, Ian. We can't cut our friends off," said Phil. "They're counting on us now, and it's been damn good for business, ain't it?" Miguel nodded his ascent.

"Fair go, mate," Ian acknowledged. "Then at least slow down. Cut ekranoplan production by two thirds, and shipments," said Ian, turning to Miguel, "by half."

"How's that gonna work?" said Phil.

"It may not, but now's the last best chance to get this thing under control."

"It's under control now, Ian. It's working for everybody. How about we don't expand from here – maintain the status quo?" Phil countered.

"It's a mistake, mates. And don't say I didn't warn you," said Ian forebodingly. "And by the way, lads," he added, suddenly changing his tone. "You'll be glad to hear Pedro's on the mend. Should be back next month."

Phil had tried, without success apparently, to keep everyone happy; and he had no idea what Ian was on about when he got all wound up about oversupply and driving down street prices, and creating overall mayhem back in the States. But Ian was impossible to ignore. For no particular reason, he gave Phil care and counsel from the start, and Phil would probably have listened even without Ian's stranglehold on supplies. So he took Ian's guidance on faith, enlisting Miguel to help him shrink the operation.

They sent a bunch of the *Americanos* home to reduce the camp's production capacity, and Miguel scaled back the number and size of cocaine shipments. Together, they tamed the camp's runaway growth, and the right-sized operation achieved a comfortable equilibrium. Phil and Miguel, said Ian, would be handsomely rewarded for preserving the status quo.

"You should be proud," said Ian, "that the Guajira, or *Americanos*, as you lot are starting to be called, are respected, even revered without being bullies, like the Zeta."

But it didn't last long. Soon enough, the Zeta placed an order for a dozen twin engine gas turbine powered ekranoplans. When Phil declined the order for lack of supplies and production aircraft to convert, the planes appeared like an airwing in the sky overhead, and taxied straight into the building sites for conversion after landing. A number carried the work crews Phil sent home only weeks before, and cash to pay for the order, a million dollars per vehicle, in advance. In all his days Phil never saw so much money. Cash had never changed hands in camp. He didn't know what to do with it all, and feared it would lead to trouble.

With twelve million dollars in cash stacked on pallets in his cabin, Guajira leaders unwilling to accept it, and bound to insult the Zeta by telling them to come back and get it, Phil and Miguel found themselves in a pickle. The best they could do, Phil reckoned, was buy time by slowing production, and hope Ian could help. But Ian was no help at all. He told Phil to put the Zeta pilots and their money back in their planes, and send them home. Easy for Ian to say, at a safe distance from camp.

For the first time since Lost Lake faded in Pedro Morales' rearview mirror, Phil felt the walls close in. Manuela was fixin' to burst. Ian gave him nowhere to send the money except back to the Zeta, and the Zeta weren't likely to receive it in any form other than a dozen new ekranoplans.

"What will you do?" asked Miguel, looking worried.

"Well, she reckons she's due in a month," Phil replied, studiously avoiding the subject.

"All the men, they are glad Manuela and you back together, Patron," said Miguel, using the term of deference with which he and the men used to address Pedro. "You and Manuela make the camp a family. The men are always missing their families, and a new baby – well there is nothing so exciting as a new baby," Miguel concluded, with a piteous look on his face.

"Why you lookin' at me that way?"

"You are not looking so good, Patron."

"I reckon I ain't so good, Miguel." Miguel knew what he meant. The Zeta were not to be denied, and filling the order was out of the question – to renege on Ian was to betray the Guajira, especially after winning their confidence. It was suicide.

If his time in Colombia had taught him anything, it was that life in the underworld was black or white. You were with us or against us, and the only thing worse than opposing us was treachery, defecting when you used to be with us. He'd be marked now and forever as a traitor. He wanted to stall, but even with time there was no way out. The men knew their work and were anxious to do it, if not for the satisfying practice of their craft, then to impress their archrivals, the Zeta.

"No good deed goes unpunished," said Phil to Miguel as the men started tearing down the planes. "How the hell are we gonna explain this?"

"Bad guys win, caballeros lose," said Miguel, mounting his ATV. "I go find Ian, Patron. Maybe he will listen face-to-face. Be back in a couple of days."

CHAPTER 29

Guajira Peninsula, Colombia

Miguel did not return for a week, and when he arrived it was by plane accompanied by Ian and Pedro. Phil could barely believe his eyes as they disembarked the plane. Gaunt, hobbled, and skinny as a rail, Pedro was virtually unrecognizable. He walked with a cane, trailing Ian and Miguel, and scowled at Phil remorselessly as they assembled in the shade of the bodega.

"Fookin' Mr. Phil," said Pedro under his breath as Ian looked over the bustling camp.

"This has gotta stop, mate. It's all gotta stop right now," Ian declared.

"How, Ian? How do we stop it without getting ourselves killed?"

"Look, mate," Ian said unforgivingly. "*We* are not going to do anything. *You* are gonna shut this down. It doesn't matter how. Send the men home, blow the planes up. Pedro's staying behind to see that it's done."

"And what am I supposed to do, Ian? What the *fuck* am I supposed to do?" He glanced at Miguel for support. Miguel looked sheepishly away.

"I don't care, mate. Get lost, as far as I'm concerned. You should never have taken the order in the first place."

"Sí," said Pedro, nodding his head, "You estúpido, gringo." His voice was raspy and weak.

Phil was no stranger to loneliness - he had felt alone before - but never with so many enemies so completely arrayed against him.

"I understand," he replied contritely. And then something foreign welled up deep inside him, something white and hot and untamed. "I'll take care of it," he heard himself say through a gathering storm of rage that stirred his sympathies, like Emerson before him, for Napoleon at the Battle of Messina, *waking his powers of combination and putting on terror and victory as a robe.*

"No, mate, I don't think you do," Ian was saying as he threw his arm around Phil's neck and walked him forcibly toward the worksites.

"You're outta time," he whispered in Phil's ear when he thought he was out of earshot. "There's a contract on your life, mate. Pedro will kill you as soon as the planes are destroyed and you send the men home. He knows the men won't obey him, so he'll wait 'til they're gone and snuff you like a candle. Order the men to dismantle this place right now while you collect your things, and tell them to go home in the morning. You get out tonight."

They walked back to Pedro and Miguel in silence.

"I'm having a walk around," announced Ian, "to see what our friend Phil has gotten himself into. Don't leave his side, Miguel, until he's followed his orders – you know what they are - understand?" As Phil had already inferred from Miguel's earlier sheepishness, Miguel had been coopted. Ian loped off in the direction of the worksites, leaving Pedro, Miguel, and Phil standing uncomfortably together on the airstrip until Ian disappeared. The moment Ian vanished, Phil rounded on Pedro without thinking and kicked him hard in his bad leg, relieving him of the fire arm in the small of his back as he fell. Pedro wheezed in pain on the ground, as shocked as Phil by the easy brutality with which Phil disarmed him.

There was no going back now, Phil reckoned, as he gagged and bound Pedro and carried him on his back, accompanied by Miguel, to the rear of José's old cabin, where he deposited Pedro in a crawl space beneath the building. He had gambled on Miguel's tendency to bend opportunistically to the upper hand – a trait common to underworld survivors – and that he would be just as easily swayed by Phil and the changing course of events. Miguel would side with the Guajira again when the time came, if only for self-preservation, but for the next few hours, Phil was counting on him.

It had been pure luck, Phil assumed, that Jim Bartsch, a kindred spirit from the deep south, and pilot of the *Roll Tide,* had been in camp when Ian returned with Pedro. Apparently, Jim had seen Phil kick Pedro to the ground, and followed him and Miguel to José's cabin.

"What *the fuck* is going on?" asked Bartsch as Phil emerged from the crawlspace beneath the building.

"We're shutting this place down, Jim, orders from on high. I gotta get outta here tonight."

"What's the deal with Pedro? Why'd you stuff him in there?"

"Long story, Jimbo. Higher-ups think I betrayed them. Pedro's supposed to kill me. I'll be gone before he gets the chance."

"The Zeta will hunt you down and kill you for stiffin' 'em," Jim warned him.

"And the Guajira 'll kill me if I don't."

"Well ain't that a predicament," said Jim.

No stranger to improvising, Phil reckoned, after years of flying for the cartels, Jim found his bearings quickly.

"I guess I best be goin', too. You take my ship. She's all yours. I'll top her off now and meet you down by the canal at sundown. You'll nuke with no cargo in her holds, and have six, maybe seven hours of range. Weather is good. Take her where you want."

"What about you?" Phil asked, grateful for Jim's help.

"I'll grab a plane, soon as you're off. See ya at sundown," and he dashed into the jungle down the path toward the canal.

No sooner was Jim gone than Phil proceeded to the worksites with Miguel by his side. He called the men together and followed Ian's orders, instructing them to wait for dark before destroying the aircraft, and to head for home at first light, before word reached the Zeta. He thanked them for their loyalty, hard work and goodwill, and told them he would miss them – it had been the time of his life.

"And what about Manuela?" asked Miguel as the men dispersed. "She will not be safe when you are gone." Yes, Manuela. Whatever his calculus had been in the moment he clobbered Pedro and stuffed him beneath José's, it hadn't accounted for Manuela, and he had set in motion events he couldn't reverse. Once again, and for no apparent reason, Jim Bartsch rose to the occasion.

Soon after sundown, Phil rendezvoused with Bartsch at the canal aboard the *Roll Tide*. Bartsch insisted he orient Phil to the considerable avionics upgrades to which the *Roll Tide* had been treated since Phil flew her check-out flights. Where Bartsch procured his state-of-the-art electronics was something of a mystery, and most were beyond Phil's mastery in the little time he had before putting to sea. He was seated in the lone pilot seat, working his way across the instrument panel when a whelp arose from down the path along the canal. In the dusk, two silhouettes were staggering in the direction of the *Roll Tide*. Jim crouched on one knee beside Phil, who ducked low in the cockpit.

"Hey, Mr. Phil, you fookin' perro. You look what I have here!" Pedro shouted as best he could, hobbling down the path, dragging Manuela by the hair. When she tried to look up, he jerked her solidly to the ground.

Miguel must have shifted his loyalties even sooner than Phil expected, freeing Pedro in a gambit to strengthen his hand in the long run with the Guajira. Ears throbbing and heart pounding, because he reckoned the time had come, Phil reached slowly for the small of his back. Pedro beat him to it, brandishing a massive revolver and placing it squarely beneath Manuela's chin.

"You comin' with me, Mr. Phil or I blow you fookin' hoar brains all over the jungle," Pedro said coolly.

"Don't move," Jim whispered, kneeling close by. "He's baked. He'll do anything." Jim was right.

"Pedro!" came Ian's familiar Australian voice, issuing from the jungle, the sound of his footfalls through the brush closing rapidly on the standoff. "What's going on, mate?"

Ian stopped in his tracks when he saw Pedro's gun to Manuela's head. Pedro turned on him, leveled his revolver, and fired three rounds in quick succession, dropping Ian like a sand bag with three holes to his chest.

Phil reckoned Pedro turned back around just fast enough to see the muzzle flash of Jim's gun. It was just one round, and caught Pedro directly between the eyes. The gun was back in Jim's sock before Phil could see what happened. Phil leapt ashore from the cockpit, landing by Manuela's side. She was holding her belly, heaving in silent sobs, the back of Pedro's head scattered like smashed pumpkin in pieces beside her on the ground. Poor old Ian lay splayed like a citizen of Pompeii nearby. The next thing he felt was Jim's hand on his shoulder, and the hot breath of his whisper.

"You get out a here, Phil, *now*. I'll take Manuela. She'll be safer with me than with you. We'll find you later. Now, *git*." Manuela composed herself long enough to rise to her feet and throw herself around Phil.

"Te amo," she said as Jim took her by the hand.

"Te amo también," he replied, turning for the *Roll Tide* and pushing her off gently from the bank. As he clambered aboard he turned for a parting last look, but Jim and Manuela were gone. Immersed in darkness, and adrift on the canal, he found himself alone again, pointed at the open ocean.

CHAPTER 30

U.S. Coast Guard Greater Antilles Section, Caribbean Sea

The eyes and ears of GANTSEC were trained across the Caribbean basin, ready to pounce at the first sign of the fast-moving, low-signature, new and mysterious delivery vehicle the experts were calling ekranoplans. Buldoc and the *Osprey* had been ordered southwest, closer to shore, to guard the exits to the Mona Passage, the gateway to the Atlantic. *Melissa* was aloft, at the surveillance controls of the C130J, flying grids over the eastern Caribbean, her high-resolution cameras and night sensors trained on the south shore of the Dominican Republic, west coast of Puerto Rico, and the approaches to the Mona Passage. Seas were calm and the night sky clear, the ocean surface flickering in the light of a harvest moon. The *Osprey* HITRON team and three other HITRON teams attached to Coast Guard cutters around the Caribbean were deployed on their flight decks, crews strapped in, ready to take flight in hot pursuit. But only a fool dared sally forth with a shipment of drugs on such a clear, calm night, and over the most closely surveilled body of water in the world. Which is why Casey Tindall was the only member of his crew still awake in his harness when

Melissa's dulcet voice crackled over the comms. And Casey was only awake because Gutterson's snore was triggering the voice activated intercom. Dougie and Gutterson were slumped like rag dolls in the cockpit.

A hundred miles south southwest, Phil milled along at a decent clip, which is to say he had throttled back to seventy-five per cent power to conserve fuel and extend his range. Approximately thirty-five minutes into his flight north from the mouth of the Guajira camp canal, he had banked thirty degrees right, bearing north northeast for the Mona Passage. With smooth seas and fair winds he soon left Colombia far behind, with range enough to reach the Bahamas or maybe even Florida; and if he poured on the coals he had fifty knots of speed to spare over and above the one hundred and fifty knots at which he was already skimming the surface, but it would shorten his range considerably. An hour later the lights of Puerto Rico were twinkling brightly at one o'clock. Just a scattering of dim beacons at eleven o'clock illuminated the less populated eastern shore of the Dominican Republic. Straight ahead lay the emptiness of the Mona Passage, and beyond it, the open Atlantic.

He had little to do but let the *Roll Tide* carry him to freedom. Trimmed and pointed in the right direction, she flew herself. It was a long, lonely ride, with plenty of time to think on the world he had left behind. He felt cold. The sweat he broke, fearing for Manuela, watching Pedro kill Ian, and Jim kill Pedro, had dried. The adrenalin that flooded his system in the chaos of his departure had subsided, and he lingered in his thoughts through the moonlit night - on Manuela, where Jim Bartsch was taking her, and when he would see her again. Maybe she'd be scared, more likely she wasn't, accustomed as she was to life among rough men.

He also thought of Miguel and all the others who lived day-to-day between shifting allegiances, struggling for survival. And Vlad, whose belief in him turned the tables for everyone – for the Guajira, the cartelitos, and even the Zeta - Vlad, who armed him, mentored him, and even protected Manuela. Was he dead, or back at work in the jungle somewhere building narco subs again? It was all behind him now. As he rode to freedom through the crystal-clear night, with fuel and cash enough to save himself, he realized it was over. For better or worse, he was done.

* * * * *

"Oscar Bravo Whiskey, this is flight control," *Melissa* crooned from eighteen thousand feet, "I have a target, low and fast, heading for the south entrance to the Mona Channel. Definitely airborne, right on the deck, could be one of these new ekranoplans, copy?" Gutterson barely stirred.

"Roger that, flight control, we're spinning up now," Dougie replied, elbowing Gutterson and eliciting a grunt. Gutterson sat up, rubbed his eyes, and cinched his harness tight.

"Here we go, boys," he said dreamily through the intercom as he flicked on the avionics and Dougie ran the check list as the engines moaned to life.

"Oscar Bravo Whiskey, flight control, I have a visual. Report when you're airborne. I'll give you a lateral vector. No delay. You'll never catchup circling in from behind."

"What's got *her* all hot and bothered?" Gutterson mused to his team. He yanked the *Dolphin* free in usual fashion from the *Osprey's* flight deck, banking right and staying low on *Melissa's* orders against the western shore of Puerto Rico. The closing speeds and distance meant the timing would be tight, presenting just one opportunity if they were lucky to intercept the fleeing aircraft. The element of surprise would be everything, which is why they approached low from the east, navigation lights doused, camouflaged against the lights of Puerto Rico.

* * * * *

Something was moving, low against the Puerto Rican coastline, as Phil entered the Mona Passage. He couldn't make it out, a ship, maybe a tanker, passing across the lights onshore. It was giving him a wide berth, whatever it was, and would pass far off his starboard wing on its present course. Not as practiced as a regular drug runner, a non-descript object passing in the night failed to arouse his suspicion.

* * * * *

"Eyes on target," Dougie reported mechanically as Gutterson completed his turn, coming to course to intercept the small fast flying vehicle. Buldoc eavesdropped on the radio traffic from the bridge of the *Osprey*.

"Damn, it's fast," said Gutterson, tipping the *Dolphin's* nose forward to accelerate. "Tell Buldoc to douse the boat's lights," he purred to Dougie. "We don't want this guy jinking when he sees the ship. If we can't get Casey a shot, maybe *Osprey* can shoot him down as he goes by."

With the moon overhead, the speeding ekranoplan was almost as easy to see through the cockpit glass as it was through night vision and infrared. Dougie manned the flood light as Gutterson brought the *Dolphin* to within a hundred feet of the ocean, and started his count.

"Five, four, three, two...." Casey cleared his gun.

* * * * *

From the corner of his eye, Phil saw the muzzle flash, and turned to see the perfectly silhouetted form of the *Dolphin* on top of him. The helicopter was so close he could see the faces of its pilots, illuminated by their instrument lights. He was instantly bathed in brilliant light, and slammed by the helicopter's rotor wash. Through the din of his engine and the overhead helicopter, he thought he heard words, burbling and incoherent.

"Free to fire, fire at will," advised *Melissa*, watching the action overhead. Phil reached for the throttle and smoothly applied more power to bring the engine to maximum RPM. Trimming the nose down to counter the additional lift, the *Roll Tide* stretched her legs, and he entered the Mona Passage pulling cleanly ahead of the *Dolphin*.

"Did you see that?" Gutterson said to Dougie, who was adjusting the flood light to keep it trained on the fleeing target.

"He must be going two hundred knots," said Gutterson as he opened the *Dolphin's* throttles. "We can't keep up."

"Shoot him down," ordered *Melissa*, "before he gets away." Gutterson edged the *Dolphin* to the left of the target's track to give Tindall a firing angle while the target was still in range.

"Weapons free," *Melissa* broadcast insistently, "Shoot to kill," she ordered, "while you can."

"Before putting a warning shot across his bow?" Casey asked Gutterson over the intercom. It was not strictly procedure, and he couldn't afford to wait, leveling a stream of tracer-laced lead on the water ahead of the target. Two more seconds and he would deliver the coup de grâce.

* * * * *

"You're a smart man," said Gregson to Phil, now warm and dry and shackled on a stool in *Osprey's* brig. "Good thing you stopped. Not a lot of your kind do."

"Yes, sir," said Phil, remembering his manners.

"You're not kiddin'" Dougie added as he and Gutterson stepped through the bulkhead.

"That's some kind of toy, you got there," Gregson continued. "Mind telling me where you got it?"

"I built it, sir."

"Sure you did," said Gregson.

"Hey, you're no wetback," Dougie interjected. "You're American." He looked at Gregson. "You one of them so-called *Americanos*?"

"I'm American, if that's what you mean, sir."

"And a true southern gentleman, at that," Dougie marveled.

"Lucky our chief was a preacher and gave you a chance," Gutterson added, "or you'd'a met your maker by now. The air boss," Gutterson continued, glancing at Gregson, "wanted his sorry ass dead."

"I reckon most folks do, sir," said Phil.

"No kidding," said Gutterson.

"And why do you suppose?" Gregson continued.

Phil told them his story, sweeping and far-fetched as it was, and it landed him in the pen. Coleman U.S. Federal Penitentiary in Sumter County central Florida was a lock-up well known for its population of informants, gang members, corrupt police officers, disgraced government officials, and *check-ins* - prisoners who voluntarily checked themselves in to solitary confinement for their own protection. He spent a year in the pen waiting to be tried - and *not* for aiding and abetting a notorious drug cartel, nor even for facilitating the surge in drugs flooding American streets, but for the premeditated murder of a federal agent, a crime punishable by death. He spent another year indulging the futile attempts of well-intended public defenders trying to appeal his death penalty. He could never have known that Ian MacKenzie had been a federal agent, nor that Jim Bartsch would turn government witness and testify against him, saying that Phil, not Pedro, had shot Ian MacKenzie dead.

PART 2

CHAPTER 31

Coleman U.S. Federal Penitentiary, Sumter County, Florida

With the next scheduled date for his execution fast approaching, Phil wondered at his newfound popularity. Katie McLean's step-sister had posed as a journalist, trying to get him to talk. Even Sheriff Dunbar had written to say he planned on visiting - more to pay his last respects, Phil reckoned, than to hear the case for his innocence. The last person he expected or wanted to see was the government's witness against him, Jim Bartsch, but that's who was waiting for him on the other side of the glass in the cramped, paneled visitors' booth that morning. He had nothing to say to Bartsch. He knew only that Bartsch was part of something bigger than himself, and so was Moira McLean. When he declined to see Bartsch and moved to return to his cell, the prison guard forcibly escorted him back to the chair facing Bartsch through the glass.

"Fuck you," mouthed Phil, looking Bartsch straight in the eye, even before lifting the handset. Bartsch held his gaze, handset to his ear, waiting for Phil to engage.

"She's O.K.," Jim began when Phil finally picked up the handset, "and so's your little boy," he continued. "But it's not safe to bring them here." Phil swallowed hard, his pasty tongue clinging to the roof of his bone-dry mouth. "I know you want to see them, and they want to see you, Phil," said Bartsch, but empathy wasn't his strong suit, and Phil wasn't buying it anyway.

"What the fuck are you gettin' at, Jim? I ain't ever seein' 'em again, thanks to you."

"You might if you play your cards right," said Jim. Phil rolled his eyes.

"What cards is those, exactly, Jim?" said Phil, "and why would I trust a lyin' bastard like you?"

But Phil reckoned anything was possible. Two years in the pen to reflect on three years in Colombia had been long enough to consider the angles. If Ian had been a federal agent for all the years Phil knew him before he died, Ian must have been laying for something big – that, or not doing his job. He had warned Phil all along to keep his head down, like he was protecting him from something, right up until the end when he warned him about Pedro. And Ian had probably saved his life by drawing Pedro's fire that night, and paid for it with his own. Phil reckoned it was even odds Ian and Jim were in cahoots all along, and that's why Jim had been in camp the same day. It was thinking of Manuela, how Jim was using her against him now, how Ian had warned him about Pedro, and Jim had prepped the *Roll Tide* to carry him to safety, that made him realize Jim was back because he needed something. The whole thing had been a set-up from which two surprising truths became clear - Jim and Ian were the law, and the law would keep him alive.

"Why did you help me get out, Jim?" asked Phil, as though it hardly mattered, "and why convict me and sentence me to death, when you know goddamned well who shot Ian." Bartsch stared him coldly in the eye. Phil realized Jim wasn't about to concede on the recorded visitors line that he had lied under oath to convict Phil, but Phil pressed him anyway.

"Two years in the joint is a long time to think about that night, Jim. You know, you're a damn good shot with a handgun. What are you? Special forces or something?"

"Sort of, and it isn't *Special Forces*. That's Hollywood-speak, what the media call us. It's *Special Warfare*."

This was getting better and better. Who the hell were all these people, and why wouldn't they leave him alone?

"*Why?*" Phil continued, urgency taking hold. "Why all the effort to sentence me to death?"

"To get you to talk, obviously. We thought you knew."

"Knew *what*, dadgummit, Jim?"

"Easy, Phil. You convinced us."

"First off," said Phil, building a head of steam, "who the hell is *us*? And second, *what* is it I'm supposed to know?"

"It's not just the *what*, Phil, it's the *who*. Who's running Guajira operations from inside the U.S., and what's happening to all the money making its way back stateside."

"Fuck if I know, Jim."

"That's why you're going back."

"*What?*"

"To find out. That's the deal. I can come back later if you want more time to think about it." Phil reckoned he'd been here before, holding no cards at all. "Go back, find out," Jim was saying, "and maybe we'll cut you a deal, and you and Manuela and your boy can safely and quietly disappear into witness protection."

So *that's* why they took Manuela, to keep her in reach for bait. With friends like Jim, who needed enemies?

"Witness protection, hunh?" said Phil dismissively. "That didn't work out so good for my uncle."

"What?" Jim countered.

"My uncle! My fake uncle, you asshole! Pedro killed him while he was *safely and quietly* enjoying life in witness protection, and framed me for the murder." He saw Jim blink. "Or didn't you know that?" Jim demurred. "Your fake reporter from the *Atlanta Constitution* knew that. That's how *she* tried to make me talk."

Jim denied knowing Moira McLean, because he was protecting her cover, Phil reckoned. How did they do it - people like Jim and Ian and Moira - how did they keep all their stories straight? The only thing Phil knew for sure was that whatever made them tick was in fits about the Guajira, about where they got their orders, and where they sent their money – things that never crossed his mind. Why did where they lived matter? Pedro was Colombian but lived in Georgia. Vlad was Russian. Ian was both Australian and apparently a U.S. federal agent, and Jim was as red-blooded an Alabamian as they come – former *Special Warfare*, whatever that meant - and now DEA, or something like it. And Manuela's uncle, José, God rest his soul, looked Colombian, spoke perfect English, and went to school in Houston, if the yearbooks on his bookshelf were anything to go by. If Phil had learned anything it was that drug trafficking was multinational, and allegiances were fluid. Why should Jim care where the Guajira called home, and why was *he* the choice to solve for Jim's unanswered questions? Or maybe that was just how the DEA worked, and all the cartels were crawling with agents like Jim, picking on dispensable bystanders like himself to root out secretive drug lords.

The prosecution had gone to extraordinary lengths to ensure Jim's anonymity during testimony, disguising his voice, and limiting his appearances to silhouetted on screen profiles – easy for *him* to say *go back, find out*. Jim had no doubt returned to active duty as a trusted drug runner the day after they took Phil into custody, reassuming command of the *Roll Tide* before he was missed, and to ensure uninterrupted service. Phil, by comparison, had fled in the night, leaving Ian and Pedro dead before turning himself into U.S. authorities. If he managed against all odds to survive getting back into Colombia, no one would trust him, however he explained himself, and that's before he turned to whatever cockamamie mission Jim had in mind.

While Jim's proposition held little allure, it beat growing old or dying young in prison. Jim, bless his ol' *Special Warfare* heart, had offered him a way out, albeit light on growing old, if past was prolog - Harry Halliday, José, Ian MacKenzie and Pedro Morales, to name just a few died young. *We do what we must, and call it by the best names we can* his daddy had lifted time and again out of context, to ennoble the cause of unsung endeavors. That was not, by Phil's reckoning, what Emerson intended. It was the supremacy of chaos, the power of unintended consequences, that Phil reckoned Emerson meant by the whole phrase taken in context. *We do what we must, and call it by the best names we can and would fain have the praise of having intended the result which ensues.* No matter the chaos, whatever the consequences, he saw no choice but to do as Jim asked.

CHAPTER 32

Coleman U.S. Federal Penitentiary, Sumter County, Florida

Jim reappeared the day after Phil submitted to his plan. He was hurried, and signed Phil out of the Coleman Federal Penitentiary by noon, dressing him like a local in a hoodie, high-tops and sweats.

"Don't do anything stupid, Phil. You know I won't miss if you make a run for it," Jim said as they exited the gates, walking in the direction of a black SUV with its engine running. Phil's keen eye went straight to the truck's unusual contours, the heavy door frames, diminished dark windows, and exaggerated hood. He knew right away what he was seeing.

"Why the armor and bullet proof glass?" asked Phil.

"You're not exactly Mr. Popular," Jim assured him. "Folks in Colombia, and distributors around here, and probably everywhere, are afraid you talked. We leaked it that you didn't, but we figure they'd rather be safe than sorry. Wouldn't you?" said Jim, double-timing it towards the back door of the SUV. He opened the door and shoved Phil inside, slamming it hard on Phil's heels before leaping into the front seat.

"Let's roll," he told the driver. "Meet Zeke," said Jim, looking at Phil in the rearview mirror. He was referring to the man sitting in the seat beside Phil. "Old friend of mine. Served together. He's a good shot, too." Zeke turned and smiled, three days of stubble accentuating the squareness of his chin and his dimples. He stared from behind the impenetrable black lenses of his wraparound sunglasses. His t-shirt, pants and bullet-proof vest were black, too. A colt was strapped to his thigh. He had in his hands a long gun identical to the gun Miguel carried back in Guajira. Phil took stock of his protection, and wondered how long he might live.

"If I'm in danger on the drive to wherever it is we're going, what makes you think I stand a chance in Colombia?" Jim didn't answer.

"Okay, where *are* we going?"

"Shut-up, Phil," said Jim impatiently. "You'll know soon enough."

It was a bracing thirty-five-minute ride north on interstate seventy-five to the Ocala International Airport, where the black SUV paused at a closely guarded, razor wire gate, before proceeding on to the tarmac and pulling up beside a Gulfstream V dressed in Coast Guard orange. Forty minutes after wheels up, accompanied by Jim and Zeke, the Gulfstream touched down at Naval Air Station Key West, and taxied to a hangar at the northeast side of the field. Just before the Gulfstream rolled into the shade of the hangar, Phil spied through his window a large Coast Guard Jay-Hawk helicopter, the Coast Guard cousin of the venerable Army Black-Hawk. Its blades were ablur. It appeared to be waiting.

As the plane came to a stop, Zeke rose to his feet from the row behind Phil and grabbed him by the scruff of his neck, lifting him and marching him to the cabin door that a uniformed flight crew was opening. Jim was out the door first as the stairs locked into place, with Phil close behind on the end of Zeke's freakishly muscular arm. They double timed it for a door in the side of the hangar.

"You mind takin' your hands off me?" Phil shouted in the din of the spinning down jet engines.

"Sorry, Phil," Jim bellowed. "That's how this works. He won't let go 'til you get where you're going." Why should he be surprised – there was always someone's hands on him.

"Zeke, here, will accompany you to your destination. Then you're on your own," said Jim standing at the hangar door with the Jay-Hawk helicopter waiting outside. Phil stared at Jim hard, Zeke's unrelenting fist pressed tight against his neck.

"What do I do when I get there, Jim?" Phil hollered, figuring this was goodbye. "Start asking around for who's calling the shots, and where they're laundering money?" he asked impertinently.

"You'll figure it out," said Jim, blowing through the hangar door and shielding his face from the rotor wash. Jim crouched and scuttled to the steps at the threshold of the helipad, waving Phil and Zeke forward. The pilot glanced sideways through his visor from the cockpit and snapped a thumbs-up.

Phil was on his way, heading for the Jay-Hawk's open fuselage door at the end of Zeke's arm before he knew it. He could have sworn Jim slapped him on the ass and said "good luck" as he departed for the helicopter. Zeke placed him forcibly in the bench seat at the back of the cabin, and strapped him in tight to a four-point harness. With Phil secure, Zeke rolled the fuselage door shut, leaned forward into the cockpit, and rapped the pilot's helmet with his fist. He sat beside Phil, flashing a smile, as the Jay-Hawk grew light on her wheels.

"It's fun, isn't it?" Zeke shouted through the deafening noise, and off they whirled into the tropical sun.

They were over the water as soon as they cleared the airbase, flying low and fast above the crystal-clear shallows radiating outward in every direction from Key West. Phil peered between the pilots into the cockpit, taking interest in the instrument displays.

They were headed southeast at a hundred and twenty-five knots. He knew his Caribbean geography well enough by now to know the only destination for a Coast Guard helicopter in this direction, about five hundred miles away, was Guantanamo Bay, Cuba, and he settled in for a long, loud ride.

When the Jay-Hawk nosed up, interrupting his sleep, he knew they hadn't been airborne long enough to begin the approach to Cuba. He craned his neck from the back of the cabin to see through the fuselage window. With the nose up and hovering almost in place, there was nothing to see but sky, until the Jay-Hawk commenced her descent. Then the radio and radar antennae towers of a large vessel appeared in the cockpit windshield. They were touching down on a ship somewhere north of Cuba and south of the Bahamas, and when the pilot feathered the blades to let the wheels take the Jay-Hawk's weight, he stayed on the power. He wasn't staying long.

"This is where you get off!" Zeke shouted, releasing himself from his harness and sliding open the cabin door. He punched the quick release button at the center of Phil's buckle, and grabbed him again by the scruff of his neck. Phil was on his feet, stepping down from the Jay-Hawk and heading for the edge of the boat's flight deck, when he recognized where he was.

"He's all yours, sir!" Zeke shouted at a stout man dressed in black like Zeke, who was there to receive Phil. Zeke released Phil's collar, stepped back on the flight deck, and bolted for the Jay-Hawk's open cabin door. The Jay-Hawk was back in the air before the cabin door closed, banking left for home back in Florida.

The scrolling, turquoise sea unfurled to the horizon in every direction, the sun and fresh salt air a welcome relief from prison yard blacktop and chain-link, razor-wire fence.

"I don't know why the hell we're doing this," said Gregson, "and I don't wanna know," he added quickly, "but welcome back, I guess."

"Tell you what, Mike," said Phil, recalling how Gregson said to call him by his first name when first they met in the *Osprey's* brig more than two years before, "beats the hell out of sitting on death row at Coleman." Gregson had played "good cop" back then. They always asked you to use their first names, just like the fictitious *Elaine* - to make you feel safe, safe enough to tell them something - and Phil reckoned it worked both ways.

That he was headed back the way he came, under Border Patrol escort this time, must have raised him in Gregson's eyes, for Gregson looked glad to see him. There was none of the man-handling he received from the likes of Zeke and the prison guards. Maybe Gregson knew the odds where Phil was going, and didn't see the point in anymore harassment.

"You're still a prisoner," Gregson said when he led Phil below decks. "I still got to lock you in the brig, but you'll be well fed and watered before we turn you loose," he continued hospitably. "Plan is to infill you at night, probably tomorrow night, since we won't be in range until then," he concluded, handing Phil a new Coast Guard sweat shirt and blanket to fend off in the *Osprey's* chill. Then he locked him unrepentantly in the brig.

CHAPTER 33

U.S. Coast Guard Cutter *Osprey*, Caribbean Sea

"We're *what*?" said Gutterson, sitting in the briefing room with Captain Buldoc, Dougie Burbank, Casey Tindall and Mike Gregson. Their routine daylight mission had been mysteriously canceled. Now they knew why.

"You mean that little booger is onboard right now?" Gutterson asked incredulously. Gregson nodded. "And you want *us*," Gutterson continued, looking at Buldoc, "to fly him in, put him on the beach, and return to the ship, that's it?"

"That's it," Buldoc confirmed. "Mount-up at midnight, we'll do a quick radar sweep to make sure the coast is clear, and off you go."

"What about *Melissa*, won't *she* see us do all this?" Gutterson asked.

"Not tonight," Buldoc said perfunctorily. "We're on our own. I want you in and out like it never happened."

"No shit," Gutterson observed suspiciously.

"No shit," Buldoc confirmed. "I'll uplink the infill coordinates to you when you're in the air."

"*Really,*" Gutterson growled, twisting his handlebar moustache, "why all the cloak and dagger?"

"Don't overthink it," said Buldoc, heading for the bulkhead exit.

Dougie and Casey sensed Gutterson's wariness.

"What is it, Hank?" Dougie inquired after Buldoc and Gregson departed.

"Something's up, boys. It's no accident we're on deck for this mission, no accident there's no overwatch tonight. Nobody wants nobody to know about this."

"What are you thinking, Hank. Why us?" Dougie asked.

"Just a guess, but it's 'cause we ain't bent. Whoever set this up wants it kept down low. You heard Buldoc...*like it never happened.* I just hope we're not being set-up."

"Set-up?" said Casey.

"You know," quipped Gutterson, "aiding and abetting the escape of a convicted prisoner."

Phil had counted his blessings on the second of his daily late afternoon walking tours of the flight deck with Gregson. Compulsory exercise aboard *Osprey* was a world apart from the Colson prison yard, and he turned in early, forewarned of his midnight departure. Sated by a full belly, and safe for the few hours he remained in custody, he had just drifted off when he heard a tap on the bars of his cell.

"Hey kid, you awake?" Gutterson said softly.

"Sure," replied Phil, though he wasn't, not really.

"Not sure where you're going or why we're taking you back, but don't you trust any other Coasties, understand?"

"What?" said Phil, coming smartly to his senses.

"Whatever it is you're doing, we're the only Coasties on your side. You get picked up, you bite your tongue - about who took you back, and whatever you're doing, understand?"

"Yeah. I understand," said Phil. He never *had* trusted the Coast

Guard anyway. How could he forget how proudly Pedro boasted of bribing them? And surely the drug trade still paid better than the U.S. government, not that he counted on encountering the Coast Guard, seeing U.S. soil again, or even on surviving for more than a few days in Colombia.

A few minutes past midnight he dropped from the HITRON *Dolphin* gunship cabin into the smooth soft sand of a deserted Colombian beach. He stooped and ran clear of the blades spinning overhead, hitting the dirt in a fetal crouch just the way Casey instructed him. When the air around him settled, he raised his head and watched the dark silhouette of the *Dolphin*, her running lights doused, slip out to sea. A final report of her slapping blades dissolved in the sound of the surf.

When the cloud cover broke the sky filled with stars. A waxing, gibbous moon hung low on the horizon casting a luminous pall over virgin seashore as far as the eye could see. They left him with nothing, in the middle of nowhere, to find his own way as he pleased. No guards, no bars, no stiff arms with fists, he basked in the novelty of liberty. High in the night over the jungle an incandescent glow marked the lights of a distant town, and he set off in that direction. He was but a handful of strides into his journey when the familiar sound of an ATV ignition burbled from the tree-line across the beach. A distant headlight flickered to life and turned in his direction as the engine revved into high gear. Phil froze as the ATV accelerated, closing on him fast. So much for solitude, so much for liberty, he thought, raising his hands in surrender. As the ATV drew close, headlights in his eyes, he heard the clutch disengage, and it coasted to a halt before him. The engine died, the lights flickered out, and the rider took shape in the moonlight.

"Señor Phil," hailed a familiar voice.

"Jesus, Miguel!" Phil exclaimed. "Man, am I glad to see you!"

CHAPTER 34

Lost Lake, Georgia

"He's either tellin' a whopper, or your Phil's in a heap of trouble," J.D. whined.

"You glad you went?" said Marion.

"Yes, ma'am. Thank you for making me go. But what do I do now?"

"Well, what'd he say?"

"He said Pedro Morales murdered Harry Halliday, and did it to make it look like he done it – just like we thought. He said Pedro was dead, and before he died, he killed the federal agent Phil's convicted of murderin'. He says they know the federal agent was killed by Pedro, and convicted him instead to get him to tell them something he don't know."

"Hold on, hold on, J.D. Slow down," said Marion soothingly as the sheriff wound himself up. "Start at the beginning." J.D. obliged.

"And that's not all," he finally came around to saying, after repeating Phil's account of the shoot-out and his escape from Colombia.

"What more could there *be*?" Marion entreated.

"He said he has a girl, and she was carrying his baby. She was there at the shoot-out, saw what happened and could corroborate his side of the story."

"And where is *she*?" asked Marion.

"He don't know. He said the same guy who helped him escape, and who testified against him, took her."

"Well, is she safe? What about the baby, J.D.?" Marion pleaded, as if J.D. and his whole sex had no sense at all.

"I reckon so. Phil says this feller visited with him in prison, and said she'd had the baby and they were both fine."

"A girl or a boy?" asked Marion. J.D. groaned. The things women thought of at times like this.

"A boy. Does it matter?"

"Of course, it does," Marion sighed.

By the time J.D. was done, even Marion's well of hope had run dry.

"He needs help, J.D. What'll we do?"

"I don't rightly know. I'm rackin' my brain," J.D. replied, looking out the window across the yard.

"How about the Marshals Service, can anyone there help?"

"No. I wouldn't know who to trust. If Halliday weren't safe in witness protection, nobody's safe. I won't have another one on my conscience."

What began as J.D.'s predicament, taken as he was into Phil's confidence, now became Marion's. How and to whom could they tell Phil's story without sealing his fate. They would never forgive themselves for blabbing something around that brought Phil to more harm, though worse harm than a sentence to capital punishment was hard to imagine. J.D. was stumped, too, and with something more to lose. Coming to Phil's rescue now was only bound to revive suspicions that had followed him since Halliday's murder. As they sat together in silence, the kitchen walls closing, contemplating their dismal conundrum, Marion broke the silence.

"Remember, summer before last, some fella came to visit from Washington? Said the town was rife with money laundering? I know you didn't take much of a liking to him, but..."

"No, I surely didn't. And nothing ever came of it, did it," J.D. countered, by which he meant *that's enough of that.* "Typical blow-hard Fed. All hat no cattle, though I ain't forgotten what he said about the bank. And it weren't long after that that Pedro turned up missing."

It hadn't dawned on J.D. until he said it that Pedro's disappearance had coincided with receiving the obnoxious visitor from Fusion, Lenny Marks, and he pondered a connection. He should have thought of it before, only he hadn't missed Pedro, and was happy the sting operation Marks promised never came to pass – he'd let sleeping dogs lie. The truth was Pedro never crossed his mind again until his visit with Phil at the Coleman pen, when Phil told him Pedro was dead.

"Just listen to me, J.D.," Marion persisted. "He came here lookin' for something, and he knew about Halliday and the arrest warrant for Phil before he arrived. Isn't that right?"

"So?" said J.D.

"So, don't you think he already knows more than we do, and if he doesn't, he can find out? Don't you think *he* might hear you out if you tell him Phil's side of the story?"

"Come on," J.D. whined, "if he knows anything at all, he already knows Phil's side of the story. And besides, we didn't exactly part on cordial terms."

"We just *gotta* do something, J.D., and that's the best I can think," said Marion hopelessly. "What do we have to lose?"

J.D. reckoned Marion was right. He already knew what Lenny Marks thought of him, and he also vaguely recalled Marks entertaining his suspicions of Pedro. Perhaps his currency with Marks would appreciate with Phil's account of Pedro's murder in Colombia. If he could just get Marks to consider Phil's story, to hear the boy out, that would be something.

"I'll call him," J.D. relented begrudgingly, not that Marion left him a choice.

* * * * *

"Marks," answered Lenny with signature abruptness.

"Hey, Mr. Marks. U.S. Federal Marshal Dunbar, here, from Lost Lake. How y'all doin' today?"

"Fine, Dunbar. What is it?"

Until very recently, Lenny had made no progress since his fruitless trip to Lost Lake almost two years before. The conclusions he'd drawn about the crooked sheriff, his ties to South American criminal enterprise, and the enterprise's connection to U.S. banking and domestic politics had planted a brooding contempt that sprouted like a rough stalactite in the darkness of his vulnerability to Moira.

Like his disdain for the sheriff, the scandal and professional disgrace to which he imagined his dalliance with Moira left him exposed had done anything but fade. All the many ways he could have implicated himself in the untoward dealings of the McLean family and the Atlanta Guaranty and Trust Company, N.A., had coalesced and hardened like Damocles' sword, hanging over the job for which he was meant.

Naturally, Moira had stonewalled him, and SOD had outright rejected Sam's PATT reports on executives of the Atlanta Guaranty and Trust Corporation, N.A., just as Lenny and Sam expected SOD would. All avenues to further investigation had been closed, making the whole episode more suspicious. It also made Lenny more paranoid about his vulnerability to a conspiracy whose scale he feared grew with time and his inability to investigate it. He had conceded resentfully to biding his time, because the truth was bound to out he consoled himself in his darkest hours. Never would he shrink, never would he bow, but wait like a spider in the corner of his web - until a misstep begot struggle, and struggle entanglement, and with entanglement the wrath of his bite.

Just when Lenny thought it might haunt him forever, the DEA hauled in the loose end for whom no one could account – the mysterious and elusive Pheonix Perdue – and convicted him of premeditated murder of a federal agent in proceedings closed to the public *for the safety of the defendant,* and to conceal the identity of witnesses. The defendant was sentenced to death, notwithstanding the court's earlier concern for his safety.

It was the opening for which Lenny had waited, a golden opportunity to draw Moira in and get to the bottom of her dubious associations and family ties. He knew she was a sucker for sob stories, even after law school, and he anticipated she would sympathize with Perdue, both because Lost Lake was common ground, and because Perdue claimed he was falsely accused and convicted. If she were mixed up with her father, and they were laundering money through Perdue's old boat business, she would have difficulty concealing their acquaintance in the scenario Lenny had cooked up to catch her.

To get her to play, Lenny tried something he had never tried before. He apologized, and then he doubled down and asked Moira for help, though he would never admit openly to going *that* far. This was her chance to make a difference, Lenny said, to clear a good citizen of Lost Lake of Harry Halliday's unsolved murder, if not overturn the conviction for which Perdue claimed he was falsely accused. She just had to get Perdue talking about his years in Colombia.

Moira had been conspicuously receptive. He wanted to believe it was because, deep inside, she harbored a smoldering longing for him, but the reason she gave rang truer. Being a second-year associate working eighteen-hour days, seven days a week at a prestigious beltway law firm hadn't been nearly so glamorous or fulfilling as she imagined, and she hungered for distraction and excitement – and *meaning*, whatever that meant. He hoped she wasn't interested for a third reason, the reason he always feared – that she was probing again – this time for what Phil might have divulged.

She took the bait, and together they staged her encounter with Perdue. She felt sure he wouldn't know her, and at first, she was right. He struggled valiantly but without success to place her, or delivered a brilliant appearance of doing so throughout the meeting. His performance cleared her, in Lenny's mind, and even Sam's, of suspicion when he succeeded at the end, with evident triumph, to see through her guise and name her. It was hard to conclude from their interaction, which Lenny had observed from behind the one-way mirror in the interrogation room, that they shared more than their connection to Lost Lake. Phil had shown Moira's heart was true, which made Lenny suspect Phil's could be, too.

"Mr. Marks?" said J.D., "you still there?"

"Sure. Do you mind repeating that, sheriff?"

"I said, I know it's been two years since we visited, but I have new information." J.D. went on to describe events as they were recounted to him by Phil, the same as he had to Marion.

"Thanks, sheriff," said Lenny. "'ppreciate the call. Wish I could tell you any of this is news," he quipped, doubting the sheriff's intent.

"So, you already looked into it?" said J.D., sounding discouraged.

"As much as I can, sheriff. I don't need to tell you about inter-agency politics."

"But I thought you were *Fusion*." J.D. interjected. "Don't that by definition mean you can cross lines?"

"Technically, I suppose," Lenny replied dismissively, "but once you're in the hands of the DEA, it's hard to unwind how you got yourself there. But *you* know that, don't you sheriff?" Lenny said caustically. "And this kid, Perdue," Lenny continued, picturing Phil in his mind, "doesn't come with a clean slate, does he. I mean, given how he ran from the scene, took up with drug runners, and got picked up by Border Patrol coming out of Colombia."

J.D. knew they hadn't parted friends, but this Marks' hostility was something. Of all the grudge-holders, Marks was one of them.

"Don't it bother you at all that the whole proceeding was closed?" J.D. pressed.

"No," said Lenny, reluctant to hear more unless the sheriff caught himself out. That would be worth waiting for, and he started recording the call.

"But why would the feller Phil says saved him, turn around and testify *against* him? It's not like Phil did him wrong. What does *he* get out of it?"

"Who?" said Lenny, momentarily confused.

"The witness, the feller Phil said saved him. What does *he* get out of it?"

"Maybe it's the truth, sheriff," Lenny replied. "Maybe he's doing his job, and Perdue is guilty."

"The kid's on death row, Mr. Marks. What's to lose by askin' a few questions?"

The sheriff had given Perdue a free pass five years ago in the Halliday murder, thought Lenny. Maybe he had a mind to set Perdue free this time, too.

"Wouldn't know where to start," said Lenny, feigning indifference, to see how much it meant to Dunbar.

"How 'bout with the witness who testified against him?"

"The witness with the concealed identity?" Lenny posed. "You mean, *that* witness..." Was Dunbar scouting a revenge plot? The cartels had balls.

"Yes, Mr. Marks. You got a pencil ready? Here's two names, the name of the witness and the name of the agent Phil is convicted of killing. Make a few calls. Please. Something ain't right." So much for the revenge theory. The sheriff already had the names.

Moira *had* fallen for the sob story, and her failed attempt to deceive Phil into saying something implicating had probably left her feeling bad about herself, and worse about Phil's predicament. And she had liked being tapped by Lenny, no doubt in his mind about that, even though her empathy for bad guys was undiminished. He feared she would ask to come back. But he wouldn't make that mistake again, even though it was generally acknowledged that her performance as the reporter, *Elaine,* cleared her of suspicion. While that mostly eased Lenny's fears, he never lost track of his scars. The years he spent suspecting her haunted him no less than the wrongs he avenged as a teenager. A clear conscience was reward enough, and the idea of a rapprochement was a minefield. Never again would he mix business with pleasure.

What a shame. With no stomach himself for lost causes, like the crooked sheriff's plaintiff inquiry to look into Phil's trial, he could use an associate like Moira, a veritable fanatic for lost causes. With no one else to do it, he swallowed hard, and suborned himself to personally obliging the sheriff's request, clicking on the DICE data base icon and searching on the two names J.D. had given him – *Jim Bartsch* and *Ian MacKenzie.*

He knew from the moment he pressed *Enter* he was way beyond his paygrade. Even with more than a billion potential matches, DICE took him straight to the sub directory requiring the highest security authentication, *Top Secret/Sensitive Compartmented Information,* or SCI. He used his SCI code so infrequently that he had to look it up.

Jim Bartsch, to no surprise, was an alias, the designated name of a highly decorated former Navy SEAL, one of the few with advanced flight training in enemy combat aircraft, which meant he had stolen a few, either by design for inspection by the U.S. military, or because it was the chosen method of exfiltration for one mission or another. He had assumed his alias after leaving the teams and joining SOD, where he was remanded to the DEA. The DEA had formed a new, elite tactical interdiction unit called Foreign-deployed Advisory and Support Teams - FAST to agency insiders. Their mission was counter narcotics, counter terrorism, and direct action. That's where Jim Bartsch's records ended, five years ago, right about the time the Office of the Inspector General, or OIG, issued the unflattering report about the dysfunctional relationship between the DEA and the FBI, the same summer Moira came to work for Lenny. He couldn't be sure it was the same Jim Bartsch, whose name Perdue gave the sheriff, the name being an alias, and the recent record silent. It was easy to imagine the bearer of the original alias was dead, killed in the line of duty as long ago as five years, where his record trailed off.

There were a total of five FAST teams, and they saw plenty of action, living on permanent standby. Four of the teams functioned as rapid reaction forces operating from Marine Corp Base Quantico, Virginia. The fifth was on perpetual rotation in Afghanistan fighting the opium trade. Killed in action would explain the silence in Bartsch's record, though he was not reported deceased.

Then there was Ian MacKenzie. Lenny traced him back easily through DICE to the Australian Federal Police. MacKenzie spent almost a decade at the AFP in anti-narcotics before going undercover and posing as a Qantas mechanic to infiltrate a heroin smuggling ring that came to be known as the *Bali Nine* – nine Australians employed by a national catering company that served high-end venues including the Sydney Cricket Grounds and various airlines.

Members of the *Nine* eventually testified they were recruited by an Indonesian drug kingpin at a local karaoke bar. The two ring leaders were sentenced to death and executed by firing squad in April, 2015. One died of natural causes in prison, another was released after fourteen years served. Five remained incarcerated at three separate prisons in Bali, and a fourth prison in East Java. Some considered the sentences harsh for smuggling eighteen pounds of heroin worth four million dollars, but Lenny admired the conviction of his foreign counterparts.

And then he noticed the conspicuous similarity between MacKenzie's and Bartsch's service records. They both went silent five years ago, at almost exactly the same time. Lenny was no believer in coincidences, and these were top flight operatives from opposite ends of the earth with deep knowledge and experience of narcotics interdiction. What the hell were they up to together with Perdue in Colombia, and how was he going to find out?

CHAPTER 35

Zeta Territory, Colombia

"I had your back then, Mr. Phil," said Miguel through the dark, "and I have it now. Climb aboard." That's not exactly how Phil remembered his last hours in the Guajira camp two years before, and he'd had a long time to think about it.

"Sure," said Phil. "Where we goin'?"

"To see some old friends," said Miguel, scooting forward on the seat of the ATV to make room for Phil behind him.

Old friends – Phil couldn't think of any, or friends of any kind. He felt pretty much played by everyone he'd encountered since even before Pedro took him from Lost Lake. He wanted to exclude his daddy, but the facts were the facts, and he knew it was making him mean. *Old friends – we'll just see about that* he thought to himself as he climbed aboard behind Miguel and grabbed the handle bars ringing the seat.

Miguel gunned the engine and they tore off across the flats toward the tree line. A low, sinister moon filled the beach with eerie light, casting long dark shadows of their fused shape far across the sand, until they reached the tree line where the jungle swallowed them whole. Moving at breakneck speed from the endless open moonlit shore to the pitch-black darkness of the jungle gave Phil the funny feeling of falling down a well. But Miguel never took his foot off the gas, cleaving to a smooth straight track with no resemblance whatsoever to the jarring, root-gnarled, rut-pocked goat trails of Guajira. Phil had settled in for a ride of indefinite duration when Miguel slowed to a crawl and guided the ATV up a short incline, alighting at the top on a two-lane paved road. The reflector of a large vehicle looming in the dark on the shoulder blinked in the headlights. Miguel guided the ATV to the open-ended bed of what revealed itself to be a pickup truck jacked high above the ground on ruddy all-terrain treads.

"You can get off now, Mr. Phil," said Miguel over the clatter of the idling engine. Phil dismounted and saw in the headlights a pair of crenelated stainless-steel ramps rising from the road to the bed of the truck. Miguel gunned the engine and the ATV scaled the ramps, coming to a halt against the back of the truck's cab. He cut the engine, dismounted, and vaulted from the flatbed to the ground, stowing the ramps in purpose-built recessed holes beneath the flatbed, and securing the ATV with wheel chalks and a nylon come-along.

"Nice rig," said Phil, admiring the engineering.

"Better roads," Miguel countered, smiling, as he made his way around to the driver's side door.

"Come on. Get in. You're going to like where we're going *mucho* better than the last place."

They mounted the cab and Miguel cranked the ignition.

"Wow Miguel," said Phil, caressing the soft leather seats and admiring the instrument panel as he and Miguel glowed together in the light of the touchscreen dash. "What'd you do to get this?" he asked.

"You like it?" Miguel asked. "I'll get you one."

This was a new Miguel, Phil reckoned. He must have risen in the ranks. With a truck like this in Lost Lake, tricked out with an ATV, he'd be the talk of the town. How could he begrudge Miguel the fresh start he needed so badly himself.

"How'd you know?" asked Phil as Miguel pulled off the shoulder on to the road.

"Know what?"

"It weren't hardly a regularly scheduled flight," said Phil, "so don't tell me you just happened by."

Miguel's silence in the moments that followed left Phil contemplating the potential range of Miguel's ties – was he on the side of the law, with Ian and Jim Bartsch and maybe even his new-found friend Gutterson, or was he running at the same time with the likes of Pedro, making and taking bribes, and killing and kidnapping innocents. Or did he change sides with the weather, adapting to circumstances. Truth and deceit, ends and means, the law and the lawless, they were all of a part with Miguel, ebbing and flowing for self-preservation in ways he'd come to appreciate if not completely understand. He refrained from repeating his question to save Miguel the embarrassment of losing even more face than he already had.

Slowly, the road climbed until it broke through the canopy into the open, skirting a hillside overlooking the ocean. Ominous moonlight filled the landscape, painting a flickering path of glistening gold on an empty, undulating sea. The dark deserted jungle unfurled beneath them to the coastline, only the dimming lights of a distant ship on the horizon hinting at the existence of humanity. He was luxuriating in the desolation, drifting in quiet contemplation, and speculating on Jim Bartsch's assignment and whose malign intent it served, when Miguel turned right off the road and on to a drive that dove into darkness beneath the jungle. A half mile on, Miguel stopped at tall wrought iron gates set between high rock walls that vanished into the dark on both sides. A sentry in camouflage with a gun across his back stepped forward from the shadows into the headlights.

"Miguel?" he said, shining a light into Miguel's eyes.

"Sí," said Miguel.

"And who is the Gringo?" said the sentry, training his light on Phil.

"You will know soon enough," Miguel assured the sentry, who stepped back, rolled open the gates, and waved them ahead.

A winding gravel drive bordered by craggy, freestanding trees bisected a moonlit expanse of clear-cut manicured grounds. Where the drive split, the avenue of trees extended up towards a vanishing peak. Miguel bore right, following the road across a gently rolling grass plain before arriving at a small, one-story house that rose from the shadows of the nearby jungle. Warm soft lamplight spilled from the windows beneath the cold, white light of the moon.

"Come on, Mr. Phil," said Miguel.

"How about just *Phil*, Miguel. I reckon we known each other long enough."

"Gracias, Phil. Welcome to your quarters. No hammock in the jungle this time," said Miguel, marching for the entrance.

He pushed on the knob of the heavy paneled door and it swung easily into a welcoming, brightly lit vestibule. A plume of luxurious cool air spilled out in the humid night. Miguel led him into the house, past gayly pastel painted walls, a furnished sitting room, and a well-appointed kitchenette, where Miguel opened a fully stocked refrigerator the contents of which he proceeded to recite. There were cushioned bamboo seats and sofas like nothing Phil ever saw, and paintings and prints in tropical palates ornamenting every wall. Things were improving, there was no denying that.

Miguel led him to a room at the end of the house with a four-poster canopy bamboo bed bigger than Miguel's truck, an adjoining tile bathroom with separate tub and glass walled shower, and towels - as clean and soft and plump as the towels he remembered from Guajira – a standard cartel creature comfort, apparently, that reminded him unexpectedly of Manuela.

"Where the hell are we, Miguel?"

"The guest house, my friend." Miguel checked his watch. "It is late. Get some sleep," he said, passing through the bedroom and pausing at a pair of mullioned French doors.

"These open to a terrace," he said, flicking on outdoor lights, "if you prefer fresh air," he continued as he swung the doors open and stepped out. Phil followed him into the moonlight, where two distant sentries silhouetted in the dark paced past the back of the house.

"Nothing changes, hunh Miguel?"

"No, Phil. Not so much changes, except the guards!" he exclaimed with a friendly slap to Phil's back. "I see you in the morning, mi amigo. Pick you up at seven for café with the patron, and all your questions will be answered." *All?* thought Phil. That would take some doing.

CHAPTER 36

Zeta Territory, Colombia

Miguel arrived at quarter of six, catching Phil with one of the brilliant white towels still riding low around his waist after a long, hot rejuvenating shower. He was shaving in the bathroom with a real metal razor.

"Come on, mi amigo. We will be late. Fresh clothes in the dresser. Help yourself." Phil reckoned he hadn't been this clean or felt this good for as long as he could remember, and nothing sounded better than a potent, percolated Colombian coffee, an extravagance he learned to appreciate after the discolored brown bilge water to which he was subjected in prison. He had decided overnight that he hoped he could help Bartsch, and by so doing return to the straight and narrow, but things could be worse if he didn't. The only thing left was to find Manuela, and if he knew anything about cartels by now it was that they could find anyone, anywhere.

They departed the guest house, ascending the gravel drive in Miguel's truck, crossing the grass plain to where it converged with the tree-lined avenue that rose towards the distant peak.

"What's that?" said Phil, pointing to a small red flag snapping smartly from a springy staff in the breeze.

"Sixth hole," said Miguel with a smile.

"We're on a golf course?" Phil asked, bewildered.

"No," said Miguel, shaking his head, and proceeding gingerly into the tree-lined avenue as if to preserve something precarious about the curated tranquility. "This is the house of the Patron, Phil," he said, stealing a glance through the passenger side window beside Phil. The golf course fell away from the tree-lined drive to the edge of the primeval jungle, which rolled on in vast undulating serenity for another five miles to the sea. The breeze was sweet with flower and fruit, none individually discernible to Phil, but together cleansing his lungs, and clearing his head, and even restoring his soul, he reckoned.

"We done our time, ain't we Miguel?" said Phil wistfully, like they'd found in this paradise their due.

Miguel steered delicately through a series of gentle turns before pulling to a stop before a grand, two-story, white clapboard plantation house. Set high above ground level, the house possessed commanding views of the ocean and surrounding wilderness in all directions. A majestic course of painted wooden stairs descended from a magnificent veranda that encircled the first floor in a geometric white hoopskirt of rails and lattice and newels. Each corner was shaded by wafting palm fronds that spilled like fountains from arching trunks as thick and round as field artillery.

"It ain't like the old days," said Phil as he and Miguel left the truck. Miguel accompanied him to the base of the veranda stairs.

"This is where I leave you, Phil. Good luck," said Miguel. He gripped Phil's hand and looked him straight in the eyes, dipping his head reverently as he turned for his truck to go. It was almost enough to convince him it wasn't Miguel who set Pedro free the night of the shootout in Guajira, the night Ian and Pedro died, and Jim absconded with Manuela.

Phil had reached the second step on the stairs to the veranda when he heard someone call his name. The sonorous voice sounded foreign and friendly, a combination he had learned to suspect.

"Señor Phil," the voice boomed from the landing above.

"Welcome to Hacienda Xixim. I am Humberto Gallardo. You dignify us with your presence!" he declared, his arms spread wide like a televangelist.

"Thank you," said Phil, taking umbrage. "Much obliged." But for the jewelry, Gallardo looked a lot to Phil like the Latin version of a Lost Lake home owner from Atlanta. He wore a white linen suit with a pink collared shirt open wide enough at the neck to display heavy gold chains. His black, wraparound sunglasses, that looked suspiciously like Zeke's, rode comfortably amidst the swirls of his oily black hair. The welcome act was uncannily familiar.

Phil had converged with Gallardo at the top step of the veranda when he spied the man he knew all too well by now, seated comfortably in the shadows. The close shave and unfamiliar clothes - pastel blue polo shirt and pressed white chinos – successfully distracted him, but only for a moment. There was no mistaking the profile of the silhouette that testified against him by remote, voice-altered video feed. It was Jim Bartsch at the end of the veranda, in a peacock cane arm chair, gazing wistfully out at the sea. He looked removed and benign and lost in his thoughts until Humberto took Phil's hand, which he held a beat too long, before stealing a glance in Jim's direction down the veranda.

"I think you know Jim, yes?" Humberto said solicitously. "He's a big fan of yours, Señor Phil. But I think you know that," he concluded with the sureness of a confidant.

"He is?" said Phil as Jim turned his gaze from the sea to Phil, and Humberto resumed his monologue.

“You are the hero of the Zeta, Señor Phil, and the spirit of the *Americanos*, and you are welcome here for the rest of your days,” Humberto gushed with admiration.

“I am?” said Phil, looking quizzically past Humberto at Jim.

“Because...” said Humberto with a dramatic flourish, his back turned to Jim, “you killed the dog, Pedro Morales.”

From the comfort of his magnificent cane chair and the obscurity of his position behind Humberto, Jim smiled and winked.

“It’s true,” Jim rejoined with pitiless sincerity as Humberto looked on admiringly. “The bastard had it coming to him.”

“And you build these invisible flying boats, and make sure to share with all of us,” Humberto added incredulously. “I hope you will enjoy your stay,” said Humberto sincerely. “You are welcome as long as you wish,” he finished with a flick of his wrist.

“Look, guys, I really appreciate all the happy talk,” said Phil looking doubtfully at Jim, “but what the hell am I doing here?” He knew by now to dispense with the pleasantries because they always foreshadowed a plan.

CHAPTER 37

Organized Crime Drug Enforcement Task Forces Fusion Center, Washington, D.C.

"Can you check these guys out with SOD, Sam?" Lenny asked, handing Sam the Jim Bartsch and Ian MacKenzie files he'd pulled from DICE, "without raising eyebrows?"

Lenny hadn't burned *all* his bridges at SOD when he left to join Fusion, but his inquiries were still treated cautiously. It made more sense for Sam, who kept frequent contact with lower-level SOD staff reviewing PATT reports, to ask the questions. SOD commanded the FAST teams, and one of Sam's pals was bound to know someone in the field ops group, someone who had heard of Jim Bartsch.

"I can try," said Sam, glancing at the Bartsch file. "FAST, hunh? What do you want to know?"

"Where he's been for the last five years, and if he's still on our side."

"*Our* side? or SOD's side?" Sam asked. "I can never tell the difference." Sam glanced at the file again. "Where'd you find these guys?"

"Couple a names our hayseed sheriff friend from Lost Lake gave me. Said our convicted boat boy, Phoenix Perdue, gave him the names. Boat boy says he worked with them in Colombia, as recently as two years ago."

"Doesn't sound good."

"I know it, Sam. Do the best you can, and be discrete. Maybe it's a sanctioned operation, maybe it's off the books. We don't want SOD thinking we know about it either way."

"And maybe these characters have gone to the dark side," Sam added forebodingly. "They always seem to, eventually."

"Maybe. I'm going back to Florida to talk to Perdue myself this time, to see what our friend can tell us. Maybe he knows more than the sheriff is telling."

Twenty minutes later, after a brief phone call with the Coleman Federal Penitentiary to schedule a visit, Lenny discovered Perdue was gone. "Moved," is what the visitation officer said, but he couldn't, or wouldn't tell Lenny where.

"You ever get the feeling someone's trying to hide something from us, Sam?"

"Don't you always have that feeling, Lenny?"

"While you're inquiring after Bartsch, maybe you can ask SOD where they misplaced Perdue."

"...without raising eyebrows?" Sam asked skeptically.

Lenny's intuition about Moira was bang on. In the days following her performance as a reporter, pretending to interview Perdue for posterity, she asked to come back to Fusion. Lenny hated saying no, but he had no choice. Sam didn't think he did either, whether or not she had cleared herself of suspicion.

"Still don't trust me, hunh?" she said, standing at his desk at Fusion, sounding defeated. She was gazing outside through the slats in the blinds at the window beside his desk. It was trying to be spring in Washington, D.C., but the sky was a ferris wheel of dark and light as heavy low clouds scudded fast over the District, pulsing Lenny's office with short bursts of sunlight.

"It's not that, Moira."

"I thought I might change your mind by interviewing Phil Perdue, but..." She cut herself off.

"But what?" He could see her think something through. "Say what's on your mind."

"You don't really think I believed it was Perdue you were after when you asked me to question him?"

"What?" said Lenny defensively.

"I knew it was me, you know. I knew you were testing *me*, to see if we were accomplices. Why do you think I agreed to do it?" she posed, hoping Lenny would see. "I wasn't probing, Lenny. Not then, not now. I never even met Phil before the interview, and I wish I'd never tagged the Lost Lake Farmers Building and Loan in that damn report."

"Then why did you?" Lenny asked.

"Who knows, Lenny? I felt like being a brat. I felt like giving my father trouble. Girls do that, you know... No, forget it, you probably don't... You're just paranoid, Lenny," she said as a cloud darkened the room, "and probably right to say *no*," she continued unpersuasively. "It's a bad idea. I'm desperate to do anything besides proof reading documents eighteen hours a day." She looked out the window again, lost in her thoughts.

"Maybe I can find you something else," he suggested, though the offer was presumptuous, even by Lenny's standards.

Moira's access to influence inside the beltway, if that's what she wanted, far exceeded his. Senator Charles Wingate's star was rising in the Republican party, not least because, thanks to Moira's father, he had an exceptionally well-funded campaign for the coming presidential election. No one doubted Malcolm McLean was up for a cabinet position or ambassadorship if Wingate were elected.

Ever since Dan Thorne at FinCEN cautioned Lenny about investigating the Atlanta Guaranty and Trust Company, N.A., and Sam intercepted the call to a Wingate staffer originating in Colombia, Sam's hunch had raised tantalizing possibilities. Was the bank not just laundering money, but channeling it into Wingate's campaign? Why Dan at FinCEN and SOD had let it continue, when they had to know from Sam's PATT report requests that Fusion was tracking it, presented a quandary. They were sitting on their hands for a reason. Were they still building a case, or waiting to bring it at the most politically opportune time? Or was blind political ambition fed by the prospect of advancement in a Wingate administration causing them to hold their cards? There had to be an explanation for such calculated neglect, especially in light of Dan's warning to keep his head down. He could hardly afford, as the leader of Fusion, to compromise a continuing operation.

"Forget it, Lenny," she was saying, "Anyway, I need some time," she continued, turning from the window. "I'm going home, back to Georgia for a while."

"To see the old man?" said Lenny, McLean on his mind.

"Hell, no! To see my mother. It's been years and she hasn't been well. It's long overdue." He could see she was finished, mentally checked out, and she turned for the door to go.

"You know, Moira, there *is* something," he said with studied indifference, "if you'll be near Lost Lake," he said, as if the thought just crossed his mind. "In an unofficial capacity, of course," he added with a wry, self-satisfied smile.

After confessing to the ploy of which she accused him, he defended it by saying the exercise had cleared the air, at least of suspicion, if not the impropriety of the liberties they took as colleagues. What hadn't changed was his suspicions of the sheriff, J.D. Dunbar, nor of the money laundering activity taking place in Lost Lake, that he couldn't pursue, "...until I was sure you weren't...what I was afraid you were."

The sheriff, said Lenny, was a problem, and recent events had done little to absolve him. Dunbar had called him out of nowhere to plead Perdue's case, who's predicament had been surprising enough when Lenny called Moira to interview him on death row. Now things were even more complicated. It all began, Lenny told her, when he disinformed the sheriff to see with whom he might confer. The disinformation traveled at light speed, intercepted on a call originating from a burner phone in Lost Lake to Bogotá in less than twenty-four hours.

"That can't be," said Moira. "It just can't be."

"Maybe now you understand why I was worried," said Lenny, feeling vindicated. He elected to omit both the last leg of the trip the information took from Bogotá back to Wingate's congressional staffer, *and* the warning from Dan Thorne to stay clear of Atlanta Guaranty and Trust. The truth would out in time. There was no need to tell her now.

"Care to drop in on Sheriff Dunbar?" Lenny asked.

"What do you want me to ask him?"

"You don't work for me anymore, Moira, I can't tell you what to ask him. And you already know more than you should. Just follow your nose. He's unnaturally interested in Perdue. Might be worth knowing why."

Moira made the nine-hour drive from Washington, D.C. to Lost Lake, Georgia the next day. She left at daybreak to leave herself time to walk Main Street before dropping in on J.D., whose culpability she sincerely doubted. She would reach her mother's in time for supper, even if J.D. did go on, as often he did. It was good to leave the beltway behind. Spring advanced the deeper south she drove, warm temperatures and sunshine bathing hillsides of tobacco and fields of white fenced blue ridge horse farms with the promise of new life. She looked forward to being home, to sipping sweet tea on her mother's porch swing two lakes up from Lost Lake, and to dispensing with Lenny's long-shot request.

She arrived on schedule, pleasantly reminded that parking on Main Street was free. Some things had changed, but many remained reassuringly constant, like the General Store that stocked anything and everything, from groceries to gardening tools. She picked up a coffee to-go along with the weekly town newspaper, *The Intelligencer*, scanning the pages as she ambled down Main Street moving in the direction of the police station. On page two she found the story about Phil. *No Hometown Hero He* read the headline. A wire service had picked up a two-line summary of Phil's trial, conviction and sentence, which *The Intelligencer* reporter had embellished with impressive flourish. With a cursory nod to his father's venerable boat business, and disparaging remarks about the debts to which it owed its demise, the story pronounced Phil a discredit to his father, his family and the town – *"a flesh and blood instance of the evil that lurks among us,"* the article concluded. Moira turned the page and smiled. Some things like small town sensationalism and the need to sell newspapers never changed.

"*Hey!*" Betty Dunphy cried as Moira appeared at the counter of the police station.

"*Hey!*" Moira replied, rediscovering her Southern.

"Why, you ain't changed one bit, Miss Moira. *So* good to *see* you. What all brings you to town, honey?"

"I was hopin' to visit with J.D." she said, unleashing her lilt and dropping her *g*'s, much to her own surprise. Betty raised J.D. on the radio and let him know he had a visitor. He said he was tickled Moira was in town, but he couldn't be back to the station before six, unless it was urgent. With Betty's able assistance Moira relayed that the matter could wait. She was staying at her momma's, and would come back *later*, when J.D.'s schedule permitted. Then J.D. had an idea.

"Why don't I carry you to Boat Church Sunday?" he suggested. "We'll have us a real nice visit." There was no declining such a heart-felt invitation, and she could probably do worse, albeit not *much* worse than being captive to J.D. on his police boat for the observance of Boat Church. So they agreed to meet at French's early Sunday morning.

CHAPTER 38

Lost Lake, Georgia

"It's with heavy heart I stand here before you today," Preacher Small began with darkening foreshadow. His crisp voice and dire tone echoed down the lake, amplified by a modern high-fidelity sound system that came with the well-appointed pontoon boat the McLeans gave the church about the time Phil disappeared. The robed, teenage choir squinted in the sun, waiting on the call to song, conveying, by their distraction Small's intent to carry on for a while. The audience knew it, too, by the gravity in Small's voice. Solemn openings portended long sermons, and restlessness gripped the fleet.

"I reckon we're in for it," J.D. whispered to Moira as they rocked side by side in the front seats of the Lost Lake Kingfisher patrol boat.

"*Now*," said Preacher Small with consternation, "I know y'all have read the heart-breaking story in *The Intelligencer* this week about Phil Perdue, a boy born and reared in the bosom of this God-fearing Christian community." Moira couldn't believe her luck. The preacher himself was raising the subject of Phil, the opening she needed with J.D. "Raised at his daddy's knee because he had no momma, God rest her soul, and who was took from us by the *Devil!*" Preacher Small spat derisively.

Moira heard something low and resonant approaching the drifting flotilla from behind. She turned and saw the very thing she had hoped to avoid, the *General Lee*, inbound, her father at the helm surrounded by her siblings, full and half-blooded, and her stepmother, Ana-Maria. She sank in her seat and pulled her hat low.

"Why, here comes your daddy, Moira," J.D. barely whispered. He was caught off guard by Moira's vanishing act until he remembered her estrangement from her father. The approaching vessel caught Reverend Small's wary eye, too, and he lifted his voice and hurried his cadence to rise above the surging throb. He realized too late, when his voice and tone carried in the silence after the *General Lee* suddenly cut her engine, that he sounded like a madman railing against the storm, and he checked himself, recovered his poise, and delivered the reproving glare for which he was duly dreaded, and it found the *General Lee.*

Moira peeked out from the brim of her hat to observe the terrible beauty of the *General Lee* coasting silently past the prow of the drifting Kingfisher. She raised her eyes high enough to take in Katie, seated on the engine cover behind the second cockpit, her careless legs on the soft green leather, and a baby squirming clumsily in her lap.

"Since when your baby sister have a young 'un of her own?" asked J.D., as surprised as Moira at the sight of the child.

"And who's that other girl?" Moira added, referring to a woman seated directly beside Katie. "They could be identical twins," she said staring from beneath her brim.

"I reckon they *could,*" J.D. added, as he raised a hand in perfunctory greeting that McLean declined to acknowledge.

"And let's face it," said the preacher, his voice rising with ire, "it's

Perdue who forsook *us*! ...Like the prodigal son!" he pronounced, for which he was heartily rewarded with a chorus of earnest *Amens*!

The baby started squirming more energetically, catching Katie unprepared. It arched its back and raised its arms, and whelped as it tried to twist free. At first, she clutched it tight like a football, pressing it hard against her torso, but when that failed, she lateralled it into the arms of the woman beside her where it went limp in the woman's familiar embrace.

"I see," said J.D., like he was an old hand with children. "That *there's* the momma. I'd a known if it were Katie's," he assured himself.

"Duncan will know who she is," said Moira beneath her breath, still rapt by the mother's resemblance to Katie.

"Original *sin*!" said Preacher Small, finding new ground. "Who among us dare say deep inside a Phil Perdue don't lurk...that deep in our *hearts*... we don't *all* of us harbor a Phil Perdue!" A restive fidget rippled through the congregants.

"He wasn't *that* bad, was he?" Moira said to J.D.

"I reckon not, but who knows, Miss Moira?" J.D. whispered deferentially as Preacher Small whipped up rapture. J.D. knew better than to distract the preacher now.

The sermon closed with something about saving the fatted calf for someone more deserving than Phil Perdue, and the collection was taken and the congregation blessed. J.D. set the Kingfisher's course for his ritual tour of the lake, and Moira asked him to go by any way that avoided her family. It just wasn't fittin', thought J.D., that parent and child should be at such odds, but who was he to say.

"How do you think Phil ended up in Colombia, J.D.?" asked Moira, pretending to reflect on the sermon.

"No tellin', Miss Moira," J.D. replied. "There's still a warrant out for his arrest for the murder of Mort Ashton, his own uncle, and that was five years ago. Who knows how far down the path he gone since then. Nothing surprises me anymore."

"*You* keep a close eye on things around here, J.D., don't you? Did you have any inkling?"

"Well, I ain't with Preacher Small, if that's what you're askin'."

"And why is that?" Moira asked innocently enough.

"Pedro Morales," J.D. muttered, low and direct. "A vagrant grifter, with no place in these parts. Plenty of his ilk come around since the days you been here, Miss Moira," said J.D., tipping his hat and smiling solicitously as they passed sunbathers on a dock.

"Pedro Morales?" she asked, verging on progress.

"Pedro Morales," J.D. repeated, all scorn and contempt. "He gone now, I don't mind tellin' you. But he were runnin' with Phil in the days before Mort's murder," he said, cutting himself short and studying Moira quizzically. "Phil h'aint found all that trouble all on his own," he assured her.

"Where there's smoke there's fire, though J.D., isn't that what they say?" said Moira, to keep J.D. talking.

"I suppose," he said, waving to a passing boat.

"And no one's seen him since the murder?" Moira persisted, to see if J.D. would lie.

"You sure ask a lot of questions, Miss Moira, for someone who ain't come around for a while," said J.D., now on full alert, "or is you comin' to see me have somethin' to do with Phil?" Barely concealed in J.D.'s circumspect manner, Moira sensed an explosive tale - a tale about Phil she doubted he would tell. They completed their tour of the lake, J.D. dispensing salutations, and drawing occasional looks for the lady sitting low in his boat as mares' tails and mackerel scales filled the sky overhead. Soon, distant thunder sent half the boats on the water running for shelter, and the lake was left to the hearty, daring the rain to come.

It was against a cool, damp wind that they finally returned to

French's. They had set the Kingfisher in her hoists and were exiting the covered docks when Moira turned a corner and ran headlong into her father. She nearly knocked him off his feet as he strode to the *General Lee,* which was taking on fuel at the pumps with the full complement of her church goers still aboard.

"Pardon me, young lady!" said McLean before recognizing Moira. "Good grief!" he exclaimed, astonished and pleased, before he spied the sheriff standing behind her. "To whatever do we owe this happy surprise?" he asked, his eyes shifting testily to J.D.

"Howdy, Mr. McLean," said J.D., injecting himself sacrificially.

"I was on my way to see Momma," Moira blurted, "and..."

"And the good sheriff," McLean interrupted, to save her from herself, "knowing of your ardor for the Lord, offered you a ride to Boat Church," said McLean, clasping his hands. "How good of you," he observed, smiling at J.D. "Since I'm quite sure you intended sooner or later to visit with us at the house, why don't you come and say hello to everyone now?" McLean offered disingenuously. "Everyone will be so excited."

"I'll wait for you," said J.D., sensing Moira's distress.

"Why Moira!" Ana-Maria exclaimed with a simpering smile as Moira followed her father on to the fuel dock. "How lovely to see you," she fawned through her fluttering fake eyelashes. A large, fat raindrop plonked like a dropping on the gunwale beside her.

"Hey, Sis'" said Duncan.

"Hi Dunks," replied Moira, "and Katie. You're *so* grown up since the last time I saw you," she said, softening. Another rain drop plonked on the foredeck and spattered the windshield. The water surrounding the docks suddenly flowered with rippling circles.

"Hi, Moira...." said Katie, looking nervously overhead.

"Introduce your cousin," said Ana-Maria hastily, forcing a smile from her place in the center cockpit.

"This is my cousin, Manuela," said Katie self-consciously.

"From Colombia," Ana-Maria added in her deep, husky voice.

"And who's the little one?" Moira asked, squatting low at the edge of the dock to admire the baby.

"This is," said Katie, with a cartoon-character-stuffed-animal voice, "Phillipé."

"Quite some sermon about our old friend Phil Perdue," Malcolm interjected as the automatic shut-off on the gas pump clunked.

"I'm sorry," said Moira to Katie sympathetically. "I know you were friends." And by chance, in the moment, she saw Manuela's eyes drop.

"Poor blighter," said Malcolm, stepping the nozzle back into the gas pump. "Shouldn't wonder that his father isn't turning in his grave."

CHAPTER 39

Zeta Territory, Colombia

Phil couldn't believe his eyes as he stared through the gaping barn doors of a gleaming airplane hangar the size of a football field. It was set at the water's edge between two decrepit finger piers extending far into a protected cove, with a gently graded concrete boat ramp that rose to meet the production floor. It beat the hell out of the makeshift rails and cart they used back in Guajira. The finger piers abutting the hangar appeared to cater to a local fishing fleet. Brightly painted dories rode lazily on their mooring lines as fishing nets swayed from the rickety pilings, drying in the heat of the equatorial sun. A pelican hung like a sentinel high in the air, waiting for unsuspecting fish to stray from the shadows of the piers.

The cavernous interior of the hangar was a beehive of activity. Men in clean overalls milled in clutches around heavy wheeled cradles that carried ekranoplan skeletons in various stages of gestation. The painted concrete floor shined like a luxury car showroom, on which the men rolled the cradles between numbered assembly stations. There was even a paint shop where finished ekranoplans were dressed in matt black paint, which made them invisible at night, if not elegant by day, as Phil originally intended.

"You ain't in Kansas anymore," said Jim Bartsch as the hair pricked in Phil's nostrils. Then his startled salivary glands oozed at the odor he recognized instantly – the rich caustic smoke of Russian loose-leaf tobacco.

"Come on," said Jim, tapping Phil lightly on the shoulder. "I know someone who's going to be happy to see you."

Familiar faces among the men tracked his progress as he followed in Jim's footsteps across the production floor, a few standing in silence like an honor guard as he passed. The smell of Russian tobacco grew stronger as they approached the far corner of the hangar, where Vlad, as usual, stood hunched at a table. He was poring over blueprints, the way Phil remembered him, bathed in brilliant white light from articulated drafting lamps, and surrounded in abundance by unfamiliar stainless-steel tools.

"You son-of-a-gun," said Phil just loud enough for Vlad to hear him.

"Dis boy," said Vlad, turning from his work, and spreading his arms as he took Phil in. "Why you take so long?" Vlad demanded. Before Phil knew it, he was in the grip of a big Russian bearhug, the bulge in Vlad's belly pressed hard against his waist.

"How in tarnation did y'all pull *this* together?" asked Phil, gazing across the buzzing production floor.

"Ahh," said Vlad, waving a finger. "The Zeta. They have the money."

"They also control Maquiladora towns along the Mexican border," Jim added. "We pulled some talent from a few of the big car assembly plants."

"I reckon you did," said Phil, standing in awe before the extraordinary undertaking. Just beyond the open barn doors, the pelican dropped from the sky and crashed through the sunlit waters rocking gently beneath the piers.

"I'm hungry, too," said Jim. "I'll get us some lunch," he declared as the pelican beat its way back into the air, the tail of a luckless fish swaying from the corner of its bill.

"Look here, Mr. Phil" said Vlad, "at what we working on now."

It was almost three years since Vlad disappeared in the Zeta's midnight raid on the Guajira camp – and something Ian said the morning after the attack, when it appeared Vlad had been taken without a struggle, had stuck word-for-word in Phil's craw. *Who says his bags weren't packed? Who says he didn't help plan the attack? You're in the cartel world,* Ian had said. *More goes on than meets the eye.*

In sweltering prison yards and dank cinder block cells, in wood-paneled court rooms, and on slow-moving food lines with partitioned tin trays in his hands, Phil had pondered - how much did Vlad know, and when did he know it. The size and scale of the operation humming all around him offered precious little comfort that Vlad hadn't been in on it from the start. While Vlad thrived, Phil had done time, more recently awaiting execution.

"Hey Vlad?" he said, diverting Vlad from his blueprints. "It's been real long, I know, and I'm real interested in what you're workin' on here, but there's something I gotta know...that I gotta know right now." Vlad faced him slowly and reached for his pate. Phil reckoned by the look on Vlad's face that he knew what was coming, and that he had dreaded facing Phil since he vanished with the Zeta in the dark that night.

"Did y'all know they were comin' fer you that night, Vlad? the night they attacked the camp?" Vlad eyed him cautiously, brooding and silent, searching Phil's eyes for any hint of understanding.

"What you talking about?" he grumbled.

"*You* know what I'm askin', Vlad. Did you *know*...they were comin' fer us?"

"Why you think dis?" Vlad asked, retreat in his eyes.

"'Cause you're here, safe and sound, happy as a pig in shit. And Miguel, and Jim, too. It's worked out real good fer you. And they come and shot up and killed a bunch of us, and would a killed me and Manuela, too, if we ain't been lucky. Did – you – know?"

"No," said Vlad, shaking his head slowly.

"You a federal agent, too?" Phil asked, sounding betrayed, "like Ian?"

"Why you think dis? Why you say dese things?" asked Vlad defensively.

"'Cause I been convicted of murderin' Ian, no thanks to Jim," said Phil, "though I didn't. And Ian said, when you up and disappeared with no sign of a struggle, your bags could a been packed, just waitin' on them," said Phil, feeling hollow and heartless for accusing an old friend. "Were your bags packed, Vlad? Cause..." said Phil, taking stock of the busy airplane hangar, "you sure did land nice, based on what's goin' on around here."

"Here," said Vlad, extracting from his back pocket a soft leather tobacco-filled pouch and a small sheaf of rolling papers, "you have smoke, Phil, and we talk."

"I reckon not," said Phil. "I quit, in *prison*," he said, stabbing Vlad with his ire. "*Prison* gives you time, Vlad. 'Specially when it comes with an expiration date, like when you're sentenced to death for somethin' you *ain't done*," said Phil indignantly. "Lots of time to think, Vlad, on your life, on your people, who's your friends and who ain't. I don't reckon I have as many friends as I thought... *do* I?" Vlad looked shamed, shamed into submission.

"Jim, he explain," said Vlad, hanging his head. "He tell you why."

Jim soon reappeared with a bulging Cuban cigar clenched in his teeth, and two large grocery bags overflowing with south American cuisine. What he found was not the happy reunion for which he had hoped. Vlad had his nose deep in his blueprints, and Phil had climbed the catwalk over the work floor, from where he gazed aimlessly on the assembly operation below.

"It's like this, Phil," said Jim, standing beside him on the catwalk, looking out through the doors on the emerald waters of the cove. "The Guajira haven't been around that long, one of dozens of cartelitos to spin out of the Cali and Medellin cartels," he began. Skittering angular shapes of bright reflected sunlight moved all about them on the hangar's inside walls. "But they were different from the start. Small, scrappy, smart, slick – a highly professional organization. It's a compliment they drafted you, really," said Jim with authority.

"*Drafted* me?" said Phil. "You mean, it was planned from the start, Pedro always meant to take me away?"

"Of course," said Jim without hesitation. "Same for Vlad. They plucked him right out of Severomorsk, home base for the Russian northern fleet. Told him they had his missing son," Jim recounted sinisterly. "That's how they do it," Jim continued. "What'd they have on you?"

"How do you know this shit, Jim, and why should I trust you?"

"You don't have to trust me, Phil, but what are your options?" observed Jim, staring him hard in the face. "You didn't make a lot friends walking out on the Guajira. They want you dead, and odds are they already know you're here. You're sentenced to death back home, so where you gonna go?" Jim continued, holding the best for last. "And you're never seeing Manuela again, or the kid, if you don't cooperate."

"Well, *fuck*, Jimbo. I ain't done *nothin'* but cooperate - with Pedro, with you, even the Zeta before I escaped," said Phil righteously.

"Hold the phone, boy wonder." Jim interjected. "You'd be long dead, and Manuela, too, if Ian hadn't warned you to get out, and *Roll Tide* wasn't there, fueled up and waiting for you. *You* didn't escape, Phil. We *broke* you out, and Ian paid with his life for it, so just cut the shit."

"Well, thanks for nothin', Jim. Then you testified against me and got me sentenced to death. Whose side are you on?"

"Yours, Phil. You have to trust me on this one," he said soberly. "This is what I do. You build boats, I infiltrate cartels. Something's happening here, and you can help. But I'm not asking, Phil. I'm telling you. You're freedom, your girl, your boy, they're all in your hands. It's up to you."

It's up to you, Phil reflected. Just like that, Jim Bartsch had said what Emerson said, only Jim said it plainer, in not so many words, and in a way he now understood. No rules, no laws, no loyalties, no friendships – just you, what you do with your hands to follow your heart – as simple as that. A beam of glinting sunlight danced across the ceiling from the water, finding Phil's eyes before he could cover them.

"You were saying?" said Phil, recovering his sight.

"Ian was a very old wing man of mine, Phil, as you probably figured out by how quickly I dropped Pedro that night. We worked together a long time doing this stuff," Jim reminisced. "It's not Vlad's fault. You can't hold it against him. Ian got to Vlad and convinced him, enticed him, really, to plant GPS antennas in the subs, so we could track them. When that didn't work..."

"*Didn't work?*" Phil interrupted. "I thought a sub got caught, and Pedro shot José fer it," said Phil, remembering José's kindness, and his resistance to Phil's interest in Manuela before Pedro's mother prevailed on him to relent.

"Apparently that was a mistake. One of our Coast Guard interdiction units didn't get the memo and did their job, but a bunch of other subs got through, and that's how we knew we had a bigger problem."

"What kinda problem?" asked Phil.

"Our own surveillance was compromised. The Guajira were paying off Border Patrol to look the other way. We weren't stopping them, even when the subs were lit-up on our scopes like the fourth of July. And that's why we pulled Vlad out. He wasn't safe anymore."

"*You* pulled Vlad out, not the Zeta?" Phil asked in disbelief.

"Sure. We can look like anybody," said Jim, as if he assumed cartel identities for sport.

"And that's why you blew up our cradles and building sites? And killed Pedro's mother? To look like the Zeta?"

"They'd been feuding for years. They'd a blamed the Zeta anyway."

"Pedro's mother was *innocent*, Jim! *You* know that as well as I do, and she kept you fed, and in clean clothes. I guess killin' sweet old ladies is *what you do*, too."

Jim wasn't listening. He'd already moved on.

"*How* the hell did you think of ekranoplans, anyway?" Jim asked wondrously.

"It's what *I* do," said Phil.

"And whatever made you think supplying the whole damn cartel world was a good idea?"

It's not like he had cooked up the whole plan for fun, he explained to Jim. It had been a gambit for survival. The men had been spooked by the attack, and together with Phil they feared the recriminations that would follow Pedro's recovery. But for their labors, they all felt doomed, by enemies both inside and out. So they took a risk on the one thing they had, the thing they reckoned other cartels would want, too. Ekranoplans. And things started changing, slowly at first, like the subtle, imperceptible turn of the tide, until there was no going back.

"It was the only way to stop the killin', Jimbo," Phil finally said. "Give the Zeta what they want, and maybe they'd go away, 'cept now I know it weren't the Zeta. It were *you*."

"When we figured out the Guajira were behind our lines, inside Border Patrol," said Jim, without skipping a beat, "it got our attention. You tread a lot lighter when they're inside the perimeter because you can't tell who's in on it, or how far it goes, so we did the next logical thing, so as not to let on we were on to them."

"The next logical thing..." Phil repeated doubtfully.

"We looked for the money, and it was nowhere to be found. The drugs went out, nothing came back," said Jim sounding flummoxed. "We couldn't find the money and we couldn't find the moles inside Border Patrol, which put the masterminds running the show out of reach. And then you came up with something we never thought of."

"I did?"

"Yes. Flood the market with drugs by distributing an undefeatable delivery platform, drive down prices, destabilize the distributers and retailers, and wait for the bosses to cry foul. And that's what you did, and that's why we think the Guajira are an American run enterprise. *That* explains why we couldn't find the money."

"Why couldn't you find the money?"

"Because we were looking in the wrong places. Because it never leaves the States. Users buy with cash, and through a very slick money laundering operation we haven't cracked yet, it goes right back into a local bank, could even be the same cash machine it came out of hours before. The ones we're after could even *be* the banks, for all we know, but the Guajira aren't Colombian. They're American, that much we know. You made them cry uncle. That's how we found them...almost."

"Why...*almost.*"

"Non-specific intercepts originating in the States to Bogotá, most perturbed by the oversupply with no uncertain instructions to put a lid on it."

"Because prices dropped?" asked Phil, getting the gist of it.

"*And*, here's the punchline, the political cost of escalating street violence between distributors. *That* was a new one. We never heard it before. Someone in the States wanted you dead, not for your run-of-the-mill price war or territorial dispute, but for the *political cost* of street violence. Behind our lines, inside the banking system, and worried about political repercussions... the triple crown of bad actors. I told you they were slick."

"And you reckon you can find them," said Phil. Jim nodded.

"You were our secret weapon, Phil. You got them to surface, which is why Ian and I were both in camp when Pedro came back to kill you. We had to get you out, like Vlad, figuring you knew the bosses who wanted you dead."

"Dadgummit, Jim. I'd a told you if I knew," said Phil. "Why didn't you believe me?"

"We had to be sure, and the optics were right. If we got the U.S. Justice system to sentence you to death, we thought the Guajira would go back to their ways, and maybe let their guard down and make a mistake. But it didn't work. We can't get ahead of them. They're too good. Won't be long now 'til they hear you're back in town."

"Well ain't *that* fuckin' great, Jimbo. So you're usin' me for bait?"

"Hell no, Phil, we got much bigger plans than that."

There was always a plan and he was always a part of it – they just always neglected to tell him. How far could you take *Self-Reliance* invisibly possessed by opposing, malign forces that kept you bobbing like a puppet on a string?

"We're going to threaten to use your play book again, Phil," Jim was saying, "to flood the market. We'll let it out that you and Vlad are reunited, working for the Zeta. That will give it teeth."

"You're outta your fuckin' mind, Jim. I ain't yourn, or anybody's anymore," said Phil, looking over the men, and admiring the gleaming forms of spontoons taking shape in the cradles beneath him.

"Sure, you're not," said Jim patronizing him. "Go on. Just walk outta here. See how far you get."

The brilliant sun-splashed cove beyond the hangar doors beckoned him to freedom, and standing between the cove and the catwalk, a vision of ekranoplan production that was, at its heart of his making.

"Why y'all pickin' on me?" asked Phil, "and why the Zeta, for fuck's sake, Jim?"

"The enemy of my enemy is my friend," Jim said soberly.

"They know you're DEA?" asked Phil. "Humberto good with that?"

"We do it all the time, Phil, when they cross the line. Humberto's good people. It's not his first rodeo."

"*Cross the line*, Jim? What in tarnation are you talkin' about? Aren't they all crossin' the line?"

"Overreaching," said Jim, "sticken their noses in things that go beyond drug trafficking, like wars and politics. What do you think finally did in the Contras, and Pablo Escobar? They should have stuck to drug trafficking."

"And that's what the Guajira done," Phil said flatly, getting the lay of the land. "They got a hankering for politics?"

"We think so. You're going to find out."

"Why ain't they gonna shoot me dead, soon as they lay eyes on me?" said Phil, impressed by the ridiculousness.

"Didn't you hear what Humberto said? Didn't you see the way these men looked at you walking across the floor? Every one of them looked like they'd seen the Goddamn Virgin Mary."

"So *I'm* gonna ride over to the Guajira camp like it's Sunday-go-to-meetin' and say *take me to your leader*?"

"Not exactly. Humberto's going to threaten to turn loose all these beautiful ekranoplans to all takers, every cartelito we can find, flood the market, drive down prices, foment violence in the streets back home, just like you did, unless the Zeta get the same safe passage protections from Border Patrol as the Guajira seem to have."

"And you think they'll go for it," said Phil.

"Don't know," said Jim, "but it'll be hard as hell to put the genie back in the bottle when fifty of these things with as many different owners start making daily crossings of the Caribbean."

"That *would* be a sight," said Phil wistfully.

"They'll offer Humberto assurances they can deliver," Jim continued "but he won't accept anything less than a direct channel, a face-to-face meeting between you as his emissary and the Guajira's U.S. leaders. You'll identify them for us, and we'll take it from there."

"You reckon?" said Phil, taken by Jim's plan.

"Yes, Phil. I reckon. It's what I do, remember?"

"And I'll live to see Manuela again?"

"Sure, you will. That's the deal. They won't kill Humberto's emissary, unless they're looking for all-out war, and they won't dare kill – what did Humberto call you? The spirit of the *Americanos*."

CHAPTER 40

Organized Crime Drug Enforcement Task Forces Fusion Center, Washington, D.C.

"Bartsch, hunh?" said Grover, Sam's confidant at Special Operations Division, the clearing house for Sam's Proactive Asset Targeting Team, or PATT, Reports. "Rings a bell. Last known operating theater?"

"Central America," Sam floated, "but that's unofficial."

"Ain't it always. I'll take a look. Standby." Sam heard his line placed on hold.

"Yup, he's the real deal, Sam," said Grover when he came back on the line. "Went from FAST to Internal Affairs. Last known assignment was Anti-Corruption unit, went off the grid about three years ago. They keep the files on the Internal Affairs guys locked down, so guys like you and me can't find out when they're watching us. He's either operating deep-cover running an operation, or he turned."

"What kind of deep-cover operation?" asked Sam, trying not to sound naïve.

"Remember, like ten years ago, the DOJ authorized something

called Attorney General Exempted Operations?" It sounded familiar, but Sam couldn't place it.

"Sure, I remember," said Sam. "Whatever happened to those?"

"They got out of hand. There was no supervision, and the approved institutions took full advantage – surprise, surprise. A lot of them made bank without ever catching the crime syndicates they were targeting." Now Sam remembered. The DOJ issued free passes to a handful of credible institutions to launder money, hoping to draw in the crime syndicates eluding them.

"Anyway," Grover continued, "your friend Bartsch could be working enforcement on one of the exempted operations. If he's not doing that, I'm stumped. Or, like I said, he turned. Happens all the time. SOD can't compete on women or money, and cartels speak the language of cowboys like Bartsch. I'll have to get clearance to dig deeper."

"No!" said Sam, knowing the call was monitored. "There's no context. It's non-specific. I'm running in circles looking for a break."

"Sure?"

"Yeah, I'm sure. I'll poke you again if there's something concrete," said Sam, following Lenny's orders not to raise eyebrows.

* * * * *

"You ever wonder why your pal at FinCEN, Dan Thorne, never did more with the tip we gave him on Atlanta Guaranty and Trust?" posed Sam. Of course Lenny had wondered, but a part of him was relieved, until Moira had cleared herself of suspicion. Now their affair was just embarrassing rather than professional suicide.

"I'll tell you why," said Sam.

"Tell me why what?" Lenny snapped, contemplating Dan Thorne's failure to act.

"Why FinCEN went dark after the thing with the boat business in Lost Lake."

"Why?" asked Lenny, ashamed of himself all over again for letting Moira hold him hostage for so long.

"Attorney General Exempted Operations. That explains Atlanta Guaranty and Trust, it explains the inactivity after the SAR on the boat business, and explains why Thorne at FinCEN told you to stay away. DOJ and FinCEN were laying a trap. It explains the whole damn thing. Of course, they're laundering money. They were told to, hoping to land a big one."

"How does it explain how fast the disinformation we fed Sheriff Dunbar moved?" Lenny countered, rearranging the pieces in his head.

"That's easy, boss. It almost worked. I hope we didn't blow an operation with disinformation." Lenny hoped not, too. Sam's logic was unassailable, and embarrassing and ironic, especially for Fusion, if true.

"How'd you come up with that?" Lenny asked defensively.

"I didn't. Bartsch. You asked me to look into Bartsch," said Sam.

"And he's a part of it? Working it from inside the cartels?"

"Can't say. My SOD contact told me Bartsch's last hitch was Internal Affairs, Anti-Corruption, that he'd have to get clearance to find out more, so I told him to back off."

"So how does that square with an AG Exempted Operation?" asked Lenny.

"My contact thought he heard AG Exempted Operations were under scrutiny for going off the rails. For helping themselves to legitimately laundered money while they waited to spring the trap. He thought Bartsch was either running enforcement on an AG Exempted Operation, or could have turned altogether and gone off the grid to assist the cartels."

"Doesn't leave much middle ground, does it?" said Lenny doubtfully.

"No," said Sam. "We don't know much, but we know this. Bartsch is real, or was two years ago, and Phil Perdue knows him. What we need now is news from Moira, and the results of her parlay with the good sheriff."

Several days passed with no word from Moira. It was making Lenny twitchy. Lingering suspicions of Moira's treachery stirred deep and unwelcomed in his soul. He feared Moira hadn't trod lightly enough, and warned J.D. they were on to him and his Colombian connection. Then he received an unexpected call from his old friend, Dan Thorne, Director at FinCEN. Thorne rambled on uncharacteristically long and with no apparent purpose, except to drop a cryptic hint about some sort of disruption taking place at SOD.

"Sam!" Lenny barked across Fusion's office bull pens. "Call down to SOD. Find out what's going on." Sam soon appeared, white as a ghost, standing at the threshold of Lenny's office door.

"I don't like it," Sam said fearfully. "I'm getting *incorrect extension* recordings from both my guys." Just then his cell phone twanged, his personal setting for an encrypted Signal App alert.

"It's Grover," Sam said to Lenny, panic in his eyes, as he finished reading the message. "He's gone," said Sam, "so is most of his department. He says stop asking questions and destroy whatever we have on Bartsch." It could only mean that some combination of Moira and Sam's inquiries had blown an Internal Affairs operation. Caught in the crosshairs with their pants down, the elements of SOD that Lenny and Sam always suspected, were covering. But everyone ran for cover Lenny tried to assure himself when Internal Affairs came to town.

Once again, Lenny feared, he had been his own worst enemy. He had more than a sinking feeling he had blown someone's cover, exposing the good guys, alerting the bad guys, and painting himself and Sam in bullseye red.

"What do we do now, Lenny?" Sam whined. "Do we try to warn Bartsch we just ratted him out?" said Sam searchingly. "Or is it goodbye, good luck, nice knowing you." Lenny knew all too well it was the latter. Wherever Bartsch was, he was now on his own, and not for the first time, Lenny figured.

"You know better than to ask me that, Sam," said Lenny discouragingly with his head in his hands. "We've done enough for today, don't you think?"

CHAPTER 41

U.S. Coast Guard Cutter *Osprey*, Caribbean Sea

"As you can tell," Buldoc said standing before the HITRON team in the *Osprey's* ready room, "we poured on the coals about four hours ago and headed southwest. Our orders are to link-up with units supporting a big anti-narcotics operation on the Colombian coast, right here," he said, pointing to a map on the illuminated projection screen. "It's a regular flotilla of support elements moving fast from all points into the area."

"GANTSEC support elements?" asked Gutterson suspiciously.

"Who do you think, Gutterson? Yes, GANTSEC elements. Another HITRON team and two cutters."

"What's the mission, shake down go-fasts to collect the rent?" Gutterson chirped.

"The intel picture is still evolving," said Buldoc, studiously avoiding Gutterson's barbs, "so things are fluid. We'll be on station seven miles off the beach in about five hours. The weather will get shitty. We have tropical storm warnings over the area beginning in three hours. Gregson will brief you up once we know the plan.

That's all," he concluded, extinguishing the projector and departing the room.

"Aren't we heading back to where we infilled that kid a few months ago?" Casey asked.

"Yes," said Gutterson darkly.

"You think they're connected?" Dougie asked. "He didn't seem the type to bring this much heat."

"I don't like it, Dougie," Gutterson replied. "We took him in all cloak-and-dagger, and now we're back with the whole damn fleet. Maybe something went wrong. Looks like a brute force mop up operation to me," Gutterson hazarded.

"That's not our mission," said Casey primly.

"It is tonight," replied Gutterson, "with GANTSEC watching to see we do our jobs."

The *Osprey* surfed on a following sea deep into the Caribbean basin as the cloud breaks filled, the sunlight dissolved, and daylight gave way to an eerie yellow dusk. The hours passed slowly and the HITRON team took to their bunks, a fitful rest being better than none before embarking on what they expected to be a long evening. Dougie thought he might have been sleeping when the call burbled from the ship's PA for HITRON to assemble in the ready room at seventeen hundred. There was no point in lying around watching the clock, and he was out of his bunk, dressed in his flight suit, and splashing water on his face in less than five minutes. A few minutes later he was sitting in his regular ready room chair beside Gutterson, who was already there, and Casey, who followed closely on Dougie's heels as the *Osprey's* transom corkscrewed on the heavy quartering sea. Gregson and Buldoc looked stern standing shoulder-to-shoulder by the screen at the front of the room.

"Please close the door," Gregson instructed Casey before igniting the projector. "These were taken this morning," Gregson continued. He focused the projector lens to sharpen the lines on the screen.

"It doesn't look like much from the air, maybe a warehouse, or a fish sorting and processing plant for the local commercial fleet," he said, circling the football field sized building cradled in the bend of a cove. "But this is the target."

"Target for what?" Casey blurted. He thought he left combat operations behind in the army.

"Colombian anti-narcotics says this is a state-of-the-art manufacturing facility for the ekranoplans we've had so much trouble stopping, and they're pumping 'em out by the dozen."

"Now I get it," said Gutterson. "That kid we sent back in? He was flying one when we picked him up a few years back. He told us he built it, remember?"

"This is a Colombian army operation, supported by a couple of our FAST teams," Gregson continued. "It may go down without a shot, but I wouldn't count on it. It's Zeta territory. They won't mind getting bloody."

"Are you telling us we're flying combat air support?" Dougie asked in distress.

"Hardly," said Gregson, chuffing at the preposterousness of the idea. Casey shot Gutterson a meaningful glance. Between the two of them, they were up to it.

"Our assignment is cutting off squirters, if they take to the water," said Gregson, clearly underwhelmed by the weightiness of the job.

"And Medivac," added Buldoc, "the cutter sickbays will be the closest medical facilities."

"That reminds me," added Gregson. "If you take ground fire and need to defend yourselves, our guys will have infrared combat identification beacons. You'll have no trouble picking them up on night vision. Everything else is fair game."

"Roger that," snapped Gutterson, mocking Gregson's bravado. Gregson eyed Gutterson menacingly before standing down and taking a seat in the ready room front row. Buldoc took Gregson's place beside the screen.

"Everything on the water is friendly," said Buldoc, projecting on the screen active surface radar contacts. "These are all GANTSEC elements," he continued, waving his hand over half a dozen blips forming a semi-circle to the left and right of the *Osprey*.

"Wow," said Gutterson. "That's quite a dragnet."

"I don't plan or design the tactics," said Buldoc. "Neither do you, Gutterson."

"I've seen this drill before. They're looking for somebody," Gutterson replied, "nobody gets out, not no way, not no how."

"That's right," Casey added impulsively, "it's a classic catch or kill formation."

"Someone hasn't paid the piper," Gutterson added cynically.

"What the hell do you mean by that?" demanded Buldoc.

"Isn't it obvious? Nobody needs a GANTSEC hall pass anymore because they're building their own ekranoplans, though why we helped them by sending the kid back in beats the hell out of me." When Gutterson realized he had the room's attention he continued. "Look, this is a shakedown, a friendly reminder from GANTSEC of certain obligations to Border Patrol," Gutterson concluded. "An *enforcement action*, isn't that what they call it?"

"That's what you think?" posed Gregson uncertainly, weighing Gutterson's argument as he stared at the radar contacts on the screen.

"Just a guess," Gutterson replied, "but that's how it looks to me," he continued, because Gregson was listening. "Aren't these raids usually stealthy, precision strike affairs? This looks like the fucking Normandy invasion. Why?"

CHAPTER 42

Zeta Territory, Colombia

Only a few hours before, the fishing nets had hung in listless coils, drying in the baking sun, while the dories swayed easily on their lines; but now the nets curled and cracked in the wind, and the dories tossed, bucking like colts at their lines, their colorful paintjobs dimming in the dusk. Mangroves guarding the wind-whipped cove billowed in convulsive supplication to gusts landing hard off the steel grey ocean, and angry little foam-crested waves licked and lapped at the decaying pilings.

Inside the hangar the work day was done, and the big barn doors were fastened tightly against the closing storm. The men milled about their assembly stations, squaring up tools, and wiping down work surfaces, drifting off in ones and twos to head for the exits at the back of the hangar.

"Let's head back to Hacienda Xixim and check-in with Humberto," Jim called to Phil from the door. "See if he's heard back from our Guajira friends about setting up your meeting." They climbed into Jim's open air Land Rover with the windshield laid flat on the hood. As Jim cranked the engine a clear white flair climbed on the wind from the trees on the hill up the road.

"That's not right," Jim said ominously, staring into the sky. "Let's take a look." He threw the truck in gear and popped the clutch, spinning its wheels and spraying loose dirt in his haste to reach the road. They had traveled no more than a few hundred yards when another flair rose in the sky, this one off to the left, zig-zagging like lightening on the gusty air. Jim braked hard, put the engine in neutral, and surveyed the hills, left, right and center. In the fading light, the silhouetted crowns of wind tossed palms broke the crisp clear lines of the hillsides. *Tak-tak-tak-tak-tak-tak* came the unmistakable sound of gunfire from the darkness on the hill-side to the right.

"This ain't good," said Jim, jamming the gearshift in reverse and punching the gas. *Tak-tak-tak-tak-tak-tak* came the gunfire again, this time from the left, where the second flair had risen.

"What a mistake," said Jim to no one in particular, "...if this is the Guajira's idea of a quick answer. Come on, Phil, get inside," Jim yelled, retreating from the vehicle to the hangar.

"Our guys are ready for this shit," Jim said calmly. "They won't make it down the hillside, whoever it is," he reassured Phil, quick-ening his pace for the lockers where the men stored their personal effects during the day. He stopped at one with a padlock and di-aled in a combination, yanking down hard to release the lock, and swinging the locker door wide.

"You know how this goes," said Jim routinely, passing Phil a handgun. "Take a couple extra clips," he added, placing them in Phil's free hand.

Jim helped himself to a combat vest packing six crescent shaped magazines and an assortment of other menacing gadgetry, all of it foreign to Phil. He pulled from a stand at the rear of the locker an angular black long gun of the variety Zeke had carried, and hung it on his chest by a strap around his neck. On his head he placed a black hockey helmet looking contraption with night vision goggles that made him look like a beekeeper by how the hardware jutted from his forehead. Then he slammed shut the locker door, replaced the padlock, and spun the combination dial.

"I doubt we'll need any of this shit," he said with a smile to Phil. "But there won't be time to come back and get it if we do. Let's go," he finished, double timing it to the end of the hangar overlooking the cove.

The sound of gunfire from the hills intensified, traveling in muffled waves through the blustery twilight.

"It's getting closer," said Phil as Jim led him by a side door into the night.

"That it is, my friend," said Jim. "Stay on your toes."

"How many guys are up there guarding this place?" Phil asked.

"A lot," said Jim, "more than they need. I'd hate to think they've met their match." Jim craned his head, turning his ear to the wind and closing his eyes. The sound of more gun fire carried in the dusk, muffled by gusts from the cove. "Not good," Jim whispered.

"What," said Phil.

"*Hush*," said Jim with his finger to his lips. "Listen." *Tak-tak-tak-tak-tak-tak* carried from the left to where they crouched behind the hangar by the water. "That's Colombian regular army, spraying their shit everywhere. Keep listening." Suddenly, close by, from the right *Tak-tak, Tak-tak, Tak-tak*.

"Fuck," Jim said. "Those are operators. We need to move."

"Operators?" Phil asked.

"Yeah, either U.S. or U.S.-trained. You can tell by the double taps. They're conserving ammo, and putting it on target, you can bet. Let's just take a gander," said Jim, dropping the night vision goggles on his helmet over his eyes. "Yeah, they're lighted," he said, reaching for a puck shaped device attached at the shoulder to his vest. He twisted it like a bottle top. "That should keep us safe, at least from them," said Jim, "though why they're here beats the crap out of me. Let's move. Nothing good is happening here. Can you crank an outboard on one of those dories on the pier?" he said, the dull roar of distant surf deadening the sound of fresh gunfire descending from the hills.

"Can *I* crank an outboard? Are you kidding me?" said Phil, vaguely amused.

"Then get to it! I'll divert them until you're cranked up and ready to push off," said Jim, sighting his gun up the hill from the hangar. Phil bolted for the pier. The aging boards bent beneath his weight as he neared the last course of pilings in the dark. He was eying a long, wide dory with a peaked prow and plenty of freeboard, when the sound of lead raining on metal echoed from where he left Jim by the hangar.

* * * * *

"HITRON Two, air traffic control, you're cleared for take-off," crackled *Melissa's* familiar voice through Hank Gutterson's helmet. "Wind at zero-six-five degrees, steady at thirty, gusting forty," she continued from her command center twelve thousand feet overhead. "We have two souls outbound in an open vessel heading for open water from the cove. Be advised, HITRON One is airborne with a medivac, maintain separation."

"Roger that," Gutterson gurgled in his gravelly voice through the comms. "Here we go, boys," he advised Dougie and Casey as he flicked on the avionics, ran through the checklist, and lit the flame on the *Dolphin's* twin gas turbine engines.

"They'll be in the water as soon as they hit the surf," said Dougie as Hank engaged the blades.

CHAPTER 43

Lost Lake, Georgia

Marion was on J.D. like a duck on a June bug when nothing came of his call to Lenny Marks. It was no surprise to J.D. that Marks never called back. Fusion wasn't the sort of place known for doing favors, and Marks didn't seem the willing type. So J.D. and Marion reckoned Phil was done for - that is, until Betty Dunphy called J.D. at home on Saturday night.

"Why hey, Betty," J.D. said. "Everything alright?" Marion perked up, muting the volume without taking her eyes off the TV screen. It was third and goal with the Bulldogs in possession and they were only trailing by three. "Why that *is* unusual, Betty. Did he leave a number?" Tech called a time out, to make the Bulldogs think about it, and Marion sat up and looked at J.D. *What is going on* she mouthed with upturned palms. "Got it," said J.D., I'll call him right now. Thank you, Betty. Y'all have nice evenin' now. Goodnight."

"What is going on," Marion demanded.

"Not sure. Let me make a call."

An old stone patio behind the *Gaslight Bar* two miles down the road from HITRON's home base on Cecil Field, Florida, glowed in the pastel hues of paper lanterns that hung by extension cords from the nearby trees. Hank Gutterson had parked himself deep in a back corner to assure himself privacy, and his cell phone was in hand when the call from J.D. came through.

"And Phil told y'all that?" said J.D. when Gutterson was done.

"No, sheriff. The agent accompanying him, who died of his wounds, said it. Phil just wanted you to hear it from me. I wouldn't have gone to the trouble unless I believed it, which I do, but there's not much I can do with it except to say it sounds credible, very consistent with the shenanigans we see day-in, day-out at Border Patrol. Phil said he trusted you, and you'd know what to do."

"Phil said that?"

"Yes, sir," said Gutterson unequivocally. Marion knew trouble by the look on J.D.'s face, and she leaned in close to his cheek, eavesdropping. It was trouble J.D. could live without, the kind of trouble for which he knew but one man. "Then I'll leave it with you, sheriff," said Gutterson, "and I've kept my end of the bargain," Gutterson finished, promptly ending the call.

"What all was *that* about?" Marion demanded. J.D.'s head swam. Last he knew, J.D. explained to Marion, Phil was where he left him four months back, in the Coleman Federal Penitentiary in Florida. Then, at Marion's insistence, J.D. had called Lenny Marks at Fusion, and given Marks the names Phil mentioned, and described how Phil said he knew them from Colombia. That was the last he'd heard of it, and just assumed Phil had been in prison all this time, but not according to the feller on the phone.

"Well, *who* was on the phone?" Marion frothed. "And *what* in tarnation did *he* say?" It was so far-fetched J.D. could barely believe it, and he gathered himself before retelling it, so the high points comported with what he knew Marion already overheard.

The man on the phone claimed to be a member of a Coast Guard tactical drug interdiction unit. He'd picked up Phil the first time more than two years ago flying some high-speed contraption the likes of which nobody had ever seen, "which *does* sound like our Phil, don't it," J.D. felt compelled to add, to reassure Marion he thought the story held up. That's how Phil landed in prison the first time, where he did two years on the way to being tried, convicted and sentenced to death. Now, this same feller, one Lieutenant Colonel Gutterson, picked Phil up again last week fleeing an anti-narcotics operation on the north coast of Colombia. Gutterson had called J.D.'s office at Phil's request to vouch for the last testament of a federal agent who died escaping Colombia with Phil, who had drafted Phil to identify the leaders of a crafty cartel operating from inside the United States. The Coast Guard turned Phil over to federal authorities as soon as they made port.

By the time J.D. finished, Marion was speechless. They sat in despondent silence on the sofa together, even as the Bulldogs ran for a two-point conversion putting the game all but out of reach for Tech. The only person with any knowledge of such matters, or power to get at the truth, had been discourteous, unresponsive, and flat out belligerent the first time he came around. And yet, this was his field, his kind of trouble, entailing the menacing sort of murkiness for which paranoids like Lenny Marks were meant.

"Is there any way to tell, before you call him, whose side he's on?" Marion bleated plaintively, seeing for the first time how J.D. could be in danger.

"There's just no tellin'," J.D. said despairingly. "Not before I call him, and you can be damn sure not *after* I call him. But I don't see as I have another choice, on account of Phil's date with the electric chair if nobody does nothin'." She knew he was right, reminded once more why she loved him.

When J.D. finally picked up the phone to Fusion, Lenny was more surprised to hear Phil was *back* in jail than J.D. had been to hear Phil was let out. Lenny knew Phil had been *moved,* but he never imagined that meant he had been released.

"And *who* told you all this, sheriff?"

"A feller who goes by Gutterson. Says he flies with a Coast Guard tactical interdiction unit that picked Phil up two years ago, reinserted him into Colombia a few months back, then picked him up again just recently fleeing a major anti-narcotics operation with this feller, Bartsch, whose name I already gave you." It wasn't the moment to observe that Lenny never called him back. Nor did Lenny feel compelled to report that Sam's inquiries after Bartsch had done more harm than good.

"And you think Gutterson is credible?" Lenny asked.

"Hell, *I* don't know, Mr. Marks. *That* shouldn't be hard to find out. The question is was *Bartsch* credible, on account of Gutterson said this all came from *him*."

Lenny and Sam already knew enough about Bartsch from the accessible parts of his file to respect his jobs and talents. Highly trained, proven in countless missions, in continuous demand by ever more clandestine units performing ever more discrete operations. And Perdue had been captured, convicted, released and reinserted, only to surface in the company of Bartsch fleeing an anti-narcotics operation. It gave Lenny hope - hope that someone the caliber of Bartsch had been assigned to Internal Affairs, according to Sam's source, and might be working Anti-Corruption. It only made sense that such an operation would start *inside* a cartel, and work its way back to who was paying and taking bribes. It also made sense of Perdue's release back to the cartels. Perdue must have cut a deal working with Bartsch to expose the compromised factions of Homeland Security.

"Where can we find him," Lenny asked.

"He says he's stationed at Cecil Field in Florida."

"Bartsch?" asked Lenny, momentarily confused.

"No, Gutterson."

"I want to talk to Bartsch," Lenny snapped, impatient with the sheriff again.

"Well that will take some doin'," said J.D. firmly, "on account of he's dead."

Lenny hadn't wanted to believe that Sam's inquiry about Bartsch had tipped SOD to an Internal Affairs Anti-Corruption operation, but it was hard to ignore the facts. The unit to which Sam's contact was attached was scrubbed within hours of Sam mentioning Bartsch, and Sam was warned by his terminated contact to destroy everything he had on Bartsch. Then Bartsch had been killed in an anti-narcotics sweep in which he should have been participating. It strained credibility that so seasoned an operative would die in a routine operation – unless that had been the plan.

There was no ignoring either how persistently this character Perdue resurfaced, nor how poorly his company fared – first, an informant in witness protection, and now a highly experienced operator. The pattern was incontrovertible. He moved with conspicuous ease between the drug trade and the legal system, between the U.S. and Colombia, accompanied if not escorted by U.S. authorities of one kind or another. Perdue was connected, to whom and for what purpose Lenny aimed to find out. Nobody else could possibly know what Bartsch had really been up to.

"Where's Perdue?' Lenny asked.

"I don't know, Mr. Marks. I called you just as soon as I hung up with Gutterson. Back at Coleman Federal Pen would be my bet. That's where I visited with him."

Coleman - from where Perdue disappeared without a trace once before. Lenny was done asking questions that got people killed, but he needed Perdue to talk before SOD or anybody else reached him and sent his secrets, like Bartsch's, to the grave.

"How do you feel about an all-expenses paid roundtrip ticket to

Coleman, sheriff?" asked Lenny as sweetly as he knew how. "Sounds like you're the last man standing he'll talk to."

"I reckon I'm willing, Mr. Marks, but what you want him to tell me?"

"I want him to tell you everything he knows, and I need you to go as soon as possible, tonight if you can still catch a flight."

"I don't need no roundtrip ticket, Mr. Marks," said J.D. - it always surprised him how limited was the Yankee imagination in the use of cars. "Hell, Mr. Marks, I can be in the truck in twenty minutes, and standing at the front gates of Coleman by daybreak. But *why*? Is it *that* important?"

"I think so," said Lenny. "Coleman isn't safe for anyone who knows as much as Perdue."

"Then let's get him outta there, for crying out loud," said J.D., "to someplace safe, where we can take our time, set a spell, and visit."

"And how are you going to do that, sheriff? Fly in on Chitty-Chitty-Bang-Bang? He's on death row." J.D. chuckled.

"That's good, Mr. Marks. Chitty-Chitty-Bang-Bang," said J.D. "But I don't need me no Chitty-Chitty-Bang-Bang, Mr. Marks. I'm a federal marshal. I can take prisoners wherever I want."

"You'll need a warrant. How long's that going to take?"

"I *have* a warrant, Mr. Marks, for the murder of Harry Halliday. What I need is a judge's order to transfer him," said J.D., demonstrating to Lenny that it wasn't *his* first rodeo.

"That 'll take forever," said Lenny, sounding exasperated.

"Not in Lost Lake, Mr. Marks. Judge Dawson's in my Bible study group. I'll call over there tonight. She'll have me an order by morning, to remand Phil Perdue to Georgia to face the charge of murder in the death of Harry Halliday," said J.D. proudly. It was just as Lenny suspected – exactly how he'd always thought things worked in backwater towns like Lost Lake, and for once he was glad.

J.D. gave Lenny assurances he would have Perdue in the Lost Lake lock-up by sundown tomorrow. And there he would stay "under my personal supervision," said J.D., until he "spoke his piece." It was a perilous sounding end to an otherwise promising exchange, thought Lenny, for wasn't it under J.D.'s personal supervision that Halliday met his gruesome fate?

CHAPTER 44

Lost Lake, Georgia

Forty-five minutes after hanging up with Lenny Marks, J.D. was fueled up and on the road heading for Florida to bring Phil home. It would have been thirty minutes, except Marion wasn't about to let him go alone, and she needed more time to pull together the right clothes. He always felt better when she was there, and she'd keep him awake for the seven-hour drive, talking. She wanted to know everything, as usual. Who was Gutterson, what was a tactical interdiction unit, what could Phil have gotten himself into, and what did Marks say? Did Marks know anything about the men Phil told J.D. about when he visited Phil in prison, how did Phil get out of prison, how did he end up back in Colombia, who was the girl Phil had talked about, and where could *she* have gotten to? There were times when the questions and complexities left J.D. plum overwhelmed. Long car rides and country music generally rejuvenated him, but not this time, because that's not how Marion worked. It was one big scrambled mystery she was determined to solve, with no prospect of quiet anywhere in J.D.'s immediate future. They checked into a rundown motel in Sumterville, two miles west of Coleman Federal Penitentiary, at three a.m., enough time to sleep a few hours and be at the prison gates in uniform when Judge Dawson's order came through.

It went without a hitch. The guards and deputies were busy, Sunday being a popular visiting day, and they were more inclined to accommodate a federal marshal acting on the order of a judge than conduct the countless searches required of visitors before they entered prison grounds. Marion waited anxiously in the rear seat of J.D.'s king cab pickup. She had dressed the same as she would for the opening day of school, it being Sunday, and because she thought looking the way Phil remembered her would comfort him after everything he'd been through. When she lost sight of her charges from Lost Lake Regional High, and especially when they turned up on the other side of the law, Marion assumed she had lost them forever. She never did try her hand at recovery because she'd never had the chance. But now, with just such an opportunity, she would not shrink from it.

J.D. showed his badge and jumped the visitors line forming at the prison gates. Twenty minutes later he reemerged with Phil, squinting in the sun, shuffling clumsily in leg irons with his hands cuffed behind his back. J.D. had him clasped like a vice by the armpit as he guided him toward the truck. By gum, thought Marion, he looked the same. No, he looked better. Strong and loose and rested, and like to charm you silly if he wanted. How could it be he'd spent years running drugs, two more years in prison, and been sentenced to death for murdering a federal agent. It pained her to admit that in all the wrong ways he had taken her teaching to heart - striking out on his own in the world, albeit in an unprescribed way, he was *Self-Reliance* embodied – and looking the better for it, she dared say, despite his crimes. She could barely wait to put her hands on him, there being nothing more important now than carrying him home to Lost Lake and setting him on the path to mending his ways.

J.D. opened the passenger side front door and bent Phil over the hood. He unlocked one cuff, directed Phil to the passenger's seat, and locked the free cuff to the dashboard handle.

"Don't try nothin' with your free hand," said J.D. swinging his billy-club, "or I'll break it," he said, bringing the club down hard on the handle.

"*Well*, I'm *sure* there's no reason for *that*," said Marion.

"Hey, Ms. B," said Phil, the way he used to when he breezed by her in the school library. He turned as much as his cuffed hand allowed to look her in the eye. "Real nice of y'all to come get me. I hope this ain't puttin' y'all out none." They were kind, familiar faces, the sort he used to trust. "I can't believe you're here. What brought you all this way?" he asked guardedly.

"Why you, of course, Phil," said Marion. "We been worried sick about you for years now, and thought you were lost," she said, as if bygones were bygones.

"I reckon I *am* lost, Ms. B," said Phil smiling. "And if I ain't, there's no such thing."

"How you talk, Phil. You're not lost as long as J.D. and I are here, you just remember that. Now start at the beginning, and tell us everything."

"Everything?" Phil asked J.D. nervously, "you sure?" J.D. looked him in the eye and nodded.

Marion's knack for interrogation was about to come in handy, J.D. reckoned. At this rate she'd have all of Lenny Marks' questions answered before reaching the lake road.

"I reckon we got time," J.D. assured Phil. "It's seven hours back home, where you'll await trial for the murder of Harry Halliday."

"You *mean* my Uncle Mort," Phil said earnestly.

"Nah, you can dispense with the bull, Phil. Marion knows who he was," said J.D., "and the truth will come out at trial."

"Woulda been nice to know myself," said Phil, "than learn it from Pedro, who know'd when he done it who he was killin', and planned it all along."

"*See*?" Marion crowed triumphantly. "I *knew* you could never have done that, Phil. I just knew it, and said so myself, didn't I, J.D.?"

"Yes, indeed," said J.D., "that's what you said. But how's Phil gonna prove it?"

"We'll worry about that later, J.D.," said Marion reassuringly, like *there goes J.D. again being nit-picky.* "Now, you start at the beginning, Phil, like I said. Go on. Tell us everything."

Start at the beginning Phil did, with the debts his father owed. The bank had called the loans without notice, almost like they meant to force him off the land, because he had no reasonable prospect of repaying them on such short notice. It had been the first of many inexplicable twists of fate in a long, strange five-year journey. He had sought help the places he knew to look, among folks like Mr. McLean, with money to burn, whose boats were treated like family by him and his father, but they all turned their backs on him, his customers and the bank alike. And then, on the same morning his fake Uncle Mort showed up to foreclose, rescue arrived in the unlikely figure of Pedro Morales, wanting to do a lot of business, and all in cash. But Mort wouldn't have it, and that cost him his life, or so it seemed at the time.

Phil reckoned Pedro had been pretty good to him until just before the end, and a darn sight better than McLean or the bank. Pedro had understood how Phil would be blamed for Mort's killing, the motive being plain, and ushered him out of the country to safety in Colombia. There'd be nothing left for him in Lost Lake, after all, when the bank took his business, and with nowhere to go and nothing to do, and Mort lying dead in his house, he ran off with Pedro, never reckoning on coming back – because it would land him in jail – which is what happened, but that was for killing another man, who he didn't kill either. Marion lost her breath trying to keep pace.

Truth was, Colombia had been an adventure. He had made friends easily, and with people from everywhere, like Russia and Australia, and what a place! There was no describing it. The plants, the animals, the colors, and the ocean – there was just nothing like it.

"And I reckon *one thing* I learned, Ms. B. Be careful when folks start bein' nice to you. There's a reason." She resisted the urge to soothe his world-weariness with platitudes, on account of it ringing somewhat of the truth.

"I won't be so quick to think it's because they like you that folks treat you good. I reckon it's more what you can do fer 'em they like, and that's where things get complicated. Sometimes you cain't see how doin' what you're good at leads to trouble, and how good work for bad people makes them worse," said Phil, sounding regretful and puzzled. "I couldn't hardly see what buildin' fast boats could *do*, and then there was no undoing what I done, to where I wished I'd never built a boat in all my life."

"It's called unintended consequences," said Marion gravely. "*You do your best...*"

"I know, I know," interrupted Phil, "*And call it by the best names we can...* My daddy said that, too. Ralph Waldo Emerson."

"Why, yes," said Marion admiringly. "That's very good, Phil."

"It don't take you too far, Ms. B, if you don't mind me sayin'. When good is bad, and bad is good, what's the difference? All you got is what you done – for better or worse – and you cain't undo it, whatever you meant by it."

"It doesn't have to be that way, Phil," said Marion, trying to sound hopeful. Phil pondered how it could have been different, and decided she was wrong. What's done was done, never mind what he meant by building fast boats.

When he got to the part about the shootout in the jungle, and Manuela being taken away, he allowed as how he still missed her a good deal, and was promised he would see her again if he cooperated, though he reckoned that promise wasn't worth much anymore having come from a dead man. She was probably safe somewhere, the better for being as far away from him and Guajira as possible.

The thing he never reckoned on was the following he built, or the best way to use it, besides urging his men on to build more ekranoplans, and to use them to make peace with the Zeta. But that had put him crossways with the Guajira, so you couldn't win for losing, the way he saw it, until Jim Bartsch came along. He never did know right up until the very end what Jim and Ian had been up to.

"What *were* they up to, Phil?" J.D. interrupted.

"Trying to take down the Guajira, who came around to wanting me dead on account of building ekranoplans for the Zeta. Jim and Ian reckoned I knew the Guajira bosses, and they helped me escape thinking I could tell 'em, which I couldn't. Well, you know what happened to Ian..."

"No," Marion interrupted. "What happened to Ian?" she demanded, her head spinning.

"Well Pedro shot him, of course, but then Jim Bartsch testifies that *I* killed Ian on account of Jim was sure I would remember who the Guajira bosses was once I'd been sentenced to death."

"Who they *were,*" said Marion, unable any longer to contain her objection to poor grammar. "Who the Guajira bosses *were*, Phil," she repeated for good measure

"Like Ms. B, said. Jim thought I'd remember who they *were,*" said Phil for no other reason than to please Marion, "and he finally accepted *I didn't*. Jim knew all along Pedro killed Ian, not me."

"So why in tarnation were you back in Colombia?" J.D. asked as Marion exhaled behind him. "Jim allowed as how he might recant his testimony if I went along with his plan to find the Guajira."

"And what was his plan?" asked J.D. Finally, they were making progress.

"To play one cartel against the other," said Phil. "Simple as pie. Jim said they did it all the time."

"How?"

"By threatening to flood the drug market, unless the one got what it wanted from the other."

"And what did they *want*?" J.D. persisted.

"Border Patrol protection, same as the Guajira," said Phil. Marion gasped.

"No lie?" J.D. interjected in disbelief.

"No lie, J.D. Jim reckoned the Guajira - the ones Pedro ran with, and where I spent a few years - were here, in the States, bribin' U.S. Border Patrol to see their drugs got through, and launderin' their money right here, before it ever left the country. Jim and Ian was with some double-secret DEA unit, I think, tryin' to figure who these Guajira fellers were and how they did it. Now, when we built all them ekranoplans to make peace with the Zeta, it had the *unintended consequence* – see, Ms. B, I'm learnin' – of flooding the drug market, which upset the Guajira plenty. And that's how Jim got the idea to make them show themselves. What with Ian dead and not a lick of quit in him, Jim set out to do it again - threaten to flood the market unless the Guajira come to the table and agree to give the Zeta the same Border Patrol protection as the Guajira is gettin', and nab 'em at the table when they come."

"Well, I'll be...." said J.D.

"Yup. Cartels hate low prices, J.D. If I learned anything, I learned that."

"So why take *you* back?" J.D. prompted.

"Standing, I reckon. Sad-to-say, J.D., and I know I should be ashamed, Ms. B, but I got standin' in the drug world - for some things that's true, and others that ain't."

"Mother of God," said Marion, recognizing the full scale of the task before her.

"Well, go on, Phil. You can't stop now," J.D. cajoled.

"So Jim has me dropped on a beach in the middle of nowhere at night, and lo and behold, it's all set up so the Zeta, arch-enemies of Pedro and the Guajira, take me in. And who's with 'em but Vlad and Miguel and most all the ekranoplan builders from the old Guajira camp, and they're turnin' out ekranoplans one after t'other, like cars off an assembly line. Jim reckoned that ekranoplans is the secret to floodin' the market. He reckoned the one thing the Guajira could count on, with me on the side of the Zeta and back together with Vlad and our men, is that we'd turn out ekranoplans by the bushel, and the Guajira would know we're serious. The plan was fer me to meet face-to-face with the Guajira, as Humberto Gallardo's 'emissary,' Humberto bein' the big Zeta boss who thinks I hung the damn moon cause Jim gone and told him *I* killed Pedro, which I didn't. But the Zeta hated Pedro, so now they love me."

"Oh dear," said Marion, cracking the rear window.

"'Cept, somethin' went wrong before the meeting could happen and we high-tailed it out of Colombia. We got out, but Jim got shot real bad on the way out, and died, but not before tellin' every word of this to the Coast Guard. You check if you don't believe me."

"Two wrongs don't make a right," Marion muttered, finding her center.

"What?" said J.D.

"Using one drug cartel to catch another. Two wrongs don't make a right," she repeated, shaking her head.

"I heard *that,* Ms. B. Didn't sound like such a great idea to me neither, but Jim said it were regular practice – *the enemy of my enemy is my friend* – is how he said it."

"So now what?" J.D. continued.

"You tell me, J.D. I'm sentenced to death in one state for a murder I didn't commit, and now Jim's gone with only Manuela to testify I'm innocent, if anyone can find her, that is. *Now* you're taking me to *another* state to be tried fer *another* murder I didn't commit, and only Pedro knew the truth of that one, and *he's* dead, not that he'd a told the truth," said Phil, sounding genuinely defeated. "So, you see, Ms. B, you can see why I started all this by sayin' *I'm lost.*"

"People make mistakes, Phil," said Marion understandingly.

"I reckon that's so, Ms. B, but Jim was my last best chance to make things right, and maybe stay out of jail and find Manuela and our boy, too."

"Of all the mistakes, Phil, you sure made some," said J.D., shaking his head discouragingly.

"Thing is, Ms. B," craning his neck to see her, "I love buildin' boats, and I build pretty fast boats, but it hain't been good fer me, nor anyone near me, nor lots of others, too. How do you square lovin' what you do with the harm it does? It's a curse, I'm tellin' you, and I wished I'd never learned it. I wish my momma had lived and my daddy died, so he never learned me this darned profession."

"Taught me," said Marion. "You wish he never *taught* you," she corrected him, cleaving in her mind to the long road to mending Phil.

"That's right, Ms. B. It's a curse, and was from the start. You can see that cain't you? He never should have *taught* me."

"Depends on how you use it, don't it?" asked J.D., making Marion cringe. He was long past minding her corrections, grammatical and otherwise. It made Phil think about Jim's and J.D.'s and Marion's lives, and wonder what made *them* tick.

"Hey, Mr. Marks," said J.D., answering his cell phone. "Yessir, I have him sittin' right here beside me," J.D. assured Lenny. "Yessir, we're havin' ourselves a nice ol' visit, ain't we Phil," said J.D. looking and smiling at him. "We're gettin' to that right now... well, I don't see why not. Hold on a second and let's get you hooked up," J.D. said, placing his phone in its dock on the dash, and activating the speaker phone. "You hear me, Mr. Marks?" J.D. bellowed.

"Yes," Lenny replied curtly.

"Phil, this here's Mr. Marks from...." Lenny cut him off.

"I knew Jim Bartsch," said Lenny. "You want to say what happened?" Phil looked searchingly at J.D.

"He's alright, Phil, I think," said J.D., wanting slightly for conviction. "He's the one who wanted you out of Coleman, pronto, and put me up to drivin' all night to carry you home."

"That's right," said Lenny. "Bartsch was a good man."

"Mostly," said Phil. "He had a bad habit of lying under oath."

"I'm sure he had a reason," said Lenny. "You didn't do much time."

"He had a reason alright," Phil said quietly.

"Look, Perdue. We don't have time. *You* don't have time. Bartsch wanted you to do something for him. What was it?" Phil looked suspiciously at J.D. The brief hiatus of his car ride with J.D. and Marion was over. Here was someone else, wanting something new.

"Like I just said to J.D.," Phil began, "he was huntin' the Guajira since before I got picked up by the Coast Guard two years back. He was flyin' my ekranoplans full of drugs to wherever, a trusted hand, or so we thought. He were really DEA or somethin' like it, turns out. He said the Guajira bosses operated from here, in the States. He thought I knew 'em and was holdin' out, so got me convicted of murderin' his buddy, another federal agent, thinkin' a death sentence would get me to talk. He knew I didn't kill his buddy," said

Phil. "I told him then, and I'm tellin' you now, I-don't-know who the Guajira bosses is."

"Are," Marion whispered.

"I *still* don't know who they *are*," said Phil.

"And you'll never know if they have it their way, Perdue. They caught on to Bartsch," said Lenny, ashamed for his part in it, "and killed him for it. It's a sure thing they're on to you, too."

"You see what I mean, Ms. B," said Phil, craning his head again to look at her. "There's no stoppin' it. The trouble won't quit." And I'll be damned, he thought, if I'll keep runnin' from it. I'm a find these bastards and square it once and fer all.

"You take him someplace no one will find him," Lenny Marks was saying to J.D. on the speaker phone. "And not the town jail, for Chrissake. A duck blind or hunting shack off deep in the woods – wherever it is you guys play at Jeremiah Johnson – and I'll come to you. I'll be there tomorrow," said Lenny, and then he was gone. J.D. turned to Phil and smiled.

"I reckon I know right where to put you," said J.D. looking smug. "I have just the place."

CHAPTER 45

Lost Lake, Georgia

The hours remaining in the drive north to Lost Lake passed in the blink of an eye. There was no denying Phil missed part of his life in Colombia. He spoke of the people wistfully, including a Russian naval architect and submarine builder, an Australian with a complicated background, and Pedro's mother, who was killed in the crossfire of a gun fight with their rivals, the Zeta, or so it seemed at the time – it turned out later to be a DEA operation in disguise. He sounded to Marion more like Peter Pan than a fugitive, and the Guajira camp like the land of lost boys. There had been tragedy and joy, friendship and heartbreak.

"Tell us more about your girl," Marion pried gently. "Where is she?" He wished he knew. Bartsch took that secret with him to the grave. Phil had no future to offer her anyway, he assured Marion.

"Don't do that, Phil," said Marion. "You've been doing it since you were a kid."

"Ma'am?" he said.

"Counting yourself out. It's not over. If you say you're innocent, then I believe you. So does J.D., don't you, J.D."

"Yes'm," said J.D., keeping his eyes on the road.

Before he knew it they were on the lake road, in the series of hairpin, compass-spinning switchbacks. It looked like home, but didn't much feel like it anymore.

"Here," said J.D., handing Phil a pair of wraparound sunglasses and a black baseball cap with an embroidered federal marshals five-point star on the peak. "Put these on. We don't want no one knowin' you're in town." Phil put on the cap just as they rounded the turn where the lake came into view. The water was rough with scores of carefree joyriders kicking up chaotic wakes that showered the shores with blinding reflected sunlight.

"I see Sunday afternoons ain't got no quieter," said Phil, as he peered across through J.D.'s window at the lake.

He could still pick out the boats by their profiles, even looking into the sun, and none better than the *General Lee*, on account of her sleek silhouette and smooth, solemn progress, even in turbulent waters. He also knew how her passengers looked, how they rode and where they sat - so the visitor aboard caught his eye. Having guests for Sunday evening boat rides was altogether unremarkable, but the one beside Katie looked uncannily familiar. He was craning his neck for closer inspection, when J.D. shoved him back into his seat.

"Put the damn glasses on and keep your eyes forward, Phil. We're comin' up on French's."

Two more turns past French's and they'd be on the straightaway passing Perdue Landing and the old Perdue homestead on the left. More than five years separated who he was now from the terrified truant who sallied forth with Pedro Morales' along this very road in a very different time. The bank would have sold the old place by now, to recover his father's debts, and mansions would stand in its place. No matter, thought Phil, unsentimentally. Things change, the world moves on, and where you're going counts more than where you've been, or so he hoped. But it would be hard not to steal a glance as they crested the hill where the lake road rose up to meet Perdue Landing.

It looked a might washed out at the margins and the underbrush had grown thick and unkempt to each side, but the entrance to Perdue Landing still looked surprisingly the way he remembered it.

"Why we turnin' here, J.D.?" asked Phil. "I don't got no need to see this place again."

"*Any* need," said Marion. "You don't have *any* need," she said, bound and determined. He could drive Perdue Landing in the dark with his eyes closed. A turn to the right and a slow climb left, followed by a shallow decent into a hollow, and they'd be out of sight from the road. It was there Phil saw the padlocked gates and the chain link fence with the signs - *Environmental Cleanup Site – Danger - Keep Out.*

"What's all this about, J.D.? What happened?" Phil asked as J.D. got down from the truck with a jailer's hoop of keys swinging from his hand. He approached the gate, singled out a key, and unlatched a padlock the size of a pocket bible.

"After the bank seized the property," said J.D., putting himself back behind the steering wheel, "soil tests they ran, to resell the property, showed you and your daddy poured enough gasoline and turpentine in the dirt 'round here to turn this place into a hazardous waste site. I guess y'all had an inground gas tank that rusted through and leaked out, too. It ain't worth the lick on a stamp," said J.D., closing his door and clearing the gates. "You'll stay here tonight, Phil. No one will bother you. I'll bring you dinner and a sleeping bag later. You stay put, and outta sight, you hear?"

"Until when?"

"Until tomorrow, when Mr. Marks from Washington, D.C. will hear your whole story."

"We'll be watching over you from here on out," Marion added

for good measure. "Don't you worry about a thing. It's all going to be just fine," she assured him devotedly.

Phil watched the taillights on J.D.'s truck fade down the drive in the dusk, smeared in the grime of the cloudy, cob-webbed windows. It looked the way he left it the day Pedro killed Mort. The filmy dust of time had settled on everything, including the blood stain from Mort's cut throat. Mouse droppings speckled the corners and windowsills, and daylight pocked the eaves. The roof never was all that watertight, and depended now more than ever on the immutable stone fireplace to stand. Phil timed his sprint to the workshop between passing boats to avoid being seen from the water, and found there a time capsule of memories and objects.

A patchwork of yellowed newspaper clippings and curling polaroid photographs celebrated the heyday of the Perdue family business. They had hung like a family crest on the walls for decades, but the fading colors and vanishing newsprint told a tale of fleeting glory. It was the time and place of his father, he reckoned, however vividly he recalled the events or closely he guarded the stories. The legends and tales like the colors and print had already all but faded, and would soon enough be gone. He sifted through the varnish-stained tool drawers of the old workbench searching for something familiar to hold, and found there a set of meticulously sharpened scrolling chisels, for carving ornate details. In better days these chisels had played their part in shaping the *General Lee*. Now they looked small and delicate like play tools in his hands, compared to the trade tools he wielded in Colombia. His hands themselves looked different, too, more scarred and gnarled and worn than the precision instruments he remembered. There was no escaping the pull of where he began, nor the promise it held of new beginnings. But with no more belief by now in new beginnings than fairy-tales, he paid the idea no mind.

There was strange satisfaction, however, in knowing the earth the bank had been so anxious to take from him had been toxic. The bank got what it deserved for forcing him off his land, and out of an honest living in the one trade he knew. He wasn't one to revel in the misfortunes of others, especially not with the cards he held now, but it was hard not to savor the irony, to relish the justice, and pleasing to have the last laugh. A pity, he reckoned, watching the lake settle in the gathering dusk through the sawdust-caked workshop windows, that he counted such shallow satisfaction among life's few meaningful rewards.

CHAPTER 46

Lost Lake, Georgia – the Abandoned Perdue Boat Business

J.D. had returned as he promised after dark with a basket of fried chicken, slaw, sweet tea and biscuits from Ms. B, and a sleeping bag, toothbrush and other toiletries and essentials to see Phil through the night.

"Remember what I said, Phil," he had warned. "You stay put and out of sight, until this Mr. Marks gets here from Washington."

Phil woke to the morning light, dreaming of the *General Lee* coming for him, the soft melancholy throb of a distant antique lake boat that he thought at first he knew but didn't, carrying through the morning mist. It was nice not to wake to the buzzing and clanging of opening and closing steel prison doors, to hear instead water lap at the shoreline and songbirds call, and squirrels scuffle. Rising up from far corners of the lake and pouring through the eaves with the dawn came soothing sounds of daily life. The bass boats were already afoot, the soft voices of fisherman carrying from inlets and shoreline where wilderness still reached between manicured lawns to the water's edge. He could almost feel nature hold its breath, as if for clearing winds, or improving fortune to unfold.

The intensifying throb of the distant vessel foretold of its inexorable advance. She sounded like hell, which is why he had failed to place her when she first set out from her boathouse. But he knew her now by her throaty vintage World War I V-12 aircraft engine - the only one of its kind on the lake or anywhere, misfiring on cylinder eight, and maybe ten, if he wasn't mistaken. Her messy timing was the unmistakable ham-handed handiwork of Logan French, but the *General Lee* was abroad, albeit prone to coming up lame.

Standing in the window behind the covered porch, where the shadows kept him hidden, he gazed expectantly over the bend in the lake. He reckoned the vaunted old vessel would accelerate through the turn and open up into the straightaway, the way most joyriders did, rising on her chines in a gawdy display of her fetching showgirl flanks. In time, as he expected, she alighted idly on the bend, the lazy curl of her exhaust rising and falling and rising again on the mist, where she started her turn. But her turn was not in the usual direction, and moments later through the clearing mist appeared the unmistakable silhouette of Malcolm McLean's bust, alone at the wheel behind her windshield, bound for Phil's dock.

Good God, thought Phil. Of all the citizens of Lost Lake the very last he expected to see was McLean. He must be stopping to relieve himself, or walk his dog, or simply to find seclusion in the fenced-in, posted land. Phil made himself scarce deep in the shadows as memories of McLean's rebuke those many years ago and the trouble it caused him burned fresh in his heart.

The gurgling *General Lee* crept gingerly alongside his dock before stopping in her tracks with a nudge in reverse from the helm. McLean leapt gamely from the cockpit with dock lines in hand, snubbed her up short, and made her fast to the pilings. He eyed the house with expectant curiosity before abandoning the dock for the shore.

"Master Perdue!" he called, skipping spryly up the path from the dock to the house. "I know you're up there," he said, studying the house for movement. How the heck did he know, Phil wondered, baffled by his unexplained appearance.

"Come now, young man, let's dispense with the formalities, shall we," he called as he approached the house. "I heard you were in town. I wanted to be the first to welcome you home," he continued cheerfully, stopping by the porch and peering in at the front window. Phil had retreated to the darkness at the center of the house, his back to a corner against the cold stone chimney. He could easily outrun McLean if he bolted for the drive. He knew the woods and where to hide, and waiting McLean out until J.D. arrived is what he should have done.

"I know this has been hard for you Phil, and for that I'm sorry," said McLean, sounding genuinely contrite, "but you must hear me out. You must understand why." The treetops stirred on disconsolate mountain drafts that flowed down the bank and ended in soft ripples on the water.

"The hard part's done, old friend. You are ready."

"Ready for what, sir," said Phil, stepping defiantly out from the shadows.

"Hello there, young man," said McLean with a welcoming smile.

"Pardon me for asking, sir, but what the heck are you talkin' about, and how did you know I was here?"

"Always the ingénue, Phil. Explains your winning ways," said McLean proudly. "You look well, if I may be so bold. Life has been good to you, I trust?"

"I reckon," said Phil. "No complaints."

"Still and always the stoic, too," said McLean admiringly. "Let's be honest with each other, shall we? It's been a long road, hasn't it, and a difficult one, according to the *Intelligencer*. Preacher Small delivered quite a sermon in your name some weeks ago."

"Sir?"

"Oh yes, warning of evil lurking in the hearts of men and all that sort of rubbish. Rather ungenerous, if you ask me, in light of your accomplishments."

"What accomplishments, Mr. McLean?"

"Spirit of the *Americanos* and all that sort of thing. It was all covered in the papers. I always had high hopes for you, Phil, but you far surpassed my expectations."

"As a death row inmate, Mr. McLean? Did the papers say that?"

"People make these mistakes all the time, Phil. And you're not in prison now, are you? No, you're back here, on *your* land, where *you* belong, with powerful friends in the most unlikely of places. You've made a man of yourself, you have, with the world at your fingertips. Aren't you glad I didn't bail you out the way you wanted all those years ago?" said McLean, beaming.

"Sir?" said Phil.

McLean was off his rocker. He knew it happened to old people sometimes.

"Who do you think sent Pedro for you?" McLean continued cheerfully. "I'm sure it came as a shock – he was never the delicate sort – but got the job done, mind you." And there it was. He had come right out and said it, just like that, out of the blue. By God, McLean wasn't off his rocker either, and maybe he could know some of these things by reading the papers, but not all of them, Phil reckoned. And that's when he realized he had known it all along, or at least since Pedro said things weren't always as they appeared.

His blood rose and his strength swelled and his head filled spontaneously with the madness of Pedro's sickbed rantings. Incapacitated, morphine-addled, and angry, Pedro had never wanted for grievances to launch himself into tyrannical tirades. Yet, on the subject of his first meeting with Phil, right here on these grounds, he had been consistently clear – he came to Phil's to murder Harry Halliday, because Phil would be the natural suspect, and because it simplified the task of enlisting Phil. He had never given Pedro credit for being more than fair to middling smart, which had stirred in him the sense of an invisible hand – a hand that wasn't so invisible when he thought of his last parting from McLean, and how it drove him into Pedro's hands the next day.

"Tell me you knew you had what it took," McLean was saying. "*I* certainly didn't. But there was no other way, and let me assure you, not one in ten lads would have coped as you did. It's not the sort of risk you take with your own flesh and blood, after all, especially not with the likes of Duncan, poor pampered sod. The plight of all scions of great enterprise, sheltered to no meaningful purpose from the storm. He wouldn't have stood a chance. Believe me when I tell you this is the only way. A bit like tempering steel."

"The only way for *what*, dadgummit?" said Phil, stepping back, the pressure in his head blurring his vision and the sound of his heart in his ears.

"Probably not fair to you, my boy. But fairness has its limits, and success is never assured. I put my money on the underdog every day of the week, and look what you've accomplished."

"Who says I was lookin' for *accomplishments*?" Phil countered. "Who says I wanted any of what all happened since then?"

"Who ever wants to be what they become, young man? Who has the freedom to decide, or to control what the world makes them?"

"*I* did, Mr. McLean. *I* had the freedom. Right here, where I'm standing now, five years ago, I was *free!*"

"Debatable," McLean countered indifferently, "with all the money you owed - the freedom to wander off and live like a hobo, maybe."

"Beats the hell outta where I am now, Mr. McLean. On death row for one murder, and like to be convicted right here back home fer another. I got freedom alright, Mr. McLean, the freedom to count the days before they light me up in the chair like a Christmas tree, or put me down with a needle like a horse."

"I shouldn't think it's quite so dark as that."

"Ánd why not?"

"Are you guilty of these murders, Master Perdue?"

"Heck, no, I ain't!"

"Then what have you to fear. You have many supporters on all sides," said McLean encouragingly.

"With respect, sir, your words won't truck with the Feds, and there ain't nobody left on *my* side."

"That's not so, Phil. Don't discount me - I have more influence than you might imagine. And the good Sheriff Dunbar, Humberto Gallardo, probably even Judge Dawson, who signed your transfer order to the county house of corrections. With so many for you, who could be against you?"

"Humberto Gallardo?" Phil replied in disbelief. "How the heck do *you* know *him*?"

"Master Perdue," McLean began with evident pleasure, "who do you suppose those good federal agents pressed you into service to find?"

The way he said it, plain as the nose on Phil's face, made Phil wonder if the door to freedom by which he thought he recently passed had subtly closed behind him. The chain link fence encircling the toxic grounds did not seem so much suited now to keeping tormentors out as holding him in, to be found by McLean, or anyone in his infinite reach. Had J.D. placed him here at McLean's direction? Was J.D. even planning to return? Phil paused to make a murky mental calculus that struggled to make sense of his situation. How far did the influence of McLean, elusive Patron of the Guajira, reach?

"You can't simply step off the bus now," McLean was saying as he eyed Phil queerly, like he'd missed the point. "Who will be left?

The whole damned exercise will have been for naught. No, it's time you got straight back to work, did your part, assumed your duties, in line to take over in time from me."

"You're outta your gourd, McLean. I done my time in your crazy world. I ain't doin' no more."

"Leave? Abandon the enterprise at the height of its powers, when you're the perfect man in the perfect place at the perfect time? It's madness."

"No it ain't, McLean. It's wrong."

"First the ingénue, then the stoic, and now the idealist? Don't you know by now there's no such thing, Perdue? There are only the things I have labored like a coolie all my life to acquire – power, money, influence - the things everyone wants but fears having. Not me, Perdue, and not you. See for yourself. Here we are together, old acquaintances at a summit for two dividing and conquering the cartels. Soon you will learn the art of finance, and eventually, political influence. All in good time," McLean concluded optimistically.

"It ain't that easy, Mr. McLean,"

"Oh? And why is that?"

For the first time in his life Phil had the sense of seeing around corners, and all he could see was trouble – trouble for himself, and trouble for McLean. J.D., and Ms. B, and the Coast Guard crew that took Jim's statement, and this feller Marks, who was on his way from Washington, D.C. – they all had the picture, or most of the picture – the one missing piece was McLean.

"I don't want to, McLean."

"Poppycock, Perdue. You're in danger of being ungrateful."

"I don't want to, McLean, plain and simple. And I ain't gonna. Find someone else."

"You'll be off to the electric chair, I dare say."

"So be it, Mr. McLean."

"If you won't save yourself," McLean posed ominously, "perhaps there are others worth saving. Is there not *anyone* you know worth saving?"

"I beg your pardon, sir?"

"Manuela, for example" said McLean, like a menu selection. Phil knew at once by the striking familiarity of the unexplained rider on the *General Lee* the day before that McLean wasn't kidding. McLean had Manuela and their son.

"How's that?" said Phil.

"Did it never cross your mind why she bears such a close resemblance to my Katie?" McLean taunted. "Yes, Phil, your eyes don't deceive. She's Katie's half-sister. We tell people they're cousins, but the truth is somewhat darker, I'm afraid." The air in Phil's chest grew dense and hot, and defied his exertions to expel it. "She's Mrs. McLean's illegitimate daughter, conceived unfortunately when Mrs. McLean was a teenager. She was raised by Mrs. McLean's brother, whom you knew, if I'm not mistaken – José," McLean intimated cagily. "So, you see, you have many things to live for if not yourself," he said like a Delphic prophecy.

"It's too late, Mr. McLean. I already told too many people," blurted Phil, realizing when he said it that but for revealing himself to Phil, the Patron of the Guajira remained unknown.

"For both our sakes, Mr. McLean, you best be gettin' on," said Phil unmoved. "J.D. could be here any minute."

"And so could Manuela," said McLean with a smile.